"No ambula___, _____ ___ _ ___

She pushed Redmond's hands away and turned toward the wall, trying for privacy, but Redmond circled around until he was facing her again.

"Don't be stupid," he said. "I don't need you dying on me."

"That's ridiculous. I'm not going to die."

"You're *shot*," he pointed out. "I can't believe you're still standing."

Brynna realized there was no way he was going to leave her alone. Fine. Let him watch. She reached under her T-shirt and found the wound just below the ribs.

"Hey!" Redmond said in surprise. "Don't do that! Just put pressure on."

She ignored him and dug into the hole with her forefinger, hissing as fresh pain scissored through her muscles. The misshapen piece of offending metal came out with a fresh pulse of new blood. Brynna pressed her fist against it, warming the flesh until it heated and swelled, temporarily closing beneath her touch.

"No," Redmond said. His voice sounded dull, almost mechanical. "You can't have done what I think you just did."

HIGHBORN

THE DARK REDEMPTION SERIES

BOOK 1

YVONNE NAVARRO

POCKET BOOKS

New York   London   Toronto   Sydney

The sale of this book without its cover is unauthorized. If you purchased this book without a cover, you should be aware that it was reported to the publisher as "unsold and destroyed." Neither the author nor the publisher has received payment for the sale of this "stripped book."

Pocket Books
A Division of Simon & Schuster, Inc.
1230 Avenue of the Americas
New York, NY 10020

This book is a work of fiction. Names, characters, places, and incidents either are products of the author's imagination or are used fictitiously. Any resemblance to actual events or locales or persons, living or dead, is entirely coincidental.

Copyright © 2010 by Yvonne Navarro

All rights reserved, including the right to reproduce this book or portions thereof in any form whatsoever. For information address Pocket Books Subsidiary Rights Department,
1230 Avenue of the Americas, New York, NY 10020.

First Juno Books/Pocket Books paperback edition November 2010

JUNO BOOKS and colophon are trademarks of Wildside Press LLC used under license by Simon & Schuster, Inc., the publisher of this work.

POCKET and colophon are registered trademarks of Simon & Schuster, Inc.

For information about special discounts for bulk purchases, please contact Simon & Schuster Special Sales at 1-866-506-1949 or business@simonandschuster.com.

The Simon & Schuster Speakers Bureau can bring authors to your live event. For more information or to book an event contact the Simon & Schuster Speakers Bureau at 1-866-248-3049 or visit our website at www.simonspeakers.com.

Designed by Jacquelynne Hudson
Cover design by Anna Dorfman
Cover illustration by Craig White

Manufactured in the United States of America

10 9 8 7 6 5 4 3 2 1

ISBN 978-1-4391-9173-6
ISBN 978-1-4391-9174-3 (ebook)

For Wes
because of everything.

Acknowledgments

In no particular order, thank you to:
Weston Ochse
Martin Cochran
Don VanderSluis
Wayne Allen Sallee
Wayne Barlowe
Jerrett Cook
Scott Soukup
Laura Jiménez
Lucy Snyder
Tod Goldberg
Michael Whelan
Chris Golden
and
Mike Klesowitch, who is a real person but not
the person in this book. He wanted me to use his
name as long as he could be "anything but a soul-
sucking baby-killer." So now you know: There
is no soul-sucking baby-killer in this book.

Prologue

Most of the time, Astarte could smell the souls burning.

Accompanying the heavy fragrance, the tortured screams below her window endlessly swelled and receded, strung together like notes pried from a twisted violin and seething with the burned-sugar scent of agony.

There had been a time, early on, when she had enjoyed this, had relished the eternal punishment being hammered upon the spirits of those creatures she and her longtime lover considered no better than the rats that infested their earthly world. No, not rats; *mice,* tiny, insignificant rodents worthy only of being food for those beings not much better than themselves. The shrieks had been musical back then, filled with blood and retribution, but eventually Astarte found that she barely heard the sounds—they faded to the background like the constant buzzing of ever-present insects.

But now the soul cries had changed. They should have been as natural as the blood that constantly oozed from the cracks in the walls of her opulent rooms, nothing more unusual than the eternity of time one second took to pass to another. But no; lately the undulating waves of suffering had begun to eat at her, stinging her psyche like hungry, biting blowflies diving relentlessly at the wounds of a dying beast. Sometimes she would lash out and silence the ones within range, her rage and impatience incinerating them instantly and giving her a few moments—just that—of heavy, anticipatory silence.

Then, of course, the next shrieks would ripple across the plains as more souls were pushed forward to fill the void left by those she had temporarily destroyed. A hundred or a thousand seconds from now, the same souls she had just obliterated would be reborn into another cycle of their punishment and would be heard yet again. If she was lucky, their wails would fall upon the ears of another rather than herself, one who would grin rather than flinch at the sound.

But who in Hell was ever lucky?

She turned away from the sill and its vista of glowing scarlet rivers, a landscape that was dark but forever well lit. It was an arena filled with abominations that were always new and unspeakably dangerous, things that even now continued to surprise her when they crossed her royal path.

Everything in Hell watched everything else; it was a living thing, encompassing all, missing nothing, revealing everything to everyone. Even so, she neither knew nor cared who or what watched as her cracked and blackened fingertips lifted the only thing that remained of what she had once been.

A feather.

Its quill still glowed white, crystalline and pure—even the fires of Hell could not dim the light within its center. That the edges of the vane were singed and stained with sulfur and smoke took nothing away from the power it held over her. The pain she felt each time she held it was worse than anything a thousand demons could inflict, and the agony grew deeper and more overwhelming every time. The feather's light was an aberration in this room, a single spot of perfection that was impossible to disguise or hide in this city of sheer obscenity; as if to prove that, the screams of the damned would swell to an unbearable cadence of want if she held it toward the unshuttered window. That the feather had not been ripped from her possession was a testament to the fact that even she, with all her vile, hallowed standing in this place, was not above being personally tormented. Nothing reminded an immortal being of its own eternity like an everlasting memento of that which could never again come to be.

Hell had taught her many things, not the least of which was how to wait. She had spent countless days, each like a century, with one elbow resting on her knees as she contemplated the feather, that glorious relic of the time before her fall from Grace. As the heat of Hell swirled inside and outside of her, she had to wonder—

Could she be redeemed?

It was said that nothing and no one could truly return from Hell, that time ceased to exist once those colossal black gates closed behind a weeping spirit. Any chance of salvation or forgiveness was left behind, as eternally unreachable as the Great Light of God Himself. But Lucifer was the King of Lies, and what better way to intensify

One

A butterfly saved her.

Being what she was, she'd always been partial to anything with wings, and the fireball missed her only because she leaned sideways to look at the creature where it was balanced on the back of a park bench in Chicago's Lincoln Park. Two inches wide at best, the butterfly was orange and yellow, plus a couple more colors that never registered because of the agony that suddenly ran up one arm and nearly spread to her neck and jawline.

A Hunter had already found her!

She dropped forward and rolled away from the next fireball, then scrambled around and behind the bench. A third fireball, small and white-hot, arced across the space in which she'd been standing only a second before, then disintegrated against a massive old tree. It made a sound like a fast-moving forest fire, then instantly burned out, leaving a smoking, circular scar on the tree's thick trunk. On its heels was a scream from a woman who had come around the bend in the path just in time to see the miniature blast.

Good. Getting humans involved would put the balance on her side, give her a chance to escape while her pursuer was forced to hide. He wouldn't kill her, but it was glaringly obvious he was going to have fun hurting her before he dragged her back.

Like she was ever going to let *that* happen.

It wasn't difficult to lose herself in the trees off the path while the Hunter tried to follow without being seen. Once he made it into the trees, she could hear her attacker crashing after her, and all it took to leave him behind was stealth—he was overconfident and noisy; she was neither. She stayed close to the ground, almost on all fours, and moved as fast as she could, intentionally weaving in and out of the populated areas. In these she was barely more than a blur that made passersby frown and blink, and when she got to the edge of a body of water next to a sign that said SOUTH POND, she sucked in air and slipped into the warm mud- and leaf-choked liquid without hesitating. She didn't breathe for a long, long time, swimming blindly away from the danger and coming up like an alligator at the water's edge several hundred feet later, slow and cautious as only the top of her head and her eyes broke the surface.

She was safe.

For now.

SHE WASHED HER FACE and hands at a water fountain in the park, then pulled clean water through her hair until she felt reasonably presentable. Water was such an amazing thing—refreshing and clear, sweet against her skin despite the chemicals added by the city's processing system. Although she hadn't been able to stay and appreciate it, she'd even enjoyed the dirty, slightly polluted water in the pond.

Quickly moving west and away from the upscale lakefront area, she found some clothes hanging on a line in a small backyard. In this world of modern conveniences, she didn't think people did that anymore—hang clothes out to dry—but perhaps this person wanted the smell of fresh air in the fabric. To her sensitive nose, Chicago's exhaust-choked air wasn't truly fresh, but people here were used to it.

Taking the simple T-shirt and denim jeans and the worn pair of athletic shoes she found by the back door was stealing, but she was out of options and that, surely, was not even a blip on the chart of her many crimes. Besides, walking around in rags stinking of pond water and streaked with dried mud wasn't going to help her accomplish her task. The stolen jeans fit her tall frame surprisingly well, although the T-shirt was stretched snugly across her wide back and small breasts. The fabric was tight around her biceps, and every movement of her right arm sent a hot jolt down the flesh burned earlier. The side of her neck and face were deep pink from the heat spillover, but the pain was minor; her hair was singed and still smelled of fire. But she was quite used to that smell.

"That's a pretty nasty burn on your arm."

The voice came from her right and belonged to a nice-looking guy in his late thirties, who was a good four inches taller than her own six foot two. She was in Walgreens, a store like a twenty-first-century apothecary, staring at a shelf full of gauze and burn salve and thinking about the products on display. Her own physical pain was something she hadn't had to contemplate in quite awhile. The last time she'd paid it any mind, human medicine had been little more than someone waving burning clumps of herbs over a wound and uttering a meaningless chant. Was there anything among the brightly colored boxes on these shelves that would actually soothe the monstrous stinging on her arm, or would it simply be a waste of time? Humans were certainly good at that. Because of what she was, a lot of things—how to dress, how to talk, even a culture's customs and slang, just *came* to her automatically. But for this, she really had no idea, simply because she'd never needed such a thing. And in the meantime, here was this man.

No, not a man.

A *nephilim*.

A child fathered by an angel and born of a human mother.

She could *smell* him, in the way that only her kind could. It was an unmistakable thing, deep and alluring, as though he were surrounded by a mist of clean ocean water. The scent was so strong and so unexpected that all she could do for an overly long moment was breathe it in, pull it deep into her lungs and hold it there while she reveled in his nearness as his essence spread throughout her body.

A double heartbeat later, she exhaled. Without conscious thought, her tongue flicked over her lips, seeking the last trace.

He was looking at her expectantly. The burn—right. He'd said something about it. "Yeah," she responded at last.

Her voice was low and husky, a bit hoarse. She hadn't actually spoken in centuries—it simply hadn't been necessary—and she certainly hadn't carried on a conversation with a human. Was there something else she should say about her injuries? What would this nephilim want to hear?

No, she reminded herself. Don't think of him as nephilim, think of him as a man. After all, that's all he knows that he is. Just a man.

The guy looked down at her arm again, then his gaze skimmed along the display. "This," he said, pointing to a small blue-and-white box labeled BURN JEL. "If you're not going to see a doctor, this is your best bet. Wash the entire area thoroughly every morning and evening, then spread this stuff on a piece of sterile gauze and scrub off the newly formed skin until all the dead skin is gone and the new is growing in evenly. It's called debriding. It'll be painful but it will help it heal and keep scarring to a minimum."

She shrugged, then winced as the movement pulled the fabric of the shirt against her arm. "I don't care about that," she said. She wanted to keep him talking, but her people skills sucked. "It just . . . hurts."

He nodded. "I'm sure it does, but there's not much over the counter that's going to help the pain. The ointment has a small amount of lidocaine in it, and you could take some aspirin along with that. You could also try one of the burn sprays, but I wouldn't expect much out of it, not at that level." He nodded at her arm, then fell silent for a moment. "You know," he added finally, "that's a fresh second-degree burn. I can't believe you're not going to see a doctor."

She managed a small, strained smile. The pain made that easy, even if normal conversation was a challenge. "I thought you were one."

He looked momentarily surprised, then shook his head. "Me? No, I'm an EMT."

She squinted at him. "What does that stand for?"

"Emergency medical technician. I drive an ambulance."

"Next best thing."

"To a doctor?" He shook his head again, this time more emphatically. "Not at all."

"Well," she said. She hesitated, finally stepping back from the shelf. She'd run out of creativity and couldn't think of anything else to talk about. "Thanks for the advice."

His eyes widened. "Wait—aren't you going to pick up some supplies?"

"Maybe later."

"Ah." He frowned at her, then his expression smoothed. She realized instantly that he knew she had no money. As much as he dealt with people, he was probably an expert at reading situations. "I'm Toby. What's your name?"

Name? Of course—she should have one of those, yet she hadn't given it a moment's thought. Giving her real name was unthinkable, but what should she call herself? Twice before she had been formally named, and she had used thousands of others through the millennia; for the first time, now she could choose her own. A million alternatives flashed through her brain, letters and languages with little rhyme or reason, still others with hidden purpose—

"Brynna," she blurted.

All right. That would do.

"Very nice," he said, but it was clear he was thinking about anything but that as his hand dug in his back pocket and brought out a worn leather wallet. "Listen, Brynna. I think you could use a little hel—"

The left side of his head caved in.

There wasn't much sound with it, just a sort of *thump* and a crystalline tinkling that seemed to come *afterward,* almost as an addendum to the actual event. One moment Brynna was gazing at Toby, whose expression was sincere and vaguely like that of an eager-to-please child as he prepared to offer her money; in the next, she was blinking at a misshapen red hole easily two inches around. It was a huge and ugly thing that gouted blood down his shoulder; even more hideous was the way the right side of his skull had suddenly bulged outward, like someone had forced air into a balloon then let only part of it out. Toby's knees buckled and he turned and fell in front of her, leaving a pattern of bloody mist and vaporized skin in his wake. He went down as quickly and gracelessly as a dropped wooden puppet.

Brynna scowled and bent over him, but it was a useless gesture. He'd been gone and sent to glory in the millisecond between when the bullet had touched his left temple and slammed against the inside of his skull on the right. If she touched him, she might be able to see at least a hint of the duty his destiny had demanded, but why bother? Whatever task had been assigned to this gentle and generous nephilim soul would never be completed. Now he was just an empty husk ready to be returned to the dust of the earth. "For dust thou art, and unto dust shalt thou return," she murmured.

Brynna straightened, then realized someone was screaming. It was an older man in a white coat behind the counter at the end of the aisle, and the only reason she even noticed was because it was so odd to her senses that there was just one man screaming instead of thousands. He was frozen in place, his sight locked on her as his mouth gaped and howled, and he gave no sign of stopping anytime soon. She sent him a puzzled look, then it hit her that this must be a terrible shock—most humans simply weren't used to blood and death on the same scale she was.

As if to underscore that, something red and moist dribbled down Brynna's forehead and slid across the bridge of her nose. When she reached to flick at it, her fingers came away washed in the familiar hue of scarlet. Her hair and face were splattered with Toby's blood. Nothing new historically, but it was really kind of admirable, the way humans had come up with so many deadly methods of killing one another. Twenty thousand years ago she never would have thought them capable of much more than desperate hunting with rudimentary tools, yet look at them now.

Brynna sighed and automatically tuned out the old man's screeching as she turned away from the nephilim's corpse. There was nothing to be done for Toby now, and she didn't have currency or anything else that seemed likely to be accepted in trade for the medicine the dead EMT had recommended. She had an idea that Toby's death was going to throw off the normal rhythm of things, anyway. From where she stood, Brynna could see the front window of the drugstore, or what had been the window before it, too, had been shattered by the same bullet that had killed her nephilim. Glass fragments sparkled in the sun where they weren't shadowed by the flapping remains of the advertising posters that had been taped to the inside surface. She glanced back at Toby one more time before starting toward the door. As she did, her gaze skimmed across the people gathering on the sidewalk; she stopped short as her eyes locked with those of a single young man.

Brown hair cut very short, hazel eyes. Tall and overly thin, all arms and legs underneath a hip-length denim jacket that was too heavy for the hot afternoon and bulky along one side—

The escalating sound of a siren cut through the jabber of conversation outside. The man jerked his gaze away from Brynna's, then backed up and disappeared behind the gawkers crowding up to the broken window.

Brynna stared at the space where he'd been, considering, before she quickly left the drugstore. There was no reason to stay here, and she certainly didn't want to be involved in any police investigation. The man outside, though, he was another story; there was something about him that intrigued her. Was he also a nephilim? Nephilim weren't common but they also weren't rare; still, to see one at the moment of another's death . . . that was certainly on the side of odd.

The people standing on the sidewalk stepped aside to let her pass, and it took Brynna a couple of seconds to figure out why—she was bloody, her face and shoulders splattered with the last moments of Toby's earthly life. With her history, it was ridiculously easy for her not to notice something like this; the sensation, the sticky, heavy copper scent, the warmth—it was all just one more part of a bigger normalcy. But that had to change if she was going to blend into *this* world. Judging from the appalled expressions of the onlookers and the way they backstepped, she really needed to work harder on remembering her surroundings. It was damned ironic—all the mayhem, murder, and devastation that mankind had wrought throughout the ages, yet now people in some of the most densely populated areas on the globe couldn't seem to stomach the sight of blood. How had the human race ever gotten through the Dark Ages? The Inquisition? The countless, never-ending wars they waged upon one another?

There wasn't any place she could wash as she had in the park, so the best Brynna could do was stay close to the buildings and duck her head when someone came toward her on the sidewalk. She didn't miss that she was essentially skulking in broad daylight, and she hated having to do that. Skulking reminded her of the alley demons from Below, hideously filthy creatures that looked like a cross between hyenas and Komodo dragons. They prowled the blood-soaked passageways of the undercities and preyed on fleeing souls, darting forward to snap and drag a fugitive into the darkest shadows. There they chewed on the screaming victim until nothing remained but ragged, twitching puddles of ripped and half-digested soul-flesh. When the soul finally died, they moved onto the next and left the ruined spirit to disintegrate and re-form back at the original location it had so stupidly thought it had escaped. Hell was nothing if not repetitious.

Finally Brynna found a service station with outside restrooms. She waited, and when an older man came out of one door, she ducked inside; the sarcastic comment he started to utter died in his throat at the sight of her blood-smeared cheeks.

With her face and hands cleaned a few minutes later, Brynna came out and studied her surroundings. There was a big yellow Shell symbol above her, and on the corner was a dual street sign that read HALSTED on one side and WRIGHTWOOD on the other. The air was heavy with the smell of gasoline, but Brynna barely noticed. She'd smelled a lot worse.

The slight breeze tingled the places on her face that were still wet and Brynna let herself soak in the feeling for a few seconds. But only that—she wasn't here, standing on this particular corner in the city, by happenstance; even as she'd tried to make herself as invisible as possible, she'd been tracking the man she'd seen staring at her through the drugstore's broken window. There wasn't much to go on but the slightest hint of his body odor; by itself it wouldn't have been enough—there were too many other scents in the city that smothered it. But there was something unnatural mixed with it, something much stronger and heavier and impossible to miss.

Gunpowder.

Feeling less conspicuous now that she'd been able to clean up, Brynna lifted her head to the sunshine as she turned onto Wrightwood and followed the acrid scent west. She'd only gone two blocks before her sharp sense of smell made her turn north onto a heavily tree-lined street called Mildred Avenue.

The thick canopy of leaves from hundred-year-old oaks made the air cooler and dimmer; instead of heavy summer sunshine, the sidewalks and buildings were mottled with thousands of sunlit circles that moved and danced as the breeze cut through the leaf-laden branches. It gave the old apartment buildings a softer, more appealing look than they would have normally had. On an overcast day, Brynna knew they would appear as they really were: worn and overused brick and crumbling mortar fronted by cracked sidewalks and lawns dotted with weeds. Here and there were halfhearted splashes of color, geraniums, petunias, and marigolds planted along borders that weren't particularly straight. Right now there wasn't much going on and the street was devoid of people. That made it easy for Brynna to follow the stink of gunpowder down a shadowed walkway to where it ended at the glass-fronted door of an apartment building.

Brynna stood there for a moment, then tried the door. It was locked, which wasn't much of a surprise. Humans always thought they could keep out their version of the Big Bad with things like flimsy metal fastenings. It was a useless effort, but she wasn't here to be the evil anymore, was she?

She was pretty sure her target was a nephilim—he'd paused at the door and she was almost positive an ocean scent lingered beneath the caustic smell of gunpowder. There were names and doorbells along one side, but unless he made a habit of pushing his own bell, she had no way of sensing which one belonged to him. It was a big building, at least thirty-six units, but once she was inside, it would be easy to find the door to his apartment.

Brynna tried the door again. The handle was nothing but decoration; the lock mechanism above was what kept it closed. To force it, she'd only have to break the jamb on the side.

"What are you doing down there?"

A sudden gravelly voice somewhere above her head made Brynna jump. She backed away from the door and looked up to where a wrinkled old woman with fuzzy, iron-colored hair was glaring down at her from two stories above. "This is a Neighborhood Watch area, missy, and you'd better believe I watch it all the time." The woman's voice climbed higher and took on a threatening tone as she squinted at Brynna. "Never seen you here before."

"I was looking for a friend of mine," Brynna explained.

"Then ring the damned doorbell instead of hanging around like a hoodlum!"

"I don't know his last name," Brynna said without thinking.

"Then you're not much of a friend," the woman snapped back. "You get out of here or I'm calling the police. This is a Neighborhood Watch area!"

"I heard you the first time," Brynna said. She gave the door a final look, then shrugged. If the murderer who'd gone into this building really was a nephilim, he'd been corrupted, led astray from the path God had set out for him. It was unlikely Brynna would do herself any good by finding him anyway. Let the humans deal with the killer in their midst. She wanted nothing more than to forget he existed.

"I'm warning you!" the elderly woman screeched.

Brynna turned to follow the sidewalk back to the street. "You have a nice day, ma'am," she said as sweetly as she could. The woman muttered something cantankerous in return as Brynna touched her forehead in a gesture of farewell. A moment later the crone gasped and backed away from her concrete windowsill.

Brynna grinned darkly. Stone was always so good at soaking up heat. Maybe that would keep the old bat away from her Neighborhood Watch area for a while so her fellow tenants could go in and out in peace.

Two

Spending her first night in human form was definitely a learning experience for Brynna. It might have gone better except for the burn on her arm; the wound was healing rapidly, more so than any normal person's would have, but it still hurt. The swift healing process also had a downside: the growing skin itched ferociously, yet if Brynna gave it the smallest rub, the itch morphed into a deep, savage sting.

She didn't notice the summer night's cooler temperatures; her heat came from within, stored from millennia spent in Hell. Had it been winter, Brynna could have slept in the snow and her body temperature would have melted a circle around her. But the weather wasn't the problem— she had nowhere to go, nowhere to sleep, nowhere *safe* to be. Still out there somewhere was the Hunter that had tried to capture her earlier, and although she might have a demon's soul, this was a human body, more or less, and it had human requirements. It screamed for things like food, rest, and bodily comfort.

Tomorrow, she decided, she would figure out how to

get some money and go back to that drugstore for some of the ointment the dead nephilim had recommended. She could ignore the feeling of hunger in her belly, but this body had been injured and overtaxed. It required rest to heal, so she couldn't put off the need to sleep. When Brynna thought back, today's events didn't seem all that taxing; on the other hand, it wasn't every day that a high-level demon escaped from Lucifer's Kingdom and re-formed herself on earth as a human woman.

She was *tired*.

Brynna had endured a lot in Hell, and although a soft bed with silk sheets would have been nice, there was absolutely nothing wrong with the dark niche she found between a Dumpster and the back wall of a dinky neighborhood restaurant. She settled herself beneath the dubious cover of a torn, dirty cardboard box and thought wearily about Toby, the dead nephilim. She didn't know if it had been the sight of the horror on the faces of the onlookers outside the drugstore's broken window or the memory of his blood trickling down her sun-warmed cheeks, but as her eyelids fluttered closed, all Brynna could think about was that it was a shame Toby's already short human life had been cut even shorter.

When she finally slept, Brynna dreamed of scarlet lakes of fire beneath the coolness of a glowing and mad-deningly out-of-reach blue sky.

BRYNNA HAD BEEN HALF expecting to find the Walgreens closed the next morning, but although the window was boarded up, it was open by the time she wandered over at a little past nine o'clock. She still didn't have any money, but that didn't stop her from going inside and heading to the aisle where the burn medicine was. The floor had been cleaned but her overly sensitive nose could still pick up the scent of blood, and she could see it, too. Nothing man-made would erase the blood shadow where Toby's life had leaked onto the floor. Humans couldn't see it, but her kind could pick it up in an instant.

Brynna glanced over at the prescription counter and saw the same old man who'd been there yesterday; he recognized her and his eyes widened, but she paid no attention to him as he turned and pressed a telephone against his ear. What was it Toby had recommended? Gauze and burn salve. Her gaze skimmed the shelves until she found the stuff he'd pointed to, but she was no longer sure she wanted it. Her arm stung, yes, but the pain had diminished to the point where it was bearable and would probably be gone by tomorrow . . . well, provided that damned Hunter didn't find her and toss another fireball or ten her way.

She wasted another twenty minutes browsing around the aisles, fascinated at the variety of goods, the things humans had come up with. She couldn't remember the last time she'd physically been on earth—perhaps it had been in the sixteenth or seventeenth century. Medicine, electricity, *flying* . . . so many things had grown out of what she and her angelic brethren had believed were little more than dull-minded creatures who might *look* like their Creator but would never accomplish more than warfare-based survival. They—

"Excuse me, ma'am."

Brynna looked up from her study of something called a giant bone sponge in the auto accessory department. It looked nothing like a bone and it certainly wasn't a giant anything, so she was trying to wrap her brain around why it was called that.

"Ma'am," the man standing in front of her said again.

"Yes?" He was a nice enough looking man but ordinary, not nephilim. At six feet tall, with blue eyes, pale skin, and slightly shaggy brown hair, he reminded her vaguely—*very* vaguely—of the ancient images of an angel. Well, except for the round glasses (another incredible thing man had invented) and the scruff growing on his cheeks and chin— angels never had to shave.

He took something out of his jacket pocket and offered it to her, but when Brynna went to take it, he pulled it just out of reach. All she could do was look at it. It was a piece of metal in the shape of a star, with numbers on it and the words CHICAGO POLICE DEPARTMENT and DETECTIVE. Ah, a policeman.

"I'm Detective Redmond. I need to ask you a few questions." Brynna lifted one eyebrow, but he didn't wait for permission. "Yesterday a man named Tobias Gallagher was shot and killed in this store." His unwavering gaze was fixed on her. "You were talking to him when he died."

Tobias Gallagher—Toby. Of course. "Yes."

"What were you talking about?"

"Burn medicine," she replied without hesitation. She nodded toward her arm.

"Uh-huh." He stared at her and frowned slightly. "And when he was shot right in front of you, what did you do?"

"I left." Despite an instant effort to hide it, she still caught his expression of surprise. She added, "Other than that conversation, I didn't know him. So . . ."

"So you just left." He pulled a small notebook out of another pocket. "Did it ever occur to you, Miss—"

"Brynna," she said.

"Okay, *Brynna*. Did it ever occur to you that you were just leaving a crime scene?"

Crime scene? She hadn't thought about that. She'd seen and grown used to countless instances of death in her existence, so Toby's death was just that to her: a death. But to these humans, having one of their own die like that was something else entirely. It was a murder. And for that they had police, and laws, and repercussions. Well, none of that concerned her—she hadn't killed the nephilim. But he was waiting for her to answer his question. "No," she said. "It didn't."

"Right." He ran a hand over his hair. "I'm going to need you to come down to the station with me."

"The station?"

"Yes, ma'am. The police station."

Brynna considered this, then shook her head. No, she didn't want to go anyplace with this man. It was too dangerous—if a Hunter caught up with her, she might not be able to escape in time. "No, I don't want to do that."

Standing not far from the police detective was another man. This one was shorter and darker-skinned. His skin tone and dark eyes made Brynna think of the exotic men in ancient Persia, back when Alexander the Great had defeated the Persian Empire. He stepped behind Brynna and stopped, then turned to look at Redmond.

"It's not a request," Detective Redmond replied. He put a hand on her wrist and she slapped it away instinctively. He yelped in surprise and stumbled backward—she'd forgotten her more-than-human strength. Even so, she raised her hand to strike him again if he dared to touch her once more. Suddenly there was an ominous, metallic-sounding click behind her right ear.

"Please do not move," said a soft, thickly accented voice, "or I will be forced to shoot you. You are under arrest."

Brynna opened her mouth to argue, then shut it. There were too many people around for a Hunter to take advantage of her unfortunate situation, and while her demon essence might go a long way toward strengthening this human female form, it was still little beyond a fragile shell. The gun at her head also brought back the unpleasant memory of the way Toby's skull had pushed outward when the killer's bullet had gone into his brain.

"All right," she said.

Redmond scowled at her as he brought out a pair of steel handcuffs. He pulled her arms around to her back and snapped the cuffs around her wrists before the other man reholstered his revolver. With a detective on either side of her, Brynna was led none too gently to an unmarked police car parked outside. "You have the right to remain silent," Detective Redmond told her in a rigid voice. Then he kept on talking, droning about courts and the law and more things she paid no attention to as he opened the door and his partner guided her into the automobile's back compartment. The door closed and locked, leaving her feeling trapped if not vulnerable; the windows were tinted, so at least she wasn't on display inside a glass bowl. It was more comfortable than Brynna had expected, and having her hands restrained behind her back bothered her not a bit. She was limber enough to easily wriggle her backside and legs through and get her wrists to the front, but ultimately she decided that wouldn't be a good idea; she'd swatted that detective harder than she'd intended. She could see him favoring a wrist that was showing a deep bruise along one side. Clearly, hurting him hadn't been a good move on her part.

With traffic, it took almost forty-five minutes to get to the Criminal Courthouse, a big, multistory gray building that the street signs noted was at 26th and California. The front of the structure on California Avenue had eight stone columns, and while Brynna thought they were poor copies of ancient Grecian architecture, they did give it an imposing façade.

Inside, the place was crowded and noisy, filled with uniformed and plainclothes policemen and criminals of all kinds. It was fascinating, the sight and scents of so many different aspects of humanity, all jammed into a relatively small space and with one group—the law enforcers—trying to maintain control over the other. While a lot of the people seemed to be in a hurry, Redmond and his partner were not: they took their time about getting her seated at a table in a room surrounded by windows, then uncuffed her and left her there for several hours as she wondered what the next step in her arrest would be.

When Detective Redmond finally came back, he was alone. He settled himself on a chair across from her and pulled out a pen and a notebook, then looked at her expectantly. "Name?"

"Brynna," she said promptly. Cooperation seemed like a good thing.

He sighed. "*Last* name?"

Brynna sat back. Last name? Damn, she should have expected this—almost all the humans used them now. "Malak," she blurted. The Arabic word for *angel* was the first thing that came to mind.

"Malak," Redmond repeated, then spelled it out loud and waited for her confirmation that he was correct. "Address?"

This was going to be a lot harder than she'd thought. If she tried to make something up, he'd find out. "I . . . don't have one," she answered. "I just got here."

"Where did you come from?"

Crap, it was just getting worse. "You wouldn't know it."

Redmond tapped his pen impatiently. "Just give me the address."

"Caina," she said after a moment of indecision. He scowled, and she added quickly, "1224 Maple Street." It sounded fake even as she said it, but it was too late to take it back. "It's down south, very . . . out of the way."

"Down south," Redmond repeated. "Where down south? Georgia? Florida? Tennessee? Where?"

"Georgia," Brynna said.

He glanced at her as he was writing. "You don't look like the Southern-girl type."

"Appearances can be deceiving."

"Uh-huh." He stared at her for a long time without speaking, but she only stared back. "You know, I could charge you with assaulting a police officer and leaving the scene of a crime."

Brynna resisted the urge to point out that she'd only slapped him on the wrist. Sarcasm was probably not the way to go. Instead she said, "But I didn't commit the crime. I didn't even know there *was* a crime." His look of surprise made her instantly realize her mistake—of course it was a crime to kill someone. This was Earth, not Hell, and everyone would know that. "I mean, I knew there was a crime, obviously, but I didn't do it, so I didn't know I was supposed to stay." She hoped that would somehow cancel out her blunder, but the expression on the detective's face said otherwise. If only propriety came to her as easily as words.

Finally he leaned forward. "Let me explain something, Ms. Malak. This is the fifth shooting like this, where some poor sucker—and they've come in all ages—seems to be just minding his or her own business, and *kablaam!*" He slammed his fist on the table, but Brynna didn't even flinch. "Shot in the head, right out of the blue. No reason, no motive, no connection between the victims."

Brynna opened her mouth to ask if five was a lot, then wisely shut it.

"One was a middle-aged homeless woman, another was a fourteen-year-old boy going home from a soccer game." He glared at her. "One was a science professor about to retire, another was a secretary at an advertising firm. And the only thing they have in common is that they were all killed by the same gun." Redmond half stood and leaned across the table. "And here you are, the closest thing to a witness that we've had, standing right in front of the latest victim. But you don't have an address here in the city, and I'd bet my next paycheck you don't have any identification. In fact, I'd bet you don't have a driver's license or even a social security card. Do you?"

All Brynna could do was look at him. "I don't drive."

"And a social security number ? How have you held a job without one?"

"Well, I've never really worked . . ." Her voice trailed off.

Redmond stood up so quickly that his chair toppled over behind him, but he didn't seem to notice as he made a sharp gesture toward the two-way glass. "I've had enough of your bullshit," he said roughly. "You don't have any identification, you don't have a local address. A man dies right in front of you, and you have this screwed-up attitude like it's no big deal. Maybe a night or two in lockup will put you a little more on the cooperative side." By the time he'd finished speaking, two female police officers had come into the room and taken a position on each side of her.

"I don't know what you want me to cooperate *about*," she countered. "I didn't kill Toby, and I don't . . . know who did."

Redmond had already turned his back to her, but he picked up instantly on her hesitation. He spun and pushed his face close to hers. "You saw something, didn't you? Something or someone. And out of all these killings, you are the *only* one who did. So why don't you help us out, huh?"

She wasn't sure why, but Brynna wasn't ready to talk about the killer or the fact that she'd followed him back to what was mostly likely his apartment building. She might need this information to help herself, and giving it out to this cop could change everything, could put her into the public eye in a way that would be devastatingly unsafe. She shook her head. "No. I can't."

"You're lying," Redmond said flatly. He jerked his head at the uniformed women. "Take her to booking. For now, just make it a twenty-four-hour hold."

Brynna didn't bother watching Detective Redmond as he walked out. In another moment, the two officers had rehandcuffed her and were leading her out. She was more interested in the next twenty-four hours. Did he think she would be frightened? That was ridiculous—it was such a short period of time, not even a twitch of her eyelid in the passage that had been her existence. It had been a long time since she'd been on Earth, and she'd already decided that being in the belly of this building was a safe enough place. Like being in the belly of a whale, protected from the sharks circling in the dangerous waters of the outside sea. Spending the next day here would, Brynna believed, go a long way toward bringing her up-to-date on part of the culture that modern mankind had developed.

"MAYBE THIS WILL MAKE her more cooperative," Eran Redmond said as he and Sathi watched Brynna Malak being led away by two policewomen, both of whom were considerably shorter than their prisoner.

"Perhaps," his partner agreed.

Redmond turned to look at him. "You don't sound convinced."

Still watching as Brynna and her escorts disappeared around a corner, Sathi crossed his arms. "There is something . . . *strange* about that woman," he finally noted. "I can't quite figure it out."

"She's very attractive," Redmond said without thinking.

When his friend sent him a wry glance, Redmond shrugged. "Come on, it's not like you didn't notice, too."

"I did," Sathi admitted. "But I think it would be a grave mistake to do anything about it."

"Yeah," Redmond said. He pushed open the main door and headed out to the parking lot and their waiting car. His face darkened and he couldn't keep a hint of bitterness from edging out with his words. "It always is."

A corner of Sathi's mouth lifted. "In your love life, that does seem to be the unfortunate truth, my friend. But in this instance . . ." He didn't finish.

Redmond started to prod him, then decided not to. It wouldn't do any good to put Sathi on the spot when Redmond had a feeling the man couldn't explain himself. Just as Redmond himself couldn't explain that even though his partner had never finished what he was saying about Brynna Malak, Redmond knew *exactly* what he was talking about. To start with, there was the obvious: A cop never, *ever* hooked up with someone involved in a case. Redmond couldn't think of any faster way to screwed-up, and although anyone with a brain would say it was a no-brainer, he'd seen plenty of good cops take their careers right into the crapper by doing just that. He didn't need any personal education on it, thank you very much. He already had enough of a family history to know what the flipside of being one of the good guys could get you.

But as Sathi had noted, there was, indeed, *something* about Brynna Malak.

Setting his jaw, Eran forced away his thoughts of her as he climbed into his car and went about the rest of his day.

Three

The two policewomen took Brynna to a lower level, then through a locked door where there were four holding cells fronted by a long hallway. The cells weren't particularly large, each only about fifteen by fifteen feet, with an exposed metal toilet in a back corner. The fronts and sides of each cell were made of steel bars. A layer of steel mesh woven between the sides gave the occupants something to lean against without being grabbed by someone else from behind. The back wall was dirty gray and covered in stains and graffiti, and the air stank of urine and unwashed flesh.

A female guard sat on a chair by the entry door, occasionally glancing at the occupants with a bored but experience-sharp gaze. Her belt was laden with tools and weapons, including a stun gun and a long billy club with a well-worn handle and scarred surface. Once the handcuffs were removed, Brynna was shoved inside one of the center cells and promptly forgotten. The two cops left and the guard never tried to talk to her. Brynna didn't have anything to say anyway.

The short benches along each wall were taken and

there was nowhere else to sit besides the dirty floor. Brynna was used to being looked at, so the stares of the other women—desire mixed with appraisal—didn't bother her. She settled against the back wall on the right side, where she could observe her cellmates as well as the women in the holding area next to her. It was an unsavory group, and more than a few of them knew each other. Brynna watched all of them, drinking in the different accents, languages, and personalities, soaking up as much as she could in such a restricted situation.

"You don't look like a whore." The woman who moved to stand next to her was short but sturdily built. Her hair was a flat, dyed black that showed lighter roots, and her heavy eye makeup was smudged. She was wearing a red vinyl miniskirt and her muscular legs looked out of place above spike high heels that were a not-quite-matching scarlet. Across the backside of the too-tight skirt, the word *Candy* was stitched in flowery pink script. Glimpsed from a cruising car, little Candy—if that was really her name—might look eighteen, but up close her face showed her to be more like forty. Brynna figured the woman was actually in her late twenties, weak willed and already thoroughly corrupted. It wasn't surprising she was attracted to Brynna. "So what're you in here for?"

Brynna barely gave her a glance. "I guess they don't like me."

Candy's mouth twisted at the unspoken rejection. "I get it. A smart-ass."

Brynna finally looked at her. "If that's what you want to call it."

"Hey, I'm just trying to be friendly!" Candy's voice rose

enough to make a couple of the other women look her way. She stepped closer to where Brynna was seated. Predictably, the guard ignored all of them.

"I'm not looking for friends," Brynna retorted. "And if I was, I wouldn't pick you."

"Well, just *fuck* you, then!" Candy's face flushed. "You snotty-ass bitch, just who the hell do you think you are?" When Brynna didn't bother to answer, Candy bent forward slightly. "I oughta teach you a lesson, that's what I oughta do. You stupid cunt, you don't know nothing about nothing."

"Go away," Brynna finally said. All she wanted to do was sit and watch the interaction among the others. She didn't want to be a part of anything, she certainly didn't want to have a conversation with this twit, and she was starting to get annoyed.

"Fuck you," Candy said again. She drew one foot back and aimed a kick at Brynna's leg.

Bad idea.

Brynna caught Candy's ankle long before the pointy toe of her shoe connected with anything. She was going to dump the woman on her backside, then decided that wouldn't be a good idea—it would cause a ruckus and get the guard's attention. Any police presence in the holding cells would affect the behavior of the women. Since she wanted to see how things happened on their own, it was better to keep the guard out of it. Of course, the issue with Candy itself was just another lesson in how humans treated one another. Rather than take the little prostitute to the ground, Brynna used one hand to simply pin her foot to the floor.

Candy grunted and wobbled on her other foot, try-ing to maintain her balance. "Hey, let go!" She scowled, not understanding how Brynna was able to hold her. She hopped slightly, trying to get into a better position. "Bitch!"

Brynna sighed, then pressed harder. There was a faint *crack* as the arched part of the woman's shoe broke and flattened against the floor. Candy gasped in pain and tried futilely to jerk her foot free. Brynna sent a dark glance in Candy's direction. "Of all the people in here, I'm the one you *least* want to fuck with," Brynna said in a low voice. "Go *away*."

"Fine," Candy spat. "What*ever*." This time when she pulled, Brynna let her go. Candy tripped backward, then stomped off to another corner in the holding cell, although her attempt to look haughty was made comical by her lopsided, broken-shoed gait. Every now and then she'd shoot a poisonous glance in Brynna's direction, but at least she'd learned to keep her distance.

The hours passed, measured unceasingly by a clock on the wall opposite the holding cells. For some, the time obviously went more slowly. Brynna watched in amuse-ment as a few of the better-dressed prostitutes repeatedly banged on the bars and called out to the guard, who was very good at ignoring nearly everything and got up only to open the holding cell door when necessary. Various cops came and went, sometimes bringing someone new, occa-sionally selecting someone for release or whatever other fate awaited them. Once in a great while the guard would push a tray laden with flimsy plastic cups of water—no food—into each holding cell. Listening to the prisoners' constant loud complaints, Brynna thought they should count their blessings. Five hundred years ago being taken away by a prison guard had been a guaranteed death sentence, and the suffering endured before the killing itself had been unspeakable.

Midnight came and went, then another round of cops came in, this time steering in front of them a terrified-looking girl who probably wasn't yet out of her teens. Her blond hair was long and tangled and her face and hands were dirty. Brynna could see clean spots on her cheeks where tears had washed away the grime. "Please," the girl kept saying to the two stone-faced officers. "This is all just a big mistake. If you'd just get my dad on the phone, he'll straighten it all out. I just—"

"Daddy's not home," one of them said coldly. "Spend the night in here and see how you like it."

"But—"

"Save it."

The guard pulled the door open and one of the cops pushed the girl inside the holding cell. She stumbled against one of the older prostitutes, a thin Hispanic with leathery skin and unreadable dark eyes. "Watch where you're going, dumb shit," she snapped and gave the girl a hard shove. The hooker pulled on the straps of her dirty tank top like she was straightening a major wardrobe mishap.

"S-Sorry." The teenager backed away and looked around. Her eyes were slightly wild but Brynna could see her fighting to stay calm. "Sorry." She turned to plead with the cops again, but they were disappearing through the exit door at the far end of the hallway. She hung on the bars for a moment, then wisely decided it was a better idea not to have her back to the other occupants.

"Well, ain't you just a pretty little thing." The Latina sidled up to the newcomer, then reached out and fingered some of the light-colored hair spilling down the girl's back. "I'd make a lot of points with my man for turning you out." She gave the girl a sly, tobacco-stained smile, then let her thin fingers drop to the teen's shoulder. "What's your name, *chica*? You and me, we'll hook up once we get out of here. What do you say?"

"No, I don't think so." The teenager stepped sideways to get out of reach, then shook her head. A look of horror skittered across her features before she could disguise it.

The hooker didn't miss a beat. "You in our world now, girl." One hand whipped forward and snagged a fistful of the young woman's hair. "You need to think real hard about where your ass currently is before you get all high-end. This ain't the North Shore."

The teen gasped and tried unsuccessfully to get her fingers between the woman's hand and her scalp to stop the pulling. "Stop it!"

The older woman just sneered at her. "Don't be telling me what to do." She sent a sideways glance to the hallway to make sure the guard wasn't looking their way, then pulled down on the girl's head at the same time she brought her knee up and into the younger woman's ribs. The teenager gasped and opened her mouth to yell, but the hooker's other hand cut the cry short when they wrapped around her target's throat and squeezed. "Shhhh," she said. She jerked her head at another one of the women, who hurried over to join in the fun. "We're just going to show you a few things. Call it a reality check. You don't want to make any noise, see, because if the guard gets pissed at us, we'll get pissed at you."

Watching from the corner as the two started taking halfhearted jabs at their victim, Brynna frowned as a third woman, heavier built and with old needle scars along her elbows, grinned nastily and ambled toward the group. It really wasn't Brynna's responsibility to step in, but this girl was in trouble and, from the looks of it, things were going to get worse. This pretty young woman probably represented everything these hard cases could never have: youth, wealth, opportunity. For some those choices had never existed at all and they did what they could with what they'd been born into; for others—and maybe these were worse—she was the picture of the lives they'd once had and thrown away. Either way, Brynna thought that although the girl had walked in, she'd be going out on a stretcher.

The group had grown to four or five, and now they were scuffling quietly in the corner. One of the prostitutes did something, but the girl's shriek was muffled by a hand slammed over her mouth. The guard didn't even notice—her attention was on the glossy pages of some magazine. Brynna saw the teen being bent backward. If the women took her to the floor, they might end up permanently disfiguring her . . . or worse.

"Shit," Brynna muttered as she stood. What the hell—maybe she'd get a few celestial brownie points for playing rescuer.

"Oh, lookie here." Candy's sarcastic voice slid into her ear as she moved to walk with Brynna. "Ms. Snotty decides to participate." She gave a little extra push to the last syllable—par-ti-ci-*pate.*

Brynna ignored her, and when she got to the women crowded around the hapless teenager, she jammed one arm between the two closest backs, then rammed her elbow first in one direction, then the other. The impact sent two of the hookers stumbling and the others were startled enough to pause. Brynna needed only a second to wrap her fingers around the girl's arm and haul her out from the middle of the vicious group.

"Fun's over," she said. They stared at her as if she should say something more, but Brynna didn't feel obligated to explain herself. The girl was already a mess, with one eye swollen shut, a split lip, and the left side of her face gouged by someone's artificial fingernails. The way she was hunched over hinted she might have a cracked rib or two. Brynna pushed her none-too-gently to the back corner, where she slid down the wall and cowered like a beaten dog.

"What the *fuck*?" the Hispanic woman demanded. "I'll break your ugly face, bitch!"

"I doubt that."

"I don't," someone else said. The added comment came from the biggest gal in the holding cell, the one with needle scars on the dark brown skin of her arms. She was a couple of inches shorter than Brynna but outweighed her by a good thirty pounds; that put her at close to two hundred, so despite whatever toll the drugs had taken on her body, nothing had affected her appetite. Besides being tall, strong, and street-smart, she was confident and undoubtedly believed she was as mean as a starving wolf.

Brynna loved it when humans thought that.

Wait—she was supposed to be doing good here, not breaking heads. Plus she needed to remember her human body—although she could do many things not written in the *Homo sapiens* rule book and this shell wasn't nearly as fragile as a normal body, she could still be hurt. If she needed a reminder, all she had to do was glance at the substantial expanse of scabbed-over skin on her right arm.

The sturdy black woman stepped close enough to almost touch Brynna, but Brynna didn't move. When the prostitute spoke, her words came out with the scents of old onions and older meat. "You gonna step aside and we gonna continue our fun with Miz Preppie over there. Then it's your turn." Her mouth turned up. "But first, lemme give you something to look forward to."

Brynna had almost decided to just take whatever blow Meat Mouth was going to give, but at the last instant she changed her mind. She'd had enough pain—maybe not so much here on Earth, but more than enough for a million lifetimes in Hell. What these hookers could deal out was nothing in the scheme of eternity, but there was that one big question, wasn't there?

Why should she?

As Astarte she'd had power in Hell, but there had always been those with more than she had—Lucifer himself, of course, and those demons charged by him to oversee the oceans of agony and ensure that no corner of Lucifer's Kingdom ever ran dry. And what had she been? Only one more of Lucifer's possessions over which he could gloat, the most prized, the best, she who had to dance to his every whim as she waited for the current never-ending moment to pass so that the next could begin. Even as she was, a Highborn angel fallen to demon, she knew what it felt like to shrink beneath the shadow of torment, to cringe away from creatures the concept of which would drive those around her now instantly insane. She knew the feel, smell and taste of her own blood, the pain of the spirit, and the true suffering of the flesh.

And she would not stand still and experience so much as a droplet of it from the woman standing in front of her. No human would ever have that kind of power over her. The very notion of it made heat flare up within her skull.

A *lot* of heat.

Brynna's eyes flashed briefly red and she stepped forward so fast that one knee was between the other woman's legs before she could do anything about it. There was barely time to blink, then Brynna's face was right *there,* almost touching the other's, and the breath—and there was so *much* of it—that Brynna exhaled as she spoke suddenly smelled dark and sweet, like hot, rotting cherries, all the while promising so much more.

"Do you think that you frighten me, little streetwalker?" Brynna whispered. The big woman instinctively tried to backpedal at the same time that her body was drawn of its own accord to Brynna's, but two of Brynna's fingers had already found the low neckline of the prostitute's red T-shirt. Her forefinger slipped over the fabric's edge, then went deeper, digging into sweaty cleavage. "I have eaten the hearts of men who've murdered a thousand whores like you, then sewn up their chests just so I could tear them apart again." Brynna's lips were so close to the other woman's that they brushed as she spoke; her tongue flicked out, like a snake's, and she tasted the fear and unbidden lust that oozed from the nicotine-scented flesh of the hooker's mouth. Brynna tilted her head and stared into her opponent's eyes, feeling the fire behind her own beckoning. "Would you like me to show you how it's done?"

Her prisoner—because really, that's what the hooker had become—swallowed, then coughed as fear smothered longing and made her choke on her own saliva. She whimpered as the skin between her breasts started to blister. "Yo, honey, I was just fucking with you. Didn't mean no harm. It's all right. We're good." She was nearly babbling. "Yeah, we're real good, I swear."

"I've had just about enough of your white-bread ass," the Latina suddenly snarled. She launched herself in Brynna's direction with a tight, experienced swing, then found herself crumpling as Brynna's other hand whipped out and her fist was covered over by Brynna's very, *very* hot fingers. A faint wisp of oily black smoke wafted upward from the joined hands, and Brynna noticed that the Hispanic woman was the one with the clawlike fingernails. They were pretty damned ineffective right now. In fact, they seemed to be melting along the edges. "I-I—" Whatever the working girl had planned to say was lost in a garbled moan of pain and the smell of charring human flesh.

She'd been going to let the Hispanic hooker fall, but instead Brynna decided to introduce her two annoyances to each other. A satisfying jerk sent the two women crashing together face-first, hard enough to make teeth snap and bones bruise. Brynna held them there so she could study them for a few seconds, then let go. Both women went down, clutching at each other like stumbling mountain climbers.

She looked around, but the other occupants had backed away. She could feel heat painting the inside of her body, the exhilarating anticipation of violence. Her skin was probably a nice rosy red. "Anyone else care to introduce yourself?"

Her question got a lot of head shaking and negative noises, but one woman's muttering wasn't difficult for Brynna's sensitive hearing to pick up. "Bitch's gotta sleep sometime."

Brynna laughed harshly, and the sound, a bastard cross between blackboard scratches and a hyena's cry, made her cell companions wince. "Actually, that's incorrect. I'd *like* to sleep, but I don't *have* to." She turned her head quickly enough so that her gaze met and held that of the woman who'd spoken. Once pretty, this young streetwalker had brown hair and lifeless eyes. Night living had aged her way beyond her years. The hooker tried bravely to hold it, but after only a few seconds she had to look away from Brynna's smoldering stare.

"My hand," groaned the Latina. She was still on the floor next to her would-be battle companion, but now she was sitting with her knees drawn tightly against her chest while she cradled one hand with the other. "It's burned—God, it hurts so *bad*."

"Stop whining," Brynna said offhandedly. "You have no idea what a *real* burn feels like." She felt the stares of the others, most of whom were just now noticing the scabby expanse of skin on Brynna's upper arm. She only grinned at them.

No one stepped forward to defend the two women she'd put down or to get to the childish one she was protecting, so Brynna finally went over and sat beside the teenager. The girl was quiet and withdrawn—in shock, maybe—and Brynna was inclined to leave her that way. She wasn't interested in a life story that would come with an obligatory chapter about how *a girl like me suddenly found myself in a place like this.* The lack of conversation suited her just fine.

She was, Brynna discovered, vaguely disappointed at the lack of fight all these women had. She'd been gearing up for a lengthy, all-out and bloody brawl, maybe something akin to a fight at an English country pub in the thirteenth century. But no, not in this day and age. That she yearned for a confrontation like that disturbed her all the more. She'd come back to Earth to be the opposite of what she'd become in Lucifer's Kingdom, to return to the light of Grace and leave the lure of the dark behind forever. Instead, she had been fully willing to reopen her shadow side, or at least a bit of it on a smaller, earthly scale. She was disappointed in herself, and if she felt that way, someone with much more rigid standards was likely displeased as well . . . that is, if He had even noticed.

Then again, the attitude, habits and lifestyle learned after an uncountable passage of time weren't so easily banished, so maybe she needed to give herself a break, chalk it up to the learning curve. After all, the humans she was surrounded by certainly weren't going to sympathize, and from what she'd seen so far—witness how she'd ended up in here because of one of society's so-called protectors—the ones on the outside wouldn't either. So often there was a purpose to the things that happened; maybe she'd been put in here for a reason, even if it was only to protect the withdrawn young woman sitting next to her.

REDMOND AND HIS PARTNER came for Brynna at about eight the next morning. She caught his scent—fresh bath and laundry soap and a pleasantly scented aftershave—before anyone saw him, but apparently he was quite a familiar face to the ladies of the night with whom she had spent the last eighteen or so hours. The two detectives kept their expressions emotionless and ignored the cat-calls and jeering flirtations leveled at them by the hookers. Redmond jerked his head in Brynna's direction, and it wasn't until she stood and came to the front of the holding cell with the battered teenager scrambling after her that his stony countenance gave way.

"Please," the girl whimpered as she clutched at Brynna's arm. "Please don't leave me here. *Please.*"

Brynna opened her mouth but didn't know what to say. This, she suddenly realized, was likely to be only the first of many situations in her new world over which she would have little control.

"What the hell happened to you?" Redmond demanded.

His tone of voice made the teenager shrink backward, but not far enough to release her hold on Brynna. Redmond scowled when she didn't answer, then motioned at the duty cop. A moment later the policewoman was unlocking the holding cell's door. "Let's go, Brynna."

The teenager gasped and her hold went from tight to desperate. Brynna started to pry her loose, then hesitated. "They'll kill her," she said in a low voice.

Redmond and his partner stared at Brynna, then Redmond's gaze flicked over the teenager's face again and his eyes narrowed. During the night the skin around the younger woman's battered eye had gone purplish-blue, and the gouges along her cheek had taken on an angry red tinge around the edges. "Fuck," he muttered. "Asher!" he snapped. The guard looked up in surprise at Redmond's tone. "Maybe you ought to keep your attention on the prisoners rather than those magazines," he ground out.

She started to snap something in return, then her gaze followed his pointing finger. Her face paled, and suddenly she was all business. "You," she ordered and motioned at the girl. "Get out here." As the girl stumbled out behind Brynna, the policewoman wrapped a hand around the teenager's wrist and her face darkened when she realized the girl had been more than a little bruised up. "I'll have you taken up to medical." She glared at the rest of the women in the holding cell, but no one looked especially concerned. "Well," Asher said to no one in particular as she made sure the cell door relocked, "I'll probably have to use the hose to stop any more altercations. And this bunch sure looks like the type who's going to need controlling."

That, Brynna noticed, wiped away most of the sneers. She saw several of the women glance at a neatly folded green hose hanging on the wall in the middle of the hallway across from the cells. Above it was a valve labeled simply ON and OFF. It wasn't hard to imagine how a powerful spray of cold water might instantly take the belligerence out of a group of fighting prisoners.

The girl sent Brynna a final grateful look and was hustled off in the other direction. Although Brynna was handcuffed again, she could sense that most of Detective Redmond's animosity toward her had dissipated. She didn't know why, but she hoped that meant she could get out of here; she'd learned all she cared to know about this part of Chicago's nighttime culture.

"We're going to turn you loose," Redmond said, almost as if he were tuned in to her thoughts. "I gave some consideration to charging you with assaulting an officer, but that's just too damned much paperwork to screw around with."

He glanced at her, expecting her to say something, but Brynna stayed silent. He looked disgusted and shook his head slightly. Belatedly Brynna wondered if she was supposed to have said thanks.

"One of the reasons I'm going to give you a break is that I want you to think about coming clean about what you saw when Gallagher was killed," Redmond continued. "A lot of people have died and we're just chasing our tails here. If more die and you could've helped identify the killer, it's going to be on your conscience. There's no correlation among the victims, Ms. Malak. For all we know, next time it might be a five-year-old kid." His blue eyes were penetrating. "Can you be okay with looking yourself in the mirror if that happens?"

Brynna opened her mouth to say it wasn't her business, but the words didn't come out. *Wasn't* it her business? She'd escaped Hell to save herself, but doing that wasn't going to be a free ride. She had some learning to do, some *giving*. Where she'd come from, fear and respect were just part of what came with her position. Here in the world of humans, if she wanted to be viewed favorably, she would have to earn it whether she liked the idea or not. "He had brown hair," she finally offered. "Kind of brownish-green eyes. And he was tall."

Redmond and his partner jerked to a stop in the middle of the hallway, then steered her into a sharp right turn and hurried her up a flight of stairs. More turns and stairs, then he was motioning her toward a chair on the other side of a desk that was one of dozens in a large, noisy room. Redmond's partner—for the first time Brynna noticed that the ID hanging from his pocket said SATHI—leaned over without comment and unlocked the handcuffs. Brynna didn't bother to rub her wrists.

Redmond nearly leaped onto the chair behind the desk, then yanked out a notebook and began scribbling in it. "What else?" he asked. "What was he wearing? Did you notice anything else about him? A weapon?"

Brynna made a show of trying to concentrate. "He had on some kind of long jacket," she said at last. "If he had a gun, I never saw it. Maybe he hid it beneath that coat." There, she thought. That was all she was going to give them. After all, there was no way for her to explain how she could follow the man to his apartment building, or even that she knew for sure it was the same person. Chicago's finest were going to have to figure out the rest for themselves.

Redmond sat back, tapping his pen against the table-top. "What the hell," he said. "It's a whole lot more than we had before yesterday."

Sathi nodded. "Cut her loose?"

"Yeah." Redmond stood. "Let's go, Ms. Malak. We'll escort you out."

Barely two minutes later, the two detectives had walked her downstairs to the front desk area. The two men turned and headed back inside and Brynna moved toward the door at a fast walk. Her eyes were on the beckoning sunlight outside when a dark-haired woman charged into the foyer and nearly knocked her over. She was speaking in rapid-fire Spanish, her words tumbling and shrieking and jumbled with panic.

"¡Que alguien nos ayude, por favor! ¡Mi marido está teniendo un ataque al corazón! ¡Por favor, por favor—ayúdenos que se me muere!"

"Ma'am—ma'am!" the desk sergeant tried to interrupt. *"No habla* Spanish! Speak English!"

The woman either didn't understand him or was too excited to comprehend what he was saying anyway. *"¡Alguien debe entenderme! ¡Por favor, él está en el coche, allí delante del edificio a la derecha! ¡No creo que podamos conseguir el hospital a tiempo—él morirá!"*

"Does anyone here speak Spanish?" the sergeant bellowed. "She's talking too fast—I need some assistance here!"

"She's saying her husband's having a heart attack," Brynna said without thinking. "She's parked out front and he's in the car. She thinks he's going to die before they can get to a hospital."

The desk sergeant's eyes widened, then he darted around the desk and ran outside. Two more uniformed officers followed as another man behind the desk yanked up a telephone handset, punched in a two-digit code, and spoke rapidly into the mouthpiece. "Dispatch, we need an ambulance stat at—"

Brynna turned back toward the door, then stopped as the Hispanic woman went to her knees in front of the desk and sobbed. *"Señora,"* Brynna said, hesitating.

She gave the woman's shoulder an awkward squeeze. *"Él tendrá todo razón."* He will be all right. She didn't know if she sounded comforting or not, but it was the best she could do—she just wasn't used to this. *"Le ayudarán."* They will help you. Within another twenty seconds one of the cops had returned and gathered up the crying woman, and by the time an ambulance wailed to a stop outside, things had calmed down enough to where Brynna thought that she might be able to finally get out of there.

"You never mentioned you spoke Spanish." She paused at the sound of Detective Redmond's voice.

Brynna considered replying that he'd never asked, but gave him a noncommittal shrug instead. "I . . . have an ear for languages."

Redmond's eyebrows raised in surprise. "So you speak more than one."

"Sure."

"Really. How many?" When she hesitated, he folded his arms and looked even more disbelieving. "Come on, either you know or you don't."

The smug tone of his voice was aggravating. "All of them," she snapped.

Redmond's mouth opened, but for a moment he couldn't say anything. "Right." It was clear he thought she was insane.

"Whether you think I'm telling the truth makes no difference to me," Brynna told him.

He studied her without saying anything for a few moments. While she waited—and she wasn't sure why she was bothering—Brynna thought that women probably found him quite attractive. The rough ladies in the holding cell hadn't kept their admiration a secret when he'd gone down there, and although the noncriminal females up here—policewomen and others—were more subtle, it wasn't hard to pick up on the vibe. "So you're going to stick with that story," he said eventually. When she only looked at him, Redmond finally added, "Claiming that you can understand any language."

"I don't have any reason to lie to you about that."

"Uh-huh." He pressed his lips together and she knew he hadn't missed the qualifier—*about that*. He carefully adjusted his glasses before he spoke again. "Tell you what. I have a meet this afternoon with a Korean guy to talk about his daughter's disappearance. He doesn't speak English very well, so you be back here at two o'clock and run interference."

"Interference?"

"Translate for me," Redmond said patiently. He kept his expression carefully bland. "Back and forth." When Brynna didn't agree right away, he leaned forward slightly. "Is there a problem?"

"I don't keep track of time," was all Brynna could think of to say.

The detective glanced at her wrists, then unbuckled the band of the watch he was wearing. "Take this."

Redmond's partner had been standing silently the entire time, but now he frowned. "Eran—"

"She'll bring it back." Redmond's gaze sought Brynna's. "Won't you?"

There was nothing for her to do but accept the watch. "Of course." She peered at the band, then fastened it clumsily around one wrist. "I'm not a thief."

"Of course," Detective Sathi echoed. He made no attempt to hide the sarcasm in his voice.

"Easy, Bheru," Redmond said. "It's a cheap sports watch." Redmond glanced back at Brynna, then pulled a twenty-dollar bill from his pocket and offered it her. "Here."

She didn't reach for the money. "Why?"

"Why not?"

"But what is it for?"

Redmond looked at her oddly. "If you insist on a reason, call it an interpreter's fee." He motioned toward the commotion out front, which was rapidly drawing to a close. "For helping us out with that lady and her husband."

Brynna pondered this for a moment, then nodded and accepted the bill. "All right." She turned to go.

"Is there somewhere we can drive you?" Detective Sathi asked her in his lilting accent. "You are supposed to be back here in"—he glanced at his own wristwatch—"just about four hours."

Brynna wondered if the man realized that she could speak Hindi better than he could. She resisted the urge, knowing it would probably irritate him. "No, thanks. I'm not going far."

"Indeed."

Brynna smiled a little, charmed by his formality in spite of herself. "I'm good," she promised. "I'll be back."

She knew they wanted to know more, but like all good things, her many, many secrets would have to wait to be revealed.

Four

True to her word, Brynna stayed in the neighborhood. It felt odd to be bound by a human schedule, but that was just one more thing she would have to adapt to in this world. Her stomach was twisting, rumbling, and rather painful, and although that could be ignored—she'd endured much worse—this was the start of the third day in this female form without something to eat and it was starting to run down—like an automobile, the body required fuel to keep going.

She found a restaurant on Cermak Road about ten blocks away from the courthouse, a tiny place with a sign that read NICKEL AND DIME DINER above the front windows. The inside was just as grubby as the outside, with a half dozen booths beneath the windows and ten or twelve stools along the counter. Brynna chose a booth toward the back where she could sit just out of sight of the street yet still see who came through the door. Redmond and Sathi had followed her, although they had no idea she knew it. They drove with their car windows open and like the nephilim killer, each had a unique scent which she would forever be able to instantly identify. Their surveillance didn't bother her, but she must never let her guard down regarding Lucifer's Hunters. Sitting at the counter closest to the door were a couple of uniformed cops, but they didn't make Brynna feel any safer.

The waitress was a tired-looking woman of about fifty, with graying blond hair and the wrinkles of a hard life showing on her face. A name tag on her chest identified her as Paige. While she waited, Brynna scanned the dingy plastic-covered menu at the table. "Coffee," Brynna finally said. "I want something without flesh, but I don't see—"

"W-What?"

The stutter made Brynna look up. Paige's eyes had widened and she was staring at Brynna. "Meat," Brynna corrected. Oddly, sometimes the stupidest details of a dialect would trip her up. "I don't eat meat."

"Oh!" Paige scribbled on her book, looking relieved. "The cook can make you a vegetarian omelet, no problem. You want potatoes? Toast?"

"Yes and yes," Brynna answered. She glanced to her right and saw an old man at the counter munching on a piece of dark-colored bread. "Rye," she added. Before Paige could leave, Brynna asked, "Can you give me change for a twenty? I want to buy a newspaper."

The woman glanced at the scarred tabletop, where someone had left three quarters and a couple of pennies. "Just take it out of that," she said wearily, then walked away.

Brynna watched her go, wondering what kind of life the waitress lived outside of this place. Paige smelled like bacon grease, cigarette smoke, and coffee, as though the restaurant had a soul and had insinuated itself into her skin. Beneath that was a faint scent of laundry detergent and a sense of wear, like every day was just one more chore.

After a few moments Brynna picked up the three quarters and went outside. There were two newspaper machines, one for the *Chicago Tribune* and one for the *Chicago Sun-Times*; she chose the *Sun-Times* for no other reason than its smaller format would be easier to manage. Back inside, she worked her way through it, stopping only to enjoy the food that Paige brought. It might not have been the best the city had to offer, but as her first meal since she'd gotten here, Brynna thought it was damned good and finished every bite.

Concentrating again on the paper, she quickly read nearly every page and used it as a learning tool—there was no faster way to acquaint herself with this city and environment. Competing with politics and gasoline prices was a big chunk of space devoted to the man who had shot the nephilim talking to Brynna in the drugstore yesterday. Advertisements, birth and wedding announcements, even the obituaries, were educational, and Brynna was a little amazed. The human life span had increased dramatically, yet what she read in the paper told her that mankind was still doing astoundingly stupid things to shorten their time on earth.

A few patrons, mostly cops, came and went, but the Nickel and Dime was anything but busy. Brynna stayed in the booth for almost three hours, with Paige clearing the dishes and refilling her coffee without comment. Brynna left the paper there for the next person and went to the register to pay; as she did, she watched one of the old men at the counter drop two dollars next to his empty coffee cup before he left. After another waitress rang up Brynna's check and handed her the change from her twenty, Brynna looked thoughtfully at the money in her hand, then walked back and dropped the ten-dollar bill on the table. Her burn was almost healed and barely even itched, and she couldn't think of anything else to buy. This would leave her with over four bucks—enough for a cheap lunch—and she owed Paige for the newspaper anyway. A ten-dollar tip would probably make Paige's day.

Even hung with car exhaust, the air outside was refreshing and warm after the smells of the stale, over-air-conditioned restaurant. The dirty concrete and trash blown along the curbs by passing cars and trucks made Brynna long to be back in the park by the lakefront, where she would have had a reason to take her time walking back to the courthouse. She thought about the butterfly that had kept her from being caught by the Hunter, but she wouldn't see anything that beautiful in this part of the city. This area was nothing but concrete and metal, broken only by tough, yellow-green weeds poking intermittently through cracks in the ground.

She knew when Redmond and his partner drove past in their car so they would get to the courthouse before her, just as she knew they were waiting down the hallway when she came out of the women's room after washing her face and hands. It was partly her sense of smell, yes, but it was also just a . . . *knowing*—what the humans might have incorrectly called a sixth sense, a term they had for trying to justify those things they would never be able to explain. The building was fairly quiet in the afternoon, the downside of the cycle before they built back up to the usual frenzy of a Chicago evening. The desk sergeant looked at her and frowned, but Redmond was there before the guy could question Brynna's presence.

"Glad you could make it, Ms. Malak," Detective Sathi said. "We were wondering if you would."

"No, you weren't," Brynna said flatly. "You knew where I was from the moment I left here." She turned toward Redmond, who looked oddly amused when his partner frowned. She unbuckled the detective's sports watch, then held it out. "Where is your . . ." Now it was her turn to frown.

Detective Redmond took his watch and strapped it back on. "Come with us, please." Brynna fell into step between the two men and they moved deeper into the building. "He's not *my* anything. He's just a regular citizen whose daughter disappeared about a week ago."

"And you think I can somehow help."

Redmond shrugged. "The guy barely understands English and I'm not doing much better with what he says. Interpreters are like cops—there's never one around when you need one." He grinned a little at his own joke. "So that's where you come in. Provided, of course, you can do what you say you can."

"I told you, I have no reason to lie to you."

"Right." Brynna glanced at him, but there was no sarcasm in Redmond's voice and his expression was placid.

"In here." Sathi pushed open a door that had a frosted-glass pane in its upper half and INTERVIEW 5 on it. A

Korean man sat at a table in the center of the nearly empty room. The turquoise-colored silk scarf he was working with his fingers was the only spot of color in the room except for the dull yellow of a new legal pad a few inches away from him. The fabric was pocked with dirt smudges and frayed from rough treatment, as though it had been stepped on.

Brynna and the two detectives filed in and Detective Sathi pulled the door shut behind him. Redmond and Brynna took seats across the table from the Korean man but Sathi stayed back, leaning against the door and folding his arms like a bouncer outside of a nightclub.

Beneath a thick salt-and-pepper crew cut, the Korean's face was angular and thin, the wrinkled skin loose as if he'd recently lost a lot of weight. When he looked at Brynna, his expression was a mixture of hope and desolation, like a man hanging on to the loose dirt along the edge of a cliff who still thinks that somehow he will survive the coming plummet.

"This is Kim Li-kang," Redmond said. "Mr. Kim speaks extremely limited English but he does understand some important words and concepts." The detective had brought a thin file folder with him, and now he flipped it open and pushed a photograph toward Brynna. "Mr. Kim's daughter is Cho-kyon. She's nineteen and a nursing student at the University of Illinois. We estimate she's been missing for about two weeks. We can't pinpoint the exact date of her disappearance because they didn't speak every day. The last time she called him was a Friday afternoon after class. Her roommate went away for the weekend, so she went missing sometime between then and Monday morning, when she didn't show up for her classes." Redmond frowned but didn't look up. "No one's seen her. Right now we have no leads."

Brynna examined the photograph, which showed a young girl with shoulder-length straight black hair and a sweet smile. She handed it back to Redmond. "And what am I doing here?"

Redmond closed the folder. "We've got a real language handicap here. I *think* Mr. Kim is trying to tell me that he has information. I don't know why he didn't find someone where he works to translate for him, but he wouldn't." He looked at her steadily. "You say you can speak Korean. I think the rest is obvious."

It was. Without bothering to look again at either detective, Brynna leaned toward Kim. *"Kim-shi, Jae irumun Brynna imnida. Hyongsa ae mal hago ship uen gosul essunmika?"* *My name is Brynna, Mr. Kim. Is there something you wish me to tell the detective?* She picked up Sathi's indrawn breath and resisted the urge to smile; the fool really *had* thought she was lying.

The Korean man looked surprised, but only for a second. Then he began speaking rapidly. *"E goes cun nae dal seu-kapeu imnida,"* he said. *This is my daughter's scarf.* His fingers clutched at it. *"Bangkok uel bang mun han chinchok uen chak nyun ae boe naesumnida. E gol kolmok an ae chajassumnida. E go bwa— irum uel ba neul jilhan gos ae essumnida."* *A relative who visited Bangkok sent it to us last year. I found this in the alley. Look—here is where she stitched her name on the edge.*

Redmond already had his pen poised over the legal pad. He scribbled rapidly as Brynna repeated what had been said and Kim pointed at the embroidered edge. "Ask him where exactly—the alley behind what?"

"*Clark gori ae rikyu jeom dwi ae kolmok essumnida. Keu nyeo ga sa neum gos aeso yak gan gu hwek molli neon. Cho-kyon eul bal gyeon ha gi wi ha yeo in guen an ae kolrokago essumnida,*" Kim replied when she did. *Behind a liquor store on Clark Street. Only a few blocks away from where she lives. I walk in the neighborhood to see if I can find Cho.* Brynna repeated the man's words in English. Before Redmond could ask his next question, Mr. Kim continued. His voice escalated with each word, becoming nearly a shriek by the time he was finished. "*Keu nom e ya—Kwan Chul-moo. Nae dal eul yoo gwae han nom e ya!*" *It is him—Kwan Chul-moo. He is the one who has my daughter!*

Mr. Kim had half risen from his chair and Sathi came forward and urged him back down as Brynna dutifully repeated the man's words. Redmond slipped his fingers beneath his glasses and rubbed his eyes. "I need more than him just saying this. I need proof, a *reason,* something more than a scarf found on a sidewalk. I can't barge into someone's house or business on hearsay. Getting a search warrant is only the second step—first he has to convince *me.*"

Brynna nodded. "Why do you say these things about Mr. Kwan?" she asked Mr. Kim in Korean. "The police need more than what you think. They need hard proof."

The older man's face twisted, and in the folds of emotion there Brynna saw fear, fury, and helplessness. His answer was long and passionate. By the end of it, he was crying and looked a decade older. The two detectives turned to her expectantly and there was silence for a few moments while Brynna tried to think how best to tell these modern-day policemen about the ways of a part of the world in which they would never believe.

"Kwan Chul-moo is a very rich man in the

neighborhood," Brynna told them. "A businessman, very respected. He has a daughter named Jin-eun, the same age as Mr. Kim's daughter, but Kwan cannot control her. She uses drugs and alcohol, and has sex with bad people. The things she has done have made her ill."

"In what manner?" Sathi asked.

"She has a disease—"

"AIDS?"

Brynna shrugged. "He didn't say—he might not actually know. Kwan has often tried to talk to Cho, to get her to work for him, to come to his jewelry shop or have lunch with him. Cho thought he was offensive and avoided him—she didn't trust his intentions. Mr. Kim believes that Kwan has kidnapped Cho to use her as a substitute for . . ." Brynna hesitated, but there was just no other way to tell it. "As a substitute for the demons that are tormenting his own daughter. Kim believes that a very powerful witch doctor has been hired to work magic that will fool the demons into believing that Cho is Jin-eun, and as long as Cho is held, this frees Jin-eun to go back to living a healthy life."

"Aw, crap," Redmond grumbled. "Now I have to deal with superstitious bullshit on top of a missing person." He was silent for a moment, then he asked, "I don't suppose Mr. Kim has any solid evidence that this guy nabbed his daughter?"

Brynna knew the answer without asking the Korean man, so she shook her head. At least now Brynna knew where Redmond would stand on this type of thing. She turned back to Mr. Kim and pointed at the scarf. "May I look at that?" she asked in Korean.

He pushed it across the table without comment, but Brynna paused before she touched it. This was a closed room, so the danger was minimal. Still, it was *always* there. If she did this, she would be opening herself, even if only for a span of seconds, to discovery. Redmond might think Kim was a crazy old Korean with Old World beliefs, but Brynna knew better. There were reasons the Korean people believed everyone's life was ruled by demons, and several of those nasty, invisible little reasons were probably squatting on his shoulder right now. If Brynna put herself in a position to see them, they would see *her* too. And they were so very, very talkative.

She reached out and laid her fingertips gently on top of the Thai silk. Her vision hazed over and she closed her eyes quickly, before she could meet the startled stares of—

Saturday morning, bright sunshine, cloying humidity already. The launderette smells of heat and soap, washers and dryers making a steady, noisy thrumming. Clothes in the washer, restroom in the back. Finished now, no hot water in the faucet, coming out the door and something stings her on the back of her neck. She reaches for the spot—

Blackness.

She wakes in terror and pain. Her vision is skewed with firelight and shadows. Chanting, cold, then hot, burning, the smell of smoking human hair, the sting of a blade, another sting—a needle? Floating, then flying, spinning, terrifying. Force-fed, poked, prodded, cut, another needle. The cycle begins again,

and again,

and again,

and again . . .

Brynna opened her eyes and Mr. Kim's two tiny demons were leering at her. They were small and fearful

creatures with leathery black skin, drooling and chittering to each other as they constantly pestered the man's
subconscious with doubts and enticements. Nothing else
could find purchase on this strong-willed old Korean,
who was no stranger to the basis for his peoples' faith and
would fight their temptations with his dying breath. She
should kill them before they ran and revealed her whereabouts to a Hunter—and they would—but this area was
too small. To do so would probably incinerate everyone in
the room but her.

Brynna lifted her hand from the silk scarf and the
demons disappeared from sight as if they'd never been
there.

"Her clothes are still in the machine," Brynna said
hoarsely. She didn't know why that was the first thing to
come out of her mouth. "At the washing house where she
was taken."

Detective Sathi stared at her as if she'd grown a second
head, while Redmond just looked flabbergasted. "What
the hell— Now you're a *psychic*?"

"No, I—"

"What washing house is this?" Sathi interrupted.
"Where is it located?"

Brynna frowned. "I don't know the address, if that's
what you mean. It's wherever she normally goes to do her
laundry. Walking distance from her apartment, I think."
When she turned back to Mr. Kim and asked, he confirmed that there was a self-service laundry only a couple
of blocks away. Most of the doorways off the alley hadn't
been marked, so he didn't know how close he'd found the
scarf to the place where Cho took her clothes.

Redmond tapped his pen hard against the legal pad. "And you say she was taken from there?"

"Yes."

"Who took her?"

"I don't know. It was a surprise. She was coming out of the restroom."

Sathi came over to the table and leaned on it, peering down at her. "How is it you can see all this?" he asked.

Redmond's jaw dropped. "You don't really believe this drivel, do you?"

Sathi shrugged. "I am open to being convinced. There are many strange things in the world." He glanced back at Brynna, and his expression made it clear he thought she was one of those strange things. "You have not answered my question."

Brynna tried to think of a way to explain. "I don't really *see* anything," she said. "Not actual images. It's more like a . . . a *feeling*. I can pick up how the girl felt at the time something was happening to her. It's kind of like being in her head during the moment." She gestured toward the scarf. "I don't know how that came off, but she was wearing it as a belt."

"Great." Redmond grabbed the scarf before Mr. Kim could retrieve it, then thrust it at Brynna. "Take this. We're gonna go find that laundromat."

Brynna jerked away from the piece of fabric. "*You* take it. I'm not touching the thing again."

"Great," Redmond muttered again. Kim tried to reach for his daughter's scarf, but Redmond wadded it up and stuffed it into a plastic evidence bag he pulled from one pocket. "Let's go take some clothes out of the washer."

THE NEIGHBORHOOD TO WHICH Detective Sathi drove the four of them was an odd mixture of cultures—Korean, Swedish, Pakistani, and more. Brynna stared out the back passenger window, fascinated by the shops, the people, the *peace*. Humans living in the world today didn't always see it the way she was perceiving it right now, of course; sometimes they focused only on the crime, fighting, wars, and plenty of evil. They thought the times were bad, and why? Because they had only a few hundred years of history to compare to their own short lives. It was too bad they couldn't have seen what would have happened two thousand years ago if just three of these nationalities had met at the apex of some primitive mountain. Each would have immediately tried to exterminate the other two for no more reason than the belief that anyone outside of their own tribe was inferior. Yes, there was still plenty of that behavior in the world, and there were still wars and fighting and murder, but here, on this one sun-filled Chicago street, people at least seemed capable of coexisting.

Brynna, however, did not blend in well.

She was taller than almost everyone, and certainly all the women. Her face was long, almost wolflike, and her features were dark and sharp. Her pale brown eyes were rimmed in shadows and her gaze was a magnet for other people's, especially men. The weaker the man, the more he vied for her attention—it was on this very weakness that the demon in her had preyed. Once upon a time, before she had grown weary of torment and fire, Brynna had walked the soil of this world as Astarte and hunted for just such souls, those ripe for corruption and the unknown lure of damnation. Now she just found that type annoying.

"Hey, sweetheart." An athletic-looking young guy of about twenty-five fell into step next to her, making a point of ignoring her two escorts. He was handsome and well-dressed; to Brynna he smelled like expensive aftershave and cocaine. His gaze swept Brynna's face and form appreciatively, then he licked his lips. His sudden hot desire thickened the air between them and gave it a honeylike scent that only Brynna and her unwanted devotee could smell. He was pathetic and weak-minded; if she didn't get rid of him fast, his lust would smother his reason and things would turn ugly. "I've been looking for you all my life. Let me buy you something beautiful."

Redmond frowned, but before he could open his mouth, Brynna's stinging gaze pinned her admirer and her irritation found voice. "You have no idea what I am. Leave me be or I will rip your head off and throw it into Lake Michigan." Something in her tone of voice—perhaps the unspoken potential for true malevolence—made her would-be suitor's eyes widen. The man stumbled backward, then blinked and pressed himself against the side of the building as Brynna kept going.

"That might have been a bit harsh," Redmond said calmly.

"He is a foolish man with a rotting soul and a polluted body," Brynna said without thinking. "He'll be dead before his thirtieth birthday."

Sathi's gaze darkened and he automatically glanced back at the man on the sidewalk, who was already moving away from them. "What makes you say that?"

Brynna started to answer, then just shrugged. She'd said too much already, and in the scheme of what was going on here, it didn't matter anyway. She really needed to get a handle on the *in-the-mind, out-the-mouth* thing. "Here." She stopped in front of a laundromat as Mr. Kim nodded. "This is where Cho was when she was kidnapped."

Redmond pushed open the door and went inside, his expression betraying nothing. Sathi motioned Brynna and Mr. Kim to go in next. Brynna was happy to oblige— being out in the open wasn't good after this morning's short mind-sink into the realm where she'd been seen by two minor demons. It wasn't hard to imagine a Hunter shadowing her at every turn, just waiting for a chance to ambush and the approval that would come from return- ing her to Lucifer's Kingdom.

There was nothing special about the inside of the laundromat. Standard-issue industrial washers and dryers lined each side of the hard-used, narrow space, and half a dozen tables divided the room. A skinny young woman sat on a chair by the front window. Music leaked from her earphones and she barely glanced up from the *People* mag- azine on her lap. The space got dimmer toward the back, where the light from the front windows didn't quite reach and two of the four overhead fluorescents were burned out.

"So which washer are they in?" Redmond asked.

Despite the blandness of his tone, Brynna heard doubt, perhaps a hint of derision. She brushed off her irritation— how could this human, born into modern times when the true roots of faith and fear had been all but forgotten, be expected to believe? Instead of answering, she walked slowly down the line of beat-up washing machines, lightly trailing her fingers along the edges. Two-thirds of the way back she caught a whiff of something sour and dry. "Here," she said. She lifted the lid, then backed away from the heavy scent of mildew.

Redmond stepped up and peered into the tub, then Kim reached around him and pulled out the topmost garment. Black spots of mold covered the still-damp underside of the pale yellow blouse. "This is my daughter's," the old man said in Korean. His voice was thick with fear. "A birthday gift from me."

Brynna repeated this to Redmond, who, with Sathi right behind him, was already moving toward the back exit. Brynna followed the two detectives and left Mr. Kim to stare morosely at the washer's contents. Redmond still had Cho's scarf, but Brynna neither needed it nor wanted to touch it again, especially in such an open and unprotected environment. When she caught up with Redmond and Sathi, they had pushed through the back door and were standing in the alley. There wasn't much for them to see besides the overflowing Dumpster by the gyro place to the north and several precariously stacked piles of boxes behind the card shop to the south. They were in the middle of the block, so the alley, empty and smelling of decomposing food, stretched in both directions.

"This is useless," Redmond muttered as Mr. Kim wandered out to join them. "What the hell are we doing here?"

Brynna eyed the alley, noting the doorways and alcoves, all the places a Hunter might hide. It wasn't too bad since it was mid-afternoon and a bright day, and the presence of the two humans took the danger level down to almost zero. Funny how these men had unknowingly become her protectors. Although it was fading, the scent of the girl was still here—she had fallen at least once and been dragged—and after a few moments, Brynna turned to the left and began walking, following the thin leftover traces of scraped skin and blood, evidence that would be impossible for these detectives to detect. The men trailed her automatically, watching carefully to see what she would do. At first there wasn't much to find, and Brynna wouldn't have been surprised if it all disappeared in a sudden drift of old car exhaust and gasoline, very possible if Cho had been forced into a vehicle.

But then the lingering smell of the Korean girl suddenly intensified, swelling into fear and sweat and more blood, mixed with—

Corruption.

Brynna stopped and looked around, careful to keep her face expressionless, working to make it seem as if she had nothing at all to give the detectives. It was stuffy and windless here, and the afternoon's increasing humidity was making them all perspire. Beneath her feet, however, the concrete radiated more than heat, and it all led up to the metal door on which she had purposely turned her back. There was a sense of darkness here, of evil and magic and a kind of menace that these two Chicago detectives would never be able to fight. To the right of the doorway was a greasy window at ground level, but it was small, barely two feet long and less than a foot high. The girl was inside this building, and she was alive—Brynna could sense that much—but to try to rescue her now would be disastrous in more ways than Brynna could measure.

Cho would have to wait.

"I'm sorry," Brynna said. "There's nothing more I can do."

Sathi peered at her. "You're not picking up anything?"

"No," she lied.

"Excuse me, but what did you expect?" Redmond asked impatiently. "An excerpt from *Psychics Today*?"

"This is the second time you've brought up psychics," Sathi pointed out. "Let me remind you that *you* were the one who decided we should come out here." Brynna thought he was doing a remarkable job of keeping his voice even.

"Yeah, well, sometimes even I let myself get caught up in the moment." Redmond shaded his eyes from the sun and scanned the alley, but there was nothing to see. "Let's get Mr. Kim and head back downtown. We'll write up what we found—not much—and take the two of them home." He glanced at Brynna. "Or wherever it is they want to go."

THE HOLY MAN HAD come to him again this afternoon, and Michael Klesowitch was, as always, honored and terrified by His visit. Although His mission in this world was dark and unpleasant, was not the fact that He could walk in God's beautiful, bright sunlight inarguable proof of His righteousness, of His right to demand unflinching obedience from one so lowly and insignificant as Michael himself? It had to be.

An hour home from work, and Michael hadn't been doing much of anything—just sitting around and trying to decide what to do to occupy himself. It might be nice to go to the lake, pack a peanut-butter-and-jelly sandwich, a bag of chips and a diet soda, and trek down to Diversey Harbor, watch the boats come and go while he stayed safely in the shade (he burned easily). Mike had been pulling the jar of grape jelly from the refrigerator when he'd heard the front door open. Although he shouldn't have been surprised—he'd given the Holy Man his spare key weeks ago—he didn't think he would ever shake that sudden sense of anticipation, of nervous elation, that came with each meeting.

"Hello, Michael."

"Hi, uh, H-Hank." It seemed so strange to address the Holy Man by such a mundane, human name. Still, Michael understood—as Hank had told him, he would never be able to pronounce Hank's heavenly name. He had a thousand questions he wanted to ask, but Mike forced himself to stay silent. It was not his place to know most of what he wanted. It had taken him awhile to understand that—after all, he wasn't some sicko lead-me-around-by-the-nose idiot. No, he was an intelligent, fairly well-educated man in his midtwenties. He knew the difference between right and wrong, had a healthy sense of conscience and ethics, wasn't paranoid, and could tell when he was being scammed. He also had enough religion in his upbringing to appreciate a miracle when he saw it, and Hank had shown him more than a few of those.

"I have another task for you."

Michael swallowed and looked down at his hands. These tasks . . . he knew they were necessary. Hank had explained that to him, had been so patient each time as Michael struggled with his own instincts.

Thou shalt not kill.

Not one of the Seven Deadly Sins—most people didn't realize that—yet still sixth on the list of those all-important Ten Commandments. Such an important rule in the game of life, and yet every time Hank came to him, he directed Michael to break it. But it was God's work, was it not? Through Hank? Through Michael?

"You should not doubt yourself and your role," Hank said. His voice was gentle and full of compassion. "It is a hard one, but you fulfill your duties well."

His duties . . . yes. Five of those "duties" so far, and here was Hank again. Who, Mike wondered, was to be the next *duty*?

As if Hank could read Michael's mind, he held out a piece of paper. Mike took it, seeing his hand reach out of its own volition and feeling like he was dreaming, or maybe watching someone else who was wearing his face and body. So odd that Hank could make Michael's sense of will and self-control just . . . evaporate.

"The information is all there," Hank said. The Holy Man actually sounded sad, and when Michael looked down at the paper, he immediately understood. It was a cheap, computer-printed image of a man who was about sixty years old. He had a soft, friendly face, and he looked vaguely like Michael's grandfather. Next to the photo was the man's name and address, plus a few sentences about his routine and where Michael was most likely to find him. He couldn't help wonder what this guy had done to mark him for celestial assassination. But the question he would have asked skittered out of his mind at Hank's next words. "You must take extra care not to be identified. The police would not understand your calling, or me, or the wisdom of eliminating those who would cause unwanted events before they have the opportunity to do so."

Michael examined the piece of paper in his hand and again considered asking what this man could possibly do to warrant his death. Instead, he folded it reverently and put it in his pocket.

Five

Faced with another night in the open, Brynna was starting to see the value in having a place to stay. She'd spent a couple of hours first as Redmond's passenger, then again as a translator while he filled out his paperwork, but what she'd been able to offer him was limited. She knew a lot about Cho's whereabouts that she had decided to leave unsaid, since the information would likely get him and his partner killed.

Later, because she had nowhere in particular to go, she rode along as they took Mr. Kim home, then asked to be let out. Redmond complied without comment, then surprised her. "I know you're transient," he said through the open car window. "But if you can come up with some identification, the department can use someone with language skills like yours—especially if you're as good at other languages as you've been so far with the Spanish and Korean."

Redmond still radiated an air of disbelief, but before he and Detective Sathi drove away, he gave her a business card with the CPD logo and a couple of telephone numbers printed on it. Brynna's first instinct was to toss the card, but logic intervened. What she held in her hand was more than a two-by-three-inch piece of paper. It was the key to fitting into this human society, to getting off the streets and having food to eat while she figured out how to redeem herself. A roof over her head would go a long way toward making her feel safe—sort of—from Hunters while she worked it all out.

But how was she going to get identification? She'd need a social security number, but she was fairly certain she couldn't walk into the appropriate government office and just ask for one. They'd want to see documentation so she could get that number, probably a birth certificate. Now *that* was funny.

Or not.

Brynna spent time walking and wandering, finally ending up in a neighborhood some twenty-five blocks south of where Kim Cho-kyon had disappeared. The mostly Hispanic residents lived in tiny run-down houses that had been subdivided into two or more tinier apartments, all within a stone's toss of the rumbling Ravenswood train line. The few trees that remained were thin and diseased looking, as if some insect or blight were slowly devouring the helpless plants. Brynna felt oddly sorry about that and wondered if these streets had once looked as lush and green as the street on which the nephilim killer lived.

She ran a hand through the choppy ends of her hair, then wished she hadn't. Every part of her felt dirty—her hair, her body, her clothes. There wasn't much she could do about it, and another night spent sleeping beneath a cardboard box wasn't going to help. The sun had set and it was cooler now, with wide pools of shadow between the streetlights. There was a discernible difference in the atmosphere of this mostly residential neighborhood. Although the daytime climate wasn't friendly by any stretch, night here held an undercurrent of something else. Not outright danger but *tension,* a knowing that something was always about to happen. Brynna could tell that it felt like this every evening.

Heading west on Lawrence Avenue, Brynna caught a glow from the window of a small late-night restaurant. The red neon sign said simply TACOS, and she remembered the money still in her pocket at about the same time the scent of spicy meat and refried beans eased past her on the otherwise stagnant night air. Her stomach clamored for food—more persistent human needs—so Brynna pushed through the front door.

If the Nickel and Dime Diner had been scraping the low end of deluxe, this place was bottoming out. It was deep and narrow and dark, with most of the light coming from the kitchen and cash register area at the far end. The battered yellow tables that lined the walls on both sides had red booth-style benches bolted to them, and a few tattered Mexico travel posters, serapes, and dusty sombreros were hung on the aged walls. Faint beneath the odors of fried meat and tortillas was the scent of bleach and cleanser.

Brynna made her way down the space between the tables, heading for the small message-board menus on the end wall. There were three men standing in front of the register and one on the other side of the counter; the hushed, heated conversation they were having ceased abruptly as she got closer.

She wasn't interested in hearing their talk anyway. She had a little over four bucks in her pocket; if she asked for water, she could get one of the combination plates, maybe the one with cheese and—

"We're closed," said one of the men in heavily accented English.

Closed? The sign on the door said the place was open until midnight, and that was still two hours away. Brynna glanced at the speaker, noting the guy was on the customer side of the counter. He was young and slender, wearing a dirty sleeveless T-shirt and a baseball cap turned backward that covered short, curly black hair.

"Yeah," echoed one of his companions. Brynna sensed his gaze go down her body then move back up to her face. It was calculating and lustful, and it felt almost like sandpaper. "Beat it, lady."

Brynna turned her attention to the man behind the counter, but he only stared at the beat-up Formica. Although he said nothing, everything about him conveyed anger—he was gripping the edge of the counter hard enough to make the ends of his fingertips white. All four men were drenched in perspiration and something else . . .

Fear.

Yeah, it was there. The older man's fright was different from that of the younger trio. His was organic, like that of prey cornered but unwilling to surrender. Theirs was . . . *anticipatory,* like hyenas running down the weakening matriarch of their pack, readying her for the kill as the younger female moved in to take over.

She should walk away, leave and let these humans go about their own natural selection process. But no, there had to be a reason she was here, some divine intervention that had made her choose this particular eatery. As always, she knew too much about the way the universe worked to believe in true coincidence. Besides, everywhere she went would always be like this—it was her appearance, her scent, the very fact of her *existence* on earth that would draw the weak to her like cockroaches to garbage. Sometimes you just had to deal with it.

Brynna pulled out her money and put it on the counter, then pushed the four rumpled dollar bills toward the man by the register. All four men stared at the money as if they'd never seen such a thing in their lives. "I'll have combination plate number three," she said. "Cheese enchiladas with verde sauce. Make it spicy. Water to drink."

"Number three?" the oldest man repeated. "I—"

"I said we're *closed!*" the one with the baseball cap yelled. Maybe he thought if he ramped up the volume, she would believe him. "Don't you understand English?"

"I do," Brynna replied. "And about seven thousand other languages as well." She glanced at the menu again, then at the man she assumed was the owner. "I think he can make my food and then close. I'll be the last customer."

"Oh, you'll be the last customer all right," Baseball Cap said nastily. He turned to fully face Brynna and one hand whipped forward; the lousy lighting gave her a flash of dull silver, then there was a stinging across her forearm. When she looked down, a line of red was seeping out of a thin three-inch gash in her flesh. She'd known he had a weapon, of course, but not that he would have the temper and the balls to use it so quickly. If he'd known the consequences, he would never have been so foolish. There was nothing to admire about stupidity.

"Next up is your face," he hissed. "You got one more chance to get the fuck *out* of here."

As Brynna looked down at the cut on her arm, the edges of it parted and spread, revealing a much deeper wound than she'd thought. The older man gasped as blood suddenly spilled out one side of it, a canvas of crimson that was startling even in the poor light. Without warning, the pain from the laceration increased in intensity and Brynna felt her temper stir. Not good.

"Please, *señorita*," the older man said. He was almost moaning. "You go now, *sí*? So you do not get more hurt." He held a hand out to the younger men in a pleading gesture. "I just give you the money, *sí*? And then you go too?"

Brynna covered her wound with one hand and pushed it closed. So that's what was going on here—a robbery. These boys—they were far too young for Brynna to think of as men—were thieves.

"Way to go, idiot." One of the other guys, a burlier youth whose hair was shaved close to a scalp gleaming with perspiration, grabbed the owner's T-shirt in one fist and yanked him halfway across the counter. The tattoos on his heavily muscled arms quivered. "Now the bitch knows what's going down and things are going to get a lot dirtier."

"Let him go," Brynna snapped. Her hand tightened around her forearm and her palm went hot. Before anyone could say something more, there was a muted burst of red light from beneath her palm, then the unpleasant smell of scorched blood. With the wound seared

closed and the blood blackened against her flesh, she felt
even angrier. Now it hurt twice as much, and she was so
damned *tired* of being burned.

"How the fuck did you do that?" Baseball Cap was
staring at her arm, everything else momentarily forgotten.

"Just get the money and go, Pablo," the third hoodlum
whined. "Enough dicking around!"

"Watch your mouth." The second guy hadn't let go
of the owner's shirt, and he yanked on it so hard that he
slammed the older man against the countertop. A flick
of his other wrist opened up his own switchblade. "Don't
be using names. But it don't matter anyway, does it, Juan?
We got a mess here. Time to clean it up."

Baseball Cap—Juan—nodded. He reached for Brynna.

She backhanded him so hard that he landed on the
floor four booths to her right. Her left hand shot forward
and closed around Pablo's wrist where it was bunched
around the owner's shirt. She squeezed viciously and
there was an audible *crack*. Suddenly Pablo was wailing
like a four-year-old with a skinned knee. He swiped at
her with his switchblade, but Brynna effortlessly plucked
it out of his hand. She slammed it against the counter at
an angle and the blade snapped in two.

"Shit," muttered the middle guy as he backed away until
he thought he was out of her range. "Something's fucked
up with this *puta*. We got to get the fuck outta here."

"Good idea," Brynna said mildly. She yanked on Pablo's broken wrist and dragged him forward. The owner
scrambled back as the young man's wail turned into
a scream and he clawed at her hand, trying to get free.
"Let me help you find the door." The force she applied

to Pablo's back sent him careening into his friend; both of them stumbled to where Baseball Cap was trying to shake some sense back into himself. He used the edge of a table to drag himself to a standing position, then glared at her. His switchblade had fallen halfway between them and Brynna could see him weighing his chances of getting to it before she could.

She was there and snatching it up before he could make that very bad decision. She held it up, snapped the blade from its base, and let it fall back to the floor. "Are you leaving, or do you want me to teach you some more about 'Thou shalt not steal'?" She took a step toward them, then watched in amusement as all three practically fell over each other as they tried to back up.

"Fucking *freak*," snarled Baseball Cap. "This ain't over!"

"It is, unless you like pain," Brynna replied. She started to move down the center aisle, but they'd finally had enough. Another three seconds and they were out the front door and disappearing into the night. The best they could offer on parting was a final, unintelligible threat growled by Juan as the door slammed behind them.

Brynna turned and walked back to the register, where the owner was standing. "How do you do that?" he asked. "Those men, three of them, and only you—"

"I know their kind from way back," Brynna answered. Her money was on the floor and she picked it up and offered it to him. "So," she said hopefully, "combination plate number three?"

He stared at her with his mouth open, then he laughed. "*Sí*, coming right up!"

>━━●━━<

HIS NAME, BRYNNA LEARNED as she ate her cheese enchiladas, was Ramiro Cocinero, and he had owned this restaurant for nearly twenty years. He paid the rent and got by, never quite getting ahead. Business had slowed recently, so he was staying open later—clearly not a good idea in the declining neighborhood. He would now go back to his old hours of closing at nine o'clock in the summertime, eight in the winter.

Cocinero didn't sit with her, preferring to lean against the apex of the seats across from her. He felt the usual attraction toward her—Brynna could sense it—but he fought it. He looked at the floor, the ceiling, even fiddled with the thin gold band on his left hand. He was a good, God-fearing and faithful man. Brynna was impressed at his steadfastness. She wished she could somehow help him more than she had already.

"So, you have job? You live close?"

She shook her head. It would be easy to lapse into Spanish and make it easier on him, but she had always been a staunch believer of *when in Rome* . . . "Neither."

He looked surprised, then thoughtful. He'd made the meal Brynna wanted, but she had insisted on paying him for the food despite his pleas that she accept it as payment for stopping the robbery. It wasn't that she didn't believe in charity. She just didn't think she should be the recipient.

"You work here," he said. He sounded utterly convinced.

A corner of her mouth lifted. "Sorry. I don't cook or wash dishes. And I suck at cleaning."

"But you could do *seguridad*—security, *sí*?" He beamed

at Brynna. "I cannot pay much, but free food and a little cash, no taxes."

Brynna sat back and pushed her now-empty plate away from the edge of the table. "No, I can't. I have . . . other things I need to do during the day."

His expression melted into disappointment, then brightened again. "At night, then, *sí*?" He gave her a knowing glance that encompassed her disheveled hair, dirty hands, and grubby clothes. "Unless you go home."

Brynna thought about this. She had no doubt that Cocinero knew instinctively that she had no place to go, but did she need a place to sleep that badly? Maybe not . . . but it sure was convenient.

"Throw in dinner every night and I'll be here from eight until six in the morning," she offered.

"Excelente!" His smile was even wider. Cocinero disappeared into the back while she finished her water, then he ushered her back there and showed her an old army cot covered with a worn but clean serape. Resting at one end was a pile of clean kitchen towels. "No shower," he explained as he pressed a key into her palm. "But clean *baño* and many towels. *Agua caliente* and you eat anything you want." He pointed at something behind her and Brynna turned to look. "Even a television."

Brynna's gaze returned to the cot and the towels. The front door and windows would secure with a metal fire gate, and the back door had a heavy metal bar across its center. It was damned near as safe as the jail at 26th and California, and she could even clean herself up.

She smiled. Yeah, this would definitely do.

Six

A good night's rest, clean skin, food in her belly, and the start of a new day. On a human level, Brynna thought there wasn't much more to be desired, at least from where she was standing.

Cocinero had been there to open the restaurant at ten to six, and had insisted on fixing her breakfast. Brynna had relented and a few minutes later her reward had been warm corn tortillas filled with scrambled eggs and cowboy-style beans with sliced jalapeños. She'd finished it all, then left him to his work and stepped out to greet the early Tuesday morning.

She had things to do today. Still wavering on her list was the nephilim killer, but if he was, indeed, the killer of all those other people, his victims were all still dead and there was nothing she could do to change the past. Yes, there would be more—she was now certain of that—but she had no way of knowing who.

Kim Cho-kyon—or Cho Kim, as she would be known to her American friends—was a lot closer to Brynna's heart. Brynna had talked to Cho's father, learned about her, seen her picture. More than that, she had *felt* the girl—the simple act of touching the silk scarf had made Brynna feel Cho's shock and disbelief as everything in her relatively uneventful existence went from summer sunshine to inexplicable terror and pain. Yes, Cho was still alive, but what her father and the two police detectives didn't know was that she would *stay* alive. Her abductor didn't plan to kill her . . . now or ever.

There was nothing quiet about Clark Street by the time Brynna made her way to the alley's entrance. Traffic was heavy and there were more than enough pedestrians to make Brynna wonder if she shouldn't have faced this problem in the night hours. She would have had the darkness to hide in, yes, but so would a lot of other creatures. Daylight sliced away her hiding places, but it put more humans on the street and made her less of a target—those who would hunt her did not want to be seen by the average Mr. and Mrs. Normal. But she didn't want to be noticed by those same humans if she had to do something decidedly *un*human.

Brynna slipped around the corner and moved down the alley. The smell of garbage was sharp and strong this morning, and judging from the overflowing containers, it was pickup day. Now and then Brynna's sensitive hearing detected the chittering of rats as they snuffled amid the leavings, but nothing else worked on her nerves. In no time at all she was past the back door of the laundromat, already open to customers and spilling the scents of cheap detergent and wet fabric into the air. A few more moments put her outside the door behind which she knew she would find Kim Cho-kyon.

Brynna pressed herself into the shallow doorway, and when she inhaled, the heavy scent of Cho's terror leaking from the thin bottom edge almost made her cough. She smothered the sound and scanned the street, mulling over her options. Was this a good idea? Was she *safe*? As far as Brynna could tell, she was still undetected by any Hunters. If she was that worried, she could change her timetable and come back tonight, or even walk away entirely. But the dark hours just didn't appeal to her—she'd had lifetimes of darkness, and now she relished the warmth of the sun and the daylight that revealed so much. Besides, abandoning Cho completely was simply . . . out of the question. Brynna wasn't so dense that she didn't realize she needed to work on her own sense of empathy, and if there was ever a girl who needed some compassion, it was this Korean teenager. Yeah, Brynna decided, there really was only one choice.

She glanced around a final time before testing the heavy metal doorknob. When it wouldn't turn, Brynna forced it, rotating it slowly in the hopes that it wouldn't make too much noise. She was lucky—there was only a low grinding sound, then a quiet *snap* as the bolt cracked. Beyond the door was a dim, stale-smelling hallway with three doors. The one on the left was a bathroom—Brynna could see the toilet from where she was standing—and the closed and locked one directly in front of her likely led to the main jewelry shop in the front. Beyond was probably an office.

The door that interested Brynna was directly on the right. It looked almost exactly like the other three, a solid wood slab covered in old white paint that was now cracked and spotted, tack holes everywhere from a thousand notes and calendars hung on it over the span of ten or more decades. The thing that set it apart was the oversized padlock, obviously new, that ensured the door would stay closed. That sort of intervention meant nothing to Brynna. She twisted the padlock off with barely any effort and pulled open the door.

The daylight from the alley sent a weak glow down a set of stairs that took a right turn into darkness. Brynna could see a hint of light from somewhere, probably a lamp, and she could hear soft, unidentifiable sounds of the sort that had no business in the course of a normal human life. Worse than that was the smell, a conglomeration of sweat, blood, mildew, herbal and chemical potions, and something else, something disturbingly familiar.

He was smiling and waiting for her across from the stairway that led into the red-smeared room.

ANN SATHER'S RESTAURANT WAS already well entrenched in a typical state of Tuesday morning madness, and Eran Redmond felt lucky to snag a small table against the north wall. He hadn't been here in years, but little had changed except for some menu items—wraps and breakfast seafood stuff—that showed the place was trying to stay in tune with Chicago's young, upscale community. He ordered eggs and Swedish potato sausage, then sipped his coffee and watched the customers while he waited for his food to arrive. Thanks to yet another sniper killing, he'd been up half the night. He was tired and unfocused, pinning way too much hope on the notion that caffeine would clear the mud from his brain.

It wasn't coincidence that he'd picked this place for a morning meal. His thoughts turned to the missing Korean girl, and then to Brynna Malak, of whom he'd also already lost track. He had a directive in to notify him if anything happened on the case, and he planned on nosing around the neighborhood, talking to Cho's landlord and neighbors, then making a visit to the jewelry store owned by Kwan Chul-moo when it opened for business at ten.

Brynna Malak . . . now there was an enigmatic woman. He'd worked the problem to death, but he could find no possible connection between her and the murdered Tobias Gallagher or to Kim Li-kang and his daughter before he'd introduced Brynna to the old man the day before. How could she have known where the teenager had spent her last moments before her abduction? If she *had* been abducted, of course—right now, all they had to go on was the scarf Kim said he'd found, his claim about the jewelry store owner, and the girl's abandoned clothes. Well, that and Brynna's supposedly second sight, or whatever his partner wanted to call it. In Eran's mind, it wasn't much. It wasn't *enough*.

And Brynna Malak? Wow. His mind spun in all directions every time he tried to sort her out. No address, no identification, but clearly educated. A person wasn't just born knowing a bunch of different languages, and although he still found her claim that she could understand anything pretty damned far-fetched, he had to admit—only to himself, of course—that he was impressed.

The Georgia address she'd given him was a total fabrication—he hadn't expected anything else—and he'd gotten zip on a name search. According to the databases,

Brynna Malak didn't exist, but the tangible version was hard to deny. Eran wouldn't have said she was pretty, but there was definitely something darkly fascinating about her. Something . . . *seductive*. In Eran's view, that, combined with the weirdness factor that clung to her, made her dangerous. Not in a physical way, but in other arenas he didn't need to explore.

Even so, his thoughts couldn't help turning to the what-ifs. What if she turned out to be on the level? They weren't common in this digital age, but paper-trail wipe-outs did happen. Chewing methodically on his sausage, Eran gave himself a mental punch. Who was he kidding? For whatever reason, Brynna Malak didn't want to be identified. He'd never formally charged her with anything, so he had no fingerprints, and he'd never get approval for any kind of a DNA test without a solid reason. Until she wanted to spill the truth, Eran knew nothing about her except for her unbelievable language skills and the unsettling instances of apparent clairvoyance.

And as for any thoughts of hooking up with her . . . he needed to turn those off right now. Something like that could only lead to disaster.

Yeah, Eran thought. *Disaster*. That was definitely the word for relationships in his life. The rest of his breakfast had suddenly lost its appeal and he pushed the remaining bites of egg around on his plate. His last attempt at dating someone—a very pretty woman in her midthirties named Monica—had ended nastily almost a year ago. He remembered very clearly, down to the word, the last thing that Monica had said before walking out of his life: *When you look in the mirror, Eran, go beneath skin deep. You can't control the*

world, and if you don't get a handle on your insecurity, you'll be alone
for the rest of your life.

Ouch.

The busboy came and took the dirty dishes, leaving Eran to stare morosely into his nearly empty coffee cup as he replayed that final Sunday evening showdown. It had been his fault—it was *always* his fault. He knew that, yet he seemed powerless to stop himself. He destroyed every perfectly good relationship by working his way into demanding to know where his partner was and what she was doing every hour of every day. Jealousy? No, not at all. Paranoia was more like it. *Safety.* Lots of cops became domineering after too many years on the job, but couple that with the problems of his childhood and Eran was doomed. Every time he let himself care about a woman, he tried, usually sooner than later, to pack her into a tight, safe package that always ended up being nothing but a prison.

Eran downed the last of his coffee and grimaced at the bottom-of-the-pot bitterness. It was only a quarter after eight, still what he considered a little too early to go kicking down the doors of Cho's neighbors. He'd kill time by checking out the area for another hour or so, then start ringing doorbells. He'd talked to most of these people after Mr. Kim had first come to him, but maybe he'd catch a break and pick up something new and useful.

He dropped a few bucks on the table, then paid his check at the register. Clark Street was still hustling with morning traffic and his cell phone rang as he stepped out of the restaurant.

"Detective Redmond, this is Sergeant Emerson. You left a marker

*to contact you if something happened on the Kim missing-person case.
I thought you should know that the silent alarm's been triggered at one
of the addresses in the file's database. It's the back entrance of a jewelry
store on Clark Street—"*

Eran said something in reply, then he was running
down the sidewalk and shouting for people to get out of
his way.

"HELLO, ASTARTE."

Brynna's head whipped around as she stepped off the
staircase and onto the filthy concrete floor. It calmed
immediately, but for a second her pulse was a huge, thick
thing in her throat—she hadn't been so startled in ages.
The closest thing had been the Hunter in Lincoln Park,
and back then she'd simply shifted into automatic survival
mode.

"Lahash." Brynna struggled, but couldn't quite keep
the surprise out of her voice. He wouldn't have the upper
hand—never—but now he would *think* he did. That would
make what was coming even more annoying. He didn't
say anything else and he didn't seem inclined to come at
her, so Brynna let herself give the dim, dreadful room a
quick scan.

There was very little light, but midway down the long
room a small lamp and a dozen or so candles flickered.
They gave out more than enough light for Brynna's night
vision to make out everything. The damp space was cav-
ernous, and in contrast to the quickly growing heat outside, eerily chilly. The concrete walls and floor ran the full
length and width of the building above, stretching away to
almost complete darkness at the far end.

It only took a millisecond for Brynna to register what was going on, and the still-present dark part of her had to admire whoever had put this together. If the magic-wielder was human (and really, he *had* to be), she had no doubt that something with a lot more knowledge and power—likely Lahash—had fueled the entire thing. But why? What could this nasty little man have that Lahash wanted so much that he would pay in power to get it?

Ah, now *there* was the question, indeed.

The girl was down here, positioned about two-thirds of the way down the left-hand wall. She was sitting in front of a small computer desk, leaning slightly forward with her head slumped onto her chest. Strips of pink-colored tape were wound around her bruised arms and legs, forcing her into a pseudo-natural position over a crud-covered keyboard. The computer in front of her was on but the screen showed nothing but a blank, black surface with a blinking green cursor. The girl's hair was tangled and her skin was streaked with dirt. Food had dried and crusted around her mouth from being force-fed. Flies crawled energetically over her cracked and bleeding lips, and there were needle marks at the bends of her elbows. Pills, papers, and empty soda cans littered the small desktop next to the keyboard.

Brynna blinked—and saw a pair of nuisance demons, ones that were very different from those that plagued the senior of the Kim family. They would have looked like any others of their kind, except these had grown large, fat, and powerful with the spoils of Jin-eun's weaknesses. Stupid, lazy creatures, they were readily fooled by the spell that had been woven around Cho Kim to make her body pass as a substitute for Kwan's daughter. Drugged and help-less, Cho was at the mercy of the creatures perched on each shoulder, and now they were heavy beings with body fat that jiggled over their joints as they pulled at her hair, poked at her eyes and ears, and made constant, invisible furrows across the ravaged skin of her face, neck and shoulders. Her soul roiled and glowed within the gaping unseen cuts, trying vainly to pull into itself and escape the pain. The corpulent little demons looked like a cross between overgrown black bats with extra teeth, and hell-ish, miniature baboons.

Brynna scowled and blinked them from her sight, but the memory of the girl's suffering made her grind her teeth. "If I was still into this sort of thing, I'd compliment you on a great job," she said evenly. "Since I'm not, I'll stick with telling you to release the spell on the girl."

The expression on Lahash's face was almost comical. "*Release* her?" When Brynna only stared back at him, the other fallen angel wiped the back of one finger daintily across his mouth. "I'll start with I can't, because I'm not the one who cast it. Then I'll move onto the more impor-tant question of why would I *want* to anyway?"

Brynna opened her mouth to answer, then real-ized how futile it would be. It wasn't a matter of under-standing; Lahash would understand everything. He just wouldn't *care*. And he would never help her—he was Luci-fer's servant all the way. "Because I want you to, and if you don't, I will tear your limbs off and burn them back on in different places." She tilted her head to one side. "Is that enough of a reason?"

Brynna hadn't thought Lahash could look more

surprised than he had a moment ago, but he did. Even so, he managed to shake it off and draw himself up almost primly. "You know I don't fight, Astarte. It's dirty work and I dislike it immensely. That sort of thing is best left to the Hunters. And the humans—they're quite good at it."

Brynna's eyes narrowed suspiciously. "Then you'll have no objections if I kill those nuisance demons and take her out of here."

Lahash shrugged. "I won't . . . but *he* might."

His gaze flicked to something behind her and Brynna whirled. Someone—some*thing*—lunged at her and she swatted it aside without thinking. It sprawled heavily against a table on the right wall, sending a couple of candles and a mishmash of other things crashing to the floor. The candles spun and went out, while her hand throbbed unexpectedly; when Brynna glanced at it, the skin was swollen and red, as though she'd been stung by a dozen bees.

She glared at the thing pulling itself up and realized it was human, a Thai man. He was older and bald, with gnarled joints and tough skin streaked with grime. Of course—this was the witch doctor Cho's father had talked about. He hissed at her like a nasty little alley cat, and Brynna balled up her fist in response. She paid for it when the skin along the knuckles grated with pain and split slightly.

"A human," she spat at Lahash. "You would use a human to do your dirty work!"

Lahash brushed away an imagined piece of lint on his jacket. He was dressed as a businessman in an expensive suit, someone who in the daylight could pass for a lawyer or banker. "I'm not doing anything," he said blandly.

He waved at the basement room. "This is Li Chin Kong's game—his spell, his motives, his . . . *arena.*"

"But you provided the implements. And the power."

The absolutely treacherous grin Lahash sent her was full of polished white teeth. "I only offered. It's all about free will, Astarte. You know that. He can reject my gifts, but if he chooses to accept . . . well, choice *is* the spice of life." He smiled wider. "And death."

"*Variety* is the spice of life," she snapped as she kept an eye on the man Lahash was talking about. He was almost back on his feet. "If you're going to quote a human saying, at least get it right."

Lahash looked absently at his fingernails. He was playing mind games with her, Brynna knew, but in a minute she was going to give him a lot more to worry about than a less-than-perfect suit and hands. "*Variety,*" he repeated. "*Choice.* Some people interpret those to mean the same thing."

Before she could argue, Kong lurched toward her. If he expected her to retreat, he was headed for enlightenment on demon attitudes—the very slight injury to her hand was already nothing but a minor annoyance. He was a stupid human dabbling in realms best left to those born with celestial powers, and the current plight of Cho Kim was enough for Brynna to decide that the man deserved whatever fate awaited at the end of her anger.

Brynna strode forward, determined to pound this piece of human excrement into eternity. She'd taken two long steps when a sudden leeriness made her glance back at Lahash; too late, she saw his impeccably manicured hand unfold gracefully in Kong's direction and a wisp of power, visible only as a thin blur of dark smoke, swept past her and into Kong too quickly for her to intervene. The elderly Thai man reached for it eagerly, wrapping himself in the energy like a freezing child taking shelter within a heavy comforter. By the time Brynna was a foot or two away from him, Kong was standing tall and straight, and his wrinkled skin was bristling with unreleased strength.

Brynna paused and studied him warily. This time the old man waited, watching her as she watched him, gauging her abilities. "Does he know what I am?" she finally asked. "Does he have any idea at all what he's facing?"

"Right now, I don't think he cares," Lahash answered. Brynna could hear the carelessness in the demon's voice. He had no regard for the lives of the humans he influenced, for their physical pain or spiritual destruction. And still Brynna had no idea why he was here and playing out his little drama with this foolish, greedy old man and the very unlucky Cho Kim. "Besides, I'm just a Searcher. It's not my job to reveal such things. Perhaps he should have paid more attention to the warnings of his elders. Deals with the devil and all that."

Brynna sighed as a slow, satisfied sneer spread across Kong's face when he flexed his fingers experimentally.

"Oh, *crap,*" she muttered, and self-preservation made her drop into a crouch before Kong sprang forward and swiped at her. The air where Brynna had been standing crackled harshly, as though a knife made of electricity had cut through it. Now Kong was within reach, so Brynna leaned to one side, balanced on her right hand and kicked her foot out in a tight arc. The top of it burned instantly—Lahash had obviously given the man some kind of shield—but she caught Kong at the ankle and pulled him off balance. He fell, landing hard. He came back up immediately, this time with an object clutched in his hand. Brynna had time to register nothing more dangerous than one of the dozens of bricks among the debris on the floor before he flung it at her. She yanked her forearm up just as the brick disintegrated and turned into sharp shards of metal. A thousand spots of agony erupted along the inside of her arm and lower face, but at least he hadn't gotten her eyes.

"I've had enough of this," Brynna snarled, and launched herself full speed at the Thai witch doctor. It hurt—more, in fact, than anything she'd experienced so far as a human being—but Brynna knew if she didn't take this guy out for good, Lahash would just keep feeding him power. She'd never planned on killing anyone, but Kong had been corrupted too much to ever return to any semblance of normality. One of them would have to die to end this, and it damned sure wasn't going to be her.

Kong wasn't quick enough to avoid her. Brynna wrapped her arms around him and held on through the feeling of fire that built up and finally surrounded her. It wasn't enough to make her change form, but it was definitely a wake-up call as to what a human could feel in the scope of torture. Instead of fighting the shield's energy, Brynna went with it, letting her body take in the heat and magnify it. Her head filled with sound—the roaring of remembered flames, the face-to-face screams of the witch doctor—then she *pushed* and gave it, *all* of it, back to the vile human being within her embrace.

There was a split second where Kong's eyes bulged and he forgot everything about where he was and why. His shrieks changed to an incomprehensible stream of noise as he flailed uselessly, trying to free himself. Sound and red light filled the room, and while to Kong it must have seemed like a lifetime, to Brynna his destruction took only a couple of moments as the heat inside her suddenly peaked—

Then everything was silent.

Brynna straightened and let her arms fall to her sides. What was left of Kong held its shape for a moment, then collapsed, sinking into nothing but fine and forever unidentifiable ash.

She turned. "Lahash—"

He was gone.

"Damn you," Brynna hissed. Her gaze quickly searched the shadows, but she could see nothing without changing her view of the human world. No matter—she would have to do that anyway to kill the demons tormenting Cho Kim. With the witch doctor dead, the spell was broken and now Cho was groaning, struggling weakly against the tape wound around her. As vulnerable as she was, the girl had to be in agony, and it was only a matter of seconds before the nuisance demons realized they had the wrong girl. They might leave and return to Chul's unfortunate daughter—bad enough—or they might decide they liked their current meal ticket and really dig in.

A hard blink and the oversized room shaded to red. Brynna saw a fast-moving silhouette dart beneath the stairs—Lahash—but hurried footsteps overhead made her ignore him in favor of obliterating the creatures clinging to Cho's neck and hair. Four long strides put her next to the girl, where the two fat demons were crazily squabbling with each other over whether to stay or return to their original target, Jin-eun. They shrieked in stupid surprise when Brynna snatched them off Cho. With one fleshy neck in each hand, she leaned away from the girl and slammed the two beasts together as hard as she could, over and over, until they were little more than limp, stringy clumps of demon slop. When she dropped the mess to the floor, what was left liquefied and sizzled away into the cracked cement until nothing remained at all. Now both Cho and Jin-eun would finally be free.

That done, Brynna whirled and went back to seeing everything with human vision. Too late—Lahash was out of reach and a set of new problems was clattering down the stairs in the form of two Korean men she'd never seen before. Both wore suits, and the younger man led the way with a large handgun that looked impressively dangerous. For a fleeting moment Brynna remembered Toby's instant, unfulfilled death—would she ever forget it?—but before she could try to conceal herself, the barrel of the weapon trained on her face.

"Stop right there," he said in flawless English. He came down the last few steps and moved toward her, with the older man right behind him. "Who the hell are you, and what are you doing in my father's building?"

Ah—this was undoubtedly Chul-moo's son, and his companion could only be the old man himself. Brynna glanced toward the stairs, but Lahash had faded into the blackness between the boxes and junk stored beneath it. He would never be spotted by humans now, and she had yet to find out what his part was in the abduction of Cho Kim.

"I'm . . . no one," Brynna said. She backed away from

him at an angle that put the north wall of the basement at her back. He scowled at her movement, but at the same time the chair that Cho was secured to made a scraping sound as she tried to free herself. The young man turned his head to look at the girl and Brynna grabbed the chance to cross the last few feet, moving between the stairs and the two Koreans; they would think she was trying to escape, but what she was really doing was making sure they would never leave this room unless she wanted them to.

The one with the gun jerked back around and glared at her. "I told you to *stop*," he snarled. "Move again and I'll shoot you."

"You must kill her anyway, Seung," the older man said in rapid-fire Korean. "Look around. She has ruined all our efforts—the witch doctor is gone, the girl is coming around. The demons will realize she is not theirs, and they will return to torment Jin-eun."

"The demons are dead," Brynna said without thinking.

Seung and Chul-moo gaped at her, then the father's eyes narrowed. "So, you understand Korean." His tone grew harsher. "But how do you know about the demons? And how do you know they are dead?"

Brynna looked at the floor without answering. Damn, but she'd done it now. If they discovered what she was, it would put Cho's life in danger—they would try to use the girl to gain power over Brynna and control her. They no longer had the witch doctor for spells, but there would always be another idiot ready and willing to take the dead man's place. They would think she was just the one for that.

As if he knew what she was thinking, Seung turned slightly so that he could swing the gun in Cho's direction.

"I think," he said slowly, "that she is a Good Samaritan. Someone with an understanding of certain things that are not common knowledge. Therefore, the question becomes not *who* she is, but how *good* she is. Will she do as we say, or will she prefer to see Kim Cho-kyon die?"

Brynna felt her lips draw back over her teeth. Sometimes these humans really knew how to push her buttons. "The girl is of no use to you now," she told him. She lifted her chin in the father's direction. "And your daughter is freed of her burden. You might as well let her go."

Chul-moo laughed, the sound like gravel underfoot. "If what you say is true, then I have no use for either of you. On the other hand, I expect the police would have a great deal to gain by spending time with you or the girl, and I cannot allow that." The corners of his eyes crinkled in cruel amusement. "Do not be so foolish as to think you can run. You are not faster than a bullet."

Brynna opened her mouth to reply, but the sound of the upstairs door slamming open cut her off. A sudden shaft of light cut through the darkness along the staircase, followed by a voice with which Brynna was growing entirely too familiar.

Redmond.

"Police—hold it right there!" he shouted. He scrambled down the stairs with his revolver trained on the two men facing Brynna. "Don't move!"

"Shoot him!" Chul-moo screamed. The change in the older man's demeanor was so sudden and shocking that Brynna gasped out loud. *"Shoot them both!"*

Brynna had an instant—only that—to register Seung's surprise and instinctive obedience. She leaped forward just as the muzzle of the gun aimed at Redmond flashed blue-white, and then a bullet bit into the right side of her chest. Pain, like deep, red fire going in and in and in, cut through her, all the way from front to back. Damn, it *hurt*. Still, she'd experienced worse, much worse . . . but she couldn't ever remember being angrier.

The sound that came out of Brynna's mouth was vaguely like an animal growl but more guttural, more *dangerous*. Seung squeezed the trigger again, but Brynna was already on top of him, and so full of fury that she barely felt the punch of the second shot that blistered through the meat of her right side and hammered the underside of one of her ribs. Seung yelped as Brynna wrenched his weapon free, then backhanded him hard enough to send him slamming into the rattletrap table the witch doctor had been using as an altar. It collapsed, sending the rest of its display of cheap candles and useless, trashy offerings to the floor; the tiny flames went out as the bits of animal bone, herbs, and paper mixed with the melted wax. Seung groaned once and was still.

Panicked, Chul-moo stumbled and swung around, but there was nowhere he could go, no avenue of escape. Brynna's gaze focused on him and she took a step forward, the spikes of misery reinforcing her rage.

"Brynna—Brynna, *stop!*"

She almost ignored Redmond. Chul-moo was a despicable example of humanity, and it would have been so good to feel the old man's bones crack beneath her fingers, would have almost been a decent trade for the pain seesawing through her earthly body. He was unworthy of the gift of life, and the sight and smell of his blood—

"Brynna!"

She clenched her teeth and stalled the forward motion of her body. No, it was not her right to make such a decision, to pass the ultimate judgment even on someone like Chul-moo. Without repentance—and how likely was that?—his final destination would be the same whether he walked the path at his appointed time or she gave him an early push along it now.

Redmond had almost caught up to her now, with several uniformed policemen hurrying down the stairs behind him. Her face was inches from the old man's, and she could see triumph and calculation in Chul-moo's eyes. She couldn't read his thoughts exactly, but she could pick up the gist: he would place the blame on his son and plead that he was only a terrified old man, then use the legal system to drag out any sentencing and trade his son's life for probation so he could live out his own in peace with his miraculously healed daughter. He had never given any credence to anything beyond this earthly existence or the concept of retribution.

Such a foolish, foolish old man.

"Someday soon, you will suffer for your sins, old one," Brynna whispered. His eyes widened as Brynna's irises suddenly filled with a dancing red fire that only he could see. "There are many creatures that wait eagerly for your arrival . . . in Hell."

As Redmond pushed past Brynna, Chul-moo suddenly gasped, then choked and grabbed at his chest. His knees buckled and Redmond reached for him, but Brynna beat the policeman to it. With her right hand, she reached under the old man's armpit and lifted. Something no one

but she and the old Korean man knew flashed from her
fingertips and through his muscles; he gasped again and
color came back into his face. The gaze he sent her was
bulging and full of terror.

"Oh, no," she said in an almost companionable voice.
"Not yet. The time will come when retribution will be
claimed, but first you must answer for your actions
here."

Redmond pushed her hand away, but now Chul-
moo was standing under his own power. The policeman
looked from her to the old man in confusion, then his gaze
dropped and his expression changed. "Jesus," he breathed
as he jerked his head toward one of the uniformed cops.
"Call another ambulance!"

Brynna blinked and looked down. Blood, lots of it,
stained her dark-colored T-shirt in two places, spiraling
outward like melting roses. Behind each dark red blotch
was a deep thrumming pain that spread and joined in the
middle until her whole center burned with it. "Crap," she
said.

More policemen hustled down the stairs until the
room, so empty just a short time ago, was crowded with
people. They clustered around Cho Kim and the two
Korean men, gentle with the former, just short of cruel
with the latter. On one side handcuffs rattled, while on
the other, Brynna heard soothing words and the sounds
of tape being carefully cut by someone's pocketknife.
Above it all rose the siren call of an ambulance, dulled by
distance and the heavy walls of the building.

Redmond reached for her and Brynna pushed his
hands away. "No ambulance," she said. "I don't need

one." She turned toward the wall, trying for privacy, but Redmond circled around until he was facing her again.

"Don't be stupid," he said. "It's going to be hard enough for me to explain what you're doing here. I don't need you dying on top of that."

"That's ridiculous. I'm not going to die."

"You're *shot*," he pointed out, then scowled. "Twice. I can't believe you're even standing."

Still facing the wall, Brynna realized there was no way he was going to leave her alone so she could do what she needed. Fine—let him watch. Without saying anything more, she reached under her T-shirt and found the wound just below the ribs on her right side.

"Hey!" Redmond said in surprise. "Don't do that! Just put pressure on—"

She ignored him and dug into the hole with her forefinger, hissing as fresh pain scissored through her muscles. Redmond's shocked face flickered across her field of vision for a moment, then she hunkered down and pushed deeper until she felt the misshapen piece of offending metal. A twist to hook it with her fingernail, then she yanked it out. It came with a fresh pulse of blood; Brynna pressed her fist against it, warming the flesh until it heated and swelled, temporarily closing beneath her touch. When she pulled her hand out and unfolded her fingers to offer him the remnants of Seung's bullet, Redmond's expression would have been comical had she not been facing the ordeal of getting out the other bullet still lodged in her shoulder.

"No," Redmond said. His voice sounded dull, almost mechanical. "You can't have done what I think you just did."

Brynna grabbed the detective's hand and forced the bloody bullet into it. "Take it," she snapped. "I'm not much good at patience right now."

"I—"

"Don't you ever shut up?" Whatever he might have answered sputtered away when she went after the bullet in her shoulder the same way. A few more seconds and she dropped a second gory bit of deformed metal onto his still-open palm, where it clinked against the other bullet. "There," she said with finality.

Redmond stared first at the bloody bullets on his palm, then at her. "You need a doctor," he said, but his voice still sounded automatic, as if he were only saying what he knew *should* be said but wasn't quite sure why.

"Nope."

The detective squeezed his eyes shut and gave a small shake of his head. "I can't possibly walk you out of here like *that*." He inclined his head toward Brynna's arms and hands, where her skin was streaked in drying rivulets of blood. "Even your face is bloody. It'll never fly."

Brynna knew better than to ask why she had to go at all. Instead, she scrubbed the backs of her hands against her jeans, swiped at her face the best she could, then folded her arms tightly together in an attempt to hide the remaining crimson stains and the myriad of tiny wounds along one forearm. "This is the best I can do."

Redmond stared at her for a long moment. Then without another word, he hustled her up the stairs and steered her into his waiting car.

Seven

Humans, Brynna decided, spent a lot of their rather short lives just waiting. She didn't mind it, but then, she was immortal. When you had only seventy or eighty years, it sure seemed like a waste.

She'd waited at the police station—again—for at least two hours before Redmond was finally able to get to her. Unlike the first time, when he'd put her in the lockup, this wasn't a game or some kind of ploy to make her cooperate. He *wanted* to talk to her—Brynna could feel it—but all the paperwork and details of Cho Kim's rescue were getting in the way. It would be interesting to see how he worked her part into the story without looking completely crazy to his superiors.

At last the door opened and Redmond came in, his partner close behind. Sathi looked wary and almost as frazzled as Redmond, so he must have gotten plastered with some of the fallout from the case.

"How's your . . ." Redmond hesitated, and Brynna hid her smile.

"I'm fine," she told him. "A little sore, but that'll pass."

She was quite a bit more than sore, but there was no sense complaining about it.

Sathi leaned across the table and peered at her arms and shirt, which was looking even more pathetic now that the blood had dried and crusted. The stains on her arms had turned dark brown, like red-tinted dried chocolate, and the skin was pocked with tiny cuts and bruises. "So Kwan Seung shot you," Sathi said. He didn't bother starting with small talk. When Brynna nodded, he pointed to her arms. "Did he do that too? The cuts? The burns?"

"No." Brynna hesitated.

"Then who did?"

She pressed her lips together, then finally answered. "The witch doctor."

Redmond's eyes widened. "Wait—witch doctor? There wasn't a fifth person in that basement. Are you saying someone got away?"

He was already starting to rise when Brynna replied, "No. He didn't get away."

"Then where the hell is he?" Redmond's voice was exasperated. "Where—"

"I destroyed him."

Both the detectives stared at her. Finally Sathi spoke. "What do you mean, you destroyed him? Where is his body?"

Brynna folded her hands in front of her. "It's gone," she said truthfully. "It burned up."

Redmond frowned. "There was no evidence of a fire down there. Nothing more than a couple of candles."

"All that was left was ashes. Like dirt."

"We'll have to send a forensics team back down there,"

Sathi said. "Damn it, that whole area's been trampled. It'll be a mess."

"It won't do you any good," Brynna said. "Your forensics won't be able to identify anything from what's left on the floor anyway."

"Evidence of human remains can be pulled from ashes. We've dealt with fire," Redmond said sharply. "The team will—"

"Not from this kind." Brynna's gaze went from one man to the other as they stared at her again. Her voice sank almost to a whisper. "For dust you are and to dust you will return."

Redmond briefly squeezed his eyes shut. "Tell you what, let's just hear what happened. Your version—*all* of it."

So Brynna told them. Well, not all of it—she left out the part about Lahash, just because she still didn't know what his part in all of this was, other than to feed power into the witch doctor. The big question was *why,* but that was something these police detectives would never be able to find out. At the end of her tale, they were silent, and it wasn't lost on Brynna that neither of them had taken any notes. Of course—they wouldn't want a written record of what she'd just told them. Come to think of it, what a coincidence that the room they'd put her in had no two-way windows.

Finally Redmond spoke. "Chul-moo and his son— were they in the room with you and the . . . witch doctor? At the same time?" He sounded as if he wanted to choke on the phrase. Brynna fought the urge to grin.

"No."

"So neither of them saw you supposedly kill this person."

"No."

Sathi raised an eyebrow, as though he knew where this was going. "What about the girl? She knew he was there, didn't she?"

Brynna shook her head. "No way. She was still unconscious."

Redmond drummed his fingers on the table with exaggerated slowness. "Since you seem to be the only person who, uh, saw this witch doctor person, who is now gone, and since there's no evidence of a body anywhere, I really don't see a need to include any reference to him in the report." He glanced at Sathi and his partner nodded in agreement.

It made no difference to Brynna what was or wasn't in their report, but when she started to stand, Redmond held up a hand. "Oh, no. We're not finished yet. You still haven't told me what you were doing there in the first place." His eyes were dark.

"I knew she was in there from when we went before, so I went back to free her." She couldn't make it any more simple than that.

Redmond's eyes were fixed on Brynna's face. "Even ignoring that you lied to us about that yesterday, why is it you didn't call me?"

"Because it was too dangerous," Brynna explained patiently. "The witch doctor would have killed you."

"And how did you know the witch doctor was there?"

"I could feel him."

Sathi tilted his head. "Did you know he was there yesterday too?"

"Yes," Brynna admitted.

"And you knew the girl was there?"

"You already figured that out," Brynna said. "But I also knew they wouldn't let her die, like I told you."

"Because of the demons."

"Yes."

More silence, then Redmond sighed. "We're done here. If I put any of this in the paperwork, you'll end up in a psych ward, Brynna."

She spread her hands. "What do you want me to say? That's the way it happened."

Redmond squeezed his eyes shut, then opened them again and rubbed his eyes behind his glasses. He seemed to do that a lot, as though he wished everything would go back to normal every time he tried it. "There was another killing last night," he said suddenly. "You wouldn't know anything about that, would you?"

Brynna sat very still. "Of course not."

"Where were you?"

"At a Mexican restaurant. I stayed there all night." Both detectives wore expressions of disbelief, and she realized how silly that sounded. It annoyed her, but if she didn't explain, they might lock her up again. She'd had enough of that. "I stopped the owner from being robbed, so he's letting me stay there nights."

Sathi flipped open his notebook. "And this can be verified?"

Brynna shrugged. "I don't see why not." She gave the detective an approximate address and the owner's name.

Across from her, Redmond rubbed his eyes again. They were shadowed and swollen, like he was running short on sleep. "I could charge you with withholding evidence, interfering with a police investigation, and probably a half dozen other things. But I guess I'm crazy, because I'm going to let you go."

"I was just trying to help."

"You already seem to get in enough trouble by yourself." He glanced pointedly at the wounds on her face and arms, frowning deeper when he noticed the cut on her arm from the night before. "We don't need your help with police business. Stay in your lane, and out of ours."

Brynna thought that the thing they needed most in the world was her help, but she said nothing.

Finally Redmond stood. "I'll show you where the ladies' room is and you can clean up. I've got an extra T-shirt in my locker."

BRYNNA STRIPPED TO THE waist in the restroom, ignoring the stares of the two women already in there. While the sight of her bare breasts and skin would usually tempt anyone, male or female, her cut, bruised flesh and seeping bullet wounds were unnerving enough to smother any unexpected impulses. They didn't stick around and soon enough Brynna had the room to herself.

The long mirror above the row of sinks gave her an unforgiving view, and Brynna saw she was a far cry from the alluring young woman who'd been "born" into this realm only a few days earlier. The burns along her arm had healed, leaving a smattering of irregular scars that were angry, ugly, and red against her light skin. In addition to last night's knife wound, which she'd closed by turning it into a long, thin burn, she was cut in dozens of places on

her face and forearm from the shrapnel the witch doctor
had tossed at her. However, none of those wounds came
close to the damage done by the two gunshots, both of
which had eased open again. Now they dribbled blood
and were a blend of purple and yellow.

"Damn," Brynna grumbled. "I thought I had enough
burning before I got here." Even as the thought crossed
her mind, she felt the fingers of her left hand start to build
heat. It took Brynna only seconds to sear first one, then
the other, but the pain was harsh, much more so than she
expected, and her vision sparkled dangerously. She fought
it—it wouldn't be a good thing to pass out half naked
in the restroom of a police station when two detectives
waited in the hall.

How much more could this human body take? It had
been poorly used, that's for sure, and she was paying the
price. But she could fix that easily . . .

All she had to do was change.

Brynna hung on to the edge of one of the sinks, letting
the feel of the cool porcelain ground her as she worked
through the curls of agony spreading from her right
shoulder to her abdomen. The simple act of reverting to
the strongest of her demon forms would be like drowning
in the healing waters of immortality—all wounds healed,
energy revitalized, spirit rejuvenated. It should be so easy,
but it wasn't, not at *all*.

She thought back to when she'd searched out Cho Kim
via her scarf, then to the killing of the demons plaguing
the girl in the jewelry store's basement. Neither time had
been a full change, and each had given her only a glimpse
of her true domain. Yet everything she saw could see *her*

too. Only the human population had kept her safe from Hunters. A full change would draw Lucifer's soldiers like water drew the damned in Hell.

No, it was too dangerous. Brynna straightened and found herself a little more steady, in a little less pain. A Hunter might be able to find her just as she was, but it would be stupid to encourage it with a homing beacon. She wasn't sure how much time had passed after she'd finished with the second bullet wound, but it must have been a while, because suddenly a sound worked its way into her brain—someone knocking on the door. It had to be one of the guys, because a woman would have just walked right in. "Yes?" was all she could get out.

"Brynna, are you all right?" Redmond's voice was muffled but growing louder—he was inching the door open. Not good; she wasn't so out of it that she couldn't smell her own burned skin in the air.

"Hold on. I'll be out in just another minute."

He didn't answer and Brynna could almost feel the way he was considering coming in anyway. Finally she heard the tiniest squeak of the hinge as he let the door close again. Another few seconds and she felt strong enough to grit her teeth through the pain as she raised her arms and pulled on Redmond's T-shirt. She smoothed the fabric, then looked in the mirror and couldn't help laughing.

Of all the things she could be wearing, the shirt Redmond had given her read CHICAGO POLICE DEPARTMENT.

Eight

Brynna spent the next couple of days lying low at the restaurant, letting her body heal and rest in an environment that was as close to safe as she was likely to get. The three men who'd tried to rob Cocinero didn't come back, although she half expected them to and still thought they might—humans could be stupid about wanting revenge when they took a slap in their pride. She should've known things were going too well and it was only a matter of time before the tidy little existence she'd set up crumbled beneath her.

The shake-up came on the third day when Cocinero motioned for her to step into the back so he could talk to her where the few customers in the place couldn't overhear.

"You can't sleep here now," he said. "I am sorry. Some-one, I don't know who, tells the Health Department. The inspector, he calls me this morning to ask if I have some-one who lives in the restaurant. I am sorry," he said again. Brynna could see the regret in his eyes.

She didn't know much about the way places like this

were run, but it was obvious that Cocinero was breaking some kind of rule by having her here overnight. There wasn't much she could say besides "Okay." She was mostly healed, so there was no reason she couldn't figure out something else. "I'll sit out front until you close tonight. Then . . ." She shrugged.

"Listen," he said. He started to reach for her arm, then thought better of touching her; his fingers wavered in the air before dropping back to his side. "I know a place you can stay. The building, it is like here, not in so good a neighborhood. Worse, maybe. But someone like you . . ." He hesitated before continuing. "They could use that. You know what I mean? The man who owns the building, I think he maybe do the same for you like I did."

She folded her arms. "Maybe," she finally said. "I'd have to see."

Cocinero nodded. "Good, good. I will take you there at closing, *sí*? In this building is where my sister lives. You will look, and then decide." He smiled widely. "I will fix you something to eat, something *especial*. Steak maybe, or—"

"No meat," Brynna interrupted.

"No meat," Cocinero repeated. *"Sí."* He hurried back to the kitchen and Brynna went out front to wait for her food and wonder what the next turn would be in her quest for redemption.

THE BUILDING COCINERO TOOK her to later that night was pretty much a shit hole by human standards. While a few of the apartments were probably kept clean and neat, most of the folks who lived here had zero money and even less potential for getting any, at least by honest means. Hopelessness and fear permeated an atmosphere smothered by neglect. With sixteen or eighteen units, it wasn't a big structure, but it seemed to loom. The building also had a smell to it, the scent of turned meat, garbage, and blood not quite washed away. That smell combined with the darkness of the sidewalks and the burned-out streetlights to make the place seem like some kind of living monster, squatting just off the street and waiting to snatch at unsuspecting passersby. To Brynna it wasn't at all intimidating, but to a fragile man or woman, or God forbid, a child, it had to be utterly terrifying.

There were doorbells but they looked disused, and although the lock on the inside door was sturdy, the door itself had become so battered that Brynna knew a couple of solid kicks would get an intruder through. The mailboxes were in decent shape, no doubt because many of the residents counted on monthly welfare, unemployment, or social security checks, but the floor was lined with dirty papers, discarded pieces of mail, and advertisements that no one wanted. A cockroach worked its way through the layers.

Brynna waited as Cocinero pulled out a cell phone and dialed a number, then told the person who answered, his sister, to come down and let him in. Thirty more seconds and Brynna saw a middle-aged woman peer from the edge of the staircase leading to the second floor. When she saw Cocinero, she hurried forward and opened the door, checking to make sure the latch clicked after they entered. She led the way to a third-floor apartment with Brynna bringing up the rear in the dimly lit, echoing hallways.

When they were safely inside her place, the woman looked quizzically from Cocinero to Brynna, then shyly introduced herself in Spanish as Cocinero made another call, this time to the owner of the building. "I am Abrienda. Ramiro is my brother. It is good to meet you."

Was it? Brynna nodded, but really didn't know what else to say. She just wasn't good at this human socialization thing, and she was still trying to come up with something when a young girl walked out of a door off the living room.

Brynna blinked, completely caught by surprise. The child was beautiful, with flawless skin, long dark hair, and eyes so dark they might've been black. She couldn't have been more than sixteen or seventeen. She was also over six feet tall and smelled like clear, clean ocean water.

Nephilim.

It was late and the girl was wearing worn pajama bottoms and a Chicago Cubs tank top. The faded pattern on the pants might have been hearts and dogs, and served as a stark reminder that no matter how tall and lovely the girl was, Brynna was still looking at barely more than a child whose eyes were puffy with sleep. "Mama? Is something wrong?"

Of course—under normal circumstances, a visitor at this late hour would never be good. "Everything is fine," the woman assured her in English. "Go back to bed, Mireva."

Mireva—*miraculous.*

"I was dreaming," Mireva said softly. "About the science fair, I think."

"Back to bed," her mother repeated.

Brynna's gaze met the girl's curious stare, then Mireva nodded obediently and disappeared gracelessly back into the other room, moving as though she didn't know what to do with her own lanky body and oversize feet. A moment later the door closed.

"This is the person I told you about," Cocinero told his sister. "Did you speak to Castel?"

"Yes. He wants to meet her. He does not believe a woman can do this."

Cocinero nodded and swallowed as he glanced at her. Brynna knew he was having his own doubts, because taking care of an entire apartment building was a much heavier task than kick-assing three punks out of his store. His judgment was on the line here, his reputation.

"Don't worry," Brynna said. Before she could say more, Cocinero's cell phone buzzed softly. He answered it and spoke a few words, then closed it and back stepped to the door. Barely ten seconds passed before someone knocked lightly. Cocinero pulled it open without checking to see who was on the other side.

The man who entered wasn't what Brynna had expected. In her existence, she'd seen a thousand versions of the building in which she now stood, always owned by greedy, uncaring men or women whose only priority was to collect as much money as possible and screw the people who got stepped on along the way. Sometimes they were ruled by pride and flashed what they owned; sometimes they tried to fit in with the common folk so they could lie about why they didn't take care of their property. But the ordinary people always knew better. So did Brynna.

This man, presumably Castel, was clean shaven and

dressed in fresh clothes, but he smelled like soap from a recent shower and his eyes were heavy-lidded with exhaustion. He was lean and muscular, like a gangbanger. His knuckles were scarred too. Brynna couldn't help raise an eyebrow as her gaze touched on his face.

"So," he said in Spanish, "you are the woman Ramiro talks about."

Brynna said nothing.

Castel shook his head and glared at Cocinero. "You are crazy, to think that a woman can keep the building safe."

"No," Cocinero insisted. "Talk to her—"

"Nice black eye you've got there," Brynna interrupted. "Regular visitors, or someone new testing the scene?"

Castel's eyes darkened. "They are only neighborhood punks, but you are no match for them. Being tall will not help you here."

She smiled at him, and something in her expression made him frown. She wondered if he realized he was barely a step away from making a deal with the devil. "I have my methods."

His eyes narrowed, but then he shook his head. "No, it is too dangerous. You have no weapons, and I don't want shoot-outs or knife fights anyway. I don't need you on my conscience."

"One night," she said. "A trial period. Then you can see if you want me to stay."

Castel started to protest again, but Cocinero cut him off. "She can do it," he argued. "I swear—just give her a chance."

"Fine," Castel said abruptly. Brynna couldn't tell if he was angry or impatient. "But don't blame me when she gets hurt. Or worse." He dug into his pocket and yanked out a key. Tied to it was a white tag on which someone had scrawled *01 Front*. "It's not much. One room, a bed, refrigerator, a hot plate. I'm not renting *Better Homes and Garden*." Brynna had no idea what he was talking about, so she accepted the key without saying anything. "You'll probably be gone by morning," he predicted. "Just don't leave too much blood behind you."

Brynna laughed. She couldn't help it.

Castel frowned again as Cocinero avoided his eyes and Abrienda rubbed her hands together nervously. He started to say something, then shrugged instead. "Whatever. It's your funeral." He left, giving the door a solid slam behind him. Brynna wondered if that made him feel better. She doubted it.

There was a long moment of uncomfortable silence, then Abrienda swallowed and stepped forward. "My brother will show you where the apartment is." She hesitated. "Are . . . are you sure you want to do this?"

Brynna nodded. "Of course. I'm not afraid."

"Maybe you should be," the other woman said softly. Cocinero waved her off and motioned for Brynna to follow him into the dark, decrepit hallway.

CASTEL HADN'T BEEN LYING about the apartment. The jail cell she'd been in was only one step lower than this. The place was small, with walls that were a dirty yellowish-brown from decades of cigarette smoke. It was bigger than she had expected, with a separate eating area and a small kitchen on the other side of a short wall that had a pass-through window in it. The refrigerator that

Castel had referred to was small, but that was okay with her. The hot plate didn't look like it worked, but there was a beat-up microwave that had possibilities. The sole light was from a dim, overhead fixture, a leftover from long ago that had somehow managed to keep working. The sheet-deprived mattress was an adventure waiting to happen, and the bathroom was dirty, but at least all the plumbing looked as if it worked.

The apartment's only window looked out onto the sidewalk. The view was obstructed by metal safety bars, but it gave Brynna a good view of the sidewalk and the entrance to the building. It hadn't been lost on her earlier that every window on the first floor was barred like hers, and a quick check of the rear hallway revealed a dead-bolted steel door. When she tested the barricade on the window, Brynna decided that any normal human was coming through the front entrance or not at all.

There were only three other pieces of furniture in the apartment besides the twin bed: a night stand next to the bed and a tiny, off-balance table with a wooden chair in the eating area. She looked around the place without saying anything while Cocinero waited awkwardly in the doorway. "It's not much," he finally said, as if he had to defend the landlord. "Abrienda can help you clean tomorrow. Tonight I will bring you sheets. And a towel."

"It's fine," Brynna said, and meant it.

"What else do you need?" Cocinero's gaze skipped around the room, then paused on the pass-through to the kitchen. "Some dishes, *sí*? We have old ones—"

"Identification," Brynna interrupted. She turned to

look at him. "That's what I need most. A social security card, a driver's license. So I can work."

Cocinero was silent for a long moment. "Your full name?" he finally asked.

"Malak," she replied, then spelled it for him while he wrote it along with a fake date of birth and the made-up address she'd given Eran Redmond on the back of a crumpled receipt he pulled from his pocket.

"I know someone who might be able to do this," he admitted at last.

She nodded. When Cocinero edged out the door, Brynna returned to the window, lifted it a couple of inches to let in the outside sounds and smells, then stared out, waiting for the night and whatever it might bring.

THE DARKNESS HERE WAS different than it was in Hell. There were no fires or smoke or screams—well, not many—filling up the empty spaces around the building. The forty-five minutes that it took for the first hints of trouble to crop up were nothing compared to the lifetimes she'd endured. A blink in time, no more, but everything humans did was accelerated out of necessity. Brynna wondered, not for the first time, why she and her fellow angels had gone through so much upheaval over organic beings who had virtually no permanence. It was the postorganic essence that mattered, of course, but these were thoughts best saved for a time when the small group of young men skulking by the front walkway were somewhere else.

No—false alarm. In the few seconds Brynna took to decide whether or not to go outside, they were gone. Brynna's hearing was more than excellent and she heard them enter with a key, then take their whispered conversation up the stairs and deeper into the building than she cared to follow.

She pulled the chair to the window and sat, letting her head droop in semisleep while her other senses watched for her and her subconscious mulled over the fact that Cocinero's niece, Mireva, was a nephilim. Brynna realized she shouldn't have been so surprised. Modern-day life had become so saturated with temptations that it was only logical that nephilim, the children of angels, would increase in number. Humans had no idea—neither did the nephilim themselves—that the very reason for the existence of angelic offspring was to accomplish a specific task, something initially known only to the ultimate Creator. Someday the nephilim would be compelled to do something for which there would be no logical explanation, something they would do anything to complete. But just as they would strive to complete their destiny, so too was Hell itself determined to stop each and every one of them.

Numbers aside, Chicago was a huge city—it had to be more than coincidence that had put Brynna so near another nephilim so soon, that had conspired all the events in her oh-so-short time on Earth to lead her to this grubby, gang-riddled tenement house. One nephilim had died just inches from her, and yet here was another, close enough for her to . . . what?

Protect.

Could she have found her road to redemption? She had no idea, and since God didn't talk to her anymore, the only thing Brynna could do was try.

Another hour passed, then two, and she was beginning

to think that the test of her first night would pass without giving her the ability to prove herself.

Finally, a sound made Brynna lift her head. Hurrying up the darkened sidewalk to the building's entrance was a woman dressed in jeans and a grease-splattered shirt. Brynna could smell her from here. Hot oil, cheap meat, eggs, and more—a waitress like the one at that restaurant near the police station, coming home from her shift. If she was lucky, she had enough in her purse to pay the electric bill and buy a few groceries. She also smelled like fear, and rightfully so, because she was being followed.

Brynna was out of her apartment in seconds. She met the woman at the front entrance and pulled her through the door. The waitress gasped in surprise when Brynna yanked her backward and stepped in front of her just as a guy with greasy dark hair and dirty hands grabbed at the air where the woman's head had just been. He flailed at nothing for a moment, then tried again. Brynna slapped his hand away. "Get lost," she snarled. "Go rob someone else."

"Get out of my way, *puta,*" the man hissed. "I want to talk to my wife."

Brynna's eyebrows rose and she glanced behind her. The woman, petite and middle-aged, had probably once been pretty, but a hard life had taken that from her. The network of scars along her left jaw and the fresh swelling and splits in her bottom lip didn't help. "N-No, Lujano. You go away." Her eyes were so wide with terror that the whites showed all the way around her black irises. "The police say you cannot talk to me anymore. The judge said so, too—they will arrest you!"

Lujano laughed softly. "Well, they are not here now, are they, *mi bonita*?" His eyes were small and mean as they passed dismissively over Brynna, then trained again on the woman behind her. "Get your ass over here, Rosamar."

Rosamar shook her head. To Brynna, the movement looked like the tremor of a petrified bird. "No," she said again. "I have filed divorce papers. I—"

Lujano's laugh was harsher this time. "*Pendeja,* there will be no divorce. *Ever.* We are going to have a talk about that."

"This is getting old," Brynna cut in. Her palm flashed forward and she shoved Lujano hard enough to make him stumble back a good six feet. He made a guttural warning sound at her and Brynna's eyes briefly glowed a scarlet warning. "*Go away.*"

Lujano didn't notice. "I don't think so," he spat. He dragged something out of his pocket and pointed it at Brynna. "Get the fuck out of my way. I have business with my wife."

Brynna saw the barest gleam of light reflect off dirty metal—a gun of some kind, smaller than the weapon the nephilim killer used, but at this close range, potentially just as deadly. She was really getting tired of having these damned things pointed at her. Even so, she didn't back up. Behind her, Rosamar made a tiny choking sound in her throat.

Before Brynna could say anything, she felt the woman's shaking fingers tug at her sleeve. "Let me go to him," she said in a small voice. "Or he *will* hurt you." She paused, then said in a whisper only Brynna could hear, "I should know." Louder, she said, "If I let you in, you will let her go, Lujano?"

Lujano had crept forward until Brynna could see the battered old revolver in his hand. He shrugged and waved the gun carelessly to one side. "I give a shit—I don't even know her."

Rosamar moved, trying to step around Brynna, and Brynna looked back at her in disbelief. Had she heard correctly? This beaten human woman was willing to sacrifice herself for Brynna's sake? A stranger whom she'd never even seen before a minute ago? The concept was almost incomprehensible, and while Brynna couldn't see the future, it wasn't difficult to imagine what the next few hours would hold for Rosamar if she did. Brynna doubted even Rosamar realized the true danger, how far gone her husband was—there was a sheen in Lujano's eyes that Brynna recognized from a hundred thousand other men whose souls had been just as black as his was tonight.

She shifted her weight before Rosamar could slip in front of her, trapping the waitress behind her. Rosamar sucked in a breath. "I'm not usually a generous person," Brynna told Lujano in an icy voice, "but I'll give you one last chance to take off."

Lujano's wavering gun steadied and fixed on the center of Brynna's chest. "Is this where I'm supposed to ask 'Or what?' Well, not this time, bitch. You—"

Brynna's left hand was a streak in the night, far too fast for Lujano's eyes to track. A spurt of hot yellow-red light severed the darkness the instant her fingers closed over his hand and gripped it; a second later the palm of her right hand slapped over his mouth, holding in the scream that would have rippled out.

"Shhhhh," Brynna said gently. Lujano went rigid, writhing upright like a man fighting to free himself from the molten embrace of fiery clothes. "You go on home and think about changing the direction of your life, Lujano. And leave Rosamar alone—she doesn't want to see you again. *Ever.*"

Brynna let her right hand drop and Lujano's eyes bulged as his wild, agony-filled eyes rolled in their sockets. His lips were burned and blackened, sealing his screams inside; the noises he made were more like frantic, nonstop grunts. Brynna pushed him and the man almost went to his knees, then righted himself and careened away.

"Don't worry," she called after him. "Your mouth will be fine in a couple of hours." She paused, then added, "Too bad about your hand, though."

But he was already out of range, cradling one hand in the other and running crookedly along the sidewalk as fast as he could. Brynna watched impassively as he disappeared down the street, leaving behind only a single, tiny spot of cooling, liquefied metal on the cracked sidewalk.

Nine

Sitting in the Nickel and Dime Diner, Eran Redmond poked half-heartedly at the french fries on his plate. He'd eaten a couple, but the grit of the place had finally gotten to him. Now he couldn't focus on the food past the stained edge of his plate—what if this was some kind of food residue rather than age discoloration? It was ridiculous—he *knew* it—but still, there it was. He hadn't set foot in this restaurant for years because the place was just too grubby for his tastes. His throat closed up every time he thought about chewing one of these limp, greasy chunks of potato. It figured that Brynna Malak would want to meet here.

When, Eran wondered as he waited, had things started to weird out with her?

If he was going to be honest, there was no "started to" about it. She'd been bizarre right from the start, all the way back when he'd introduced her to old man Kim. That fucked-up telepathic party she'd had with the daughter's scarf should have been warning enough, but then Brynna had decided on her own to dig a little deeper into the girl's disappearance. It was incredible that she had found Cho at all, and now it was demons and witch doctors and claims of burned-up bodies that Brynna couldn't prove had ever existed. She'd been shot right in front of him—okay, she'd actually *taken* a bullet for him—but blown off the injuries and apparently healed just fine without ever seeing a doctor. All of that ended up with Brynna working herself so deeply into Eran's thoughts that he was having a hard time concentrating on things, other really *important* things.

Like two more sniper killings.

Both of these had been women, and the latest victim had kicked the killer's tally up to eight. The city was in an uproar and the media was feeding off the paranoia like leeches on an open wound. No one was safe from the accusations and blame throwing permeating all levels of the department. Every time Eran turned around, he saw a reporter hounding one of his superiors; while he was just like the next guy in that he wanted to make more money, this was one time Eran was glad that there were plenty of people at his job who had higher pay grades. Those poor souls were the media targets, the saps whose names appeared in the papers, the nightly newscasts, and in a hundred scathing Internet editorials every day.

Had he not decided to pass on that last sergeant's exam, Eran would've been right there in the bull's-eye. As it was, the shit was still rolling downhill; he expected it to start flying at him soon enough. It would be the same question that ran in the papers every day in one form or another—

Why hasn't the killer been caught?

—but he didn't know how to answer it.

As for Brynna, Eran couldn't shake the feeling that she knew something about it. He didn't think she knew the killer's identity, but there was . . . *something* there. He just couldn't pinpoint exactly what that *something* was.

And there was Brynna herself. He would absolutely not give in to the notion that his interest in her was anything remotely sexual. Yeah, she was an oddly attractive woman. Not exactly beautiful but *compelling,* hard to resist. So what? Eran had passed on piles of hard-to-resist things in his time on the force, freebies that were a whole lot easier to take advantage of than a headstrong and unco-operative woman. Things that started small, like a newspaper, a pack of gum, or a bottle of booze, but could easily end up big, moving into massages, jewelry, prostitutes, cocaine, and outright bribe money. He'd had the best and worst of offers cross his path, and he wasn't above enjoying the smallest of the stuff. But he was smart enough to avoid the career killers—his honesty helped that—and he could definitely turn a cold shoulder to a little irrational attraction.

The tabletop vibrated and Eran looked up as Brynna slid into the booth across from him. She didn't smile, and that was fine with Eran; there was something off about that expression on her pale, shadow-riddled face. It always ended up dark somehow, sinister—it just didn't fit.

"How are you?" he asked, and meant it. The last time he'd seen her, she'd had two bullet wounds that would have taken even the toughest cop off his feet. Now she looked almost the same as the first time he'd met her in Walgreens—better, in fact. Although her injuries should have taken weeks to heal, the never-explained burns along one arm had faded to little more than faint, pink blotches. There were a couple of other healing wounds, but Eran could tell that soon they'd be no more than memories. Was it the same with the two gunshot holes beneath the freshly washed, dark blue CPD T-shirt?

"Good."

He waited but she didn't say anything more. He fought his automatic urge to pry, to demand if she'd seen a doctor—he doubted it. Instead, he asked, "So why did you want to meet me here? Did you remember something else about that guy you saw through the window at Walgreens?"

She looked at him blankly, then shook her head. He should have realized that hope was too farfetched. "I still have your business card," she said. She pulled it from her back pocket and placed it on the table between them. "You said to get in touch if I wanted to work as a translator for you."

Eran pushed a lock of hair around on his forehead, then carefully smoothed it back down. "Yeah, I did. But not for me. There's only so much I can do out of pocket. I know you could get something at a few of the legal places around the loop, government or private." He leaned back and studied her. "But you need identification, Brynna. A driver's license, at least. And a social security number. I told you that before."

She nodded. "I have them."

Eran's eyebrows rose as Brynna reached into her pocket a second time, then dropped two items on the tabletop. He couldn't help picking them up. The social security card was crumpled along the edges and worn from being shoved into a pocket. The driver's license was the same—ragged at the edges, scratched along the surface of the plastic. According to this, she'd turned thirty last year, born on the thirteenth of November. It had the same Georgia address she had given him the day he'd arrested her. Eran's experienced eye thought the paper and the laminated surface of the license looked a little too new, that the creases and scratches had probably been put there intentionally. If he ran these numbers, would they come back as fake IDs? Probably.

He put the cards back on the table. "I thought you said you didn't drive."

"I don't. But I never said I didn't have a license."

"And you said you'd never really worked."

"But not that I didn't actually have a social security card."

Eran made an exasperated sound. "Brynna—"

"This is what you asked for." She looked at him steadily, and Eran could imagine the rest of her unspoken words, which were probably in the scope of *Take it or leave it.*

"Fine," he said abruptly. He shouldn't, but Eran knew he was going to look the other way on this one. There was a danger that it would come back and bite him in the ass, but if she worked as an independent consultant, the risk might be minimal. He could always plead ignorance, although that wouldn't sit well with his chief. "I'll put out some feelers." He gave her a stern look. "Essentially you're going to be self-employed. You'll need a permanent address—"

"I have one."

"—and some business clothes." That, at least, got a reaction, even if it was only a quickly concealed look of dismay. Surely she had more clothes than a single pair of jeans and his extra cop shirt. "But don't worry about that yet," he added. "Let's see if we can find you a couple of jobs first." He paused and chewed the inside of one cheek momentarily. Should he ask? He had to—the concept was still making him slightly crazy. He tried to keep his voice casual, matter-of-fact. "Is there any language I should tell them you can't do?"

"No."

Such a simple answer, such an unbelievable ability. Time would tell if she came through or if he ended up with a rep tarnished by his gullibility. Yeah, she'd stepped up with the Spanish and Korean, but *every* other language? It just couldn't be true.

Could it?

Eran forced his thoughts in another direction. "So you're living somewhere." When Brynna nodded, he took out his notebook and pushed it and a pen across the table. "Address," he instructed. "And phone number."

She leaned over the notebook and carefully wrote out a number and street name. Her writing was slow and laborious, the final product almost archaic-looking. He purposely didn't look from it to the signatures on the ID cards. "I don't have a phone," she said. When he scowled, she added quickly, "I'll get one, though. After I've worked a bit."

"It should be a cell phone," he said, although he wondered how he was going to pull this off without one right now. "So you can have it with you all the time. What's your zip code?" Her expression said she had no idea. "Find out. The companies you work for will want to know."

She nodded, then glanced at his now-cold french fries. "Are you going to eat those?"

"No."

Her hand hovered over his plate. "Do you mind?"

"Go ahead."

Christ, he thought as he watched her scarf down the food. *This is all screwed-up.* She had no clothes, no business cards, no telephone number, and, from the looks of it, not even any money for food. The address she'd written down was in such a crappy neighborhood that she'd be better off using a post office box. How the hell was she going to pass as a professional? This was never going to fly unless she had some help.

I can't believe I'm going to do this.

He knew better. He really did.

Eran slid out of the booth as Brynna swallowed the last of the fries. "Come with me," he said. "We've got some stuff to do."

"ALL RIGHT," ERAN SAID. "I'll start asking around first thing Monday. With your skills, I'm pretty sure I'll have something for you by Tuesday morning."

He and Brynna were standing in front of a Sprint store downtown, and Brynna was examining the cell phone he'd just bought her. It was small, red—for whatever reason, Eran felt that suited her better than silver—and had put him on the hook for a two-year contract. Hanging from Brynna's arm were three shopping bags from their visit to the Marshalls store over on Michigan Avenue. The pile of clothes inside—everything from business attire to a purse, stockings, and undergarments—had set him back almost five hundred bucks. It was as though she'd been living in a vacuum—he'd had to help her pick out every single thing, even the bras. He'd print some kind of business card for her on his computer when he got home, meet up, and give her a handful before she went to her first job.

"This is a phone that takes pictures?" Brynna asked. "It's so small."

"Please tell me I didn't just waste a bunch of money and time on you," Eran said. He felt like a tuning fork that had been hit too hard, shaking inside from stress and uncertainty. "I will be really pissed if I go through all this and you don't show up."

She gave him a look of genuine surprise, as if the thought had never occurred to her. It was sincere, or at least that's what Eran told himself. "Why wouldn't I?"

Eran shrugged, hoping he didn't look too helpless. Did he really think she'd book? No, but he also had a hard time explaining to himself why he'd gone so far out on a limb for this woman. And he didn't want to think about what his partner or the other cops at the station would say if they found out he'd just financed a new life setup for a nearly homeless crime witness. There wasn't a single thing that served as justification for it, and dozens of others that screamed he shouldn't have. "Let's grab a bite to eat, then I'll drive you home," was all he finally said.

When Brynna's face brightened momentarily before sliding back into her normal, neutral expression, Eran realized with a start that it was nearing six o'clock, and while he'd had a good breakfast, the french fries she'd eaten earlier had probably been her only meal today. It was still fairly early, so Eran managed to get a table at Bella Bacino's Italian Bistro & Pizzeria. Half an hour later, Brynna was diving into a plate of pasta with artichokes and broccoli and he had a plate of *frutti del mare* in front of him. She seemed to enjoy her food, but when she kept eyeing his, Eran finally offered her some.

"It's not meat," he reminded her when she pulled back from the fork he wanted to hand her. He hadn't forgotten her adamant statement to the waitress when they'd ordered. "It's seafood. Fish."

"Oh, I'll eat that," she said. She tried a bit of linguini and a shrimp, then nodded. "Very good sauce. And I haven't had shrimp since . . ." Her voice faded out.

"When?" Eran prompted.

Brynna looked away. "Really too long ago to remember." She glanced at the tables around them, then at the window at the front of the restaurant. The sun had set and the soft lights inside made the darkness beyond the glass even more severe. There were patio tables filled with people in front of Bella Bacino's, but the glare of lights off the glass kept them from seeing the patrons.

They finished their meal in silence. Like many of the smaller upscale downtown restaurants, the atmosphere was busy and the noise level almost too loud for conversation. Not quite comfortable but not quite awkward—more an opportunity to learn to tolerate each other's company. Brynna seemed at ease with him but not with her surroundings, almost as if she were waiting for something, or some*one,* to happen. She checked the entrance and the window regularly and looked at the door to the kitchen every time one of the waitstaff came or went through it.

Eran studied her, trying not to be obvious about it, but she always seemed to catch him doing it; his scrutiny didn't appear to bother her at all, as if she were used to being looked at, measured, perhaps even judged.

Brynna's face was too angular to be called beautiful, and the shadows under her eyes and in the hollows of her cheekbones hinted at a harshness that was off-putting rather than mysterious. Eran found it strange that while her makeup-free skin was nearly bone white, her cheeks always held a tinge of deep pink, like she'd just come in from a long, hot run. Her hairstyle reminded him of the jagged, slept-in look popular with teenagers nowadays. While businesses had become more accepting of trendy styles, he still made a mental note to stop by a drugstore and buy her a brush and a few toiletries before he took her home. Christ, it was as though he'd adopted a seductive homeless person.

Eran gave himself a mental punch. Seductive—where had *that* come from? He was normally such a grounded guy, but if he was going to be honest with himself, he *was* drawn to her, even though he was fighting it. No big surprise there—he was a man, and a cop, and both were, in his opinion, always horny. As long as he kept it under control, things would be fine. And never mind that "under control" was going to be a really contentious subject if his partner found out how deep in his pockets he'd gone for this woman.

They declined dessert and Eran paid the check. Outside it was another hot and humid night. There was a breeze but it only picked up moisture from the river across Wacker Drive and made Eran more uncomfortable on the walk to where he'd parked the car. Although he had sweat building beneath his shirt, the sticky air didn't appear to bother Brynna at all. Oddly enough, he could tell that being in the open air *did*. She glanced this way and that, constantly checking behind them as they walked, even scanning the sky as if she thought something was going to drop on their heads.

"What's wrong?" Eran finally asked. Being with her for the last two blocks had made him feel like he was walking down the street with a skittish animal. "You're acting like a bird with a cat outside its cage."

"I don't like being out in the open," she said. "Especially at night. It's too vulnerable."

He looked at her in surprise and caught a flash of dismay on her face, as if she'd blurted out a secret without meaning to. Interesting—he'd definitely have to file this in his mental follow-up folder. "Here's the car," he said instead of commenting. When he unlocked the door to his black Galant, she slid onto the front seat with visible relief. Eran had no doubt that the tinted windows helped. Thinking back, he realized he'd never been around her at night. What was in her past that brought out this kind of fear? Whatever it was, he felt sure she wouldn't talk about it.

They made a fifteen-minute stop at a Walmart where Eran spent another fifty bucks on stuff like toothpaste, shampoo and soap, a hairbrush, all chosen by him because Brynna just stood next to him in the aisles with that I-have-no-idea expression Eran was learning to recognize. He threw in a couple of cans of soup and some chips as an afterthought, realizing she probably didn't have any food in her apartment. He didn't like to admit it, but she seemed so naive about everything that he sometimes wondered if she hadn't spent most of her life in an institution. He'd missed his one valid chance, but one of these days he'd find an excuse to get her fingerprints and run them through the computer system.

"In case you haven't been reading the paper, there were two more shootings this week," Eran told Brynna as he drove her home. "Same gun. Two women who didn't even know each other. One was a twenty-two-year-old cashier at a Brown's Chicken, the other worked at a neighborhood video store." He glanced sideways at her but she didn't say anything. "She was only thirty-five. None of the victims knew each other. It just seems random." He pressed his lips together when she stayed silent. "By the way, Cook County Hospital—your area, in case you don't know—got a really bizarre case earlier this week. A couple of beat cops brought a guy in with some kind of metal object melted into his hand. Picked him up not far from here, as a matter of fact." He paused, then looked over at her. "You wouldn't know anything about that, would you?"

"Me?"

Had he imagined it, or had a sardonic smile ghosted across her mouth? Yeah, he was pretty sure it had. Still, he couldn't imagine how she could be involved in something like that. The station had been ringing with the story all week, how nothing could be done for the guy but amputation. Eran knew more than a few people at the hospital—all the detectives did—and a phone call had verified the whole freakish thing. While the ER doctors had speculated that the object was a gun, the patient himself wasn't talking. Eran's friend had told him the guy had second-degree burns on his mouth and that his lips had to be lasered apart and propped open so they wouldn't fuse together again as they healed.

Eran let the topic drop, and as he pulled up in front of Brynna's place, he cringed inwardly—even in the dark, the building was more of a rat hole than he expected. He wasn't sure he ever wanted to see it during the daytime. "Let me help you take this stuff in," he said, opening his door as she got out of the car.

"No, thanks." She opened the back door and leaned in. "You've done more than enough already," she said as she gathered up the bags. By the time she closed the door and stood, Eran was standing outside the driver's side. "Thanks," she added. "Really."

"Sure. You have your phone?"

"Right here."

"I'll call you as soon as I get something."

Brynna nodded but didn't say anything else as she turned and hurried up the walkway. Even here, maybe more so, she sent the night sky a couple of apprehensive looks. As Eran watched the dark, dirty building swallow Brynna's figure, he wondered again what could frighten this strange and incredible woman so much.

Ten

Boring, Brynna thought. *If this is how the legal segment of humans spends their days, I think I'd rather work at Cocinero's restaurant.*

Riding the elevator down to the ground floor of the Willis Tower was, perhaps, the most fun she'd had all day. The suit she was wearing fit well enough, but the pantyhose and shoes had to have been invented as subversive methods of female physical torture. She supposed she'd get used to them, but it gave Brynna a new level of empathy for all the women she'd seen walking around downtown. Did they really spend every day stuffed into these horrible outfits?

Maybe she wouldn't feel so cantankerous if she'd been able to give this human body more sleep, but that was an issue that wasn't likely to be resolved anytime soon. The woman whose husband Brynna had dispatched last Tuesday had not been silent about her rescuer, and now everyone in the building was calling Brynna *guardia,* a nickname that was damned ironic given some of the chores with which she'd previously been charged in Hell.

The first couple of nights had been . . . interesting, to say the least, as though the local gangbangers had felt the need to test her. At least there'd been no more guns, which was fine by her. Nothing and no one in the building was really worthy of firepower anyway, although a couple of knives had flashed in Brynna's direction and a couple of faces had bled in response. Things had settled to fairly quiet, but if there was a one-to-ten scale of satisfying slumber, Brynna stayed at three . . . if she was lucky. Some wannabe evil human barely registered when compared to what Brynna was *really* worried about. Better to forgo the nightly shut-eye than to wake to the sight of a Hunter leering down at her.

Somehow she wasn't surprised to see Redmond's car parked in a red zone in front of the main Wacker Drive entrance, the same one she'd used this morning. He was driving a standard-issue black police sedan, and if he was offering, there was no question she'd accept a ride; her cell phone had rung at six-thirty a.m. and he'd rattled off an address, saying she needed to be there by nine to translate for something called a deposition.

It was a good thing she didn't require much in the way of primping, because finding a bus that would take her all the way downtown had been a challenge—she'd had help from Abrienda with directions and bus fare but had still barely made it. Now, after almost six hours of playing go-between for lawyers and a reluctant Russian-speaking guy pegged as a material witness in a corporate personal injury case, Brynna felt pretty used up. The language part was easy; it was the bland, never-ending questions that circled around and came back that had worn her down. No wonder Hell was home to so many condemned lawyers.

"Thanks for picking me up," she said as she slid onto the passenger seat and pulled the door closed.

"Beats the hell out of the bus," Redmond said. He pulled away from the curb and eased into the heavy afternoon traffic. Brynna said nothing as he navigated his way out of the downtown area; she didn't know where they were going, but right now she was simply too tired to care. Anywhere that was away from the world of business suits, power ties and cunning attorneys was fine with her, at least for the evening. "Dinner?"

"I'm not very hungry," she said truthfully. She'd made herself a good-sized sandwich of bread and a couple kinds of cheeses from a deli tray in the conference room during the lunch break. The deposition had been held at the offices of the defendants' lawyers, who were doing a not-very-subtle job of trying to intimidate the witness. That the guy was overwhelmed by the hugely expensive surroundings and ice-blooded lawyers was not Brynna's problem; she was just there to translate and get paid. The free lunch didn't hurt, either.

Redmond nodded, but she could sense his disappointment. "Then I'll just run you home." He glanced at her quickly. "Unless you need something. To run errands or whatever."

"No. I'm fine." She gazed out the window, then added, "I have to be back at nine tomorrow. They didn't finish asking the man questions."

"That's good, right? I mean, it's work." When she nodded, he pressed a little. "So, what language did you

translate? They didn't give me details and they seemed . . ."
He grinned a little. "Well, let's just say they were as startled as I was when I told them you could translate anything."

"Russian," she answered.

"Really? Damn."

Still the doubt—Brynna could hear it in his voice. And
most likely not without reason; as a policeman, he'd probably been lied to countless times. *"Zdravstvuite, Detekív Redmond. Nadeyus, shto da u vas bíl dobrí den. Bolshoe spacíba, shto ví
menya sevodnya zabral."*

He squinted at her, and Brynna had to laugh. "I said,
'Hello, Detective Redmond. I hope you had a good day.
Thank you for picking me up this afternoon.' "

Redmond hesitated, as if he wasn't sure she wasn't just
messing with him, then he finally gave in and grinned. "I
know how to say good afternoon in Spanish," he offered.

A corner of her mouth lifted. "So do I."

"Touché."

Traffic thinned as they headed southwest out of the
Loop, and Brynna realized he was going to take her all
the way home. She thought about telling him not to,
but then couldn't think of a good reason why she would.
Instead she said, "I appreciate the ride. I hate that bus
thing."

"You could get a car."

"I don't—" She cut herself off before she could finish,
remembering just in time that she'd shown him a supposedly valid driver's license. "Like driving in the city," she
finished.

"Ah."

"It makes me nervous," she added, but even to her own ears, it sounded like an excuse.

"Nothing like doing it to get you comfortable," Redmond said.

She nodded but didn't say anything. He was right, of course. The easiest thing to do would be to learn to drive—it was that or public transportation. And since she was already supposed to know how, she was going to have to bluff her way through the basics. Still, she had time. Redmond had told her what to charge per hour, and although it was a lot of money, it would still be quite awhile before she could afford to pay cash for a car. She certainly couldn't get mixed up in the world of human financing and loans. In the interim, she would build her knowledge by watching Redmond.

Studying his driving actions as he maneuvered through the city's afternoon rush-hour traffic made the time pass quickly, although in reality it took nearly an hour to get to her building. Redmond slid into a parking space and got out without being asked, intent on walking her inside. Brynna thought about arguing, then her attention was caught by something else—a movement in the shadows beyond the front door. She frowned and strode forward, and when she pushed the door open, she came face-to-face with Mireva, Cocinero's niece. The girl jerked in surprise, but Brynna was far more interested in the boy talking to the teenager.

The guy looked older than Mireva but only by a couple of years. He was tall and lanky like Brynna but with jet-black hair chopped and gel-styled into irregular spikes. A diamond crucifix sparkled in his left ear, blatant contrast to the kohl and black mascara enhancing his eyes; the black coloring that was painted across his lips made his skin look like china. Despite the heat, a leather biker's jacket was draped over his bony shoulders. Beneath that was a tank top of torn black netting tucked into skintight black denims. Heavy black boots and fingerless gloves completed the picture. His handsome face was ageless and intense, the alabaster-smooth brow broken by nothing, not even a single drop of sweat. His eyes met Brynna's without flinching. Of course, he wouldn't. He—

Redmond—damn, she'd forgotten about him—shouldered his way past her. "What are you two doing in this hallway?" he demanded. "Do you live here?"

"Mireva does," Brynna put in. "I know her uncle."

Redmond turned his glare to the young man. "And what about you?"

"T-This is Gavino," Mireva stammered. "He walked me home from the bus—"

"Mireva!" A sharp voice cut her off and an instant later Abrienda hurried into view from the stairs. The older woman's gaze flicked from her daughter to the young man in the hallway, then darkened. "Get upstairs. Now."

"But Gavino says he can help me work on my science project," Mireva protested.

"Yeah," Gavino offered. His eyes met Brynna's and he smirked. "I hear she's working on the tree of life. I got that whole life thing *down,* dude."

Before Mireva could say anything else, Abrienda turned her daughter away from the others and steered her toward the stairs. Gavino looked disappointed and reached out like he was going to take the girl's hand, but

Brynna slipped between them. "You don't need his kind of help," she said.

"My *kind*," Gavino sneered at her as the two women disappeared from view. "You should know."

"What?" Redmond looked from Brynna to Gavino. "You two have met before?"

"Oh, we're old friends." Gavino grinned again. His incisors looked vaguely sharp, like infantile vampire teeth. Nice trick, Brynna thought.

"You are?" Redmond looked at Brynna. "I thought—"

"So it's Gavino," Brynna cut in. "That's what you're going by these days." Her eyes narrowed as she looked at Gavino, then back at Redmond. "Gavino exaggerates. We've met before, but we've *never* been friends. And we never will be."

"So, like, you want to have lunch?" Gavino asked gleefully. "I know this restaurant—"

"Keep getting smart with me," Brynna warned. "Give me an excuse to pull your lungs out through your mouth."

"Hey," Redmond said, alarmed. "Hold on, Brynna."

"Touchy, touchy," Gavino said, but he was already edging past her, trying to get to the door. "But hey, I think I'll just mosey along."

"You do that," Brynna told him. "It's safer that way." Her gaze bored into Gavino's and she stepped closer to him, crowding him against the wall. "You know what I mean."

"You don't want to start no public display," Gavino reminded her. He glanced toward the stairs, but there was no fast way out in that direction. "People might find out certain things."

"What things?" Redmond demanded.

Brynna stepped forward again, this time nearly pinning Gavino against the wall. She could feel Redmond's confused stare but she had to rein in Mr. Motor-Mouth right now. Besides, being threatened really pissed her off. "I warned you already," she hissed into Gavino's face. "Push me again and see how much I *care*."

Gavino mock-grimaced and raised his hands. "Hey, lady—no worries. I'm so outta here."

"Hell wouldn't be far enough," she snapped.

Gavino gave her a caustic-looking grin. "Aw, what kind of thing is that to say? I ain't going *that* far."

Brynna glared at him. "You might consider it." Still, she backed up a couple of inches and Gavino slid around her with the quickness of a snake.

"Later." He looked at Redmond, then touched a finger mockingly to his forehead. "Have a nice day, Detective Redmond."

Redmond growled and started to follow him, but Brynna snagged his sleeve and held him back. In another moment the dark young man was gone, leaving nothing behind but a faint whiff of matches. Brynna barely noticed it, but she saw Redmond sniff the air distastefully before dismissing the scent and turning to her. "What the hell was that all about? I distinctly remember you telling me you weren't from around here. And how did he know my name?"

"It's a big world, Detective. I've been to a lot of it." She could think of no way to explain the name thing, so she purposely ignored it.

"Is that how you learned all these languages?"

Brynna had to snicker at that. "No. Call it a . . . natural ability."

"So what's *his* story?"

"Gavino is . . ." She hesitated. How much should she tell him? He already knew a lot. The question wasn't *Did he believe?* It was *Should he believe?* "He's like me," she finally said. "Sort of."

Redmond stared at her. "You mean he speaks a lot of languages?"

"Yes. But in other ways too."

"What other ways?"

Brynna shrugged. "I don't know how to describe it. Strong, maybe. I don't know."

Redmond frowned and she could tell he was trying to understand. She wanted to help him with it, but she didn't know how. His expression changed, like he'd made a sudden decision. "Maybe I ought to go talk to this guy."

"Not a good idea," Brynna said.

"And why is that?"

"For all the reasons I just said," Brynna told him. "You really don't want to mess with him."

"Look," Redmond said. "I'm a cop, okay? That means—"

"I know what that means," Brynna retorted. "I've been learning a lot from you."

"Then you should know that no one is exempt from my curiosity."

Brynna couldn't help chuckling. "Curiosity," she repeated. "Now there's a trait that gets a lot of species in trouble."

Despite everything she'd said, Redmond still pulled

away and darted outside. She let him go, but only because she knew it was too late. "Hey," she heard him exclaim. "Where the *hell* did he go?" She watched through the open door as he squinted first one way down the street, then the other. "Son of a bitch!"

"I'm going in," Brynna said. "Do you want something to drink before you head home? I have water."

"I don't believe it," Redmond said, as if he hadn't heard her. "No one can move that fast."

"*He* can, and he does," Brynna said. She made sure the door didn't quite close and had gone a dozen feet down the hall before she heard him finally come after her.

"So you know him," the detective said as he followed her into her apartment. He leaned against the wall behind the small table.

"Not really."

"Come on, Brynna. You two were talking like old friends out there."

She had to laugh at that. "Never friends, in Hell or on Earth," she said wryly.

"But you *do* know him," Redmond pushed.

"It's hard to explain."

"So try. And while you're at it, start with why you stopped me from going after him until you knew he'd be gone."

Brynna pressed her lips together and went into the tiny kitchen. Cocinero's grandmother, a wrinkled old woman who mumbled to herself constantly, had stopped by after church the day before and brought Brynna a box of things: a couple of towels, cheap sheets and a pillow, a mismatched, well-used handful of dishes. That made

Brynna able to throw out the Styrofoam fast-food cup she'd been reusing. She pulled a couple of scratched plastic glasses from a cabinet and filled them with water from the faucet, stalling and trying to think of a way to answer.

"It was for your own good," she said finally. "You don't want to tangle with him." The expression on Redmond's face made it clear her answer wasn't enough, so eventually she added, "He could—and would—kill you without even trying."

Redmond's eyebrows rose in surprise. "Sorry, but I think you're overestimating him."

Man, she sure didn't have the patience for this. "I'm not, and you shouldn't, either. If you see him again, stay out of his way and just let me know."

"Brynna, I'm the cop here. What on earth would make you think I'd be afraid of that guy? He's just a punk Goth kid trying to hook up with someone way too young for him. At best he's an annoyance; at worst he's a perv. Neither one scares me."

"And neither one applies to him," Brynna retorted.

"Then what does?" Redmond asked angrily. "I'm getting a little tired of this verbal dance. If there's something fucked-up about him, would you just spit it out and be done with it?"

"Fine." Brynna slammed the plastic tumbler on the table in front of Redmond. "First of all, Gavino isn't his real name. Secondly, he's like me, okay? But not in a good way, and for that, you ought to just run in the other direction."

Redmond stared. "And so I'll ask you *again*—like you in what way?"

"Like me," she repeated stubbornly. "Come on—think back over the last week. Don't act like you haven't seen stuff that you never imagined could happen."

Redmond's mouth stretched into a thin line. "Overseeing a couple of questionable psychic visions and watching you dig two bullets out of yourself might walk the edge of believability, but there's only so much I can accept, Brynna. I mean, I have my limits."

"That's just it," she told him pointedly. "Your limits exist only because that's what you've been taught to accept. But the world you believe in—it's not the real one. In the real world, the world *I'm* from and where all this"—she swept her arms in an all-encompassing gesture—"was created, there *are* no limits. Absolutely none at all."

"Brynna," he said. He was standing very, very still. "What are you talking about? Religion?"

"I'm not what you think I am, Detective Redmond. You've listened to me talk about demons and witch doctors, but you don't *believe.* Modern man has moved beyond the days of spells and shadows, and because you found electricity and airplanes and computers, you think the Dark Ages are gone. But all the technology in the world won't explain or protect you from what's *really* out there, from the things that existed eons before God blinked this very planet into actuality."

After her first few words, Redmond had lowered himself onto the wobbly chair a few feet away. Now he got up again and strode over to stand in front of her. His face was set, as if he'd made up his mind that he'd simply had enough of all this crap. She frowned and backstepped, but he was crowding her the way she had crowded Gavino, inching forward until the wall was at her back and she was trapped in the narrow kitchen area—well, as much as she could ever be trapped by a human man. "Don't you think this mystery-woman act is getting a little old?" he asked harshly.

"Old is a relative thing," Brynna said. Separated by the distance of a seat in a car or a table in a restaurant was one thing, but here he was way too close to her for his own good, and she could see the effects on him already. All the not-so-subtle body language was there—his pupils had dilated slightly and his nostrils had widened, she could feel the increase in the air temperature around his skin, and he doubtlessly had no idea he was breathing faster. She wasn't immune, either—for thousands of years she had existed solely for just such opportunities, the predator leaping at the prey. Her practice-trained response had been instantaneous, instinctive, *desired*. Conditioning like that just didn't disappear in a few weeks.

"Knock it off, Brynna." Redmond's voice had dropped an octave and he blinked, trying to figure out what was going on. "He's nothing more than a slimy local drug dealer. I—"

She kissed him.

Brynna had thought she was going to teach Redmond a lesson, give him the old I-told-you-so example about screwing around with something that should have been off limits. But here, away from Lucifer and Hell and the power that she had once wielded over mortals and fellow demons alike, she was definitely unprepared for the sudden and unexpected response she felt from this human female body.

There was heat—lots of it—but it wasn't her generating it. And yet it was, and it was Redmond, and it was *them,* together. Her hands reached for him at the same time his arms went around her back and pulled her tightly against his chest. Brynna felt hungry and empty and wanting, desperate to feel his touch and tongue and nearness, to be with him skin to skin, to fold herself over him—

"Stop!"

Brynna came back to herself—where she was and what she was about to do—right before the two of them could fall onto the cheaply made twin bed.

"Why?" Redmond murmured against her neck.

His lips felt so good, so *right,* but no—it was everything but. She must *not* do this.

She disentangled herself from his embrace and pushed him away, ignoring his look of confusion. "We can't."

"Why not?" He took a step toward her but Brynna danced out of his reach. "We're two consenting adults. We're not tied to anyone else." He tilted his head. His face was flushed, the skin on his cheeks almost glowing. "At least *I'm* not."

Her mouth was still tingling, still carrying the taste of him through her nerve endings, still shooting need everywhere in her senses. "But I am, in ways you wouldn't understand."

"Try me."

"It's not that simple!"

"So you're married."

This made her laugh outright. "In a word, no. But I'm . . . spoken for, I guess is how you would say it."

"By whom?" When she hesitated, he spread his hands.

"Come on, Brynna. You kissed me. At least give me a reason why you won't follow through."

"Because I'm not human."

There, it was finally out.

Redmond's mouth worked, but for a long time it was obvious he just couldn't figure out what to say to her. "Brynna—"

She held up her hand, then edged back around to stand in front of the living room window. "No, don't find a hundred reasons to disregard what I just said. You've seen enough to where you ought to realize it's true. And," she added, "fuck the whole idea of there being some kind of 'limit' to what you can believe. I already told you my thoughts about that."

"Brynna—"

"If you say my name like that one more time, I'm going to smack you," she said irritably.

"Like . . . what?"

"Like I'm some kind of crazy person with whom you have to be really patient and really careful about saying just the right thing." Brynna scowled as Redmond just kept staring at her. "This kind of thing was actually quite common back in the day, you know."

"'This kind of thing,'" he repeated. "'Back in the day.'" Redmond blinked, then rubbed his eyes as though he just couldn't believe what was happening. "All right. If you're not human, then what are you? An alien?"

"I'm . . . Highborn," Brynna said.

"I have no idea what that means."

"You know," Brynna said. She lifted her chin and shot a gaze vaguely skyward. Yeah, they were inside, but she was willing to bet Redmond caught her gist. "Highborn. As in I used to be . . ." He was watching her expectantly. "An angel," she finished at last. It actually hurt to say the words, but she made herself say them again. "I used to be an angel."

"But you're not anymore. Now you're human."

"No," she said softly. "I'm not human, not at all. Now I'm *fallen*."

Redmond was silent for a long moment. "Fallen." He tilted his head and pointed toward the floor. "As in . . . down there."

Brynna couldn't stop a dry smile from slipping over her mouth. "Well, it's not exactly where you think it is, but yes. If that's how you have to classify it, I'm from *down there*."

"Hell. And you're a fallen angel."

She was on a roll, so Brynna decided to just throw it all out at once. "Technically I'm a demon. That's what fallen angels are."

"Right."

"Think about it," she insisted. The heat between them had cooled considerably. Brynna felt it was safe enough, so she went over and gathered herself into a sitting position on the floor in front of him. "How else would I be able to speak any language known to man, to heal from injuries that would kill a normal human, to know some of the things I do?" She spread her hands out, as if the truth were some kind of physical thing that she could offer him. "Finding that Korean girl, knowing Gavino for what he is—that's all part of it. That's what I *am*."

Redmond tried to clear his throat, but his voice was

still hoarse when he spoke. "You talk like this is an every-day thing," he said. "Like—"

"The world around you is a lot more complex than you realize," Brynna told him. "People aren't necessarily what you think they are. People like Gavino."

"Who's like you. A fallen angel."

"A *demon*," she corrected. There was a string hanging from the bottom hem of her skirt, and Brynna picked at it so she wouldn't have to meet his gaze. "We lost the right a long time ago to be called angels of any kind. Gavino is a Searcher, a demon who's here to find and destroy nephilim."

"Wait—there's angels, and demons, and now nephilim? What's a nephilim?"

"A nephilim is a child born of a human mother and an angel father," Brynna told him. "They each have a spe-cial purpose, a task that has to be completed in order for the nephilim to fulfill his or her destiny." She nodded to emphasize her words. "Eventually they figure out what the task is, and then they'll do everything in their power to get it done. They're driven—it's their entire reason for existing."

For the first time since she had started explaining this, Redmond's expression changed and he leaned forward on his chair. He finally looked a little shocked, like he might really be starting to believe her. "You're saying that angels actually exist *today*?" he demanded. "And that they come down, and they . . . *mate* with people?"

"They never stopped existing," Brynna said. "It stands to reason that if you have demons, you have angels as well."

Redmond stood abruptly. "There's nothing *reasonable* about this," he snapped. "You're a demon, and that Goth kid is a demon, and he's hanging around your building *why*? Because he's got some kind of a job to do, to find out if there are any kids in the building with angelic fathers and—I assume—really religious mothers." Redmond ran a hand through his hair hard enough to yank on it. "God, Brynna, don't you hear how crazy all this sounds?"

"You've seen physical proof."

"I haven't seen shit," he said crudely. "A few weird coincidences and you as some kind of language savant—"

"And bullet wounds!"

"—and a superhigh-healing metabolism," he finished stubbornly. "Nothing more."

" 'He is able to deal gently with those who are ignorant and are going astray,' " Brynna quoted softly.

"Oh, please. Do not—*do not* start restating the Bible at me," Redmond said. Brynna's eyebrows rose at the anger in his voice. "In my job I've had that religious crap used to try and justify some of the worst things people have ever done."

"I bet you have," Brynna said calmly.

"And let's not even get started on the Inquisition and holy wars and—"

Brynna held up her hand and Redmond snapped his mouth shut. "It's not my place to explain everything," she said patiently. "I wouldn't even know where to start, and I don't know everything anyway."

"Then what *is* your place?" Redmond asked. "If you're really what you say you are, and you can do all the stuff you claim, then what the hell are you doing *here?*" He gestured at the dingy little apartment. "In this ratty building, in this city, and specifically right here with *me?*"

"I'm just trying to be forgiven."

Redmond rolled his eyes. "Right. Forgiven. For whatever it is that you supposedly did that made you a demon."

"I don't expect you to understand."

"Good call." Redmond strode to the door and yanked it open. "And I suppose Goth Boy—Gavino—wants the same thing. To be *forgiven.*"

"No," Brynna said matter-of-factly. "He just wants to kill Mireva."

Redmond had been halfway out the door, but he jerked to a stop and turned around. "Say what?"

"Mireva—the girl you saw him talking to in the hallway. Gavino wants to kill her because she's a nephilim."

He had taken two steps back into the apartment, but now Redmond halted and shook his head. "No, huh-uh. You are *not* going to twist this around back to the beginning with angels and demons and all that BS and just start this conversation all over again. You will not get me to buy into this."

"Then how do you explain—"

"I don't have to explain anything," he interrupted. "*You* have to prove it."

Brynna actually laughed. "So much for the concept of faith."

"I never said I was religious. In fact, I'm anything but. I'm a cop, which makes me a realist, which means I need to see the cold, hard evidence."

"You've seen plenty so far," Brynna pointed out.

"No," Redmond said firmly. "I haven't. I've seen circumstance and coincidence and maybe a bit of uncanny luck."

"There's no such thing as coincidence. Everything happens for a reason."

"Right." Redmond crossed his arms and gave her a hard look. "What you're saying is it's all predetermined anyway. If that's the case, then why bother?"

Brynna rose and swung the chair around to face him, then sat. "I didn't say that at all. There are always choices, but the choices are there for a reason. What happens depends on the choice someone makes. That's how the future is made."

Redmond snorted. "Double-talk, nothing more." She opened her mouth to argue, but he waved her off. "Nope, I'm going home. It's been a long day with a very confusing end to it. I need to think."

"But—"

"Good *night*, Brynna."

And he was gone, pulling the door firmly shut between them.

She sat for a long time before she finally got up and peeled off her work clothes. By human standards her unair-conditioned apartment was hot—summers in Chicago could be sweltering and miserably humid—but Brynna didn't notice. This place wasn't much, but it had one thing that for a very long time in her existence had been in extremely short supply:

Water.

Such a basic thing, but so exquisite. A hot shower was nice, but a cool one . . . perhaps the closest thing to

Heaven she'd experienced in too long to remember. And in Chicago, thanks to Lake Michigan, the tap water was always up to what she considered the best standards—cold and fabulous.

Brynna stood in the shower for twenty minutes, just letting the liquid pour over her head, feeling it sheet down her overly warm skin and soak into her pores. It calmed her spirit and relaxed her muscles, bringing her as near, perhaps, as she ever came to truly being sleepy. Afterward, dry and quiet, it was the one time of day that Brynna could chance lying on the bed and closing her eyes, late in the afternoon when the sun was still out and the night shadows had yet to offer hiding places to the human evil that sought it.

The mattress was thin and lumpy, the sheets scratchy from years of being washed in strong detergent and bleach. There were no such things in Hell and Brynna sank onto it and let her eyelids drift closed, thinking, as she did every time she settled in for a nap, that she had never felt anything so pleasing.

At least until she'd kissed Redmond.

She frowned in spite of herself, the thought worming its way onto what should have been a mental blank slate. She tried to push it away, searching for the slightly dizzy sensation that heralded oncoming sleep . . .

It was too late.

Instead of napping, she found herself staring at the cracked, stained ceiling as a sweet glow of desire spread across her skin. It was gone in only a few seconds, but it was enough to make her realize Redmond had worked his way dangerously into her psyche. What would have happened if she hadn't stopped him, if she had let the two of them fall onto the bed? The human part of her wanted to believe in the simplicity of sex, that nothing would have taken place other than an evening of lust and physical fulfillment.

The demon side of her knew better.

Eleven

Redmond woke up at six the next morning thrashing and covered in sweat, clutching at the summer-weight throw on the bed like it was a rope he was using to haul himself out of Hell itself . . . which was precisely how he felt.

He forced himself to sit up in bed and groaned aloud. He couldn't remember the last time he'd felt this hot—was he running a fever? His hair was stuck wetly to his scalp and his eyes stung from perspiration. The light-weight muscle T and boxer shorts he'd worn to bed were sodden and uncomfortable. All he wanted in the world was a long, cool shower.

Grunt, his five-year-old Great Dane, raised her head and looked at him hopefully from where she was rolled into a not-inconsiderable-size ball on the lower quarter of his queen-sized bed. "Huh-uh," Redmond said. "No way, not until I get my shower." Grunt was deaf and couldn't hear a damned thing, but she got the message from his head shake; after an overlong second she dropped her massive white head onto the covers and gave an immense, crestfallen sigh.

"Right," Redmond said over his shoulder as he shoved aside the damp sheets. "Call the animal cops if you think you're so abused." Her response was just what he expected: With Redmond finally out of the way, the dog unrolled herself and stretched out, groaning happily at all the extra room.

He climbed into the shower and stood under the spray for a long time, using the cool water to chase away the last remnants of his bad dreams, then switching to hot for a good scrub down. The details of the dream—of the *nightmare*—were long gone, but Redmond was sure fire had been involved in it somewhere, fire and sex . . . but no, that was the limit of what he still had floating around in his brain. Impressions, but not much else. It was Brynna, of course, and that line of crazy crap she'd thrown at him yesterday at her apartment. Did she really think he'd buy it? Demons and angels and Hell, oh my. Next he'd be asking who was playing Wicked Witch of the West.

Except . . .

Redmond gave himself a mental slap and twisted the temperature back to cool, then all the way to cold. When he finally took pity on himself and shut it off, his teeth were chattering as he pulled aside the shower curtain and reached for his towel. At least he wasn't thinking— much—about Hell anymore.

He shaved and cleaned up after himself, changed the sheets—something he did often because he let Grunt sleep with him—then made himself a hard-boiled egg sandwich for breakfast. By the time he'd finished eating, Grunt was at the end of her patience and was pacing between wherever Redmond happened to be standing and the door. If she'd been capable of yelling *Hurry up!* he'd have probably heard her a dozen times over.

Once they were on the street, he and Grunt headed east up Arlington. At a quarter past seven the traffic on Clark Street was already headed to a mini-jam, with cars inching along and taxis swerving around the pedestrians and buses. Redmond didn't stay on Clark for long, just the block between Arlington and Deming, because Grunt loved everyone. Should some unfortunate man or woman stop long enough to comment about her to Redmond, Grunt's way of showing affection was to jam her massive head between the stranger's knees. There she would stand, her shoulders tight against their kneecaps (provided the object of her affection could maintain a semblance of balance), and wait to be petted.

Redmond was stubborn about keeping Clark in their walk routine only because he wanted Grunt to see all the people and the cars and the activity—it was good socialization. He thought of the left turn onto Deming as a sort of safety zone, where the commotion and fuss of the Chicago morning mellowed into the quieter side of urban living and Grunt stopped being such a spaz and a suck-up to total strangers.

Deming was a beautiful street. Most of the buildings were brown- or graystones built in the late eighteen to early nineteen hundreds, spectacular two- and three-story structures with wide front steps, stone porches, and triple-width bay windows. As was typical in Chicago, there wasn't much space between them, just enough for a passageway to the postage-stamp backyards. They were handsome and imposing, like sturdy, weathered old men keeping a stern watch over this calm street.

Away from the scramble of Clark Street, Grunt walked quietly a few feet in front of him, pulling slightly on her leash as she always did. What the Great Dane lacked in hearing, she made up for in smell. Everything—from flowers to yard decorations to fence posts—was a full-fledged olfactory adventure. Her policy was smell first and ask questions later, so even the occasional mondo-sized beetle crossing their path was fair game.

As he and Grunt came up on Orchard, Redmond slowed, then stopped in front of the large plaza that was the entrance to Saint Clement Church on the corner. He'd been passing it nearly every day that he walked Grunt, and yet Redmond realized he'd never paid a bit of attention to the massive building. Below stone archways were three separate sets of double wooden doors, all of which were now opened in an unspoken invitation. In the center of the front of the church building proper was a huge ornamental stained-glass rose window set in stone, and on each side of the plaza, fading back into deep shadows, were enormous oak trees that were doubtlessly over a century old. It was quite impressive, and for the first time since he'd lived in the Lincoln Park area—nearly twenty years—Redmond wanted to go inside, to see what it looked like. To *feel* it.

Wait . . . twenty years? Had it really been that long? Redmond found himself staring at Saint Clement's in surprise, but he wasn't sure if it was because he'd never been inside or because he was so shocked that the nearly two decades had suddenly sort of . . . caught up with him. Without realizing it, he climbed the stairs and crossed the small expanse of concrete, until he and Grunt were standing at one of the open doors and staring inside. It was cool and welcoming, filled with shadows and dreamy, golden light, and Redmond could see all the way to the altar at the far end and beyond. Down there was marble and tile and gilded statues below another magnificent rose glass window, a match to the front one that soared high on a different wall. The rest of the walls were a tapestry of Old World biblical paintings and patterns in muted but still spectacular colors, culminating in a high dome on which six angels were displayed and surrounded by small arched stained-glass windows. It was, literally, a breathtaking sight.

"Go on in," said a voice from behind him. Redmond looked to his left and saw a man standing there. He was younger than Redmond by a couple of years and in cleric's clothing; below hair the color of ink, his Irish green eyes were untroubled and friendly.

"Oh, no," Redmond said. "Not with the dog. And please don't give me a quote about 'all God's creatures' or something like that."

The priest laughed pleasantly. "All right, I won't. But I will say that I don't think the dog can destroy the church." He eyed Grunt, then amended, "At least as long as you keep it on a leash."

It was Redmond's turn to laugh. "Thanks, but maybe I'll come by another time."

"No time like the present."

Redmond groaned. "You *are* going to quote, aren't you?"

The priest grinned. "Sorry. Sometimes I just can't stop myself." He offered his hand. "Father Paul Murphy."

Redmond shook the priest's hand and introduced

himself. By now Grunt had finally noticed the newcomer and Redmond was struggling to hold her back; the sudden image he had of white hair all over Father Murphy's black slacks didn't set well. He turned Grunt and headed back toward the street. "Seriously, Father, some other time. I need to get this monster back home and head to work."

"Do you mind if I walk with you?"

Redmond shrugged. "Feel free."

"So what do you do?" the priest asked after a few moments of walking alongside.

"I'm a cop," Redmond said simply. "A detective."

"Ah." Father Murphy nodded. "A noble profession. And one of the most difficult."

"I hold my own."

"We all have to."

Redmond couldn't help smiling a little. "You're like the master of one-liners, right?"

Father Murphy reached down and scratched Grunt's back. In response, the Great Dane turned her head and gave his hand a thank-you lick. "I just try to keep it simple. Have you always been a policeman?"

"Have you always been a priest?"

Another smile, one that looked a little tenuous. "No. I started out as an orphan. Then I turned into a loner, and a bully, and then I went on to become a thief. It was a long and rather unpleasant road from there to here." He gave Redmond a sidelong glance. "I have to say that I like the 'here' much better than the 'there.' "

Redmond nodded, resisting the cop's urge to ask for more details about the past at which Murphy was hinting. He thought the priest would answer, but he didn't know

Murphy well enough—he had no right to be nosy. "I've been a cop in one form or another since I got out of high school," he offered. "I started with the Army. When my time was up, I went to the police force here."

"Didn't like the Army?"

"I liked it just fine. I just didn't like traveling, and the military won't usually let you stay anywhere for more than three years. You put down too many roots and then you don't want to deploy when they tell you."

"Ah. I guess that makes sense."

"I like living in one place."

"Stability."

"Exactly."

They'd reached Arlington, and when Redmond steered Grunt to the left, Father Murphy stopped. "It's been nice talking to you, Detective Redmond."

"Eran, please. Only the perps call me 'Detective' and my coworkers call me Redmond."

"Eran, then." Father Murphy gave Redmond's hand another firm shake. "The next time, come on inside the church. I promise the doors won't close and lock behind you."

Redmond chuckled. "I'll think about it. Nice to meet you too."

Redmond and Grunt turned east and the priest headed back the way they'd come. After a second, Redmond stopped and looked back, watching Father Murphy's retreating back and thinking. Should he have said something about Brynna? He'd had his chance right there, but it seemed so far-fetched—

Without warning, the clergyman turned around and

fixed his gaze on Redmond. "Is there something else, Eran?" the priest asked quietly. He was only about twenty feet away, so despite his low tone, Redmond heard every word clearly. "Something you need to talk about?"

Redmond stared at him, unaccountably hearing Brynna's voice in his mind.

I'm not human, not at all . . . I'm a demon.

Did he dare bring this up to this man he'd just met, take that crazy statement and lay it out in the bright light of day, just to see what happened?

No, he didn't.

"No." Redmond shook his head, hoping he sounded convincing. "No . . . but thanks."

Father Murphy gave him a congenial smile. "All right, then. Remember, you know where to find me if you change your mind." He tilted his head in the direction of Saint Clement's. "I live in the rectory. In fact," he added as he closed the distance again and reached into his back pocket, "here's my card. My cell number's on it."

Redmond reached for it. "You have a cell phone?"

Father Murphy smiled. "Yes. It's been a long fight, but priests are even allowed to use twenty-first-century technology."

"Sorry," Redmond said sheepishly, "I didn't mean—"

The priest held up a hand. "Please. You're not the first person to assume we still eat out of stone bowls and perform self-flagellation."

"I wouldn't go that far."

Father Murphy grinned. "Neither would I."

"Thanks, Father." Redmond hesitated. "Maybe I'll give you a call sometime."

Father Murphy nodded, turning serious again. "Please do. Anytime." He touched his forehead and turned away. Redmond stood there with Grunt, watching until the holy man's figure was lost among the cars and greenery.

REDMOND AND SATHI SHARED an office that was barely large enough to accommodate the double-sided desk and two chairs. To make up for the lack of space, they'd pushed the end of the desk below the window and hung shelves on either side of it, starting a couple of feet from the floor and going all the way to the ceiling. Over the years those shelves had become crammed with papers, files, books, office supplies, and anything else they couldn't fit into the desk or below it. The effect was kind of like a mini-mad scientist's office, and the two oversized bulletin boards, one on each side wall behind the desk chairs, only added to the chaotic feeling.

But Redmond and Sathi were used to the clutter, used to each other, and each man knew precisely where every piece of his paper resided. The upper half of the inside wall was glass, and every now and then someone in the chain of command would do a double-take at the mess. They'd come in on some pretense or another and test the two detectives, demanding some obscure form or file that no one had thought about in months. Neither man had ever failed to find it within two minutes. Despite the piles of paper, both Redmond and Sathi kept a passable amount of space on each side of the desk clear for whatever current project was demanding their attention. Today's problem was the same one that had been dominating the entire department for the last month and on which neither of them was making a damned bit of progress.

"Today will be the fifth day without a shooting," Sathi offered.

"It's not even noon," Redmond replied. "The killings have been all over the clock, so we have another eighteen hours to go before we can really say that."

Sathi didn't blink. "I like to think positive."

"Yeah, and I'm positive we're not out of the woods yet." Redmond watched as the darker-skinned man thumbed through the incident reports, always looking for some kind of pattern. "Besides, what kind of attitude is that for a cop? We're supposed to be all doom and gloom."

Sathi's white teeth flashed as he grinned. "It is a statistical fact that people who are optimistic live longer." When Redmond looked doubtful, Sathi added, "I can show you the article. Or you can google it for yourself."

"I believe you," Redmond muttered. "I just don't think cops are figured in there. There's nothing positive about this job except knowing that every time you think you've seen it all, someone's going to prove you wrong."

"See—you *are* thinking positive!"

"Very funny." Redmond closed the folder in his hand, then pulled the rest of the papers in front of him into a pile. "Let's work on something else for a while. I've had about all the dead end I can take right now."

"All right." Sathi snagged a folder with a Post-it stuck to it that said *Pending*. He held it up where Redmond could read it. "Let's work on this one."

Redmond squinted across the desk. Sathi was holding the Kim file, the case in which the Korean girl had been held prisoner in the jewelry store basement. Crap. He'd spent all morning trying to keep his thoughts away from Brynna and her wild claims. All this case would do was bring them right back to punch him in the nose and then some.

But Sathi was right. There was a box-load of stuff still to be done on it, not the least of which was sort through all the crazy stuff they'd found in the basement and the store's office. Although it had only been a week, the lawyers for the elder Kwan's bank had jumped in to claim the jewelry inventory and the accountable cash; the only thing stopping them from sweeping through the rest of the building and putting it up for sale was the still-open investigation. To Redmond they seemed as much vultures as the old jeweler himself.

I'm not human, not at all . . . I'm a demon.

Redmond shook himself mentally and flipped open the folder. Cho, the victim, had made a nearly miraculous recovery—she was already back at school and was adamant about not remembering anything beyond being in the laudromat after having fed money into the washing machine. The crime scene team had taken more than a hundred photos of the basement and there was definitely a bunch of weird shit down there.

"There's nothing else we can learn from this stuff that we don't already know," Redmond finally said. "According to the docket, their lawyer's supposed to be in the house to meet with his clients in a little under an hour. I say we take advantage of that and go have a face-to-face with the boy."

Sathi nodded. "All right. The kid might not talk to us, though."

"He's going to have to say *something* or he'll get his ass

handed to him on a stick. It's on the books that he and the old man are going to be indicted on forcible imprisonment, so it's in his best interest to try for some kind of a deal. The old man isn't talking—he just sits there and says nothing, not even to his lawyer. It's like his mind is totally jacked up. Maybe we can get the kid to roll over on him, find out the truth of what they were doing."

Sathi gave him a level look. "As I recall, Brynna told you exactly what they were doing."

"Please," Redmond said more sharply than he intended, "let's not get into that load of fantasy all over again."

"You cannot deny there are things that are unexplainable about what happened," Sathi pointed out.

"Everything can be explained."

"Really," Sathi said. He rose and followed Redmond out but lowered his voice. "Such as Brynna being shot twice but never needing a doctor?" When Redmond stayed stubbornly silent, Sathi elbowed him. "You do realize she took those bullets for you, right? That you would otherwise be dead?"

Redmond opened his mouth, but he couldn't think of anything to say except, finally, "Yeah."

"There must be a reason for that."

"Don't be absurd. It was nothing more than reflex."

Sathi laughed. "That, my friend, I do not believe. I also do not believe that you have remained on neutral ground with her."

Redmond started. "What the hell are you talking about?"

"I believe you are sleeping with her—"

"I am not!"

"—or you soon will be." Sathi regarded him calmly.

"You're crazy," was all Redmond could think of to say, but it was a pitiful response and he felt suddenly transparent, as if all his thoughts and dreams—and boy, even if he couldn't remember them, he knew he'd had some doozies last night—had been splayed out for his partner's critical examination.

Sathi looked like he wanted to say something else, but Redmond's cell phone gave a low rattle, effectively cutting him off. Redmond grabbed at the chance to answer it, grateful for the opportunity to derail a conversation that was veering into territory that was way too personal. "Redmond," he barked.

"Hey, Redmond. It's Bello. I've been working on the computer that was pulled from that jewelry outfit on Clark Street. I got something off it—something big. Are you in the building?"

"Yeah," Redmond said. Bello Onani was one of the computer geeks in the tech department, and he could do things with computers that made Redmond damned glad the guy was on the side of the good guys. Without a password, Onani had spent the last four days fighting to get into the computer pulled from the jewelry store. A call from him had to mean he'd finally gotten past the password stops and firewall, but Onani's tone hinted at a lot more than the usual financial swindles. Redmond did an abrupt turnaround and motioned at Sathi to follow. "What've you got?"

For a long moment there was only silence on the other end. Finally, Onani gave him a three-word answer that made the skin at the back of Redmond's neck tighten.

"A hit list."

Twelve

Brynna found Mireva on the roof at seven-thirty in the morning. The heat was already blistering, the humidity nearly crippling—an older person would have probably passed out before a quarter hour had crawled by. But Mireva was young and strong and healthy, and more important, nephilim; Brynna could tell the girl hardly noticed the temperature. Instead, she was working on her science project, walking along a quadruple row of planters that she and her uncle had built out of scrap wood. Small, lush plants rose above the edges of the boxes and shifted gently in the hot breeze, sending a bouquet of herbs, flowers, and other scents along the air to mix with the smell of the roof's heated black tar surface.

"Hi," Brynna said. Being up here, with the open sky spreading in every direction, was giving her nerves a serious knock, but the alternative—grabbing the girl and hauling her back into a closed hallway—wasn't going to put out the impression Brynna was hoping for. On the other hand, having a Hunter show up and try to drag Brynna away wasn't a great answer, either. Oh well,

Brynna thought, and gave the cloudless sky a grim look. Six of one and a half dozen of another. She just loved those ironic little sayings humans had.

Mireva glanced in her direction and acknowledged her with a slight tilt of her mouth, then bent back to her work. "Hi."

Brynna moved closer, working into step with the girl so she could walk along the rows with her. "So is this the science project you mentioned?"

Mireva didn't look up. "If you mean yesterday in the hallway when you and that guy ran off Gavino, then yeah."

Brynna could feel the resentment rolling off the girl, so she didn't say anything for a moment. "Sorry about that," she finally said. "The blame is on me. All I can say in our defense is that I've known Gavino for a long time and he's a really big jerk."

"I wasn't looking for a boyfriend," Mireva muttered. "Just some help with this project."

"I guess it's pretty important to you, huh?"

"We can't afford college," Mireva said simply. As she talked, Brynna could see Mireva's shoulders stiffen with tension. "This project is my best chance at a scholarship. A *full* scholarship. If I don't get this right, I'll have other things I can apply for, but they're all partial." She was silent for a moment, feeling carefully beneath one of the plants as she checked for moisture. "Mama's been saving forever just so there'll be money to kick in for living expenses, clothes and things like that. I'm not even sure there's enough for that. We don't have the credit for any of the loans."

Brynna nodded. "It's hard."

"The stuff Gavino was talking about—I could tell he wasn't lying when he said he could help me." Mireva's eyes flashed for a moment. "I wasn't looking for him to do it *for* me, you know. Just help me make it better."

Brynna considered the rows of perfectly growing plants. "Well, I don't know the details about your project, but it looks like it's going just fine to me."

"It's doing all right. It's a lot to take care of." Mireva shot a glance at the brilliantly blue sky. "The heat's been getting to it. The world's climate is changing, and that's figured into the criteria of the project too."

"So you were thinking Gavino could what, help you water?"

Mireva shrugged. "Something like that. He was telling me about fertilizer and soil balances, stuff like that. Like I said, he knew what he was talking about."

"Gavino talks a good game, but he gets sidetracked easily," Brynna told her, choosing her words carefully. "I'm pretty sure the last thing you want is to depend on him to take care of these for you, then come home from school one day and find them all dead because he forgot to do it." The teen's eyes widened, so Brynna pushed on. "If you need help with this, I'm available. I don't work every day, plus I *live* in the building, so it's not like I'd be thinking it's too far or too much trouble to come over and do it."

Mireva frowned slightly. "Why would you help me?"

"Why not?" Brynna countered. "If you need better than that, how about because I'm a friend of your uncle's and he's been really good to me." She paused. "I gotta tell you, those are better reasons than Gavino's."

"I know he wants to get in my pants," Mireva said

bluntly. "The boys always do, but I'm not into hooking up with anyone yet." For a second she gazed in the other direction, as if she were seeing something Brynna couldn't. "I have . . . other things to do with my life. I don't know what just yet, but I'll figure it out. Anyway, he likes me." A hint of longing made its way into Mireva's voice and Brynna had to wonder if, as strict as Abrienda was, Mireva wasn't kept pretty isolated from any kind of a social life. The realization sank in that Mireva was probably an outsider in her own world—too tall, too smart, too protected. An untold number of intelligent people fell to peer pressure every day, tempted by popularity, drugs, alcohol . . . loneliness.

"Of course he does," Brynna said. "You're smart, pretty—what's not to like?" She resisted the urge to launch into a road map of Gavino criticism, knowing it would sound too much like a lecture. "So what are you doing here?" she asked, deciding to steer the subject in a more amicable direction. "You've definitely got the green thumb thing going."

"I'm concentrating on developing affordable organic food sources," Mireva said. "Taking advantage of the naturally occurring tendencies of certain types of insect DNA and pollen carriers to increase the output, but based specifically on the location of the test group and the density of the population in the growing area."

"Really." Brynna eyed the vegetation doubtfully.

Mireva gave her a tolerant smile, very much like one a tutor would give a student who just wasn't getting it. "See, it's not just about the plants. They're an important part of the experiment, of course, but the critical components are the insects. And they, in turn, depend on the location and the environment."

Brynna scrutinized the greenery again, this time letting her focus narrow. Yes, of course—bees, flies, little gnats. There were even a couple of yellow butterflies, small, bright spots of beauty flitting erratically amidst the unexpected rooftop nursery. She couldn't begin to guess the complexities involved in Mireva's project, but she had an idea that if she asked, Mireva would take the time to patiently explain it. She thought the girl would someday make a great teacher.

Brynna bent and ran her finger along the edge of one of the long planters. She could sense the water there, smell it in the air. To her, after so many centuries of deprivation, it seemed like so much. But what did she know of the requirements for something green and alive, something that gave forth fruit and life of its own? "How often do you have to water?"

"In this heat and against this dark surface, at least twice a day." Mireva nodded toward a neatly rolled hose next to the doorway that led inside. "I water in the morning before I go. It wouldn't be a big deal except I'm taking free summer courses to earn extra college credit. The topsoil needs to stay moist, but I have to study and do my homework at the library, where there's a computer. Sometimes I don't get home until late." She tried on a brave smile. "It could be worse. At least there's a faucet."

"No kidding. Hate to have to haul buckets up the stairs."

"Yeah." Mireva went over and twisted the spigot, then unrolled the hose. On the end of it was a sprayer turned to a notch labeled SHOWER. She looked at Brynna, who stood waiting. "You have to be really careful," she said finally. "Run out the water in the hose first, because it's really, really hot from the sun. Then water from the bottom so that the soil doesn't get washed to the side and expose the roots. And not too much, or the leaves'll start to turn yellow. You can give them a spray across the top to get rid of the dust, but only if the sun's already set. Otherwise the water magnifies the sun's rays and burns the leaves."

"Got it." Brynna walked with the girl again, this time watching carefully and taking note of how Mireva slipped the hose beneath the plants and how long she sprayed each one. "I'll check them every day, I promise."

Mireva looked at the ground shyly, then finally raised her gaze to meet Brynna's. "That would be a humongous help. Thanks."

"No problem." Brynna waited while Mireva finished, then walked downstairs with the teenager, following the girl into her apartment without being invited. Ramiro was there, sitting at the tiny kitchen table and having Mexican coffee and churros with his sister. A small fan labored from left to right in the far corner of the living room, pushing the hot air from one room to another. Mireva disappeared into her room without saying anything else; the three adults watched her go and didn't speak for a few moments, each wrapped in their own too-warm mantle of silence and private thoughts.

"I saw Mireva's science project on the roof," Brynna finally offered from where she leaned against the wall. "It's really something."

Abrienda glanced over her shoulder. "I hope it's enough," she said in a low voice.

Brynna raised her eyebrows. "Enough?"

"To get her the scholarship she wants," Ramiro finished.

Abrienda's cheeks flushed and she wouldn't look at Brynna as she pushed around a barely nibbled piece of churro. "She will not get to the kind of college she wants without it," the older woman said bluntly. "Even after all these years, what I have will not be enough. The tuition rises much faster than what I make. She has her heart set on the best, and they are the most expensive. But we are not in such a position to get the kind of student loans she would need in order to completely devote herself to her studies like she wants."

Ramiro patted his sister's hand awkwardly. "I can help."

"With what?" Abrienda demanded. "You barely make enough anymore to keep the restaurant open." Her gaze flicked to Brynna and she sat up straighter, as if deciding they were getting a little too personal in front of someone who wasn't family. "We'll manage," she said shortly. "One way or another."

"I'm no expert, but Mireva's work seemed to be really good," Brynna put in. "She's extremely smart, and she knows what she's doing with it."

"Yes, she is very smart," Ramiro said. "She has a good, level head."

Brynna hesitated. "There's a boy—"

"The one in the hallway!" Abrienda's chair scraped backward as she pushed abruptly to her feet. "I knew it!"

"There's nothing going on between them," Brynna said quickly, but she was afraid it was already too late. She should have found a different way to bring up the subject of Gavino, or waited for a time when the mood was better—the heat was intense and nearly overpowering, magnifying every emotion, and not at all in a good way.

"Pah," Abrienda nearly spat. "There is always something with the boys. She is too young for boys, too innocent." Her eyes darkened. "I won't have her throw everything away for a boy or make the same mistakes that I did. She will have better than me." Without asking her silent brother if he was finished, she swept up both dishes and carried them to the kitchenette. When she scraped the leavings into the trash, her movements were almost savage. "There is plenty of time for boys, but not now. She will have a good life, babies if that's what she wants, a husband who will be there for her. But some other day, not now."

Brynna leaned against the wall and said nothing. She didn't need to ask questions to know the history. It had been the same thing for thousands of years. An innocent woman, almost always a virgin, courted and swept off her feet—an archaic term, but the meaning would always be the same—by a celestial being, an angel masquerading as a human man. One night, two at the most, and then he was gone forever; seven months later, never more than that, and a child was born. Full-weight and healthy, long of limb, and always with *something* about it that made it irresistible to the mother and wiped away any notion of giving up the child for adoption.

It should have made for the ideal home life, but

Thirteen

"Look here," Bello Onani said. He was a tall and gangly African guy with a complexion the color of wet leather and almost no body fat. Right now he was hunched over a keyboard—one of four currently snaking out of his sprawling workstation—and jabbing a long finger at one of the monitors in front of him. "This screen shows the raw data I extracted from the jewelry store computer. Dude has some heavy-duty encryption going on. I wasn't getting anywhere without a password. I tried some of the obvious stuff— his birthday, family birthdays, shit like that—but no go. Then I moved on to a basic dictionary attack, even though I figured the guy was too smart for that. I worked up to a precomputation hash combined with a custom parsing algorithm to compensate for salts and memoization—"

"I don't mean to be impatient, but can we skip the geekspeak and go straight to the English part?" Redmond gestured at the hardware fragments, screws, and wires that were layered like driftwood in every available space. "I do okay with e-mail, the Internet, and the department's system, but beyond that I start sweating."

"Yeah, sure. So I finally get into the data, right? And I start going through the files, sorting them into categories."

Redmond saw Sathi's face brighten. Organization they could understand. "Such as?"

"Dull, duller, and most boring, mainly." Onani was zipping his cursor around the screen at no less than manic speed. "Lots of documents and e-mails about financial crap that might or might not be of interest to the IRS."

"Is this the list you mentioned?" Redmond asked. "You could just send that stuff over to fraud."

"I will, sure. But first I figured you guys would want to see what else I found." The display on the main monitor flashed a couple of times as he went back and forth between a couple of open folders. "In fact, I'm thinking you'd damned well *shoot* me if I sat on this."

Redmond raised one eyebrow. "What the hell's so hot that it might move me to bodily harm?"

Onani twisted his head and gave the two detectives a grin filled with crooked but brilliantly white teeth. "This," he said simply, "is the hit list I told you about." The screen was filled with short lines of text and he used the button on his mouse to scroll it up and down for effect.

Sathi scowled at the monitor, then at Onani. "Why do you call it that?"

"Stop," Redmond said abruptly. "I see it." Onani's movements with the mouse froze, then he lifted his hand and let Redmond take over. The detective went up a couple of lines and let the cursor hover over a name on the screen.

Sathi leaned over their shoulders, trying to see. "What?"

"Matthew Dann. Sound familiar?" Redmond's voice rose. "And here—Dorothy Southard."

Sathi's dark eyes widened. "Wait, those are—"

Redmond zipped the cursor down to a third name. On the surface it seemed random until he read it aloud. "Tobias Gallagher."

"These are all shooting victims," Sathi said. "What possible reason can there be for a jewelry store owner in Andersonville to have these names on his computer? Especially when one of these people is a fourteen-year-old boy from the other side of the city?"

"Now that *is* the question, isn't it?" Onani sounded almost gleeful.

"I think," Redmond said slowly, "that if we were to check, we might find all of the victims' names, right here in this file."

Onani picked up a small sheaf of papers and snapped them smartly against one palm. "And so, here is a printout for you to check exactly that. We do, of course, have to wonder about something else."

Redmond took the list from the younger man. "Which is?"

"What was he going to do with the rest of the names?"

REDMOND AND SATHI STOPPED at the entrance to the cell block, unholstered their weapons to leave them with the guard, and went inside after signing in. The jewelry store owner's son, Kwan Seung—or the more modernized Seung Kwan, as his driver's license read—had already been taken out of his cell and put into one of the consultation rooms with his lawyer. The attorney was a slender man about the same height as Redmond, maybe ten years older. He had a salt-and-pepper mustache and slightly curly hair above stylish glasses that probably cost more than one of Redmond's paychecks. Both men looked up in surprise when Redmond and Sathi opened the door.

"Afternoon," Redmond said as he shut the door behind them. "I'm Detective Redmond and this is Detective Sathi." He inclined his head toward the Asian man on the other side of the table before giving the older man his full attention. "I'm sure your client has told you that we've already met."

The attorney rose slightly and offered his hand, eyeing them warily. "James Tarina," he said. "I wasn't made aware that we would be having a conference—"

"Call it a spur-of-the-moment decision," Sathi said.

Tarina's brow furrowed slightly but he didn't protest as he settled back onto his chair. "Sometimes those are the best kind."

Redmond gave him a vague smile as he and Sathi pulled up chairs of their own. "Sometimes." He placed the manila folder he'd brought with him on the table and folded his hands on top of it. "So you have quite the dilemma here, Mr. Kwan. It seems the charges against you are racking up like symbols on a slot machine." When neither of the men across the table said anything, Redmond continued. "Kidnapping is only the beginning here, I think. Assault with a deadly weapon, attempted murder, torture—there's one we only see once in awhile."

"As I understand it, the alleged victim doesn't recall

any of the crimes you mention," Tarina put in. "The burden of proof becomes substantially more difficult without a direct witness."

Sathi stared at him. "From what I saw when I walked into that basement, it was pretty obvious the girl was being held against her will, drugged, and tortured."

"Circumstantial at best. Did you ever consider that the girl was a willing participant? That she *wanted* whatever drugs might—and note that I'm not admitting to anything on behalf of my client—have been in her system."

Redmond wasn't moved by the claims. "Then perhaps Mr. Kwan would like to explain how Miss Kim actually came to be in the basement of his father's jewelry store to begin with. We'd love to hear the details."

Seung Kwan smirked. "You cops wouldn't understand. You're not Korean. And you're in way over your head."

Sathi sat forward. "Then enlighten us."

"I have nothing to say."

Redmond studied him for a moment. "As I'm sure you expected, the computer in the store's office was seized. In the course of the investigation, we discovered that you're quite the computer whiz, Mr. Kwan. You have more than a passing familiarity with software and programming."

Kwan shrugged. "Welcome to the twenty-first century."

Sathi's dark eyes glittered. "An interesting statement, considering the items we found on the . . . what would you call it? *Altar.* Yes, that would be appropriate. The *altar* that was in the basement with Cho Kim."

The prisoner said nothing.

"Our tech found some interesting items on the computer, things that would seem to indicate your father was a little less than forthcoming to the IRS about his financial status." Redmond flipped open the manila folder but thumbed past the first couple of pages. "Kind of interesting, but really, not my department. But this—" Suddenly he thumped his forefinger hard against a stapled set of papers. "—*this* made for some *really* captivating reading."

"May I see that, please?"

Tarina reached for the document but the detective pulled it out of reach. "Not just yet." Redmond eyed Kwan. "The way things stand now, I think we could squeeze a good ten to fifteen years out of a jury." Tarina started to say something but Redmond waved off his words. "And that's just on the *circumstances.* But this little list of yours, Mr. Kwan, really ups the ante on that verdict slot machine."

"What list is that?" Kwan's voice had dropped a little and gone slightly hoarse.

Tarina was openly scowling. "Don't talk to him, Seung. Not until we see exactly what's on that document."

"In fact," Redmond continued as if neither man had spoken, "I think we might even be headed for the death-penalty jackpot."

"That's absurd," Tarina snapped. "And I'm not going to continue this conversation unless I know exactly what you're talking about."

"We're talking about a hit list, Mr. Tarina," Sathi said. His face was grim as Redmond pushed it toward the attorney, who snatched it up and began flipping through the papers. "Four single-spaced pages of names, including the names of every single person shot over the last several weeks."

"Coincidence," Tarina spat. He dropped the list on the table distastefully, as if he couldn't believe he was wasting his time on this.

"Interestingly enough, our tech picked up a pattern here," Redmond said. "A strange one, but it's definitely recognizable. Oh, and there are a number of people on the list who are also dead." This time Redmond's gaze fixed solidly on the attorney. "But not a single one of them died by natural causes."

Tarina blinked, then picked the document up again. "I'll have to look this over—"

Redmond plucked it out of his hand. "All in due time, Mr. Tarina. After all, it'll be introduced as an exhibit in discovery once we get around to filing charges. Unless, of course, Mr. Kwan wants to talk about a quid pro quo."

"Bargaining does make the world go around," Sathi put in.

"And what would you be looking for?" Tarina asked carefully.

"A name would be a good start." Redmond turned his head so that he could stare hard at the young Korean man. "We know you wrote the program that generated these names, and we know how you used it. We know the search criteria you coded into it—once you feed it all into a computer and reverse it, the commonalities are strikingly apparent. You might be good, but the department's cryptographers are better. Still, as scuzzy as you are, we're not quite convinced you've been going around the city and shooting people."

"So we are presuming that someone paid you to generate this list," Sathi put in. "Perhaps they paid you a lot, or offered you something else in return. What we don't know is why, or who, and these are the things that we are obviously expecting to find out from you."

"Expecting," Kwan said. "Isn't that a lot like assuming?"

Redmond tapped the table. "Your point?"

Kwan's answering grin was strained, but still just to the side of nasty. "Everyone knows the old saying about assuming. Ass and *you*. Need I say more?"

Redmond slammed his fist on the table in front of the prisoner, making both Kwan and his lawyer jump. "You'd better say *more*, Mr. Kwan. You'd better say a *lot* more."

But Kwan only made a motion in the air, like he was waving away an annoying insect, and settled back. "Whatever."

"We were able to connect document generation dates and print times on your computer to more than two dozen deaths," Sathi said bluntly. For the first time, Tarina looked visibly rattled. "And that's just so far. What are we going to find as we go deeper into our files?"

Tarina's face had gone a couple of shades paler. "Perhaps we could come to an arrangement," he began. "We—"

"There's no *arrangement*," Kwan interrupted. He sent his attorney a withering look. "I don't have any name to give up. And neither does my father."

"But you admit to generating the list for *someone*," Redmond pressed. "If you won't give up a name, then at least tell us why and how you passed the information."

Kwan's mouth tightened. "I don't think so. Why don't you ask your girlfriend?"

Redmond frowned. "Excuse me?"

"That redheaded bitch who was in the basement with us. She claims she knows so much—ask *her*."

Damn, Redmond thought as his mind spun. It always came back to Brynna, didn't it? No matter how much he tried not to think of her, to keep her out of his picture. "Other than having stumbled onto the place where you were keeping Cho Kim prisoner, she has nothing to do with this," he said. He hoped he didn't sound too stiff. No matter what kind of wild crap she'd tried to feed him on purpose, this was the best he could come up with on short notice.

"Right." Kwan's smile was blatantly fake. "Like I said—whatever."

When he said nothing more, Tarina sighed. "I'll talk to my client," he finally told the two detectives. "We'll work something out and I'll get back to you." He glanced sideways at the Asian man, but Kwan's gaze had shifted up and to a spot vaguely near the ceiling, as if he'd just flipped a mental switch to the I-don't-give-a-damn position.

"You do that," Redmond said. But the only thing that kept running through his mind as he and Sathi made their way back to their office was that one, loaded question:

Why don't you ask your girlfriend?

Fourteen

Brynna had just settled onto the bus seat when she glanced to her left and saw the nephilim killer through the window.

She was up and across the aisle in less than the time it took to inhale, but he was already out of sight. The hard-eyed driver, who was watching her in the rearview mirror, didn't stop or slow down when Brynna lurched to the middle exit door and yanked frantically on the call line for a stop. Brynna reached for the emergency knob, but the slightly shrill voice of the driver stopped her.

"You pull that knob, lady, and you will *never* ride my bus again!"

"I have to get off," Brynna snapped. "I have to go back!"

"It's not my fault you forgot your purse or your cell phone or whatever," the driver shot back. "That knob is for emergencies *only*, and I don't see any emergency happening right now on my bus." The woman glanced at the road, then her gaze cut back to Brynna's in the mirror. "Next stop is two blocks down. You can walk back like everyone else."

Brynna's fingers hovered below the knob, then she let her hand fall back to her side as she craned her neck and tried to see if the nephilim killer had come back onto the street. The place where she had seen him was fading fast behind her. She rode this bus to work every morning that she had an early job, and while she was building a nice bit of savings, a car was still a long way off in her future. Did this prissy-faced little woman actually have the authority to forbid her from riding it? Brynna wasn't sure but she couldn't take the chance. It was infuriating, but she could endure it because it wasn't fatal; the nephilim killer might be hanging around the building, but Mireva was long gone to school.

Brynna resisted the urge to wrench at the call line, instead giving it an exaggeratedly gentle double pull—*ding! ding!*—right before the bus reached the stop. Perhaps this sliver of say-so was all the control this woman would ever have over any part of her life. The driver coasted the bus to a stop, then pulled the lever that released the doors and waited, stony-faced, as Brynna called out a cheery "Bye!" and jumped off the bus. It roared away, but Brynna barely noticed—she was already dashing back toward her building, moving as fast as she could in her business suit and high heels. Her pace was far better than a normal person's, but it still wasn't good enough.

The building looked as it always did: dirty, run-down, and depressing, a structure that the sun's rays had somehow skipped. Brynna easily picked up the nephilim killers's scent; what should have been sweet and delightful was, as it had been that first time at the drugstore, infused with the caustic smell of gunpowder. Not as strong because he hadn't fired his weapon recently, but it was still there.

She checked the entry door but the scent was faint—he'd tried the knob but hadn't forced his way inside on finding it locked. Brynna stopped for a second, then back-tracked, following the man's unique smell until it peaked across the street, in the doorway where she'd glimpsed him through the bus's window. She couldn't pick up anything else—the air was too full of car and bus exhaust, oil, trash, and a thousand other things associated with inner-city living. Still, he shouldn't have been able to simply disappear—

Tires squealed down the block, followed by the sound of a straining automobile engine. Brynna's eyes narrowed as she focused on the sound then saw a nondescript car speed past the building. She wasn't up on makes and models, so the best she could say about it was that it was small and white—and the man driving it was definitely the nephilim killer.

Damn, Brynna thought as she stared after the car. She should have told Redmond about this guy days ago. The truth was, she'd kind of pushed him out of her mind. Yeah, Redmond had talked constantly about the serial killer, but was there any real reason to tie the guy who'd shot her drugstore nephilim with any of the other victims? None that she could find, but she was suddenly very sure that Redmond wasn't going to see it that way. That the guy had shown up here, sniffing around the building where Mireva lived, was way more than jarring—to Brynna, he couldn't have called more attention to himself had he been walking around with a five-foot, blinking red arrow pointed at his head.

It was another twenty minutes before the next bus and then an hour's ride downtown. She was barely going to get to this morning's translation job on time, but Brynna wasn't going to stress about it. If they could find another Ndonga translator to replace her, good for them. She didn't think they could pull it off, so the lawyers and their client, an Angolan immigrant fighting deportation because of allegations he was aiding the rebels in his home country, would just have to wait.

The commute gave Brynna plenty of time to think about the nephilim killer and Mireva. Although she'd have to struggle to get Redmond to believe it, there was no connection between herself and the nephilim killer. There was also no such thing as coincidence—he was here for a reason. Since that wasn't Brynna, the only person left was Mireva, and it didn't take a mathematician to figure out that he was here to kill the teenager. The only way he could have known about Mireva, who she was and her address, was if someone had given it to him. And the only way that could have happened would be via Gavino.

Using one nephilim to kill another . . . Brynna had to admit that it was an ingenious way for a demon to get to his target. Since demons were forbidden to kill nephilim outright—that would have been far too easy *and* unfairly weighted in the demon's favor—they had spent eons perfecting the dark arts of persuasion, lying, and tempting. When she'd faced off with him in the hallway, Brynna had assumed Gavino was simply trying out those age-old skills on Mireva. Apparently not. This time around the boy was going for the big guns—no pun intended—by using one hapless human to murder others. For the demon, it was a dual win—the nephilim target was killed *plus* another nephilim was corrupted. Brynna couldn't help wondering what Gavino had said to his young murderer to make it seem all right.

Funny, she'd never thought Gavino was that smart. In any event, now it was a case of double trouble: to keep Mireva safe, Brynna would have to watch out for Gavino *and* his armed nephilim flunky.

"SOMETHING'S WRONG HERE," MICHAEL Klesowitch said in a strained voice. "Something's really wrong. It's *off*, I know it is. I have to figure this out, I have to *fix* it."

A dim part of his mind was very aware that he was talking to himself as he drove, but that was all right. He wasn't crazy, he knew that—he was just trying to verbally sort it all out. He did his best thinking out loud, almost as if he were spreading out the store's paperwork at the end of the day to get it organized and tally up the day's packages and receipts. As the assistant manager of a UPS store close to downtown, Michael knew how to be organized. He was *good* at it, damn it. Methodical. Efficient. Those were the reasons he'd been able to get this work done, these unpleasant tasks, without being caught.

Well, that and the Holy Man's protection, of course.

Hank—yes, that's what he needed. He needed to talk to the Holy Man, to lay it all out, the pros, the cons, the *surprises,* and figure out what could be done to *fix* it, because something wasn't *right,* it wasn't—

The sudden blaring of a horn made Michael realize he was veering over the center line on Lincoln Avenue and into the oncoming lane. He overcorrected by wrenching the steering wheel to the right and nearly sideswiped a parked car. By the time he got the damned car heading in a straight line, he was hunched over the steering wheel like a half-blind old man and crawling along at fifteen miles an hour while sweat streamed down both sides of his face. "Jesus, Mary, and Joseph," he whispered. "That was close. *Too* close." His gun, a Chinese Type 64 silenced pistol that the Holy Man had given him, was in the trunk, and the last thing he needed right now was to have an accident. Just the thought made him shudder all over again. He felt like he was going to vomit. "Come on, Klesowitch," he hissed. "Just calm down. Breathe. Everything'll be fine, just fine."

But it wasn't *fine,* oh no. It had been, sure, up to the point that the bus had passed him. A *bus,* for God's sake. A dirty, smelly, old city *bus.* Not even a new one—the CTA saved those for downtown, where all the tourists could ride in clean, air-conditioned comfort and marvel at how the city transportation system was so awesome. No, this bus, the one that was causing him all the grief, had had all its windows open, which meant that the heat be damned, its air-conditioning wasn't working.

But something had . . . *happened* to him when it sped by on the street, something weird. Michael had been standing in the doorway of a building one number down and across the street from where his target lived, hanging around to see if she'd come out. If the information Hank had given him was correct, this was about the time she'd be going to summer school, although he wasn't sure if she took city transportation or a school bus. That was a fact he might never know, because Michael was trying very hard not to think of her as an actual person, as an actual high school *girl*. She had to be just a *target*, a thing that Hank had told him must be eliminated for the greater good. Michael had seen a printed version of her yearbook picture and that was bad enough—she was a beautiful girl with clear skin and ink-black eyes who smiled innocently at the camera. Hank had told Michael that she was tall, like Michael himself. How could she be anything as evil as the Holy Man insisted?

But she had to be, because the Holy Man had said she was. There was so much Michael didn't know, and he never would—it wasn't Michael's job to know the answers to the questions about things like this. He couldn't let it frustrate him, couldn't let it cloud his judgment. He had to make good, sensible decisions, like opting not to go to her school and eliminate her there. Nothing was guaranteed to draw the police faster than gunfire at a high school, and there was a police station only a few minutes away from Lane Tech's location at California and Fullerton. Plus, the sheer size of the girl's high school made it likely there would be cops all over the area every morning and afternoon; even in a brain factory like Lane Tech, they'd be constantly on the make for dealers, predators circling the prey just like the dealers circled the buyers.

Another horn blared and Michael jammed on the brakes reflexively, then gasped as the car behind him nearly rear-ended him. In the side mirror, he saw a guy lean out the window and scream something about speeding up, but before Michael could press the accelerator again, the man's car squealed around Michael's. With his heart racing, Michael spotted a bus stop with enough space behind it for half a car and lurched into it, hoping any cops around would have better things to do than focus on him. When no one pulled up next to him, he sat there, shaking and perspiring for a good five minutes before he could get his labored breathing to slow.

That bus—yeah, it had started with that. Like someone was *watching* him through the vehicle's dirty windows. Then, after it had driven by and he'd decided to run across the street and check the door to the target's building, he'd been hit with . . . what? A really bad *feeling*. That was it—a feeling. Nothing more, but it had been a truly spectacular one, hadn't it? Big enough to make him suddenly turn tail and flee like a rabbit trying to outrun a diving hawk. He'd never felt anything like it before. Hell, he'd never even had déjà vu or a sense of foreboding about anything, but this . . . it was like the hand of death had reached out and caressed the back of his neck. All he'd wanted to do was curl up in the doorway and try to make himself as small as possible—that rabbit thing again—but instinct had stepped in and driven him to do something to save his sad and sorry ass.

Michael was calmer by the time he finally pulled back into traffic, but he still wasn't sure what he was going to do. He had no way of contacting the Holy Man, so he was just going to have to wait. It wouldn't be long, he was sure; in the past he'd always been able to get his assignment completed in a day or so, but he was working on four days now. The Holy Man was bound to show up at his apartment at any time. That was a good thing—a *very* good thing.

Because for the first time Michael had some questions that he was going to insist be answered.

"I SHOULD HAVE CALLED first," Redmond said. "I know it's rude to just show up."

Brynna shrugged and stood to the side so he could step into her apartment. "If you want to come over, come over. I have no objections."

He stood uncertainly in the room as she closed the door behind him. "I guess sometimes it makes people think I'm checking up on them," he said uncomfortably. "It's been an issue . . . in the past."

She gestured to the table area. "Have a seat. I went to the store this afternoon. Would you like some fruit?"

"Sure," he said, but Brynna didn't think he was really listening. She would prepare a meal for him, she decided. He was always taking her out to eat, so she should repay his kindness. She didn't cook, but she had plenty of things that could be served just as they were.

As she began taking things from the tiny refrigerator, Redmond pulled a sheaf of papers from inside his jacket and placed it on the table. "What are you doing?"

"Fixing you something to eat," she said. "It's . . ." She tilted her head, searching for the word. "Sociable. I'm trying to fit in better."

"Fit in?"

"With city life." She'd started to say *human life,* then changed her mind. She had no idea why she was sugarcoating things for him, but maybe that had to do with trying to fit in, too. He'd clearly had a problem with their last conversation, so why not try to make this one easier? And in all honesty, she had an idea that he was going to be pretty ticked off at her once he found out about the nephilim killer. Maybe a meal and trying to soothe his feelings would help somehow. She didn't understand why she cared about how Redmond felt or what he thought, but she did. Some things were what they were, and you just had to deal.

He watched her in silence for a moment, fidgeting with his papers. "Can I help?" he finally asked. "I feel weird, just sitting here watching you."

"Nice thought, but it's way too small in here for two people. And I'm done anyway." She carried a plate over and set it in front of him.

Redmond eyed the contents and a smile played at the corner of his mouth. "This is interesting."

"It's all good," she promised as she offered him a paper towel and a beat-up fork. "And healthy. Grapes, olives, fish, and bread. People have been eating these same things for thousands of years." Oops, she hadn't meant to say that—she didn't want to go into that area of discussion, at least not yet.

He poked at a grape and finally put it in his mouth. "I have to say that I never thought of sardines in hot sauce as 'fish.'"

Brynna looked a little sheepish. "I like the spiciness," she admitted. "I didn't buy any of the plain."

"It's fine. And thanks."

Brynna had found an old folding chair in the basement

and now she sat across from him, watching as he ate and trying, yet again, to figure out how she was going to tell him about the nephilim killer. She hadn't come any closer to a helpful solution when Redmond pushed the paper towel aside and leaned forward.

"Listen, I didn't come over here for a free snack," Redmond said. He tapped a finger on the papers next to him. "There's something I need to show you."

"Okay."

"This list," he told her, "was printed off the computer in Kwan Chul-moo's store. It's four pages long, and we think it's a hit list. A lot of the people on here are dead, and included are the names of every one of the eight people who've been shot by the same person we're trying so hard to find. It would be an enormous breakthrough, except that the only thing we can't figure out is the connection they have to one another. There has to be something we're missing, but we can't find it. They're all different ages, races, and occupations. As far as we can determine, not a single person on here even knew each other. We're stymied." He was silent for a long moment. "The girl in this building, Mireva . . . her name is also on this list."

Brynna frowned, not liking where this was going. "You got this list from that jewelry store? The one where the Korean girl was?"

"Yes."

Lahash.

"Crap," she said unhappily.

"Whatever it is that you're not telling me needs to come out right now," Redmond said. His voice had

changed, gone to the edge of harsh, but Brynna could tell
he was trying to tone it down. He was, she realized, going
to be even angrier than she'd anticipated. The idea upset
her, a lot, although again she didn't understand why she
should care. Maybe it was a give-and-take thing; the man
had been good to her and now she wanted to be the same
for him. Unfortunately, today he was going to feel like
that was the last thing she was doing.

"The names on your list are probably all nephilim," she
said.

"Oh, Jesus. Here we go again."

"It's true," she said stubbornly. "If you don't believe me,
check your . . . records, I guess. You're going to find that
they're all physically similar—tall, like Mireva. Probably
very good-looking." She paused. "And none of them, or
their mothers, will actually know where their real fathers
are. They probably won't even be able to tell you their
fathers' names."

Redmond ran one hand through his hair, then uncon-
sciously smoothed it back into place. "Great. So according to you, all the people on this list are the children of
angels." When she nodded, he made an exasperated
sound, then shook his head. "Brynna—"

"This morning I saw the man who killed Tobias," she
blurted.

Redmond's mouth worked but no sound came out.
"What?" he finally demanded. "Where? And why didn't
you call me?"

"Here," she admitted. "Outside the building. I was
already on the bus and by the time I could get off, he was
driving away." Before he could ask, she added. "It was a

small white car, but that's all I could tell you about it." She glanced at the list again—

Lahash.

—and exhaled. "I think he was trying to find Mireva. To kill her."

"Why didn't you call me, damn it?" Redmond was practically vibrating on his chair. She could hear how furious he was.

"I was going to," she said. "I just . . . didn't know how to tell you."

"What the hell does *that* mean? You just tell me, just like now." He stared at her. "Unless there's more." When she didn't speak, he smacked the heel of one hand against his forehead. "Oh, I just don't believe this. *What*, Brynna?"

"There was someone else in the basement of the jewelry store."

"What?"

Brynna took a deep breath. "His name is Lahash. He's like Gavino, only stronger. *Much* stronger."

Redmond gripped the edge of the table. "Then where did he go? There was no way he could have gotten out of there without someone seeing him. *And*"—he held up a hand to stop her before she could answer—"why didn't you tell me about him when you were at the station that very first time that you started talking about demons and spells and witch doctors? Why not then?"

"Because I didn't know why he was there," Brynna said. She got up and put the opened can of sardines in the refrigerator. "And you never saw him, so I figured you wouldn't believe me."

"I never saw the so-called witch doctor, either."

"And if you're honest with yourself, you really don't believe *he* was there."

"But where did this Lahash *go?*" Redmond pressed. "You said you killed the witch doctor. Did you kill Lahash too?"

Brynna shook her head and lowered herself back onto the chair. "The witch doctor was nothing but an evil human. It would take a whole lot more than a little fire to get rid of Lahash. He's a demon. A Searcher."

Redmond drummed his fingers on the table. "A Searcher, like Gavino. So if I've got this right, you're telling me that Cho Kim is a nephilim."

"No," Brynna said. "She's not. Which is why I didn't mention him—I couldn't figure out why he was there in the first place, what he would want with a nobody human girl. Oh, and there's the small fact that he's unbelievably dangerous."

The detective squeezed his eyes shut, then opened them again. "So this Lahash demon is somehow tied to this list, which then ties him to the serial murderer and to Mireva—"

"And to Gavino," Brynna finished for him. "Don't you see? They're working *together.*"

"Wouldn't be the first time."

"Yes, it *would,*" Brynna insisted. "This isn't human business, Eran. Demons don't collaborate. They do for themselves and that's all. This is absolutely *unheard-of,* and I can't think of anything short of the actual apocalypse that could be worse. If I were you, I'd be terrified."

"If you say so," Eran said. "But right now I'm still trying

to figure out how Lahash got out of the basement without anyone but you knowing he was there."

Brynna sighed impatiently. "He just did, that's all. You couldn't see him because he didn't want to be seen." She paused. "Had there not been so much going on—all the noise and people running around—I really think you would have *felt* him, though. He's pure, perfect evil."

"Unlike you."

Brynna looked away, trying not to be stung by the sarcasm. "I don't know what I am," she said. "I'm just . . . trying to change."

"Right." Redmond looked around the room, but she didn't think he was really seeing anything. "And how exactly is it that he can not be seen? Last I heard, invisibility wasn't an option."

"He's a demon, Eran. He has demon abilities."

"As do you . . . supposedly."

"We each can do what we can do. That's the only way to explain it. Lahash may look human but that's just a façade at best, a game that he likes playing because he thinks human clothes are amusing. Beneath the surface, he's absolute demon and he has full access to his demon abilities." Brynna had slipped into a pair of denim jeans before going up to the roof to water Mireva's plants, and now she ran her hands lightly across the tight fabric encasing her thighs. "For him, the human form is just a sort of lightweight cloak. He can toss it off at any time. For me, it's fully shifting my form that enables me to hide from my own kind, at least until they get up close. But this shape limits me. In my real one . . . well, let's just say there's a lot about me that you'd find really surprising."

"Can you get in touch with this Lahash?" Redmond said, changing the topic. "Maybe he knows where the killer is."

"Lahash will never cooperate," Brynna said. "But it doesn't matter. I know where the killer lives."

"You know where he *lives*?" Redmond's voice was incredulous. His face went white with shock and he looked like he was going to fall off his chair. "Good God, Brynna—all this time and you didn't tell me? People have *died*!"

"I'm sorry," she said, and she meant it. Brynna spread her hands, trying to find a way to make him understand. "Don't you see? I've never had to think about stuff like this before. About people and how they feel, about how short your lives are. I'm still . . . I don't know. Learning, I guess."

"Whatever you want to call it," Redmond growled as he dragged a notebook out of his back pocket. "I call it withholding evidence." His movements were jerky, his expression furious. "What's the address?"

Brynna's eyes widened. "I don't have any idea." She stood. "But I can take you right to his door."

Fifteen

He felt calmer now.

Klesowitch had been driving all day. Not going anywhere in particular, just kind of wandering around. He'd been scheduled to start work at three o'clock, but he'd called and said he was going to be late. He'd made up an excuse—he couldn't remember what—and the day manager had accepted it. It was the second time this week he'd called in late, but at least he hadn't told his manager that he wasn't coming in at all. He'd taken sick days once early last week and once the week before that, both times that he'd had to do the Holy Man's assignments. Did he even have any medical time left? He'd been saying he had a medical issue, knowing that the manager wouldn't feel comfortable questioning on it—privacy laws and all that. Besides, the woman really didn't want to know; she didn't *care* about Michael Klesowitch other than trying to make the personnel schedule work.

Klesowitch gritted his teeth. He needed to be tougher, damn it, and not think about these problems. He needed to do his duty and walk away proud. A righteous rock in the hand of the Lord.

But he wasn't, oh no. He was weak, and he was uncertain. Instead of getting stronger as time went by, he was getting more and more hesitant, cowardly. He had to stop his wavering right now, pull himself up by the proverbial bootstraps, and get the damned job done. Not many people were chosen for this kind of thing, so he couldn't take the chance of failing. It just wasn't an option.

And see—here was the proof. All this time that he'd thought he was just driving aimlessly while thinking, and yet his car, an aging Toyota Corolla, had ended up right in front of that high school girl's building again. Yeah, there was still that . . . *feeling* about it, but it wasn't so bad now. He had beat it. Maybe it had never been there in the first place, a case of the "vapors," as his mother would have called it. Nervousness for no reason, or she'd sometimes claimed it was "sad memories." She used to have those sad memories every now and then and dose herself up good with Librium. He'd always wondered if it had something to do with the father he'd never known, a man his mother had confessed had come into her life and seduced her, then disappeared without so much as leaving behind a photograph, much less a last name. Had he inherited his mother's anxiety problems? It wasn't impossible.

Nothing was impossible.

Klesowitch pushed the thoughts of his mother from his mind and worked his car into a parking spot at the end of the main walkway to the door of the girl's building. It was tight, and he would have preferred something bigger, like a bus stop, but it was the only thing with a solid line of sight, an absolute necessity. He'd have to stay in the car and wait it out—he couldn't very well just stand in front of the building on the empty sidewalk with his pistol hidden under his coat. He'd look like some kind of pedophile.

What time was it? God, it was like a blast furnace in the car, with the sun searing through the windshield. Klesowitch had no choice but to roll down the windows—it was that or suffocate. He pulled a hand across his forehead and eyes and his fingers came away dripping with sweat. It crawled into the corners of his eyes and stung, making him squint. Did people really leave animals and kids locked inside their cars in the summer? It was unthinkable. He struggled out of his soaked denim jacket and threw it on the passenger floor. For a few minutes he felt a bit cooler, then the sauna effect began to build again. He couldn't do this, the heat was killing him. He'd have to come back in the morning, try again in the tolerable morning hours before the temperatures rose—

There.

Klesowitch jerked upright, the summer heat forgotten as he watched a city bus swerve to the curb. The vehicle's air brakes hissed as it stopped, and when it pulled away, the girl was standing on the sidewalk. Despite the oversized backpack she was hauling around, the teen stood tall and beautiful. What a difference from what Klesowitch had been expecting—the crappy printed image the Holy Man had given him might as well have been a line drawing on newsprint. Everything was incongruous. The Holy Man had insisted that no matter how young she was, she was evil and despicable, just like the others, and that horrible things would happen if Klesowitch didn't eliminate

her. But in the here and now . . . it was so *off*. It was seem-
ing more and more wrong every time he had to do one
of these tasks. The sun was shining, it was a hot summer
day—even the birds were singing. How was he supposed
to believe that this sparkling young woman, this *kid,* was
malevolent?

"Faith," Michael mumbled. "That's how."

He set his jaw and tried to bring the pistol up, but the
barrel caught beneath the steering wheel in the cramped
area of the driver's seat. He yanked it free so brutally that
he smacked the muzzle against the rearview mirror hard
enough to actually crack it. It made a loud enough sound
so that the girl glanced in his direction as she walked past
his car and turned down the sidewalk toward her building. His grip was slick with sweat and the gun slid out of
his flailing fingers and thunked to the dirty floormat. Klesowitch grabbed for it and accidentally kicked it halfway
under the driver's seat.

"Wait—hey, girl!" Michael called out. He was panicking now, overreacting in his effort to keep her in his sights
until he could get the gun up and get off a good shot.
Damn it all, he couldn't quite get hold of the weapon. "I
want to talk to you!"

The teenager was halfway to the door now, moving
with quick, long-legged strides. She paused and looked
back, then frowned. For an instant, Klesowitch imagined
what she saw—a crazed-looking older guy with a sweating red face making frantic, jerky movements out of sight
in his car. He felt suddenly deeply ashamed at what she
must think, and that in itself made him think he was going
utterly insane. How could he be afraid she might think he

was some kind of pedophile but still believe it was all right to murder her in cold blood?

For a second his gaze locked with hers, then his hand brushed against the barrel of his pistol.

She ran.

"Damn it!" Klesowitch screamed. His fingers spasmed, and instead of closing around the pistol's handle he accidentally pushed it away. He twisted and forced his body sideways under the steering wheel, slapping his hand wildly beneath the seat. There—finally, he had it.

When he clawed his way upright, the girl was already shoving her key into the lock; like his, her movements were frantic and clumsy. She glanced over her shoulder and saw him as he lunged across the driver's seat; she tried again, bending over as she struggled to get the key to go in.

Klesowitch grinned. It was a statistical fact that people under high stress lost motor control—they fell when they ran, they couldn't remember PIN numbers when a kidnapper wanted money, they dropped keys or, like the panicking girl in his sights, just couldn't get the key in the lock. Hadn't he just done the same thing with his pistol?

He took a deep, calming breath, then raised the Type 64 and fired.

REDMOND STILL WASN'T SPEAKING to her as they pushed through the hallway door and stepped into the foyer where the mailboxes were. His anger was almost palpable in the hot air, unseen but unpleasant; there was little she could do about it, but at least she could atone, to a point, by taking him to the nephilim killer's apartment.

In her ongoing quest to find acceptance as a twenty-first-century woman, perhaps she should stop thinking of the man like that and put it more in human terms: humans did not believe in nephilim, hence the shooter was a *serial* killer. If she referred to him as Redmond did, it might make conversations between them go a little smoother. It was worth a try, anyway.

There was a shadow on the other side of the full-length frosted panel on the outside door, and Brynna instantly recognized it as Mireva's. The girl was hunched over and doing something to the lock, or the door handle . . . *something*. It sounded like she was *clawing* at it.

Something was wrong. In the short time it took Brynna to cross the foyer, the teenager's shadow half turned away from the door, then came back to it. Brynna's hand was on the handle when for no apparent reason, Mireva suddenly slammed into the glass face-first.

"What the *hell?*" she heard Redmond shout, but she was already pulling on the handle. It was stuck—Mireva had managed to get her key in the old-fashioned lock but she hadn't had time to turn it; now the tumblers were locked in place around her key.

Mireva cried out and started to slide down the glass, and Brynna could see her trying to pull herself upright. She had no idea what was happening, but the teenager was trapped. "Screw this," Brynna snarled. At the far right corner of the thick window, an inch-long crack had appeared; the glass had cracked when Mireva smacked into it. *At least it's away from her face,* Brynna thought, and rammed her fist against it.

Redmond shouted something but Brynna couldn't

hear him over the sound of shattering glass. Mireva tilted inward, flailing her arms as her shins caught on the bottom sill; Brynna reached out with both hands and grabbed the backpack straps running over Mireva's shoulders, then hauled her bodily through the window. Mireva gasped as the jagged edges of glass bit into her skin but she didn't fight. A sound cut through the air, strangely soft but compelling, and Mireva was thrust forward into Brynna's arms. Brynna held her balance—just barely—as the wheels of her memory spun and gave her information. Yes, she had heard that noise before, a split second before Tobias Gallagher had been shot in the head right in front of her.

The nephilim killer!

Redmond was already shoving his way past Brynna and Mireva. The killer wasn't finished—he had to be right outside, taking aim, and as long as he could see Mireva and there was a chance he could shoot her, he would keep trying. The three of them were crammed into this tiny foyer and the detective was headed right into the line of fire.

Brynna shoved Mireva against the back wall and lunged in front of Redmond.

"Brynna, get out of my way!" He tried to untangle himself from her, but she had him by the upper arms and wouldn't let go. "What are you doing?"

That sound again, twice, and each time like a knife splitting the air with cosmic speed. The second one Brynna felt at the same time she heard it, and she understood why Mireva had been tossed against the door like a child's ball. The impact spun her at the same time it knocked her backward. She fell against Mireva and the two of them went down at the same time Brynna heard Redmond shout, "Shooter! Shooter!" This time she couldn't stop him as he charged outside, scrambling through the remains of the window with his own gun drawn. Brynna registered a new sound—

crack

—as Redmond fired, then she heard a revving engine and a series of fast noises, metal crashing against metal. Redmond bellowed from outside and the metallic sound came again, followed by tires squealing and a straining engine. Another three seconds and even that was gone, and the only thing left was the ringing in her ears, echoes of the shot Redmond had fired.

"Brynna!" Redmond was back, climbing through the window opening. She heard shouts from the hallway, tenants yelling about gunshots and demanding to know what was going on. Mireva was trapped beneath Brynna's weight, shaking and crying silently. "Are you all right? Crap, you're hit!"

Again? This was really getting old. Brynna shook her head to clear it, then pushed herself up. Pain, like someone had pressed a hot branding iron against her skin, went through her left arm, just above the elbow. When she looked at it, blood welled from a single hole with a dark, scarlet center.

"Just grazed," she said, ignoring Redmond's knowing gaze. "Come on, Mireva. He's gone now. Let's get you inside."

Before Brynna had finished her sentence, the inside foyer door burst open, revealing a crowd of tenants beyond. Mireva's mother pushed to the front, her face rigid with shock and fear. Brynna wanted to go after the nephilim killer, but she had to make herself wait and let things play out. Everyone was talking at once, with Redmond on his cell phone and Abrienda gathering up her daughter while half a dozen others swarmed around the four of them like ants taking care of their hill. Someone pressed a towel against Brynna's arm and she accepted it, then shook her head when Redmond mouthed, "Ambulance?" It hurt—this third time wasn't any easier than the first two—but at least this time she could take care of it in the privacy of her apartment. After that, she was going to the nephilim killer's building.

And with or without Redmond's approval, she was going to kill him.

Sixteen

"You shouldn't be out," Redmond said for the second time as he braked for a stoplight. "You need time to heal." He sent Brynna a sideways glance when she didn't answer, but he couldn't tell if she was focused on the street signs or ignoring him. He wanted to repeat himself, but he knew it would do no good; she'd just say she'd spent the morning doing just that and now she was ready to go. She was such a strange and independent woman. If she was a woman at all.

I'm not human . . .

He wanted to say that her words came back to him at odd times, but that wasn't true. They came back at just the *right* times, like late yesterday afternoon, after all the chaos had died down and the beat cops and the neighbors and the relatives had finally gone away and he and Brynna could retreat to her apartment.

They'd come back when, for the third time, he'd watched Brynna gouge a bullet out of her own flesh. At least this time she'd used a clean knife, even if she had taken it from a kitchen drawer and pushed it into her arm before he could do something as silly and *human* as sterilize the damned thing. She'd waved away his protests, and what could he say when, twelve hours later, her wound was clean and closed, if a little on the side of raw?

"Earth to Brynna. Anyone home?" She hadn't said anything for almost the entire trip. They were on Halsted and getting close to Wrightwood; a left turn, then a quick right onto Mildred, and she'd finally *have* to start talking because she didn't know the street number of the serial killer's apartment building. "Come on," he said. He knew he sounded exasperated, but he couldn't help it. He wasn't over his fury about her not telling him about Klesowitch, and this was just making him more frustrated. "What's going on in your head?"

Five seconds passed, then ten. Redmond was about to simply pull over and wait it out when Brynna spoke. "I feel . . . odd," she said.

Redmond sat up straighter. "Odd? Are you sick? You might have an infection from the bullet—"

She held up a hand. "No, not odd like that." She paused, and Redmond could see her trying to work it out mentally. "Regretful, I guess. Guilty." She looked at her hands. "You told me that people have died because I didn't reveal the whereabouts of the nephilim killer."

"Brynna, I didn't mean—"

"But you did," she interrupted. "And you were right. I remember you telling me that there were two women, and their ages." She still wasn't looking him in the eye. "They were both young. One wasn't much older than Mireva." Brynna turned her head and stared out the window. "They were hardly here at all, and the killer snuffed them out like their lives were no more important than candle flames."

Redmond tried to think of something to say but couldn't. Everything she'd said was true.

"It's sad to think about," Brynna continued. "Sad, and . . . *heavy* somehow. I've never felt guilt before. I've never *had* to." She scowled. "It's very difficult, and yet there are so many people in the world who don't seem to be affected by it."

"Sociopaths."

"What?"

"Sociopaths," Redmond said again. "People who feel no guilt exhibit what psychiatrists call sociopathic behavior. No matter what they do or who they hurt, they feel no guilt or regret about it. They don't care. Often they actually enjoy hurting others, and most don't see any problem with sacrificing other people to get what they want." He paused. "Maybe that's what we're dealing with here."

"I don't think so," Brynna said in a low voice. "This man is a nephilim, and nephilim are irrevocably tied to humankind. He's been misled and my guess is that this is a great struggle for him. His ties to his destiny are strong, and unless he's lost himself completely, instinct tells him it's wrong and he'll question what he's doing more and more as time passes."

"Then why do this to begin with?" Redmond asked.

"He's weak and he's making the wrong choices. It's the human part of him." Brynna's eyes were troubled when she looked at him. "You see, it's all about choices. It always has been. And it's making the wrong choices that gets us *all* in trouble."

Redmond thought about this as he neared the corner of Wrightwood and Mildred. Brynna had talked about choices before, and making the right ones was really what it all came down to. Still, he didn't think it was as black-and-white as it seemed on the surface. There were way too many things that affected decisions, especially the big ones, and if he understood what she claimed was happening here, deception was a key factor. So was circumstance. And what about those who were forced to choose something they might not have otherwise? Yeah, it was a lot more complicated. But then, wasn't everything? Choices were a part of life, and very few people had truly simple lives.

"This is Mildred," he said. "How far down?"

"Not far," she said. "Might as well park."

Redmond nodded and slid the car into a spot on the west side of the street. They got out and Redmond followed Brynna as she crossed to the east sidewalk. She was walking fast, with more determination than he thought he'd ever seen her show. Somehow he wasn't comforted by the change. "Wait up," he called when she turned into the walkway of an older apartment building. "I should go in first."

She tilted her head. "Why?"

"Because I'm the police," he explained patiently. "And you're not."

"Fine," Brynna said and moved aside to follow him. "The door in the back. But it's probably locked, and I don't know which apartment he lives in."

Redmond stopped at the entrance, considering. "But you know for sure he lives here?"

Brynna nodded. "I'm certain of it. I followed his scent." When he started to protest, she cut him off. "Before you say that's crazy, remember that's how I found Cho Kim."

What could he say to that? He tried the knob out of habit, and of course it wouldn't turn. He pointed to the right side of the door, where there was a line of doorbells with a worn label over each. "But you can't tell from here?"

"Do you push your own doorbell?"

Good point. He stared at the names again, but that certainly wasn't going to help. With nothing beyond Brynna's . . . *guidance,* he certainly hadn't been able to ask a judge for a search warrant—until now, he hadn't even had an address. No, he'd have to come up with some other way to figure out which of these people was his man. Then he had an idea. "Let's assume the killer is a nephilim like you say. Wouldn't his name be on that list, even if he isn't one of the victims?"

Brynna lifted one eyebrow. "Maybe. Actually, more than maybe. Probably."

Redmond pulled out his phone and had Onani on the line in less than a minute. "I've got some names here," he told the tech. "Run them against that hit list pulled off the jewelry store computer." When Onani was ready, Redmond read him the mailbox labels, spelling the less common ones. "Sallee, Osier—what? O-S-I-E-R. No, I have no idea how to pronounce it. Nothing yet? Then try these: Van Patten, Massie, Skinner, Klesowitch, Gallardo, Fassl—F-A-S-S-L." A grim smile swept across his mouth. "Got it. Here's the last three, just in case: deMonterice,

Hodge, Sweedlow." He listened, then nodded. "Thanks."
To Brynna he said, "We have a match. Klesowitch."

"Great." She put her hand on the doorknob. "Let's go
get him. I can open this—"

"I see you!"

The shrill voice cut through the air and both Redmond and Brynna looked up. "Fabulous," she muttered.
"Here we go again."

Above their heads, an old woman was leaning out of
her apartment window. "And I remember you, young lady.
I warned you before, this is a Neighborhood Watch area.
I should've called the police on you the first time, but you
can bet your bottom I'm going to right now!"

Brynna looked perplexed at the woman's words, but
Redmond yanked out his badge and held it up before the
woman could back away from the sill. "I *am* the police,
ma'am. May I ask you a few questions?"

The old woman's face twisted in indecision. "What're
you doing with her?"

"She's helping me locate someone," Redmond
answered.

"She didn't even know his last name when she was here
before!"

"Nothing wrong with her memory," Brynna said in a
voice low enough so that only Redmond could hear.

Redmond suppressed a smile. "But we do now, and
maybe you can help us."

The elderly woman peered down at him. "What is it?"

Redmond made a show of glancing around. "I'd rather
not shout it out, if you get my meaning."

"All right," the woman said after a moment. Her gaze

cut to the left and right, and Redmond could imagine her cooking up some great conspiracy. If only she had any real idea. "I'll ring you in. Third floor front."

There were no apartment numbers on the bells, but once the buzzer rang and they were inside, he could see who lived in which apartment. Klesowitch was on the second floor, in the rear; they would pass it on their way up, and if he heard movement inside . . . well, there would be a little delay in talking to the building busybody.

But everything was silent on the second-floor landing, and Brynna confirmed it. "There's no one in his apartment," she whispered. "If there were, I'd be able to hear." Redmond set his jaw and reluctantly kept going, but what he really wanted to do was kick down the damned door.

"In here," the old woman said impatiently from the landing above them. "Don't take all day. Having the door open is letting out my air-conditioning."

"Yes, ma'am," Redmond said agreeably. He bit back a retort about how hanging out the open window would have the same effect. Next to him Brynna actually laughed under her breath as they were going through the doorway, although he had no idea why. The apartment was fairly spacious, with flowered oval throw rugs on clean wood floors, and overstuffed antique furniture. A small air conditioner hummed in the window to the far left, and semi-sheer curtains muted the light. Dozens of framed photographs, most in black and white, were hung on walls that could have used repainting five years ago. Fresh flowers—daisies, lilies, and the like—rested in a vintage crystal vase on one of the end tables.

"Let me see your badge again," the woman demanded

before he could introduce himself. "It might be fake. And don't think I'll be fooled if it is."

Redmond held it out but kept his grip on it when she tried to pull it from his fingers. With his other hand he offered his business card. "I'm Detective Redmond and this is Ms. Malak. Sorry, but I can't let you take the badge. You're welcome to call in the badge number if you like. We'll wait. And your name is . . . ?"

She scowled at him, looking from his badge to the business card, then back to his face. Finally she gestured for them to sit. As they settled onto the couch, she announced in a voice that was too loud, "My name is Clara Sweedlow. I've been in this apartment for thirty-five years and I know everyone in this building."

I'll bet you do, Redmond thought, but outwardly he gave her as pleasant a smile as he could manage. Inside, his mind was spinning with impatience, but he knew from experience that you just couldn't push people like this old woman. They'd tell you just about everything you wanted to know, but it would be at their own pace. "Do you know Michael Klesowitch?"

"Of course I do." Clara Sweedlow lowered her ample frame onto a rocker upholstered in worn floral fabric, then folded her hands in her lap like a prim schoolteacher. "He's a very nice young man, lives on the second floor in the rear. Very polite. Very religious," she added with a small, satisfied nod. Her watery gaze focused on Brynna and her eyes narrowed. "A bit young for you, I'd think. Although he's very good-looking, so I can see why you'd be interested."

"I'm not—" Brynna began, but she stopped when Redmond cleared his throat pointedly.

"I don't think Mr. Klesowitch is at home right now," Redmond said. "Do you know where we can find him?"

"Why do you want to talk to him?" The old woman drew herself up. "He's a very nice boy, you know. He's never done anything wrong."

"We're actually looking for an acquaintance of his," Redmond said without missing a beat. "The guy is kind of a bad apple, and we're afraid he might get Michael in trouble." Not technically the truth, but not really a lie, either. If Redmond could get his hands on that Lahash character, he had more than a few questions for him, no matter what Brynna said. And according to Brynna, Lahash was the man behind the curtain regarding Michael Klesowitch's evil.

"Really? Oh, dear." Clara Sweedlow sat forward. "You know, I worked for the city for most of my life, and I've sure seen what a bad influence can do. What do you think Michael's gotten himself into?"

"I'm sorry, but I'm just not at liberty to say right now." Beside him, Brynna was fidgeting. He needed to get her out of here before something they'd both regret came out of her mouth. "Does Michael have a job?"

"Oh, yes. He works at one of those mailing stores. You know, the kind that have mailboxes and send packages."

"Which one?"

The old woman looked distressed. "Why, I don't know specifically. It's downtown, I think."

"Mail Boxes Etc.? UPS?"

"That's it—UPS. He mentions it by name every now and then. He likes his job, you know. He's a good worker."

"I'm sure he is," Redmond agreed, although he doubted

she had any facts at all on which to base that statement. He stood and Brynna did the same, clearly relieved. "Thank you for your help."

Clara Sweedlow levered herself up and followed them to the door. "Should I tell Michael to call you? I could give him your business card."

Redmond sucked in his breath. "If you don't mind, it would be better if you didn't." She nodded, but Redmond didn't think there was a chance in hell she wouldn't open her mouth the first instant she saw Klesowitch. They'd just have to make sure they got to him first.

Once the old woman had closed her door, Redmond hurried down the stairs, motioning at Brynna when she would've stopped at Klesowitch's apartment. "Why not wait for him here?" she asked. "Once he gets off work—"

"He might go straight for Mireva again," Redmond cut in. "I've got an officer over there, but that won't help much if he's out of sight and manages to get a shot at her. Come on. I'll know which UPS store he works at by the time we hit Lincoln Avenue, and I'll have a stakeout on this building before we get there."

FROM HIS VANTAGE POINT on the roof, Lahash watched Astarte and the policeman walk down the street, then climb into a car and pull away. He'd been waiting for his "nephilim tool"—his pet name for Klesowitch—to get home. It was Thursday, and Klesowitch was so ridiculously predictable. Because he opened the store on Thursdays, his shift would end at four-thirty; from work he would go to the supermarket and do his weekly shopping because he didn't like the weekend crowds. So trivial. So *human*.

Lahash straightened the cuffs of his sleeves and reposition a cuff link that had turned sideways. Now, of course, the policeman would post a sentry or a guard at the apartment to try to catch Klesowitch. Everything would have to change, and Lahash would have to find a way to intercept the nephilim before he came home and got himself arrested. Clearly, Klesowitch wasn't going to be good for much longer. It really irked Lahash to see all the effort he'd put into his nephilim tool go to waste, then to have to start all over again. Still, his little brainstorm of using nephilim as puppets was pretty good, and it just begged for another try. As of now, there was nothing he could do to change the past, so he might as well get on with manipulating the present. He wasn't quite finished with Klesowitch. Not yet.

First, though, he was going to pay a little visit to the old woman, the one who lived on the third floor and thought she had a viewpoint into the lives of every tenant in the building. She'd been such a snoop for all these years.

Now she was going to find out more than she'd ever wanted to know.

"HE WENT HOME ALREADY." The name tag on her shoulder said *May Jenkins—Day Manager,* but since she'd seen Redmond's badge, the brown-haired young woman talking to him seemed as nervous as a teenager caught shoplifting. Brynna hung off to the side, not minding that Redmond was taking the lead in the hunt for Michael Klesowitch, as they now knew he was called. Finding him was human business; stopping him was another story. It could be human business. Or it could be hers. "Is there a problem?"

"We think Michael might be able to help us," Redmond said easily. "He might've seen something and not realized it, and it's really important that we find out as soon as possible."

"What?" May Jenkins looked from Redmond to Brynna. "What did he see?"

"Well, I can't really go into that," Redmond explained. "I wouldn't want to say anything that might do what we call 'lead the witness.' He really needs to verify this on his own." Redmond glanced around the store thoughtfully. "You know, Ms. Jenkins . . . Is it okay if I call you May?" He waited for her to nod, then continued. "There *is* a way that you could help us at least know if we're on the right track."

The young woman's eyes widened and her expression brightened with self-importance. "Really?"

"Definitely. If I gave you a list of dates, do you think you could tell me if Michael was at work on those days?" Before she could answer, Redmond pulled a piece of paper from a notepad on the counter and began scribbling on it.

"Gosh, I don't know." She glanced at the only other worker in the place, a guy with spiked hair who was fighting to unjam a copy machine across the room. "I'm not really sure I'm supposed to give out that kind of information. Aren't you supposed to have a warrant or something?"

"Oh, this isn't sensitive information, May," Redmond assured her. "Not like medical or personal stuff, or even financial. See, if he was here on these dates, then he's probably not going to be able to help us out and there's no sense in even talking to him. It would save us a lot of time."

Brynna stayed silent as she watched the play of emotions across May's face. The girl seemed as though she wanted to refuse, but Redmond had created a sort of bond between them by using her first name; now she didn't know how to say no. Good thing she wasn't a nephilim.

"I—I guess so." She glanced again at her coworker, but he was swearing at the copy machine under his breath and hadn't even noticed Redmond and Brynna. "Just don't tell anyone I showed you." She slipped into the back office, then came back with a looseleaf notebook that said EMPLOYEE ATTENDANCE on the spine. Redmond reached for it, but May pulled it back. "I'll look it up," she said. Her voice was a little firmer.

"Great," Redmond said warmly. "Thanks so much." He offered her the note and she picked up a pen and flipped through the pages, scrawling something next to each date. Her handwriting was small and childishly round.

"There," she said, and slid the paper back to Redmond. "I guess he might be able to help you after all. He wasn't here most of those dates."

"Most of them?"

"He left early or came in late sometimes," she pointed out. "I wrote it all down. He's been having some kind of medical issue, but I can't say what." She raised her chin and Brynna saw a hint of rebellion in the stance. "Even if I knew, I wouldn't tell you because that's, like, private."

"Absolutely," Redmond agreed. He folded the note and put it in his jacket pocket. "You've been a huge help. Thanks again."

Brynna followed him out to the car and climbed inside, knowing the girl was watching them the whole time. "Well?"

"Bingo," Redmond said grimly. "It appears that our Mr. Klesowitch was notably absent from work on all the same days that there were daytime shootings, which means five times out of eight. What are the odds."

It wasn't a question, so Brynna didn't try to answer. "Where are we going?"

"Back to Klesowitch's apartment." He glanced at her. "Unless you're too tired—I can take you home first."

She shook her head. "I'm fine. The wound is barely noticeable now."

He opened his mouth but the ring of his cell phone cut off whatever he was about to say. "Redmond," he said into the receiver. He listened for a few seconds, his face darkening. "I'm on my way."

Brynna looked at him. "What was that all about?"

Redmond's jaw was rigid as he hit a switch on the dashboard. Blue lights began to strobe across the front of the vehicle as he pushed hard on the accelerator, weaving in and out of traffic. "There's been some kind of incident at Klesowitch's building," he told her. "The beat cop who called me said something about a fire. He wasn't making much sense and I couldn't make it all out because of the sirens and the noise in the background.

"But I think Clara Sweedlow is dead."

Seventeen

"This doesn't look promising," Redmond said.

They'd made their way past the multitude of vehicles outside, following the line of people into the building and up the stairs. The third floor hallway outside Clara Sweedlow's apartment was packed with fire department and police personnel, and yellow crime scene tape had been used to cordon off the area at the top of the stairwell. Despite all the people, there wasn't very much noise—no one, it seemed, had a whole lot to offer in the way of comments.

"Ma'am," said one of the firemen when he saw Brynna duck under the tape and follow Redmond to the apartment door, "you probably don't want to see this."

"She's fine," Redmond said, making Brynna wonder if he was finally on his way to believing her origins. She had an idea that the scene he was about to see would help push that along.

Redmond was only three feet into the apartment when he froze. "Jesus," he breathed.

Brynna stood next to him and said nothing. She'd seen

things like this before—in fact, much worse—but this was probably a first for Redmond and the rest of the people here. For them it had to be a definite jolt.

Most of the living room was untouched. The photos still hung on the walls, the curtains at the windows were clear and cream-colored, drifting gently where they were closest to the flow of the air conditioner. There was a slightly sweet scent to the air, and Brynna traced it to the flowers next to the couch. Earlier in the afternoon they had brightened up the room and given it life; now the fragrance was out of place and the cheerful colors were a mockery.

There wasn't much left of Clara Sweedlow except a foot encased in a pink leatherette slipper below a pile of gray ash and blackened cinders. Most of the old woman's remains were still in her rocking chair, although the burn marks on the floral fabric extended only a few inches around the impression of where her body had been. The sides and back of the chair were untouched, as was the throw rug beneath it. Brynna knew the humans would expect to smell burned flesh and fat, but the air was pretty clean.

"Some kind of a fire," said one of the firemen uselessly. His uniform had markings on it that Brynna assumed indicated he was some kind of official. "Probably flammable clothes. Maybe she was smoking—"

"She didn't smoke," Redmond said.

The fireman frowned. "Well, she had to have done something. It's all preliminary right now, but there's no evidence of an accelerant, and people don't just burn up by themselves."

"Spontaneous human combustion, Captain."

"What?" The captain turned toward a younger fireman who'd spoken.

"I read up on it—we all did at one time or another. In fact"—he pointed at Clara Sweedlow's foot—"this looks just like the photograph of one of the cases from back in the sixties, I think it was."

"I don't want to hear you spreading rumors like that," the captain snapped. "There's a scientific reason for what happened to this woman. We just haven't found it yet. Get back downstairs. *Now*." The captain glanced at Redmond and shook his head in disgust as his chastised fireman headed out of the apartment. "Damned kids. They'll believe anything they read on the Internet."

Redmond didn't answer, but Brynna saw him glance her way. When the captain had finally moved out of earshot, he touched her elbow. "What the hell happened here, Brynna? Do you know?"

"Lahash," she said quietly. "It's his trademark."

Redmond stared at her, horrified. *"Trademark?"*

She nodded, making sure that no one else could overhear them. "Yes. He doesn't do it often because it would call too much attention from bigger powers than him, but this is what he does to humans who really annoy him." She glanced at the doorway, but the younger fireman was gone. "That guy actually hit it right on the head. Every recorded instance of so-called spontaneous human combustion through the centuries has been Lahash's work."

"Are you *kidding* me?"

"No. Your scientists and forensics people will work

very hard to come up with an explanation, and they'll probably even come up with some chemical process. And why not? Life itself is a chemical process . . . until you get down to that very last question: What makes it start to begin with? And that same question applies here. What made the fire start to begin with? The answer is Lahash."

Redmond said nothing for a long moment. Then he asked, "And Lahash is like . . . you."

"Yes."

His gaze swept what was left of Clara Sweedlow. "Is this what you did to that witch doctor you said was in the jewelry store basement?"

"Yes," Brynna admitted. "I just didn't leave anything. Lahash likes to sign his work." She looked around the living room, and again was drawn to the photographs. She couldn't help examining them, following them from one end to the other, the oldest to the most recent. It was clear where Clara Sweedlow's life had started, from the grainy baby photographs taken almost three-quarters of a century ago to the sharp clarity of the more modern ones. Once upon a time, she'd been married and had children, and in the last one she was smiling around a couple of grandkids. It was a picture book of the old woman's life, and now she was gone, her existence snuffed out by a petulant, vengeful being who could live forever and therefore had no perception of how precious a human life could be. A being like herself.

"Let's go," Redmond said. "The uniforms will fill out all the paperwork. I've told them as much as I can."

"Yeah," she said. She knew exactly what he meant. "Let's."

They talked very little on the ride back to her apartment. Brynna watched the buildings and the people flash by as the car sped southward, still thinking about the brevity of human life. And yet the men and women kept going, most struggling to make their existences not only the best it could be for themselves but for their oh-so-short futures and their children, or sometimes just for others in general. They were tenacious and industrious, creative and inquisitive. They were *strong*.

"I'm sorry," Brynna said as Redmond eased the car into a parking spot close to her building.

He shut off the engine. "About what?"

"That Lahash killed that woman." She looked down at her hands, thinking again about how quickly her own body healed and how well she could endure pain. Clara Sweedlow hadn't had either ability. She probably hadn't even understood what was happening, and she most definitely wouldn't have known why. "She must have suffered terribly," Brynna added softly. "It's pretty unfair."

"Yes, it is," Redmond said after a moment. "Come on. I'll walk you inside. I want to check on the cop assigned to Mireva, anyway."

Brynna let Redmond go upstairs to Abrienda's apartment while she wandered around her own place, not sure what to do with herself. Since she'd moved in, the building had gained a reputation as a place *not* to hang around or mess with. The gangbangers and dealers went somewhere else and the tenants slept more soundly; even the domestic spats had all but disappeared. Every time she came back from being gone for more than three or four hours, some small gift was left in her apartment or something was cleaned or changed. She guessed it was the people in the building because she didn't bother to lock the door. But wasn't it a lot more common for things to be taken away? Now there were things hung on the walls, well-used, inexpensive pictures and small, homemade wall decorations. There were towels in the bathroom, dishes in the kitchen, knickknacks here and there. What had been a dingy little hovel was actually starting to look like a welcoming place to live. Tonight, for instance, there was a bright red throw folded neatly across the bottom third of the bed, itself made with new (to her) sheets that had shown up last week. On Monday night, she'd come in and been startled to see a worn but serviceable blue love seat against one wall.

Brynna sat on it now, settling back to wait for Redmond and kicking off her athletic shoes with enough force to send them across the small room. She was tired but not as sore as she expected; this last bullet wound had been the least troublesome. The reactions of her human body—hunger, exhaustion, and especially *emotion*—still often surprised her. The curtains, which were really nothing more than a couple of mismatched sheets, were spread across the front window to keep out the summer heat and the stares of curious children. Sometimes it didn't hit Brynna until she came home how much she was on edge outside, how she always expected a Hunter to show up at any moment. Now that she was out of the public eye, Brynna almost felt safe. Almost.

She'd become familiar with Redmond's footsteps and she heard him long before he turned the doorknob. He stepped inside and shut the door behind him, pausing for a moment before he came and sat next to her. Brynna thought he looked as tired as she felt. "What did you just do?" she asked. "At the door."

"I locked it."

"I never lock it."

He looked at her in surprise. "Oh—sorry. Habit, I guess."

Of course—that's what normal people did. Brynna wondered if Clara Sweedlow's door had been locked. It wouldn't have made any difference.

"How's your arm?"

Brynna glanced down automatically, a silly thing to do because her arm and the bandaged wound were covered by the long sleeve of her shirt. "It's okay. It'll be gone by tomorrow afternoon."

"Have you changed the dressing?"

"No. Should I have?"

"It could get infected," he said. "No matter how strong you think you are, the world is still full of bacteria. And weren't you the one who said it's all just a great big chemical reaction?"

"But it's fine."

"Wound dressings should be changed every twenty-four hours," Redmond said firmly. "No arguing." He got up and went into the tiny bathroom; she heard him rummaging around for a minute, then he came back with clean gauze and tape. "Sleeve up," he ordered.

Brynna obeyed. She didn't want to, but at the same time, she did. It wasn't a good idea to have him so close. He was just a man, a human, and it wasn't safe. Maybe by modern human standards it wasn't much, but they had a history. That first touch, that kiss . . . no one knew better than Brynna how it could work on the psyche. Memory, desire, pheromones, hormones. They all played a part in how the universe went round. Birds and the bees. Demons and angels and humans.

Redmond's touch was gentle, surprisingly adept. He frowned as he tugged the medical tape free, glancing at her to see if it hurt. Brynna met his gaze then made herself look away; the old saying about eyes being the windows to the soul was truer than humans realized, and there was too much going on in his eyes. No matter how tempting, getting involved with a human, with *Redmond,* promised too many pitfalls for a fleeting bit of pleasure. She was supposed to be seeking redemption, not thinking about delights of the flesh, but that was getting damned hard with him sitting right next to her. Brynna could smell his aftershave, something human-made but woodsy and not too sweet. It shocked her how appealing the scent was, and how much of an impact this contact was having on her. Could he hear how her breathing had increased? No—he wouldn't notice. She had to hide it, to keep herself under control. Just a few more minutes and he would leave.

"It looks good," he said after he'd switched the existing bandage for a new one, then secured it. "I'm amazed, but I have to admit that you're right. It'll probably be gone by tomorrow." Brynna could see it wasn't necessary, but he reached over and rubbed at the tape to make sure it held.

"You shouldn't be touching me," she said.

Brynna had hoped that by saying it out loud, Redmond would instinctively take his hand off her. Instead, her words had the opposite effect—rather than let go, he slid his hand down and wrapped his fingers around hers. "Why not?"

She was going to say *Because it's not safe,* but she never had the chance.

IT WAS FIRE.

It was ice.

It was like nothing Redmond had ever experienced.

The bed was a twin with a lumpy mattress and faded, overwashed sheets that were scratchy and thin with age. He hadn't been on anything like it since his Army days at Fort Riley, when he'd shivered under coarse blankets in a drafty barracks and you could see your own breath in the morning. But that bed—about the same size and appearance—had never been like this one. This one was . . .

Endless.

He had the sensation of floating, or sinking, or falling off the end of the world. And yet the edge was never there to slip over, the wall was never there to offer a solid connection to the earth. Sheets that should have been rough and uncomfortable surrounded his limbs like ocean waters, warm and tropical and fluid, that seeped into everything and caressed him in all his most secret places. Brynna's hands followed the sensation, or maybe the sensation followed her hands—her touch was cold, then hot, then cold again, until Redmond couldn't tell which was which.

At forty, Redmond had been with his share of women, but Brynna was different. Her body was lean and supple, almost hard, but it *fit* him perfectly. None of his previous

partners had looked anything like her—he'd always preferred smaller, more rounded ladies—but now they all felt
lacking, in too many ways to recount. Everything about
Brynna somehow eclipsed them, wiping their faces and
existence from his mind until all that was left were long-
ago echoes in his memory.

He felt like he was suffocating with pleasure, like all
the air was disappearing from the room but oxygen itself
was too trivial to matter. Brynna always seemed to know
exactly what to do and how to do it, and if there was anything that could have been better about their joining, it
was that she talked the entire time. Not just murmurings
of endearment or the sometimes nonsensical cooing of
sex partners, but full, odd sentences, questions that she
demanded he answer—

"You're not offering me anything, right? You're not
giving me anything?"

—but in only a negative way, when in reality he would
have given her anything in his power.

"Not now, not ever. Right? Say it, Eran Redmond, say
that you're *not* giving me anything."

Over and over, insisting that he never, ever offer her
anything more tangible than this single, ecstasy-filled
night in her apartment.

She smelled of the *darkness,* rich and heavy, like a forbidden flower from some lost and impenetrable jungle.
Her kisses were sweet and spicy-hot, her teeth and nails
sharp enough across his flesh to sting but never drawing
blood. It was fantastic and tortuous at the same time, a
ride of sensuality that did not so much rise and fall as
skyrocket and plummet, a roller coaster of the body that

always seemed to teeter on the edge of simply stopping his heartbeat.

And the night itself felt like it stretched to infinity.

"I CAN'T GO HOME? Are you *serious*?"

Michael Klesowitch stared at the Holy Man, trying to fathom the bomb he'd just dropped on Michael's head. It didn't have nearly enough time to settle before the next one came down with all the gentleness of a sledgehammer.

"You can't go back to your job, either."

Klesowitch's mouth worked, but he couldn't get his brain to slow down enough to make a coherent sound come out. This wasn't what was supposed to happen—it wasn't *right*. He was supposed to be rewarded for doing God's work, not punished. No job, no place to go—

"It's only for a little while," the Holy Man said. His voice was soothing and gentle, but it didn't make Klesowitch feel any better.

"I don't want to be a martyr," Klesowitch blurted. "I didn't sign up for that. I just wanted to help."

"Sometimes there is a high price for doing what's right."

Klesowitch blinked at him. A high price? Had the Holy Man—Hank—really just said that? This wasn't a high price. This was *everything*.

"I don't believe you," Klesowitch said suddenly. He didn't know why he'd said that, he just had. He felt like a teenager, spewing words at his parents without thinking about them, without regard for the consequences.

Hank looked wounded. "Have I ever lied to you?"

Klesowitch didn't answer. He couldn't. If Hank *had* lied, how would he know?

Can't go home. Can't go to work. Can't go home.

It just kept repeating in his head, like the chorus of a hymn. Hank had intercepted him coming out of the grocery store, walking along to Klesowitch's car and watching as he put his two bags inside. These two bags—there was nothing else. Other than his car, his gun, and the clothes on his back, this was everything he owned in the world now. Klesowitch's eyes burned with tears. He would be a street person, a homeless man sleeping on park benches and eating from the garbage cans behind restaurants, huddling beneath cardboard boxes over the steam grates on Lower Wacker Drive in the dead of winter. How had all that had been his life up to now come to this? And this man, with his pristine hair and clothes by designers whose names Klesowitch couldn't even pronounce—what did he know of homelessness and street life? Of poverty? For that matter, what did Michael himself know about it?

"I will take care of you." The Holy Man's melodious voice cut into his chaotic thoughts. "You must finish the last task assigned to you and then I will send you someplace where you will have an entirely new existence."

"I can't!" Klesowitch cried. "She isn't like the others. There are people watching her, cops—"

"She is the hardest one because she is the one who most needs to be eliminated," Hank broke in. "But I, too, have helpers. I will keep you safe and then you will finish your task. Then everything will be all right."

"It will?"

"Yes. I promise. After this is done, you will have a new start. Haven't I guided you so far? Even today, I've kept you from walking right into a trap."

Michael swallowed and considered this. He'd always thought of himself as an analytical man, but there was so much conflicting information. If the girl—his target— was so evil, why was she being protected? And why had he ended up being hunted by the police?

"There is so much going on that normal people don't understand," the Holy Man said. Again, *always,* it was as if he could read Michael's mind. "It's only the special ones, the *chosen* ones like you, who have those like me to guide them to those who must be eliminated. It's for the greater good, Michael. *You* are one of the people who make that greater good possible."

Michael exhaled, willing himself to calm down and think, dammit, *think.* "What do I do in the meantime?" he finally asked. "Where do I go?"

"There's a restaurant on Irving Park called McNamara's," the Holy Man told him. "Up near the Kennedy Expressway. It's quiet during the day. Go there and wait for me."

Klesowitch rubbed his eyes. "I'm supposed to just sit in there for what? Hours? You think they won't notice?"

"Have a sandwich," Hank said. "Read the paper. Be resourceful, Michael. I'll come for you."

Michael bit back the protest that came to his lips and focused on his shoes instead. They were Nikes, a pair he'd seen advertised on television last year but which were way out of his price range. He'd hunted around and found them on eBay, then won a late-night auction and gotten them for a great price when the original ones were three times higher.

Be resourceful. He could do that, couldn't he? Just like he had with his Nikes. He was an intelligent man. He was *resourceful.*

He looked up again, but the Holy Man was gone. The summer sun bled enough heat onto Michael's forehead to make him feel faint, and he knew the car wasn't going to be much better. There were a couple of frozen dinners and some other stuff in his bags that ought to be kept cold, but there was no help for it. He thought briefly about taking them back in and asking for his money back, then decided that was stupid. What a way to draw attention to himself.

After a minute or two of indecision, he pulled out the perishable items, dropped them on the ground next to his car, and drove away.

Eighteen

Morning's light warmed the sheets hanging at the window and brightened up the tiny, dark apartment. Brynna had marked the passing of the night by listening to Redmond's heart, a steady pulse that slowed when he slept but had pounded to his own staccato rhythm at the height of their lovemaking.

Lovemaking.

Odd that *lovemaking* was the word that had slipped into her mind when she thought of what they had done last night. She was not immune to it—no one, human or celestial, was. God had created everything out of just that, and even the least of the creatures in existence experienced their own form of it. But for Brynna, love had been so long ago it was almost beyond memory, and with a being who had so closed himself off that the only thing left in his center was an abyss filled with malevolence. Love itself had become so far out of reach that Brynna had never thought herself capable of feeling such a thing again.

She had been with countless others, male and female, since her fall from Grace, but no one had touched her like Redmond. And *touched* was something that meant so much more than the physical. Even that part of it had been exquisite and rapturous and unique, like nothing she had ever experienced. How could that be? *She* should be the one giving that to him, not the other way around. Eran Redmond had gone past her detachment and distance to reawaken a part of herself that she'd thought was forever dead. He had made her *want,* both physically and emotionally. Now, like any creature rising from a too-long hibernation, she was wide-eyed and ravenous, aching for—

"Good morning."

Brynna turned her head and saw Redmond regarding her. His eyes were puffy with sleep and relaxation, and when he stretched, he reminded her of a well-fed wolf. Looking at him made her breathing quicken and she rolled out of bed and stood before anything else could happen. She knew from experience that it wasn't a good idea to have a repeat performance so soon—even the strongest of humans faltered when faced with a creature as addictive as Brynna. She had the feeling that in the future there would be many things she wanted for Eran, but addiction to her wasn't one of them.

"I need to get dressed," she said. One of the newest additions to the apartment was an old but working wall clock in the shape of a metal sunburst; a glance at it made her realize she'd made the very human mistake of staying in bed too long. "I have to be downtown before nine."

"I'll drive you." He threw aside the sheet and stood, and before she could move away, he pulled her into his arms. "Thank you," he said against the side of her neck. "I've never . . . had a night like that before."

Brynna slipped out of his embrace quickly. She didn't know what to say, so she settled for "You're welcome" and ducked into the bathroom.

"Hey," he said from the other side of the door when she deftly closed it before he could crowd in after her. "I have to ask you."

"What?"

"What happened to your belly button?"

Brynna had to laugh. Humans could be so *dense*. "Silly— I was made, not born.

"I never had one."

"Hi."

Mireva jerked around, then relaxed when she saw Gavino leaning against the door that led from the roof to the interior of the building. "Hey." She pulled her gaze from him and went back to studying her plants, but it took effort. There was something enticing about him that she couldn't identify. Sure, he was the best eye candy she'd ever seen outside of a television screen, but it went beyond that. She couldn't figure it out. Hormones? Maybe. At seventeen Mireva was still a virgin, even though she'd been on birth control pills since she was fifteen. Her mother had told her it was to keep her from suffering from monthly cramps, but Mireva knew better. She'd never known her father and, oddly, had never wanted to, but simple math made it easy to figure out her mother had hardly been older than Mireva was now when she had conceived. Hormones could be a disastrous thing, but screw that—Mireva wasn't about to let a chemical reaction in her body make her do something that would change her entire life, no matter how cute the guy was. She was too smart for that.

Gavino watched her for a few minutes before he spoke. "So, how's it going? All ready for your science fair?"

"I'm pretty up on it," she answered. She glanced at the sky involuntarily—she always seemed to do that when thinking about the effect of the heat on the plants. "Everything will be okay if the plants can stand the heat."

"Told you I'd water for you."

Mireva intentionally didn't look at him. She'd thought long and hard about Brynna's words and decided that even if Brynna was wrong, she couldn't take the chance. At least Brynna lived in the building; for all Mireva knew, Gavino lived on the other side of the city. "I've got it covered." This time she did glance at him. "How'd you get past the cops?"

Gavino shrugged. "I have my ways. Cops have never been able to keep up with me."

"Ah." She poked her fingertips around the bases of a few plants, checking the surface moisture of the soil and pulling out the ever-present contingent of tiny weeds. Did he think she would be impressed? Some girls might be, but Mireva's thoughts ran opposite to the pubescent norm. Why, she wondered, would the police *have* to keep up with him? And what had he done in the past to gain that kind of experience?

She straightened and stretched, working the stiffness out of her back. Yeah, the more she thought about it, the more she realized Brynna had given her a good warning. She wanted to believe that Gavino would never do anything to intentionally harm her, but then, what did she really know about him? Not much. Like Brynna had said, he talked a good game, but for Mireva the history just wasn't sliding into place. Unintentional was a nice sentiment, but it wouldn't regrow her plants if he screwed up. Mireva also knew she had a tendency to think the best of people where others, like her mother and uncle, were perpetually rooted in pessimism. Her optimism could bite her in the butt if she didn't keep a handle on it.

"So, are you done here? For the day, I mean."

She frowned. "What do you mean?"

Gavino shrugged again, and Mireva had to stop herself from saying something. She hated that movement because it conveyed everything she *didn't* believe in—carelessness most of all. He met her eyes, then stepped forward and squared his shoulders, almost as if he could read in her body language that she wasn't all that high on him. "I mean there's a Cubs game this afternoon. As in Wrigley Field, peanuts, hot dogs, and good old Chicago baseball." He held up one hand and wiggled a couple pieces of brightly laminated paper in her direction. "They usually start at one-twenty, but there's some kind of road work issue on Addison, so it's not going to begin until four o'clock. And I've got tickets."

Mireva stared at the tickets, not quite believing what she'd heard. Go to an actual Cubs game? She'd been a fan ever since she could remember—and she was pretty good on the softball field herself—but actually *going* to a game had never been a possibility. It was too far, it was too expensive; it was, frankly, something done by people who had a whole lot more money than she did.

"No, thanks. I . . . I can't." It was her voice, but it wasn't. It was, however, the voice of reality.

"Aw, come on. Why not?" Gavino pointed to the rows of lush green plants behind her. "Plants are watered for the day, right? And knowing you, you've probably already done your homework three times over, plus extra-credit stuff."

Well . . . yeah, she had. But that wasn't the only thing going on, and Mireva was a long way from forgetting the bullets that had whizzed at her yesterday, right on her own front doorstep. If it hadn't been for her backpack full of books taking the first two, she'd be dead right now instead of standing on this roof. On the other hand, how likely was it that the guy—assuming it had been a male—who'd shot at her yesterday was going to be waiting out front today? There was nothing surreptitious about her security force: two squad cars out front, one out back, uniformed cops both in and out of the building. And speaking of—

"How did you get up here, anyway?"

"It wasn't hard," he said. Mireva's eyes narrowed at the indifferent tone of his voice. He caught her expression and added quickly, "The cop was on his cell phone, talking to his girlfriend or something. I mean, despite all the excitement yesterday, I don't think they really believe that person is going to come back here. And with all the cops hanging around, he'd have to be crazy to show up, right?"

Mireva poked at her plants again, her mind spinning. Everything he said sounded so reasonable. Only a fool would come back here now—the cops had checked every car parked out front, hassled every person going in and out of the building, and basically followed her everywhere but into the bathroom. The only reason she'd been able to convince them it was okay to come up to the roof was because they believed the guy who'd shot at her wasn't inclined to go above sidewalk level.

She turned to face Gavino. "But what about going out? Maybe we could have one of the cops go with us."

Gavino shook his head. "Nah, they'd never go for that. You know how paranoid cops are. They think bad guys are going to jump out of every shadow." He gave her a handsome grin. "Think about it, Mireva. Wrigley Field holds over forty-one thousand people. Even if someone was still after you—which is doubtful—how the hell would he find you? You're much more of an easy target right here."

"Forty-one thousand?" Mireva echoed.

"Forty-one thousand, one hundred and eighteen, to be exact. As of 1998." When she raised an eyebrow, Gavino's grin widened and he gave her a conspiratorial look. "Us baseball people know stuff like that." He held up the tickets again. "Come on, what do you say? You can leave your mom a note or something."

Mireva considered the idea of a note, then rejected it. She knew exactly what would happen once her mother read it, and how embarrassing would it be for her mother to send the cops to the baseball park to find her? It wasn't such a stretch, considering biometrics and the number of video cameras that were popping up nowadays. She'd once heard a politician on television say that it was easier to beg for forgiveness than ask for permission. She'd never used that principle before, but maybe she could, just this one time. She wanted to act cool and unconcerned, but in spite of everything a small churning ball of excited butterflies seemed to be banging against the walls of her stomach.

"Okay," she heard herself say. "Let me get my Cubs cap, then we'll see if you're good enough to get us out of here without getting caught."

ERAN WASN'T WAITING FOR her when Brynna got off work, so she dug out her money and rode the bus like everyone else. By the eighth stop she had a seat by a window; that gave her plenty of time to watch the world go by and think about what had rolled through her mind when she'd walked out of the Dirksen Federal Building and realized she was on her own for transportation. That was no big deal, obviously, but the disappointment she'd felt that Eran wasn't waiting troubled her. Well, that didn't really cover it. It bugged the shit out of her—he was a human, she was a fallen angel. *And never the twain shall meet,* her mind supplied snidely, but that wasn't true, wasn't it? They'd met last night, all right, and that "meeting" had opened up a whole new set of dark and dangerous doors.

It occurred to Brynna that things were going a little too smoothly. Yes, Mireva had been shot at and Brynna had taken a bullet for her, but that was all on a human level; where Brynna came from, things could, and usually did, get much, *much* worse. She was, in fact, relaxing a little *too* much—when was the last time she'd seriously thought about Hunters? Sure, she found herself glancing around now and then, but she was paying a whole lot more attention to Eran and Mireva and her nearly daily commutes downtown for interpreter jobs, really getting caught up in the human world. The sudden realization of how completely careless she'd been almost made Brynna cringe.

Was it possible that Lucifer simply wasn't looking for her anymore, that he wasn't going to bother? Such an idea brought up strangely complex emotions, the biggest of which was the one most likely to be true: it was utterly absurd. Lucifer was greedy, lustful, and possessive. While there might have been a time when he had loved her, that era was long gone. Now, as far as he was concerned, he simply owned her. And he did not allow possessions to leave.

On the other hand, what if he truly no longer cared? Part of her would rejoice in her freedom—*if* she could confirm it—while another part of her felt stung by the notion that she might have given up everything for someone who ultimately didn't even care enough to try to bring her back. She didn't want to return, of course, and she would die rather than do so, but she had literally given up God's *Grace* to stay by Lucifer's side. Ultimately it wasn't that he held her in so little regard, but that she had made an error in judgment that was so monumental it could never be equaled by anyone, in Heaven *or* on Earth. How could she have been so completely senseless?

Before Brynna could berate herself further, the bus turned onto her street and she gathered up her purse and stood. The bus slowed and she glanced forward automatically, then stiffened. Her building was about half a block down, and through the windshield she could see three squad cars pulled to the curb in front of it. As the bus slowed to a stop and the doors hissed open, Brynna realized that Eran's car was also there, sandwiched between two of the CPD's Crown Victorias. This couldn't be good.

Someone must have told him she was coming, because by the time she made it to the building's door, Eran was waiting. "What's wrong?" she asked. "Where's Mireva? Is she all right?"

"That's the problem," Eran said. His face was grim and tight. "We don't know *where* she is. Somehow Officer Cutler there managed to lose her." Eran shot an angry look toward a round-faced cop with dark hair who was staring at his shoes while his sergeant spoke to him in low, rapid tones.

Brynna sucked in a breath. "How long ago?"

"No damned idea," Eran answered. "The last time that Eagle Eye can place her, she was headed up to the roof to water her plants after she got home from class. As near as he can recall, that was about two o'clock."

Over two hours ago. "She could be anywhere."

Eran ran one hand nervously over his hair. "I was hoping you might be able to help me look for her," he finally got out. "Take a look at her room, her stuff. You know, like you did with Cho Kim."

"Absolutely. Let's go." She was already moving toward the stairs.

In the apartment, Abrienda was pacing the small living room, her movements tight and efficient, like a highstrung lioness. Sathi was stationed by the window, his sharp dark eyes watching everything that happened on the street below; a young, uniformed officer stood by the front door, and it was clear from his stance that he just wanted to avoid the trouble that Cutler had gotten himself into.

"Ramiro is on his way," Abrienda said when she saw Brynna. She waited for the span of a double heartbeat, then asked, "Do you think she is already dead?"

Eran's eyes widened and he opened his mouth to answer, but Brynna beat him to it. "It depends on where she's gone, and with whom," she answered honestly. "She has a better chance if she's by herself than with Gavino."

Abrienda's face darkened. "Gavino—that boy I saw in the hallway."

"Yes."

Her seething gaze found Eran. "If you knew he was a bad person, that he would harm my Mireva, then why did you not arrest him?"

"He hadn't done anything wrong," Eran said. "And there's no proof that he has now, or that he's even with Mireva."

Abrienda turned to glare at Brynna. "But you—you knew, didn't you?"

Careful now, Brynna thought. This was Abrienda she was talking to, not Eran. "I had a bad feeling about him," she said. "That's why I made him leave the build—"

"Ms. Cocinero," Eran cut in, "may we take a look at Mireva's room? Maybe there's something in there that will help us figure out where she is."

Abrienda folded her arms. Her back was straight, her shoulders stiff. "Fine. Do whatever you need to. Just find her. *Alive.*"

They crossed the living room and Eran pushed open

the door to Mireva's room, then reached in and flipped the switch for the ceiling light as Brynna stepped in behind him. He stood to the side as Brynna took in everything about the tiny area. Shoved against the far wall was a single bed made with fading purple sheets; at the bottom was a thin, neatly folded quilt, handmade, while a couple of heavily worn stuffed animals were arranged with the pillow at the headboard. Brynna didn't know much about teens, but this seemed like it would be a typical teenage girl's room. Adorning the walls were heart- and flower-shaped construction paper cutouts with girlish handwriting interspersed with baseball novelties and photographs cut from magazines. She recognized the images of movie stars from those in the periodicals she'd seen while standing in the grocery checkout line.

Despite the closeness of the space—not much room for anything but the bed, a small chest of drawers, and a beat-up student's desk—it was a bright, cheerful environment. There was a lot of pink and purple and blue, and an undercurrent of life and expectation, especially in the carefully rendered scientific sketches of greenery that hung above the desk, in an area clearly dedicated to schoolwork. All the drawings were meticulously labeled and filled in with colored pencil, and when Brynna looked closer, she realized she was looking at the life cycle of a stalk of corn.

She stepped farther into the room, trailing her fingers across the end of the bed and inhaling deeply. She had caught Gavino's scent out in the hallway in front of the apartment, but it hadn't carried inside—Mireva had been well taught by her mother not to let strangers into the apartment. This room was saturated with Mireva's wonderful sea-spray smell, clean and fresh, and Brynna thought it was a shame only she could enjoy it. What would it be like to be a human teenager? To be a teenager, period? Brynna had not been born, she had been created—a fully grown angel, at one point not existing, at the next, an entity gifted with eternal life. There had been no childhood, no growing up, and it had never been something she'd wondered about until now. How wonderful it must be to face each new morning and know that it was filled with new knowledge and possibilities . . .

Damn it. Where *was* Mireva?

"So?" Eran asked from behind her.

"Nothing," she had to admit. "And Gavino wasn't even in here, if that's what you're wondering."

He glanced back over his shoulder, keeping his voice low. "Where would he have taken her?"

"I don't have any idea. What I know about the things that would tempt a female teenager is next to nothing. My specialty was always adults."

Eran gave her a sideways glance then went back to studying the room. There was a narrow door against the entry wall, and when he opened it, they saw a short row of neatly hung tops and blue jeans with a couple of disused dresses against the wall in the back. The closet was barely three feet wide. Mireva's pajamas—a much-washed pair of light cotton pants and an oversized T-shirt—were draped over a hook on the inside of the door. Brynna pulled the edge of the shirt out and fingered it, then let it drop.

"Wait a minute," Eran said. He reached past her and pulled on the shirt until he could see the design on the front, then pointed at the wall opposite the desk with his other hand. "Cubs. She's a Cubs fan."

Brynna tilted her head, not following. "What?"

"The baseball team," Eran explained. "Look around. There's a pennant on the wall, she sleeps in a Cubs T-shirt, she's even got her pens and pencils in a plastic Cubs cup. She's a huge fan." He glanced at his watch and his expression turned sour. "Take a young girl who does nothing but grind away at schoolwork and offer to take her to see her most favorite thing in the world—something she'd never be able to afford on her own—for free. How long do you think she could resist?"

Brynna thought about this as she looked around the room again, this time actually noticing all the things that Eran had pointed out. Yeah, there was definitely a theme going on here, and it had the red, white, and blue Cubs logo all over it. "Good point, but where would—"

"There's a game today." Eran glanced at his watch. "I heard on the radio that it's starting late, but it's going full swing by now."

"All right, then," Brynna said. "Let's go . . . where?"

"Wrigley Field." Eran led the way out of Mireva's room. Abrienda looked at them both with a hopeful expression, but Eran only shook his head; Brynna understood that he didn't want to give the woman any false hope. It wasn't until they were clear of the apartment that they both picked up their pace and hurried to his car. When the car was moving, Brynna finally voiced the words rolling around in her mind. "You *do* know I can find her, and it doesn't matter how many people are there, right?"

Eran stared straight ahead, his concentration focused on the Friday afternoon traffic as he tried to weave around the cars. He'd flipped on the police lights but most of the drivers were staunchly ignoring them. Every now and then he hit the siren when his patience got too thin. Brynna wasn't surprised at his words when he finally answered her.

"If you say so. I guess, then, that the bigger question is—

"Can you find her in time?"

Nineteen

Klesowitch fingered the ticket stub the Holy Man had given him yesterday evening and felt his cheeks flush. Thank God he was alone now—well, as alone as one man could be in the midst of literally thousands of people— and didn't have to talk to anyone. He wished he could turn back the clock and redo the previous evening, change the memory of himself acting like a grateful little puppy when the Holy Man had finally walked into McNamara's at nine-thirty.

Michael had been sitting there for almost four hours, and the more time that passed, the more certain he'd become that the Holy Man had abandoned him, had found him unworthy and simply . . . gone away and left him to fend for himself. And Michael, of course, had no idea how to do that. His life had always been well ordered and predictable, conservative and calm. With all that obliterated, if the Holy Man didn't show up, Michael thought he might as well go outside, walk up the ramp to the Kennedy Expressway, and lie down in front of the next eighteen-wheeler coming in his direction.

He looked down at the ticket in his hand again, then gave himself a mental whack. Right now was what counted, and last night was over, gone, *adiós, amigo*. He might as well move on, and if he couldn't exactly pretend it had never happened, he could at least justify it, just get on with his task and blame his behavior on the terror and isolation he'd felt. He had things yet to do in his life, *big* things. The Holy Man had promised him that God wasn't through with him yet. He might not understand why this teenager had to die, but someday he would. That's what faith was all about—believing in something you couldn't see, knowing that it was right. Michael was living proof that a man didn't have to be a martyr to have faith.

He'd been to Wrigley Field countless times as a kid but that was years ago, and this was his first visit in too long to remember. He had a dim recollection of turnstiles and lots of impatient people at the entrances, but now the entrance was all modern glass and shine, renovated with a big Bud Light sign over it. The lines moved quickly, helped along by electronic scanning, and it took less than fifteen minutes for him to get inside the park and head to where the Holy Man had told him to wait.

But when he got there and positioned himself, he didn't think his spot halfway behind a support column and the door to a janitor's closet was much of a vantage point. It sure didn't give him much protection— was there even anywhere he could run? The park was heavy in security employees, and a gunshot in the midst of all these people might as well be a fire alarm. Michael swallowed, trying to fight off another circuit of doubts.

There were so *many* people, so much noise, so much confusion and movement. This girl was one person out of tens of thousands in Wrigley Field this afternoon, one face among the multitudes. How was he supposed to find her?

Still, the Holy Man had said that a contact would bring the girl to the game and make sure she was where Michael could get off a shot. That was all fine and good, but if there was another person involved, why couldn't *that* guy do the dirty deed? Why did it have to be Michael?

The baseball game was just beginning, and right now all he wanted in the world was to ditch the damned Type 64 digging into the waistband of his jeans beneath his supersized Cubs jersey, then grab a hot dog and an extra large Coke. Then he wanted to find himself a seat in the bleachers and watch the Cubs play—and hopefully beat— St. Louis.

But . . . no. He couldn't do that. This was just a baseball game, an afternoon that would be no more than a fading memory in a few hours. He hadn't given up his job and his apartment, his *life,* to surrender to fear and temptation now, not after all this time and effort. And not after the Holy Man's words last night, after he had answered every single one of Michael's hard questions—

"The things that this girl does, Michael, her place in the web of life, will someday affect hundreds of thousands of people. It's up to you to prevent that."

His duty, his responsibility—that was what was important. Everything else was trivial, material . . . fleeting. And besides, the Holy Man had sworn to make it all right in the end, to get Michael a fresh start in another city, somewhere far away, warm and safe, and where no one would ever ask him to do God's work again.

Michael Klesowitch set his jaw and waited.

FORTY MINUTES LATER, ERAN pulled into a no-parking zone on Clark Street. When they got out, he stood for a moment, glaring at the entrance as if he could will Mireva and Gavino to suddenly walk out of it.

Brynna touched his arm. "You need to think positive," she said. "Believing that there's no hope ruins everything. It saps the spirit and undermines all your efforts."

"Right," he said. "Just call me Norman Vincent Peale."

For a change Brynna knew who he was talking about, but she didn't bother to comment. Instead, she followed Eran as he went in, only half listening to his short conversation with one of the security guys posted at the front. Even though the game had already started, there were people everywhere on the main floor. The lines to the hot dog and beer vendors were long and restless, and Brynna could feel impatience surge and wane every time a cheer reverberated through the park. The hot, humid air swirling around them was saturated with the scents of frying beef, boiled pork, popcorn, beer, and the sweat and breath of a stadium filled to capacity with overheated fans.

Eran shot her a sardonic look. "Still insist you can find her?"

Brynna tilted her head to one side and regarded the long, crowded aisle that curved in front of them. The food vendors were on her left and lines wound out from each one like colorful snakes. "Yeah," she said. "I do."

His eyebrows raised. "Lead the way, then."

As she began working her way forward, Brynna didn't bother to point out that there was a reason no one could simply hide from their fate in Hell—souls were designed to be tracked, by both light and dark entities. How many of those here would eventually end up there? A lot, probably. Every step she took brought hungry gazes from men and women who turned to watch her, especially if she couldn't avoid brushing against someone as she passed. A few even tried to follow, backing off only when Eran snarled something under his breath. This was the last place she ought to be—the park was permeated with pheromones, overrun by the rough and tumble kind of men who, because they were prone to fanaticism, had always been the easiest of her prey. But while those days may have been over for her mentally, Brynna's physical manifestation still sent out signals advertising exactly the opposite. So much noise and humanity, so many—

But only one Mireva.

Like fingerprints or retinas, no two souls were exactly alike. Each soul had its own scent, its own track in the universe. Unique, eternal, and impossible to duplicate or counterfeit, the tracks of even those condemned to Hell were never destroyed. They burned, they were torn apart and obliterated, but they would always eventually re-form, if only to suffer the same or different agonies all over again. Mireva's soul was the same as any other human's, and yet it wasn't—the nephilim side of her made her essence stronger, brighter, and much, much *sweeter*. The scent of her, that always fresh sea-spray fragrance, could never be fully muted by the press of a human population. It wasn't easy to find it in such a mass of humanity, but it wasn't impossible either; as she had done occasionally during her uncountable years in Lucifer's Kingdom, Brynna breathed deeply and centered herself on her goal, peeling aside the remnants of everyone else like the skin of an overly strong onion as her own senses filtered through everything around her—

There.

Catching a trace of Mireva's soul was almost like following a line of invisible spider silk, one that broke now and then but always started back up. Brynna thought that if it had been visible, that infinitesimal string would be blue, the bright color of a clear winter sky on one of God's beautiful mornings. The scent floated gracefully through the crush of people like a butterfly, moving as she had moved to sidestep a group or go around a line. At one point a trip to the women's restroom nearly obliterated the scent, but it returned, steady and strong, a few feet beyond the door.

"Anything?" Eran asked. "It's got to be impossible with all these people." Brynna started to answer, then paused and scowled. "What?" Redmond pressed. "What is it?"

"Gavino," she said under her breath. "And the killer—they're both here."

"Shit." Eran look around almost wildly. "Where? I don't see—"

"Not *here* here," Brynna interrupted. "But here in the *park* somewhere."

Eran dug out his cell phone. "I'll get backup and shut the place down."

"She'll be dead by then," Brynna said flatly. She grabbed his arm and pulled him along before he could flip open the phone, heading to where the people-clogged corridor turned north. "Come on. We don't have time to waste on phone calls. I don't think they're far."

Eran followed and struggled to hang on to his phone, then gave up and shoved it in a pocket. "Please tell me they're not together."

Brynna lifted her head, testing the air. "No, not yet. But soon . . . if we don't stop them."

"I bet they've got this coordinated," Eran said. "That Lahash guy and Gavino. One of them is giving the orders—"

"That would definitely be Lahash."

"—and the other, Gavino then, is following. Kleso-witch is just doing what he's told."

It was a shame, Brynna thought as they dodged through the knots of people, that the young man hadn't followed his instincts instead, that sixth sense that humans so often talked to each other about but still insisted on ignoring. It had been there, she was sure of it, dragging at Kleso-witch's conscience with an inkling that something wasn't right, that no matter what kind of party tricks Lahash—or whatever he was having humans call him lately—could do, sending him to kill a fellow human being was just too far off the scale of wrong. Yes, sins were always forgiven. But the priceless question was how long, in terms of time and pain, was the road back to God's Grace? Sometimes it could be traveled simply by sincere regret, but most of the time absolution came at a price that was measured in eons and agony. Time was twisted in Hell, and an hour could equal a thousand years. If you were lucky.

Brynna ought to know.

"Damn it," Eran complained. "I wish there was a way we could at least figure out what section she's in. We—"

"There," Brynna said suddenly. When Eran would have plunged ahead, she threw out one arm and stopped him short. "They're coming down the steps. Careful—don't let them see you. Gavino's right next to her. Lahash's been trying to kill Mireva for awhile now, and there's no telling what he'll do if he realizes we've found them."

"I thought you said he couldn't hurt her himself. And Gavino—he's the same, right?" Still, Eran backed up to where Brynna had edged around the corner of a cart selling baseball caps in the middle of the wide passageway.

"He can't, but there's still Klesowitch to think about. He's somewhere around here, too."

Eran scanned the crowd, but there were too many people moving at once. "You know that for a fact?"

"Definitely."

"Well, we have to do *something*," Eran said impatiently. His right hand was inching up and under the edge of his T-shirt, angling toward his gun. "I'm not a sit-back-and-watch kind of guy."

"Wait," Brynna said. "What's going on?" She leaned around the corner of the vendor's cart, trying to see. A small commotion suddenly broke out on the staircase, with—wouldn't you know it?—Gavino and Mireva at its center. "I think Gavino's trying to make Mireva do something."

Eran squeezed past her, trying to see around the people clustered in the way. In another moment Mireva's clear voice rose above the growing murmurs of the crowd.

"No, I'm not going down there. Let go of me!"

Before Brynna could remind Eran to stay put, he was

around her and headed toward the stairs, moving on training and instinct. But even that wasn't much help—the noise swelled as something happened on the field and an announcer's excited voice boomed over the speakers by the ceiling. If Gavino said anything in return, it was as lost in the noise as Eran's shouts were as he tried to push his way to the stairs. Brynna cursed under her breath and followed, but there were too many damned people in the way to stop him before he got to the bottom of the stairs. "Eran—wait!"

Too late; the detective in him had gone into full operational mode and he was already drawing his gun. In the time it had taken Eran to move forward through the fans, Gavino had managed to get Mireva almost to the bottom of the stairs. Now she was outright fighting him; he had one hand wrapped around her arm and was trying to steer her around the railing toward a shadowed alcove behind it. A couple of feet away, some guy who had probably tried to help Mireva lay crumpled and groaning against one of the steel posts. There were a couple of other men inching warily toward Gavino, but they backed up when Eran yelled, "Police—stop right there!"

Gavino's face whipped in their direction and his expression contorted into one of loathing. Brynna knew Eran's gun was useless. He would never fire into this many people, but she couldn't let him get near Gavino—the demon-in-hiding was forbidden to personally hurt Mireva, but he had no such constraints for non-nephilim. If Eran got within his reach and tried to stop him, Gavino would kill him without hesitating.

Brynna finally shoved the last knot of gawkers out of the way, then surged past Eran.

"Brynna, get back!"

"I'll take care of him," she snapped. "Get Mireva—"

A *crack* split the air, and for a moment Brynna froze. Then someone behind her shrieked, *"Look out, he's got a gun!"* but the words were lost to anyone else as a roar went up from the stands and the announcer's voice blared over the speakers again. Brynna grabbed Eran and yanked him closer so he could hear her. "Klesowitch is here!" she screamed in his ear. "He's under the stairs!"

He pulled away from her and went to the right, leaving Brynna to deal with Gavino. At the bottom of the stairs, Mireva balled up her fist and whacked Gavino on one side of his head. It didn't hurt him but it was enough to pull his gaze off Brynna, who grabbed the chance to leap the last few feet and jam Gavino bodily against the steel handrail. He still didn't release Mireva, instead hauling her with him and pinning her behind his back. She fought and clawed at him, but it did no good at all.

"Hey, Astarte," Gavino panted. He slammed Mireva back against the railing again, hard enough to knock the wind out of her but not enough to actually cause the girl any pain. "How's it hanging?"

"Let go of her, you moldy piece of demon shit," Brynna snarled. "Or I'll rip your arm right out of its socket."

Gavino's grin was wide, impossibly wide for a human, and Brynna saw his teeth shift and sharpen inside the darkness of his mouth. His gaze flicked from left to right, and Brynna knew he was looking for Klesowitch while he tried to keep Mireva still enough for a killing shot. He let out a high-pitched, obnoxious giggle. "Sticks and stones, baby—sticks and stones!"

"Oh, I'm much more effective than that," Brynna said. Before he could react, she sank the fingers of one hand deep into the muscle of his shoulder, pushing in and in and in until the skin split beneath her fingernails and she dug into meat. He cried out and the grip he had on Mireva released.

The teenager didn't need an invitation to yank herself out of his range. "You jerk!" she yelled at him. Tears streaked her flushed face. "I trusted you!"

"Your bad," Gavino ground out, then backhanded Brynna hard enough to knock her off her feet. She was up and in front of Mireva instantly, but Gavino had finally given up on the nephilim girl. Instead, he crouched and faced off with Brynna as the people around them scrambled to get out of the way. With an evil smile, he ran his fingers over the blood leaking out of the wound on his shoulder, then brought his hand to his mouth and licked the fingertips. "Mmmmm, yummy." His eyes glowed. The noise grew as the fans outside went crazy over something exciting that was happening on the field; anything the people around Brynna and Gavino tried to say was drowned out, but Brynna heard Gavino's next words very, very clearly.

"Bring it, hell bitch. It's long past time for you to die."

REDMOND WANTED TO STAY with Brynna and take care of that little Goth bastard, but he couldn't. Despite the noise level—the screams of the fans and the shouts of those who were focusing on the mess created by Gavino—he recognized the sound of a second gunshot when it came, even though it could have been mistaken for the snap of a bat against a fastball. A millisecond later a man bellowed in surprise and pain as a bullet blistered a path across the side of his head. The injured guy reeled sideways and Eran scrambled around the right side of the staircase, pulling his pistol free. "Klesowitch, freeze! You're under arrest!"

At the sound of his name, Michael Klesowitch spun wildly, his oversized pistol waving in front of him. Half a dozen people dove for cover, pulling their friends with them as their shouts blended with the rest of the ballpark noise. Klesowitch lurched forward a couple of steps, then took off in earnest, twisting through the masses with the gun held in front of him like a sword.

"Son of a bitch!" Redmond ran after him, struggling to keep the guy in sight. It would be too easy to lose him— there were staircases going up the stands, restrooms, exits, dozens of ways for him to swerve away. With his teeth grinding every time the young man slipped out of his sight for a moment, Redmond could only hope that Klesowitch would try to duck out one of the exits. That would be the best end to this bad situation, to get the killer out of the park where he could try to bring him down without hurting anyone else.

No such luck.

Instead of veering right and out of the park, Klesowitch did a three-sixty and headed up one of the ramps leading to the seating sections. Twenty feet and one turn behind him, Redmond lunged between the posts at the edge, reaching through the space in the railing and trying to grab Klesowitch's ankles as he passed. No good—his path had shifted him to the far side of the ramp and out of Redmond's range, and all Redmond got for the effort was concrete-bruised ribs. Redmond chased after him, screaming *"Get out of the way! Get out of the way!"* every ten or fifteen feet in an effort to clear the ramp in front of him and close the distance.

If Klesowitch was trying to get lost in the crowd, he'd chosen badly. Most of the game-goers' attention was riveted on the playing field, where the Cubs were up and had managed to put two players on base with only one out. Despite Redmond's yelling, nobody was looking at the two men running up the ramp, and even the drawn guns didn't seem to impress anyone until after the fact—

"Hey, I think that guy had a gun."

"What? I didn't see anything. Watch the game—you're gonna miss something."

Klesowitch bounded off the ramp and swung around, scrambling across the bottom row of the bleachers, wading over the legs and feet of the people seated there like they were nothing but rocks to be stomped on. Eran had no choice but to follow, still yelling for the killer to stop but knowing he wouldn't and that he was stuck chasing Klesowitch until he either got away or turned and decided to fire at Redmond himself. Klesowitch surrendering was, of course, a possibility, but Redmond thought that was as far-fetched as an alien ship landing on the pitcher's mound in the next five minutes.

The protest from the people in the seats was immediate and heated.

"Dude, what the fuck—"

"Hey, watch where you're stepping!"

"What is your problem?"

And in a place like this, it wasn't long before someone with an unforgiving nature weighed in when Klesowitch tried to shove him aside.

"I'll break your face, you little shit!"

Redmond saw the man, a burly guy in a Rich Harden T-shirt, try to grab Klesowitch, who flailed wildly at him with his empty hand and tried to keep going. The fan's face went red with anger and he managed to catch hold of a handful of the killer's shirt. Redmond saw Klesowitch turn and imagined disaster in an instant—a bullet blowing out Mr. Tantrum's head—and then all hell really *would* break loose.

"Police!" Redmond didn't think he'd ever screamed as loudly in his life. *"Let him go right NOW!"*

The man obeyed without thinking, reflex saving his ass as Klesowitch lurched away. Redmond followed only a few seconds later, ignoring other people who were starting to pick up on the incident and giving the big guy a hard push back onto his seat as he passed. "Sit the fuck down and *stay* there," Redmond snarled, just in case visions of *I wanna be a hero* started zinging through the Harden fan's mind.

Klesowitch had made it all the way to the steps at the far side of the section then barreled downward, ramming his way through the people and sending drinks and food flying in every direction. Curses flew after him as people saw the commotion coming and tried futilely to get out of his way. Redmond was at a disadvantage, losing ground because every spot that Klesowitch opened up closed behind him as people stood or leaned out of their seats to stare after him. Klesowitch almost fell down the steps to the lower bleacher seats, then found there was no way to go but back to the right. Redmond anticipated the move and leaped over the railing, but he was a fraction of a second too late; he hit hard enough to make his teeth snap, and by the time he got back to his feet, Klesowitch was headed down again, running as fast as he could.

This time the narrow steps were fairly clear, with most folks staying in their seats and intent on watching the game. Redmond closed the distance fast and almost had him when Klesowitch actually *leaped* over the railing. He grabbed at the top of the retaining fence that angled out of the wall below the railing, then clawed his way toward the edge with his gun still in one hand.

Disbelief made Redmond thunk hard into the railing at gut height instead of jumping over it. "Klesowitch, you are under *arrest*—stop, damn it!" But he might as well have been shouting at a wall, and there was no time to do anything but thrust his pistol back into its holster and go for it himself.

Redmond's landing on the retaining fence didn't have the forward momentum that Klesowitch's had, and instead of being able to grab the killer, the detective landed on the green chain-links and slid downward, nearly wedging his feet between the fencing and the wall. The metal scraped Redmond's face and hands before he could hook his fingers into it and haul himself up. He moved as fast as he could, but it was still no good. The three feet separating them was as wide as a chasm, and even as Redmond strained to reach him, Klesowitch hauled himself over and swung into the heavy mass of vines covering the wall below.

Redmond didn't hesitate. The twelve-foot or so drop

almost put him on top of the stunned Klesowitch, and Redmond gasped when the ground rammed into him. Klesowitch rolled away and clawed his way out of the greenery, but when Redmond pulled up and tried to follow, hot pain shimmied out of his ankle and into his shin. "Son of a bitch!" he swore, and crawled out of the vines instead. Another two feet and he was up and lurching across the field like a dancer with a broken heel, but he'd be damned if he was going to give up.

"Klesowitch, this is your final chance. Stop or I'll *shoot*!"

He was only about twenty feet away. With desperation etched into his features, Klesowitch spun and tried to run backward. His gun wavered crazily in front of him as he tried to track Redmond's progress.

"Klesowitch—Mike—don't! Drop the gun before anyone else gets hurt. I'm *not* gonna ask you again."

"You're not supposed to be here," Klesowitch suddenly screamed at him. "The Holy Man told me it was all right! He told me he would take care of everything. Go *away*!"

Holy Man? That was an angle Redmond didn't have time to explore right now. "I can't do that—"

"Then have it your way!"

It all happened so fast but at the same time so slowly. Klesowitch stopped, finally, but instead of dropping his weapon he raised it and pointed it at Redmond. Something in Redmond's mind registered the motion of the man's arm as it rose and acknowledged the thousands of people sitting behind him. Klesowitch's bullet might hit him, or it might go into the vine-covered wall at his back, or it might go into the stands; then someone, a man who had a family at home, or a teenager who'd come to the game with her boyfriend, or a kid who'd come to the game with his dad, would go on record as being the ninth death at the hands of Michael Klesowitch. Almost all of the ball field was clear behind the younger man, the sight of two men with guns spilling onto the field from the bleachers sending the ballplayers sprinting for the dugouts.

Before the killer could steady his aim, Redmond pulled out his Glock and shot Michael Klesowitch in the forehead.

BRYNNA CAREFULLY BACKED AWAY from Gavino, acutely aware of all the people staring at them. There were going to be repercussions for this, but not for Gavino. She still wanted to dwell among the humans, find her redemption and forgiveness; Gavino, on the other hand, didn't give a shit who saw what—he didn't live in this world, he didn't like this world, and he knew he was on his way out, one way or another. The little bastard would love to cause as much chaos and pain as possible before he left, and that, of course, meant he'd relish taking a few (or a dozen) unprepared humans with him. Already she could see a couple of guys edging up behind the demon, thinking they'd make points by rescuing her. "Get back," she snapped at them before they could get within Gavino's range.

Gavino whirled and smirked, dancing toward them with his long-nailed fingers flexing like talons in a *Come 'ere, little human, come to Papa!* gesture. Startled by her order and Gavino's utter lack of fear, they stumbled backward, expressions confused. "So sad," Gavino pouted. "You'd spoil my fun—hey, where're you going?" he asked when he turned back and saw Brynna slipping away. "Please, please,

please—stay out here." He swept his arm at the wide area in front of the stairs that had cleared of people. "There's so much opportunity for audience participation."

"You've been watching too much television," Brynna said. She kept her voice low enough so that Gavino had to keep following her to hear. "You always were stupid and overly impressionable."

"Ooooh," he responded merrily. "How your sarcasm burns—it burns!"

She slid farther back, aiming for an alcove below the stairwell. It was filled with garbage cans and half-crushed boxes from the food vendors, rife with the smell of garbage, a fitting place for Gavino to end his stay in this world. "Lahash must have laughed when he saw how easily you became his little lackey," she told him. "How available you are to take the heat for him so that he doesn't get any dirt under his immaculate fingernails."

Gavino shrugged, trailing after her obligingly but still staying out of her range. Yeah, he was ready to see this to the end—she could see the eagerness in his eyes. "You're a little off on that one," he told her. "We worked this out together, the old two-heads-are-better-than-one." His smile was gaping and moist. "Lucifer's been pretty pleased with the results so far."

"I'll bet," Brynna said.

"And we have big plans for the future."

"You don't have a future."

"Wishful thinking, Astarte." He tilted his head and for a moment he looked bewildered. "What are you doing here, anyway? This is the wrong side of the tracks for you. Why don't you come back where you belong?"

Brynna shook her head. "No, I don't belong in Hell anymore. I—"

"Well, you sure don't belong *here*," Gavino interrupted. "Lucifer misses you, you know. And he *will* find you. Things'll go so much easier if you go to him first. He's always had a soft spot for you—he'll give you another chance."

Brynna didn't hesitate. "That's not the forgiveness I'm looking for," she said.

The demon's eyes widened, then he brayed with laughter. "You've got to be kidding me! You think *God* is going to forgive you? After the things you've *done*?" Gavino laughed harder, nearly gasping for air. "Falling from Grace was just a start, remember? You went on to do much grander things. Do I have to compile a list? Got a hundred years to *read* it?"

"God will forgive anything," Brynna said stubbornly. "Eventually."

"Sheee-yit." Gavino leaned forward and spat on the ground in front of Brynna. She backed up another few steps, willing him to follow, pleased when he did. His saliva sizzled for a few seconds on the concrete before drying up and disappearing. "What happened to you?"

"I got tired of dealing with fucktards like you," she retorted, then leaped on top of him.

They went down in a snarling mound of vicious punches. All the concerns Brynna had regarding her surroundings and the bystanders flew out of her mind as Gavino tore into her with everything he had, including his teeth. She should have expected that—in Hell he'd been little more than a scavenger with pointy teeth and a voracious appetite—but somehow she hadn't thought he would bring that nature to the forefront in a fight with a fellow demon. It was a substantial and painful underestimation of her foe, and Brynna paid dearly for her foolishness. The first thing she went for was Gavino's neck, but her attempt to grab him below the jaw and quickly snap his neck was too predictable; Gavino lowered his chin, then ripped into the meat of her upper arm like a ravenous wolf.

Brynna howled and tried to pull away, but Gavino's teeth had elongated and he was *chewing* on her, shaking and grinding and going for the bone. He was swiping wildly with the other hand, slashing at any part of her that he could reach. She had to do something or the agony in her arm was going to make her pass out. She was straddling him but that didn't mean she had the upper hand, so she gave up and threw herself backward, hauling Gavino with her. He followed her momentum but still held on, growling and cackling like a hyena, sucking madly on the blood gushing out of Brynna's growing wound as he was pulled into a position over her.

"You're *so* gonna pay for this," Brynna gasped, then buried her fingers in the long hair at the nape of Gavino's neck and kept rolling forward. As their bodies started to upend again, she dug her nails through the thin layer of flesh at the base of his skull and threw herself sideways at the same time she relaxed her injured arm and let Gavino jerk it backward.

There was a sickening, wet *rip*, then Gavino's devastating bite on her arm let go. His delighted munching sounds turned into an astonished scream as Brynna yanked the skin of his skull forward and over his face in a brutal take on scalping. Her arm was a mangled nightmare, but it was nothing compared to Gavino, who was wheeling in circles and trying to claw at the blinding, bloody covering of his inside-out skin. Blood sprayed in every direction and he was screaming something at her, but the words were incoherent and muffled. She wasn't interested in hearing them anyway.

"Well," Brynna croaked, "at least you look more like you did in Hell."

Gavino wheeled toward the sound of her voice, half of the skin shredded from his attempts to clear his vision. Another couple of seconds and he'd be able to see, and the battle would begin all over again.

"We can't have that," Brynna muttered, and brought the edge of her good hand down across the bridge of the demon's nose. Gavino bellowed as the bone shattered, but anything he might have done to retaliate was lost when she pulled back again, then rammed the heel of her hand against the center of his face as hard and fast as she could.

The demon pulled in air sharply as his head rocked back and the splinters of his broken nose were driven deep into the brain of his very human form. Then he dropped to the floor, dead.

There was no time to savor her victory. With Gavino out of the way, Brynna's attention once again shifted to her surroundings, and she could hear the murmurings of people trying to work up the courage to come around to the back of the staircase. She had to get rid of Gavino's body, and she had maybe ten seconds—if she was lucky—to do it.

Ignoring the horrendous pain in her left arm, she leaned forward and dragged the dead demon's form under the stairs, then shoved him in as deeply as she could behind the metal trash cans. A quick glance behind her confirmed that the area was still clear, but it wasn't going to stay that way for long. This dirty little task was going to be tight, and hot, and bright, but she didn't have any other option.

Brynna closed her eyes briefly, and when she opened them again, her irises were filled with the scarlet brilliance of hellfire. She held it in only long enough for a final confirmation that no one had come around the edge of the staircase . . .

Then let it surge outward and fill the space in front of her with dark fire.

REDMOND FOUND BRYNNA AND Mireva standing together at the bottom of the same staircase where the confrontation with Gavino and Klesowitch had first started. They were surrounded by Chicago cops, ballpark security officers, and a good-sized crowd of people who were forgoing the thrill of the baseball game for the much more interesting saga of Brynna.

Mireva was almost hiding behind Brynna. Brynna herself was covered in dirt and had one arm seeping blood from beneath a ragged tear in her T-shirt. Her face was set with exaggerated patience, and from the irritated tones of the cops, Redmond could tell things weren't going that well. As he got closer, he realized what he'd taken for dirt was probably soot; he'd been down that road before, so any questions about what had happened to Gavino were already answered. Still, the guy had definitely gotten his strokes in before she'd taken him out.

"Detective Redmond," he said, bringing out his star

before any of the uniforms could give him a hard time.
He'd left Klesowitch's sheet-covered body on the field
surrounded by cops and park officials who were waiting for the coroner and hoping to get this nasty business
taken care of quickly so they could resume the game.
Other than the blood, Brynna looked fine, but he was
bone tired and didn't feel like dealing with crap right now.
In reality, there was probably a lot of it to come. "Brynna,
what happened?"

"He got away," she said. A lie, of course, but there
wasn't much chance of her admitting to anyone that she'd
incinerated the guy, and oh by the way, he was an evil
demon and so it didn't really matter.

"Bull*shit*," said a man who was standing off to the side.
"I'm telling you, I *saw* that dude go under the staircase
with her. Ain't no way he could've gone anywhere."

"Ma'am?" asked one of the cops.

Brynna did her best to look innocent, but the expression didn't fit well on her face. "He hit me or something.
I really didn't see—I must've blacked out."

"What happened to your arm?" asked a female officer.

Brynna hesitated. "He . . . bit me."

The woman's eyebrows raised. "That's not good.
Human bites are the worst for infections. We'll have to
get you to a hospital right away."

"I'll take her," Redmond said, stepping into the circle.
He was pretty sure that Brynna wouldn't come back with
It's not a human bite, but he needed to cap this just to be sure.

The first cop scowled. "You two know each other?"

"She's with me," Redmond said. "Part of an ongoing
investigation."

"Something to do with the shooting out on the field?"

"Could be." Redmond glanced at Brynna and Mireva. The faster he got them out of here, the fewer questions he'd have to deal with later. News crews were on their way, and he damned sure didn't want Mireva's face splashed all over the papers and television. "Come on, you two. We have a lot of paperwork to do back at the station."

"We need to write an incident report on this," said one of the park security guys.

"What's to report?" Redmond waved his hand at Brynna. "There was a fight but the other guy is gone. There was no property damage. I'll note it as part of my investigation paperwork, spare you the trouble."

The guy looked doubtful. "Well . . ."

"If you really have to write it up, call me at this number." Redmond pulled a card out of his wallet. "But right now we have to focus on something else." The guy took the business card, but they both knew he'd never call. After all, if he let Redmond cover it, there'd be less work on his end. The guy who'd nearly gotten his head taken off by Klesowitch's shot would go down on Redmond's paperwork.

"Be sure to get that wound taken care of," the female officer said. "End up with blood poisoning. I've seen it happen." The look she sent Brynna was uneasy. "Never seen a human bite this bad, though. Procedure says I really ought to call you an ambulance."

"I hate those things," Brynna said. "It's all good, I swear."

And with that, Redmond led Brynna and Mireva out of the park and out of the spotlight.

Twenty

The week that followed educated Brynna on just how public the human race could now be.

Newspapers, televisions, the Internet—they all combined to make Eran Redmond an overnight superstar. She'd really had no concept of the speedy beast into which human communication had evolved. Although she'd seen computers everywhere, from the police station where Eran worked to the offices she visited as a translator to the stores in which she infrequently shopped, it really hadn't registered just how quickly someone's—namely Eran's—privacy could be destroyed.

And while she reluctantly admitted to herself that she *wanted* to spend time with him, now she didn't dare. There had been television crews at Wrigley Field, but since they were focusing on Detective Redmond and the dead Michael Klesowitch, she'd managed to avoid them. But now every time he turned around, some journalist was asking him questions, a photographer was snapping a photo, or a popular radio DJ or local television personality wanted an interview. When he resisted, people higher up on the police force insisted he cooperate to make the CPD look good, put it out there just how much effort had gone into the hunt for the serial killer. When Brynna pointed out that all that effort had come to fruition because of only two men, Eran and his partner, Eran had waved her off and said it didn't matter. From her perspective, she thought it was pretty hypocritical of whoever those higher-ups were.

To add to the annoyance level, it hadn't taken long for a sharp-eyed reporter to go over the police calls and reports connected with Eran, and from there tie Klesowitch to Mireva. That made publicity spill onto the teenager, which set the newshounds—exactly the kind of people Brynna wanted most to avoid—hanging around the apartment building at every turn. Part of her wanted to just take off and start over somewhere else, try a new city with a new path. The stubborn part of her rebelled instantly: she had set something up here, and if she wasn't exactly human, there was a humanly *feel* about it that she was finding more and more appealing. She had a job, an apartment, a lover—even if it had been for only that one night—and she was loath to give up any of it.

Still, she had to distance herself until the fame factor wore down. Eran's place was off-limits for obvious reasons; until she felt mentally stronger, she thought it was too dangerous to spend night after night with him. Eran had made the sarcasm-laden comment that her apartment building had turned into the *Daily Planet* newsroom, which he said was a newspaper in a movie called *Superman*. Brynna had never seen the film—she hadn't seen *any* films, although she knew what they were—but the concept was certainly clear. Thanks to her work, money was no longer a problem, but when she told Abrienda and Cocinero that she was going to go to a motel for a while, she found herself with a set of keys to the restaurant and instructions to stay as long as she wanted no matter what the Health Department had to say. Eran had reminded her that it was a big and very bad city, and that it wouldn't be long until the sharks—what he called all the reporters who kept turning up—found a different meal. If it was fairly short, Brynna supposed the restaurant was as good a place as any to wait out the storm, and she would put a little more effort into staying out of the eye view of any inspectors.

If only she could be sure that Lahash hadn't set a Hunter on her trail.

She'd crossed paths with him only one more time, outside Wrigley Field just after Mireva had gotten into Eran's car. Eran had paused to talk to a supervisor who'd pulled up, and before Brynna could climb in the passenger side, there was Lahash. He was wearing a flawless summer suit in a tan color that made him look like a cool Italian tycoon from the Amalfi Coast. His hair was GQ styled and slicked, and he had enough bling on his wrists and fingers to outshine a chandelier. The effect, alas, had been spoiled by the utter outrage on his falsely tanned face.

"You'll pay for this, Astarte," he'd told her in an acid-laden hiss. "Leaving Lucifer was bad enough, but how do you think he'll react when he finds out that you've murdered one of your own?"

"It was self-defense. And I don't give a rat's ass what

Lucifer thinks. That ought to be monumentally clear by now."

"Ah, but he cares about you. And he'll find you," Lahash growled. "Perhaps I'll even help him." The demon had turned away, then stopped to leer back at her. "And I promise: I will get that pathetic little nephilim you think you're going to save."

So there it was, the actual threat to out her to Lucifer. It didn't have much weight since Lahash didn't know where she was staying—at least, she didn't think he did—but demons had a way of finding each other, whether they wanted to or not. Especially when they had something in common.

Something like Mireva.

"MY NIECE HAS TURNED in the application for her entry in the science fair," Cocinero told Brynna the following Wednesday night as he was doing the last of his after-hours cleaning. His expression was a combination of pride and worry. "We will know by Friday if she wins a place in the competition."

"And when's that?"

"The first Saturday in August, about two and a half weeks from now." He grunted as he lifted a bucket of mop water and poured it down the utility sink.

"That's not much time to get ready," Brynna noted.

Cocinero shrugged. "It's more than enough. Those who are chosen to take part in it are supposed to have their entries completed when they turn in the application. She's ready, has all her posters and signs made up." A corner of his mouth turned up in a grin. "Except for the ones she keeps trying to improve, of course. We have to figure out how to move all those planters without damaging the plants, but I have a cousin who works at a furniture store on Lincoln Avenue. He thinks the owner will let him borrow one of the vans."

"That'll help." Cocinero had fixed her a plate of black bean tamales, and she was eating while standing at the counter so she could talk with him. "You sound pretty confident she'll be in it."

"How can she not be? She is smart and talented, and look at all the work she has put into it. She's worked with her teachers to make sure it was original, plus no one else has tried anything this complicated." He set the mop and bucket aside, then squeezed soap onto his palms and stuck his hands under the faucet. "I have never seen such dedication in a child. The world would be a better place if there were more like her."

Brynna took one of the last bites of tamale and let that comment go without adding to it.

"Besides," Cocinero added, "Mireva has been talking to a man from the sponsorship committee. He's very interested in what she's doing with the plants, says there's a lot of potential for using her ideas in a long-term study. Which is exactly what she's hoping."

Brynna swallowed the last of her food, paying more attention now. "That sounds promising."

Cocinero nodded. "I think Abrienda is finally starting to believe that Mireva will really get to go to one of the expensive colleges that she wants and that a scholarship— one that will include everything—will work out."

"This is what Mireva is saying?"

"Oh, no. It's not secondhand information. The man told us this himself—he came to my sister's apartment this afternoon. I'd stopped to check on them before coming to work, and I got to meet him. A nice-looking man, very professional and presentable. *Sí,* a businessman. His name is Lahain or Lahon. Something like that. You would like him, I think."

Damn it, Brynna thought. *Lahash.* And no, she wouldn't like him. Not at all.

ALTHOUGH BRYNNA WASN'T READY to go back to her apartment on a full-time basis, she was more than willing to make a special trip the next afternoon. She needed some fresh work clothes anyway, so that would give her the perfect reason to be there . . . and to talk to Mireva, see how she was doing and if the media madhouse was letting up enough so that Brynna could think about returning permanently.

There was no one around the front of the building, so she slipped inside and stopped at her own place only long enough to change into a clean T-shirt and jeans. Then she headed up to the roof, where she knew she'd find Mireva.

"Hey," Brynna said as she stepped through the door and onto the roof. "How's it going?"

Mireva flinched so slightly that a normal person wouldn't have caught it. Yeah, the girl was still feeling the effects of Gavino. It was unfortunate, but it was also good—hopefully she wouldn't fight too hard when she heard what Brynna had to say.

"I'm okay," Mireva said. "A little . . . jumpy sometimes."

Brynna was surprised the teenager would admit that. Mireva continued. "I don't think I ever really thanked you for, you know, taking, uh, care of that guy." She shot an almost furtive glance at Brynna. "What was his deal anyway? I barely knew him—why would he want to hurt me? He acted like he was my friend before the baseball game. Then he went all psycho."

Brynna folded her arms, trying to think of a way to explain that wouldn't sound insane. It was one thing to have blurted it out to Redmond when they first met, but she liked to think she had learned a little more about what humans in the twenty-first century could accept. The days of magic and mayhem were long gone, along with most of the willingness to believe. Mankind had become fixated on logic and science to the point of blinding itself to the mystical part of existence, the very arena that had been at the core of life itself. And with her heavy science background, Mireva was definitely a child of the Age of Reason.

"Gavino focused on you because there's something very special about you," Brynna began. "You're—"

"Oh, please don't start that stuff," Mireva interrupted. "You'll end up sounding like my mother. She's always saying weird stuff like that, going on about how I'm 'special' and she has a 'feeling' that God has great plans for me and everything."

Brynna stopped herself before she could say *He does.* That was the last thing that Mireva wanted to hear right now. Instead, Brynna offered the next best truth she could come up with. "I think people make their own lives, based on their own choices. A bad choice, just one, can change everything." She paused to see if Mireva would say something, but the girl remained silent. "It's hard to see that sometimes, though."

Mireva glanced at her, then quickly averted her gaze and went back to poking at her plants. Was she thinking about Gavino and how her handsome and mysterious "rescuer" had nearly gotten her killed? Probably, but that didn't matter anymore. Gavino was nothing but ash now, a disintegrated cinder in Mireva's past. From here on, the girl needed to think forward.

"Anyway," Brynna added, "Gavino's gone."

"I don't know that him getting away means he's gone."

When Brynna didn't respond, Mireva glanced at her. "Yeah, that's what I told them," Brynna finally said. "That he, uh, got away."

The teenager sucked in her breath before her shoulders relaxed a little. "Okay . . . yeah, I get you." Mireva was silent for a few moments. "I really have to put all my attention on my project now. The fair is coming up and it has to be the best it can be. A lot of people are going to be looking at it. The *right* people. My college advisor called my mom this morning and said they'd gotten the results a day early, and my name was on the inclusion list." For the first time since that mess at Wrigley Field, Mireva's smile was full and genuine, beautiful. "I made it."

Brynna smiled back. "Congratulations. I'll bet that makes you feel better."

Mireva nodded and scratched at her forehead, not realizing that her fingers were covered with soil. The motion left a mark on her skin that was eerily reminiscent of those made by a priest at Ash Wednesday services.

"About getting in, sure. But the most important part is still ahead." She lifted her chin. "My mom always says never to count on stuff, but I think I'll be okay. I mean, she's just stuck on believing it'll all be so hard that she's not getting it when something finally goes good."

"Like what?"

"We already talked to someone on the board of sponsors for the science fair. He's from Purdue University," Mireva said. "They have a school of agriculture, which is one of the sponsors for the fair *and* one of the universities I was hoping most to get into. He said they're really interested in my project and I'm on their final list of students under scholarship consideration."

"This is the guy your uncle told me about? The one who came to the apartment?"

"Yeah. Mom is still a little pessimistic, but I think the guy finally made an impression on her. He was showing her all the school's brochures and stuff."

Brynna hoped her smile was sincere, but she wouldn't have bet on it. "You sound pretty excited too. What's his name?"

"Mr. Lahash."

Brynna nodded. "He's a tall guy, right? Handsome, black hair, tanned. A really sharp dresser."

Mireva looked up from her plants and her eyes narrowed. "You're kidding. You know him?"

"For a very long time."

The teenager made an exasperated sound. "From where?"

"We . . . go back to before you were born."

"Great." Mireva folded her arms. She was trying to

look defiant, but Brynna heard the frustration in her voice. "Go ahead. I'm sure you can't wait to tell me something bad about him."

Brynna looked at her in surprise. "Mireva, I'm not your enemy. I'm trying to *help* you. Lahash can't be trusted. Everything he told you and your mother is a lie. It's what he does."

"But how do you *know* that?" Mireva sounded a little desperate. "I mean, you can't know everyone, and this is the second time—"

"Gavino was working for him."

Mireva's mouth became an O of shock, then her expression sagged. "Well, that's just fucking great," she said with uncharacteristic surliness. "Maybe I should get a tattoo that says *Creep Magnet*."

"I'm sorry." Brynna stepped closer. "Listen to me. You're doing *great*. You don't need anyone's help with your entry, or your grades, or your scholarship. You never have. This is where *your* hard work and *your* intelligence count. Those are the things that are going to catch the attention of the right people."

"Oh, I'm catching attention, all right."

"Sarcasm isn't going to do anything but feed on how bad you already feel. Ditto with beating yourself up over this." Brynna inclined her head at the lush rows of meticulously labeled plants. What Mireva had been doing, her research and carefully controlled fertilizing, was wildly successful; although it was only about a third of the way through summer, plant after plant was laden with perfectly formed, nearly mature fruits or vegetables. "Look at what you've accomplished. It's a fantastic job, and that's what the people at the fair will be looking at. This fair is *it*, Mireva. The first step to everything you've worked for."

Mireva looked at her fingernails for a long time, then she sighed as she picked at the soil caked underneath the edges. "If this Lahash guy is a fake, what's he trying to accomplish?"

Somehow Brynna didn't think telling the girl that Lahash just wanted her dead was the way to go. But when Mireva suddenly straightened, it turned out that Brynna didn't have to answer. "What am I going to tell my mother? And my uncle?"

"I'll talk to them," Brynna said.

"You . . ." Mireva's voice faded for a moment before she continued. "You can do stuff, can't you? Stuff that the rest of us can't." She gestured vaguely at the open stairwell door. "That's why you were able to clean up this place, why all the gangbangers are afraid of you." When Brynna didn't answer, Mireva abruptly looked at her with something like hope. "Do you . . . *know* things too? Like the future, and what's going to happen?"

Oh, man. Brynna sure didn't like where this seemed to be headed. "You're right in that I can do some things that are a little different than everyone else," she said. "But I can't tell the future. I don't know what's going to happen tomorrow or next week, or whenever, any more than the next person."

Mireva made an exasperated sound, then she shrugged. "What did I expect, anyway? I guess I should just be glad you've been around to play personal bodyguard.

"Otherwise, I'd probably be dead."

❦⋅❀⋅❦

As HE ALMOST ALWAYS did, Cocinero stopped by his sister's apartment before heading to the restaurant to take over for the day cook. Brynna was sitting at the table with Abrienda when he came in, and one look at his sister's face was enough to make him forget the cup of coffee he usually made for himself. "What's wrong?" he asked in Spanish. "What's happened?"

Abrienda scrubbed at her cheeks, trying to erase the tear tracks. "That man," she spat. "The one who came in and talked to us about the scholarship for Mireva. He is nothing but a liar. A fake!"

Cocinero's eyes widened as he looked from Abrienda to Brynna. "What?"

The brochures that Lahash had left were still lying on the table. Abrienda snatched them up, then stormed over to the trash bin and crammed them into it as hard as she could. "I think *those* are real," Brynna said.

"What does it matter?" Abrienda demanded. "These are all dreams, fantasies. And everyone knows dreams don't come true."

"Sometimes they do." Abrienda made a disgusted sound and turned away, but Brynna caught the look on her face, the barest hint of regret. She could imagine Abrienda a decade and a half ago, as a young woman barely older than Mireva was now, full of optimism and adoration as she clung to the angel who would sire her daughter. She was still an attractive woman who always gave more than she received. What a shame she had traded those early feelings for defeat and skepticism.

"What now?" Cocinero asked. His shoulders were

slumped and he suddenly looked more tired than Brynna had ever seen. "What do we do to fix this?"

"Nothing," Brynna answered. "You sit back and watch Mireva get her scholarship all on her own, without anyone's so-called help or offer of a free ride." She stood and carefully pushed her chair under the table. "Now have a little faith."

Twenty — one

If Lahash came back after Brynna outed him, no one in the Cocinero family mentioned it. After everything that had happened, Brynna was pretty sure they'd tell her— the deception had been too great, the hurt too deep, for any of them to excuse or, God forbid, ignore. Mireva was constantly on edge, but the girl had plenty of reason. How many seventeen-year-olds had to face a concentrated effort by a madman to kill her, then move from that to perfecting an academic project that could determine the course of the rest of her life? And all without a hitch or hint of the unspeakable situations that had led up to that point.

Speaking of outing someone, would Lahash do exactly that—reveal her whereabouts to Lucifer? It would certainly be an easy way for him to eliminate her from his little sphere of nephilim assassinations. Still, if Lahash did such a thing, he would also be admitting his failure with Mireva, not to mention the fact that Gavino, even lesser demon that he was, had died essentially for nothing. That Brynna didn't have Hunters grabbing at her from every shadow indicated that Lahash hadn't opened his mouth, but Lucifer was, after all, the King of Lies, more poisonous than any snake and a thousand times sneakier than a hungry crocodile. Lahash, too, was not an entity to underestimate. He was cowardly but sly, an inherently more dangerous combination, and while Gavino had always favored full-on confrontation, Lahash would disappear rather than risk getting physical . . . then ram a knife in her back at the first opportunity.

Brynna had moved back into her apartment, but the whole situation set her teeth on hard grind—if she'd been human, her blood pressure would have probably given a cardiologist a heart attack. Doing an assignment for a workmen's comp lawyer on Friday helped her mind focus on something else; she alternated between being amused and horrified as she translated for a Polish worker who'd gotten his uniform caught in an automatic press. While the man's injuries were pretty damned bad, she couldn't believe the almost comedic combination of employee ignorance and employer carelessness while working around what was clearly dangerous machinery.

But that distraction had ended at five-thirty, and now, three hours later, she was pacing like a trapped lioness, moving from one end of her small apartment to the other with long, smooth strides. Brynna's nerves were twinging as though they were electrical wires, but why? Her first impulse was to assume that Mireva's primary task was close, but what if her sense of anxiety was caused by something else entirely? What if it was born of self-preservation, the instinctive knowledge that a Hunter was closing in on her?

Before she could consider that possibility further, the cell phone on the coffee table jangled. The sound made Brynna jump, and that in itself aggravated the shit out of her. She had started existence as Highborn, and now she was a fallen angel, a *demon*. How ridiculous was it that a tiny piece of human technology could ignite such a flash of fear in her?

She snatched it up. "What?"

"Hello to you too." Redmond's voice was mild through the earpiece. *"I'm having a great evening, thank you for asking."*

Brynna stared at the wall, trying to focus on his voice. She realized her fist was clenched and forced the fingers to relax. "Sorry," she said. "I guess I'm just on edge."

"Any particular reason?"

She opened her mouth to reply, then changed her mind. He'd want to help, but she didn't need him trying to fix something when she couldn't tell him what that something was. "Maybe it's the weather."

He was silent for a moment and she could imagine him rolling his eyes. *"Right. Anyway, why don't I come by and take you out for some Greek food?"* When she didn't answer right away, he added, *"Spanakopita, stuffed grape leaves, feta cheese, and olives. What more could a vegetarian want?"*

It did sound tempting, but her mind wanted her to go somewhere else. "No Greek tonight, but I could go for Mexican."

"Mexican?"

"The truth is, I'd like to go by Cocinero's and check on him."

"Expecting trouble?"

"No, I suppose not. I just . . ." She hesitated, but he

was going to ask so she finished before he could. "I have a feeling that something bad's going to happen. I've already checked and Mireva's fine, Abrienda's fine. That leaves Ramiro."

"All right." Redmond's words had that same calm tone, but something about the tone had switched. A hint of business, of professional speculation—always the cop. But that was okay, too. *"I'll be there in five minutes."*

He hung up before she could answer, but Brynna had to shake her head and chuckle. Five minutes? Redmond was playing dumb if he thought she couldn't figure out that he was parked only a couple of blocks away.

BY THE TIME BRYNNA and Redmond made the drive across the city, Cocinero was just closing the store. Just as she'd suspected, he'd started stretching business hours again after finding out that Lahash's scholarship was nothing but a fabrication. He and Abrienda were, Brynna believed, letting pessimism dictate when patience would have served them far better; Mireva was too smart and too dedicated to maintaining her grades *not* to get a scholarship. Brynna was absolutely sure it wasn't a matter of *if* but *when*.

But in Mireva's world, Brynna's opinion carried little weight except in guarding her safety, and so here was her uncle, keeping his tiny Mexican restaurant open late in a neighborhood where anything could happen. Had he so quickly forgotten the robbery that Brynna had stopped? Yeah, but Brynna thought that was probably a very *conscious* decision.

"Good to see you." Cocinero beamed as he unlocked

the front door and waved them inside. "It was much too quiet around here."

"No customers?" Redmond's voice was mildly reproving.

"There were some just a little while ago," Cocinero told them. "But after they left, it seemed to get . . . I don't know how to word it. More silent than usual." He shrugged. Eran glanced quickly in her direction, but Brynna was careful to keep her face placid. "You are hungry, yes? I can fix you something."

"Not necessary," Redmond put in. "Let's just get this place locked up so you can head home."

Ten minutes and it was all but done—the lights were shut off, the register closed, everything checked a second time. "You guys go out the front. I'll lock up behind you and head out the back," Brynna said.

Cocinero nodded, then looked at the two of them. "Come by my sister's place, sí? We will have coffee. Or a beer."

"Sure," Redmond said. He glanced at Brynna. "I'll bring the car around back and pick you up."

She followed them to the front door, pulled the steel gate across the outside and padlocked it, then closed the door and turned the lock. As she made her way back, she thought that Cocinero had been right about the quiet. There were only six booths on each side, but the distance from front to back seemed longer than it should, filled with shades of gray that shouldn't bother her but tonight seemed ominous.

No, it was just her mind and her nerves working on overdrive. Nothing out of the ordinary happened as she finalized everything, not so much as a drip of water from the washtub faucet or a mouse scrambling across the cracked concrete of the alley as she pulled the steel back door solidly closed behind her, then tested it to make sure the bar had slid home.

"Hey, hey, hey. Lookie who came back for a visit."

Brynna spun, caught off guard. She'd been so wrapped up in the idea that something might happen to Cocinero inside the restaurant that she'd stopped looking out for herself. Not entirely—never that—but her focus had been on fellow fallen angels, demons like Lahash, or Hunters. But that was okay; the three humans she now faced were nowhere near that level of threat. Clearly they hadn't learned their lesson the first time around.

"Long time no see," said the group's leader. He was leaning against the building beneath the streetlight on the other side of the alley, a good twenty feet away. He probably thought it was a safe distance; it wasn't, but Brynna had no reason to go after him. Yet.

"You haven't changed much, Juan," Brynna said. He blinked when she used his name but stood his ground. His two sidekicks were there, one on either side of her and maintaining a more-than-generous safety zone. "Same baseball cap, even the same clothes." She sniffed the air. "I'm not entirely sure you've washed them."

He laughed and put a hand to his forehead in a mock fainting gesture. "You cut me to the heart." He grinned and his eyes glittered. "Oh, wait—I don't have one. So I guess it don't hurt so much after all." He held a good-sized bottle in one hand and he raised the dark glass toward her in a mock toast.

A corner of Brynna's mouth lifted. "You have one, all right. Want me to pull it out of you so you can see?"

"Once a bitch, always a bitch," said the guy to Brynna's left. Yet again, far enough to be out of reach. Or so he thought.

"It's an art form," she said. "Say, how's the wrist?"

He held up his arm, which was covered in dirty plaster from his hand to his elbow. "Thanks for the cast. I should use it to smash in your head."

"If you think you can, I say go for it," Brynna replied, but he made no move to come toward her.

"Hey, dude, we got company," one of them said, pointing. "Let's just do it and go."

Brynna saw headlights as Redmond's car turned into the alley. Her eyes narrowed. *Do what?*

Redmond's car accelerated—he'd seen My Three Thugs and was headed their way. Juan's head jerked toward the car, then back to Brynna, quick as a snake. "Too bad," he said. "I thought we'd have time to enjoy this." He shrugged, then suddenly hurled the bottle in her direction.

Brynna didn't move and the bottle landed at her feet and exploded. The instant the scent of the liquid that had been inside swept through the air, she realized Juan's sidewalk-level aim had been intentional—he'd *wanted* the bottle to break so that the gasoline inside would thoroughly splatter her clothes.

Oh, shit.

Redmond's car slammed to a stop about ten feet from their position and he threw open the door. "Just hold it right there," he snapped. "Police—"

"Let's split!" one of the other guys yelled. They scrambled away, but Juan held out for another moment. "You don't need me, po-po," he called out to Redmond. He took a couple of steps, angling toward Brynna. "You got better fish to *fry.*"

There was a sound, just a tiny thing, but it came with such big consequences and that ancient, oh-so-familiar smell—

Sulfur.

Something small and flaming—a wooden matchstick—arced through the air and looped down, falling neatly on the edge of the thin layer of gasoline surrounding Brynna.

WHUMP!

Her transformation to demon form was instinctive and instantaneous, almost faster than the blaze that wanted to devour her. She had to change, *had* to, because somewhere in the core of her being, Brynna knew this woman form would never survive the conflagration. The flare-up was hot and wild, and the flames enveloped her like an old lover, the touch of Lucifer himself. Everything earthly disappeared—hair, fragile skin, thin nails, the soft moist flesh of her lips, her eyes. She could take many forms, but this one—yes, it was best. The blackened, carbonized skin that coated her true self soaked the fire into itself and reveled in it, making the flames bigger and better and hotter; her back extended and stretched into a set of translucent, dirt-colored wings strong enough to withstand the hurricanes of Hell itself. She folded them around herself and smiled—she couldn't help it. Then, cradled within a circular wall of flame, she distantly heard the high, cruel laughter of the young men as they ran away. Below that came Redmond's panicked shouts—she had never heard him sound so terrified.

His voice, more than anything, pulled her back. Brynna pushed away from the lure of the fire, the siren symphony of the heat, and forced herself to reestablish her earthly form. Ten seconds, twenty, and then the flare-up dwindled to nothing but straggling flickers within the smoking, ashy remnants of the clothes she'd been wearing just moments before.

She wanted to be human flesh again, she *reached* for it, but it was not so easy to return, not so fast. Demon flesh would not relinquish its hold so readily. Maybe someday, with practice, but right now Brynna had to force it, push and rend and sculpt her true body until it conceded to her will. She had to do this, and as quickly as possible. As darkly sweet as being in her original form might be, every second that she remained that way increased the danger of being seen by other demons, of a Hunter being alerted, or that—

Redmond's hoarse cries ended abruptly, choking off in shock. "What—what *are* you?"

—Eran Redmond, her human lover, might see her as she really was.

Most of the smoke had cleared but her metamorphosis was not yet complete. There was nothing Brynna could do, nowhere she could go to hide from his sight. She pulled her arms forward and her wings, gray-brown and veined with black, unfolded behind her of their own volition, impossibly strong, beautiful in Hell but hideous on Earth. Her flesh was still nearly as black as her veins and her body was stronger and fuller, oozing sexuality and full of the temptations experienced by millennia of men.

Eran took a step toward her. He couldn't help it.

She held up a hand and he halted, staring at the overly long fingers tipped with razor-sharp nails the color of heart's blood. "I told you before," she rasped. "I'm a—" Brynna started to say *demon* but the word wouldn't come out. It was locked in her throat and chest like an abomination, something that was never meant to be heard by this imperfect yet well-intentioned man.

Her skin was changing, bending to her will and melding downward toward human; she dragged her fingers across the mottled black and pink flesh below her ribs and her nails opened a furrow in her belly. There, deep within the bloodless gash, was that most precious of objects, the one thing in all of eternity she truly felt she could call her own.

Her feather.

Brynna pulled it out and held it up, almost like an offering. In the smoke-fouled air, it gleamed between her sooty fingertips like a star plucked from Heaven itself.

"Fallen angel," she finished in a whisper.

Then she was done talking, because she had to concentrate if she was going to make herself human again, to break the connection between the here and now and her demon essence from before.

Brynna couldn't have said if it was a minute or an hour later, but her feather was once more safely secreted and she was finally human again. Barely covered by burned remnants of fabric, shaking with the effort as she stood face-to-face with Redmond, she could see the amazement and reluctant belief—finally—in his eyes. The change had taken so long and so much effort, and had created so much potential for danger, and yet the only thing she was worried about was what he would think of her now.

How disgustingly human was that?

And when the pain buckled her knees and drove her to the alley's pavement, Brynna realized that as rapidly as she had transformed from human to demon, it had been neither fast enough nor into the right demon form that would keep completely safe that human part of her that was never meant to touch hellfire.

ERAN HAD NEVER DONE anything so difficult in his life as reaching out and pulling Brynna to her feet so he could guide her to his car. Had he really seen . . . what *had* he seen? Already his mind was fogging over, his thoughts questioning his memory. Psychiatrists probably had some kind of fancy name for it—post-traumatic memory modification or some such crap, a switch in a person's mind that was supposed to protect them from themselves. But that was bullshit, because nothing kept you safer than remembering, really *remembering*, something you damn well ought to avoid in the future.

Wings, he thought. *She had wings—*

"Come on, Brynna," he managed. "We have to get you to a hospital."

—*and skin as black and cracked as the charred surface of an old, overused backyard grill.*

Something whistled past their heads. It made an odd flapping sound, like a giant bat—

Wings

—sailing through the channel between the buildings.

Beneath his touch, Brynna shuddered suddenly and gasped for air. "Got to . . . get *out* of here." Her voice was smoke-choked and thin, like oxygen was making its way from lungs lined with fragments of singed cardboard. "Hunter . . ."

"Hunter?" Eran repeated. "What's that mean?" They were almost at the passenger door, and Brynna surprised him by pitching forward and clutching at the door handle in an effort to get inside more quickly. "Wait," he said automatically. "You're going to hurt yourself even more. Let me—"

"Must *go*," she ground out. "*Now*, before he takes me—" "*Back to Lucifer.*"

Eran whirled, his skin suddenly crawling. Everything inside him, every cell in his body, screamed *Run!* but he couldn't. He was stuck, paralyzed by some sort of primeval fear he hadn't known still existed in his lower brain's memory. For a too-long moment, his eyes wouldn't focus; his gaze swept the alley like a drunk's, swinging and disjointed, making everything in front of him skewed almost beyond recognition. And maybe he wanted it to be that way, maybe it should have *stayed* that way, because the creature coming toward them was quite probably something never meant to be seen by a living human being.

It was tall, almost seven feet, and just short of a living skeleton. It had skin, yes, but the covering over its bones would never be mistaken for actual flesh. Its red-gold surface was grooved and rough, like hardened, living corduroy. The color never stopped shifting, even when the demon paused to study Eran. It took Eran a few seconds to identify the visual perception that flames were rippling beneath the textured covering; they glowed a darker, richer red when the creature—the Hunter Brynna had referenced—inhaled, then faded to burnished gold when it exhaled. Its hands were bigger than Eran's head, and that wasn't even counting the long, curving claws that tipped each finger.

It lifted its chin and stared down at him from liquid crimson eyes set wide above a skeletal nose. *"Step aside, human. Astarte and I have plans for the evening."* The demon's voice bubbled through Eran's ears like poison seeping from the surface of his skin into his veins. Eran had a brief mental image of spidery black lines expanding throughout his body, each one drawing cold and death with it, but he shook it off. In the biggest act of willpower he'd ever managed, he stepped in front of the beast as it advanced on the cowering, burned Brynna.

"No," he said. "Go back . . . where you came from."

The demon paused and tilted its head, as though it were trying to understand. In a dog, the movement would have been comical; in this abomination, the gesture, and the revolting smile that came with it, was unspeakable. Bony spikes rose from the center of its skull and wavered in an uneven line that looked like something from a mutated aquarium. Its heavy bottom jaw stretched into a wide smile lined with so many stocky teeth that its upper lip—if that's what it could be called—was completely hidden. *"You are nothing to me,"* it hissed at Eran. *"A speck of cat shit I once stepped in."* One arm, impossibly long and corded with lean, smoldering muscles, lifted and extended a hand toward Eran. Instead of moving, Eran pulled his 9mm out and aimed at the thing's head. *"I will rip out your eyes and suck your soul away through the bloody holes."*

Suddenly something dragged at his arm, nearly making him squeeze the trigger. "No," Brynna gasped. She had crawled forward, actually *crawled,* and Eran lost his aim as he instinctively leaned over to help her. "He'll kill you. I'll go back. I'll go."

"Not in my lifetime," Eran said grimly. He stepped around her, blocking her progress as he raised his gun again. "Go back where you came from," he repeated. "She's *not* going with you."

The creature opened its mouth and growled at him. The sound was unimaginable and it filled him with dread. All at once he understood that his gun was useless—even if he emptied the entire magazine into the beast's head, it would still keep coming, it would grab him and do exactly what it had promised—

There was movement at the mouth of the alley, then sirens and horns echoed across the bricks on either side as a fire truck lumbered into the turn from the street on the opposite side of Eran's car. Right behind its bumper was a squad car, blue and white lights rotating. In the space of a single second, everything was washed in red and white and blue as firemen and cops surged from their vehicles.

The demon's face jerked toward the commotion and it hunched over, then bent forward even more. Was it trying to hide from the other humans? Did it not want to be seen? *"Remember what you said, human,"* it sneered at him. *"Your lifetime can be made very, very short. Astarte will come back where she belongs."*

Before Eran could retort, the fiend was gone—either

it had the ability to move so quickly he couldn't see it, or it had simply vanished into the night air. Whatever the answer, he would have to dwell on it later; right now, he had to get Brynna into the car before anyone else came around to this side of it and saw her. After the fact, he didn't think taking her to a hospital was such a great and grand idea.

Eran bent and grabbed Brynna under the shoulders, then pulled her back up. She tried to help, pushing with her feet to gain speed even as Eran ground his teeth against the mewling sounds of agony coming out of her mouth. She might be a demon, or a fallen angel, or whatever, but there was no denying that she was in the kind of pain he couldn't begin to imagine or endure. But he had to move fast, he had to keep going. Just a few feet beyond the driver's side of his car, two firemen were running toward the scorched circle of bricks where Brynna had been only minutes before. Their puzzled faces turned in his direction just as he managed to get the door open with his right hand and Brynna dragged herself inside and rolled into a ball on the seat, keeping her head below the tinted window. The Mitsubishi wasn't that big and she didn't have much room; it would get hot in there awfully fast. Could she take the heat? Of course she could. Eran closed the door and drew a ragged breath as one of the fireman hurried around the front of the car.

"Hey, man, you all right?" one of them yelled. "What the hell happened here?"

"I'm not sure," he replied. He met the guy before he got to the car's window then kept going, heading back to the burned spot where another fireman was squatting and examining the scorched ground. Just as Eran had hoped, the first one followed him automatically as Eran dug his star out of his pocket. "Three punks screwing around with gasoline or something, just as I turned into the alley."

The first fireman tilted his hat and peered down the alley beyond Eran's car. "Where did they go?"

A couple of uniformed cops had climbed out of their cars and were now poking around the area, checking the recessed doorways and the darker areas behind the Dumpsters, trash cans and boxes piled here and there. "I have no idea. They were jumping around something that was burning, and they took off when I got out of my car. By the time I checked out the fire, they were gone."

"Yeah?" The second fireman looked dubious. "What'd they set on fire?"

"Nothing that I could make out. Maybe paper—I'm not sure."

"Don't see any pieces," one said. The firemen looked at each other, then the first one—maybe he was the higher rank—glanced pointedly at Eran's hands. "You're bleeding. You get burned?"

Eran started and inspected his fingers. They were covered in soot and a glint of Brynna's blood showed here and there. "It's nothing," he said. "A few scrapes. I tripped at the edge of the fire. Trying to see."

"Uh-huh." The guy looked like he wanted to say more but the two cops were closing in. Eran knew they'd want to talk to him, get the details on what had gone down. Saved by the badges, he thought, but he hoped they wouldn't take too long. He really needed to get Brynna out of that car, take her somewhere so he could clean her up and see how badly she was hurt. The *where* of that was going to be the biggest challenge.

"So what happened here?" One of the policemen stepped up, notebook in hand. "One of the guys back there said you're on the job. I'm Jade, and my partner is Steckley." He offered his hand, but Eran held up his in apology.

"Sorry. I got into the ashes," Eran said. "Anyway, yeah—Detective Redmond. I was driving down the alley, just doing a drive-by, when I saw these three guys. They had a fire going, but I couldn't see what was burning. I got out of the car and ran over, but they took off. I smelled gasoline but by the time I checked out the fire, they were gone."

"Ever see them before?"

"No." At least he could answer that truthfully.

"What brings you down here?"

"I know the guy who runs this taco place," Eran said. "He's a friend of my girlfriend's." The word came easily, but in retrospect it also felt strange, especially after what he'd witnessed. "Sometimes I check on him."

"What's his name?"

"Ramiro Cocinero."

"That's me," a familiar voice interrupted. Cocinero must've come back to see what was going on when Eran and Brynna hadn't caught up to him. "I own this restaurant." Cocinero pointed at the back door of his shop, then looked at the fire truck and the police cars—there were two now—that blocked one end of the alley. "Señor Redmond, what happened here? I thought you and—"

"Some hoodlums," Eran interrupted. "They set something on fire right behind your place. But no one was hurt." He put a little extra emphasis on *no one*, hoping Cocinero would keep his mouth shut about Brynna.

The restaurant owner blinked and looked confused, but only for a moment. "You said there were three of them? I think maybe they were the ones who tried to rob me two or three weeks ago."

"Yeah?" The second cop's interest picked up. "What happened with that? Did you file a police report?"

"No. They ran off and didn't take anything. I had a friend in the store with me—"

"Detective Redmond here?"

Cocinero shook his head. "No, not him. My friend knows martial arts. She scared them away. Like I said, they didn't get anything."

Officer Steckley raised an eyebrow. "She?"

Cocinero shrugged, his gaze flicking nervously to Eran. This, Eran decided, would be a good time to turn the conversation in another direction. "Maybe these are the same guys," he suggested. "Maybe you can ID them."

"Would you be willing to come down to the station and look at some photos?" Steckley asked. "We wouldn't make you go through all the mug books, but there's a certain group of perps who are always causing situations around this neighborhood. I bet it wouldn't take you more than twenty minutes."

"Sure," Cocinero said. "I would do that." Eran had been around the man enough to hear the slightest hint of relief in his voice. He didn't want to bring Brynna into this, either.

"And you'll come with us, Detective?"

"Let me head home, get cleaned up, and I'll come by later," he said. "I smell like smoke. An hour, ninety minutes tops. We'll see if I peg the same guys as Ramiro."

The cops nodded and Jade put away his notebook. "You'll want to take care of those hands too."

"Scrapes," Eran repeated. "No big deal." He made a point of glancing at his watch. "I'll see you at the Foster Avenue Station."

They nodded, watching as he went back to his car and got in. The area was filling up with people, residents who wanted to know what the hell had happened, gawkers who were just curious. The more the merrier—they would keep the cops and the rest of the crew busy. Eran tilted his head in acknowledgment as he shifted the Mitsubishi into reverse and backed out, hoping they wouldn't think of something and wave at him to stop. He couldn't let them come up to the car, because he couldn't roll down the window.

He'd just have to breathe through the heavy, nauseating smell of burned flesh.

"Brynna? Brynna, can you hear me?"

A Hunter stabbed her in the shoulder, sending a rivulet of fire down her arm. She almost struck back, but at the last minute a sliver of logic wormed into her flame-ridden thoughts—

Brynna, the voice had said. Not a Hunter, no—it was Eran, not stabbing her, just a tiny touch to try to rouse her. Just that.

"Y-Yes," she managed. "I . . . yes."

"I'm going to take you to my place," he said. His words

were soft and regulated, but strained. He was under pressure, nervous—of course he would be. He had seen her in true form, hadn't he? No, not her *true* form. That image was painful in its own way, glorious to behold, but it was also one she'd left behind long ago. The one into which she'd instinctively changed was one of many she'd evolved after countless millennia in Hell, the one best suited to endure flames. Each fallen angel had her own form, her own indescribable monstrosity. In that respect, Brynna—no, Astarte—was no different, and yet she was. She was so much more sexual, ever darker and more dangerous because of it. Any reasonable person would see one of her brethren and flee, at least *try* to save his or her sanity and soul. But with Astarte . . . oh, no. She was mankind's innermost, irresistible addiction: she was *lust*.

Wait—what had he said?

"No," she gasped.

Where was she? In the backseat of Eran's car, wadded up like a sickly human rag. She tried to move and pain shot through her body, a thousand hot irons cutting across the surface of her human skin. It didn't matter, she mustn't let him—

"Not there," she grated. "Not safe. The Hunter will come back." She didn't bother to add that a single human death or two mattered not at all to those who came from Hell. Lucifer's soldier would kill Eran without blinking, and the only thing that had saved him tonight was the arrival of his fellow humans—too many witnesses.

"There has to be *someone* who can help you," Eran said. Despite the agony pulsing through her body—or perhaps because of it—Brynna could hear the desperation in his voice. "If not a doctor, then . . ." His voice trailed off, but before she could ask, his tone changed. "I know someone," he said. Then, more to himself than to her, "Yeah, we'll go there. That's perfect. It *has* to be."

Brynna swallowed, trying to find enough saliva to get her question out. Her throat felt like a tube lined with hot glass. "Where?" she finally managed.

"Saint Clement Church," Eran answered.

"A c-church?"

"I know one of the priests there. Father Murphy."

"Church," Brynna repeated. The notion made a thousand questions bubble through her mind, not the least of which was could she even go inside? She thought she could . . . but what if she was wrong? Once upon a time she and her kind had been considered Highborn, the first children of God. But now . . . now she was one of the fallen, a demon. Setting foot in the Creator's house was a privilege, not a right. Did her quest for redemption give her back that privilege, even in her most dire hour of need?

Well, if that was where Eran was determined to take her, she was certainly going to find out.

And what about Eran's friend, this Father Murphy? She'd never heard Eran mention him before and had, through some pretty close contact with Eran over these past weeks, gotten the clear impression that Eran and religion were two distinct and unrelated entities.

Before she could form a question for him, one of the car's back tires sank hard into a pothole. The jolt bounced her sharply on the backseat, launching more pain into Brynna's human body than it could handle. Whatever question might have come out was lost to unconsciousness as Brynna sank into a very comfortable and pain-free blackness.

THE RECTORY WAS A majestic stone building that had been originally constructed in the 1800s as a mansion, then bought by the parish and used as a convent before eventually being converted into the parish center and rectory. Eran remembered that much from looking up information on the church after he'd met Father Murphy, but the recollection didn't help him much in navigating, especially under pressure.

He double-parked, crossing his fingers that no one would sideswipe him, then fumbled around until he found a gate in the waist-high iron fence. Once inside, he followed a long, narrow concrete walkway that finally led to the rectory door. The doorbell was difficult to find in the dark. By the time Eran located it, he'd lost all pretenses of trying to be low-key. Besides, if another one of those things—a Hunter—was following them, he *needed* the company of others to keep it from attacking; he might be good at acting brave in front of Brynna, but after what he'd witnessed in the alley, his firm belief in his own invincibility now rested on damned shaky ground.

By the time Father Murphy finally answered, Eran had given up ringing the bell in favor of pounding on the heavy wooden door until the side of his hand was bruised. He was sweating and fidgeting and couldn't stop himself from glancing at the sky every few seconds. But then, if that creature did come back, it wouldn't be concerned about him, it would be back at the car where Brynna was—

"Detective Redmond?"

Eran whirled, realizing he'd actually started to turn away and move back toward the car. "Father Murphy!"

The priest gave him a perplexed smile, but it disappeared when he looked a little more closely at Eran. "Detective, is something wrong? You look—"

"I need your help," Eran blurted. "I have a friend in the car who's hurt. I can't take her to a hospital—it's complicated. But I'll explain everything, I swear. If you'll just help me get her off the street and inside where it's safe, I'll explain." After a second's pause, he added, "And this doesn't involve anything illegal, so there's nothing to worry about there."

Father Murphy opened his mouth, then closed it. "All right. Where—"

"Here," Eran said. He was already pulling on the priest's arm, guiding him to the car as quickly as he could get the other man to move. "Right out front. I need someplace to put her, and I can't take her to my place." The priest glanced at him as they hurried down the walkway. "It's a long story. I'll tell you everything if we can just get her inside where it's safe."

"That's the second time you've mentioned *safe*," the priest said. But they had reached Eran's car and there was no more time for questions or speculation, because when Eran yanked open the back door, Brynna's arm, pocked with blackened patches of skin and smelling like burned meat, slid into view. Father Murphy gasped, but as Eran leaned in and slid his arms under Brynna's shoulders, the priest pitched in to help without hesitating. She'd been unconscious for most of the ride but had started to wake up toward the end. Now she moaned as the two men got her out of the car, upright, and supported between the two of them.

"Detective, this woman needs more care than I can provide," Murphy protested when Eran steered them back in the direction of the rectory. "A trauma doctor—a burn unit."

"She can't go there," Eran told him without slowing. "And we have to get her inside. It's dangerous for her to be out in the open."

"But she's too badly hurt—she'll die!"

"No," Brynna said. Her voice was low but still strong enough so that they could both hear her. "I won't die. I just need to c-clean up a little, that's all. Some water. S-Sleep."

They were at the rectory door now. The priest had left it ajar and Eran nudged it open with his foot. He helped get Brynna inside, then twisted back and pushed the door closed so hard that it slammed against the frame. There was a heavy-looking lock about a foot above the brass doorknob and Eran used one hand to turn it until the cylinders clattered into place. It wasn't much comfort, but at least it was something.

"Where to?" he asked Father Murphy. "Do you have a bed, or a guest room or something? Someplace where visitors don't usually go?"

The priest frowned but inclined his head in the direction of a long hallway. "At the end," he told Eran. "Down-stairs. There's a room in the basement with a couple of twin beds in it. It's more of a storeroom now, hasn't been used in awhile so there's lots of boxes and junk, but I think one of the beds is clear."

"That'll do."

IT WASN'T UNTIL THEY had Brynna lying on the bed that Eran and Father Murphy could see the full range of her burns in the mellow light cast by a small lamp. Father Murphy hurried away and returned in a couple of minutes with scissors, clean linens, and a big bowl of cool water. Wordlessly, Eran helped him cut away what little was left of Brynna's charred clothes, then they covered her midsection with a sheet and carefully began to wash her scorched skin. Somehow she kept silent; perhaps she realized that if she cried out, Father Murphy would break and insist on outside help. The worst of the wounds were at her feet, where the gasoline had thoroughly soaked the bottoms of her jeans and her shoes; the burns lessened higher up on her body, but her clothing had provided great fuel. There were a few singed spots on her shoulders and neck, but not much on her face.

Finally they were finished. The sheet below Brynna was speckled with blood and blackened bits of skin and fabric. "We should change that," Father Murphy said, staring downward. "We have to keep the wounds clean or they'll get infected." He raised his bleary, shocked gaze to Eran. "These injuries—I don't see how she'll survive."

"She will," Eran said. He blinked as he realized he believed that, had absolutely no doubt. She really *was* what she'd claimed all along, and who better to withstand fire than a woman from Hell itself? How ironic that to save her, he'd brought her to a church.

"Is there water?" Brynna murmured. Even though her voice was low, Eran thought it sounded clearer.

"Absolutely," Father Murphy said. He hurried out of the room and Eran heard water running—there must be a bathroom on this level. The priest came back with a plastic tumbler; when Brynna reached for it, Eran took it and knelt next to the bed so that he could hold her head while she sipped. When she'd finished the entire tumbler, he eased her head back and she sighed. "Thank you. I just need to sleep now, so I can heal." Her eyes were already closing before she finished the sentence. Changing the sheets was best left for another time.

Eran and the priest eased out of the room, and Father Murphy left the door open slightly. They'd walked only about five feet down the hall before the priest turned and fixed his stern gaze on Eran. "We'll go upstairs," he told Eran. "I'll start some coffee. And you'll fill me in. On *everything*. I'll keep an open mind and you won't leave anything out. Understand?"

Eran nodded. He wondered if the priest realized just how open his mind needed to be.

Twenty – two

Brynna came awake with enough of a jerk to send a jagged swipe of pain through her ankles. Sitting up took a lot of effort, but it was worth it when the prize was the full tumbler of cool water on a small table next to the bed. She drank it all, forcing herself not to gulp when the first sensation of liquid on her tongue made thirst explode in her mouth. There was something else on the table, a small plate of tomato wedges and soft cheese; like the first sip of water, the initial taste of a tangy tomato wedge made her mouth water and her very empty stomach grumble.

After finishing the simple meal, Brynna peered down at her feet. How long had she been here? She had a dim memory of Eran and someone else—a priest—bringing her in then washing her burns, but there was nothing after that except shadows that occasionally lightened at the edges.

She was groggy, still tired in a way that told her she wasn't quite where she needed to be as far as healing was concerned. When her mind searched out the last memories she had before passing out on this bed, she wasn't surprised. It had been quite the pyre, and her ankles and shins were still raw and glistening, dribbling fluids that soaked into a thick pad below them. The burns climbed up her bare shins, where they had finally started to heal just above her knees. She thought back to the burns she'd gotten from the Hunter's fireballs right after she'd taken this human form, but there was really no comparison. Those had been not much more than grazes on the surface of her skin; this time, great chunks of flesh had been grilled right off her body. Damage like that didn't fix itself overnight, even for her.

So again, how long had she been here?

On the heels of that thought:

Is Mireva all right?

Brynna ground her teeth and swung her legs over the side of the bed, hissing at the fresh misery that billowed up her nerve endings when her bare feet pressed against the floor. More memories were reasserting themselves now: the priest helping Eran get her out of the car, the long, agonizing walk inside and down the stairs. She wasn't in the church proper but the rectory, where the priest and, sometimes, church employees lived and worked. Eran's choice had been excellent—it was a good place, a *safe* place. But now she had to get back to her apartment and find out about Mireva.

Moving more slowly than she'd ever thought possible, Brynna worked her way to the door, then out into the hallway. The lower the burn on her body, the worse the pain; every step made her want to scream. But she would not give up, and she would not be stopped.

Brynna fixed her gaze on the staircase at the far end

of what seemed like the longest hallway in the world, and headed toward it.

"GOING SOMEWHERE?"

Brynna turned a little too sharply and got a much nastier jolt up one of her ankles than she expected. She had been so intent on getting to the stairs that she hadn't paid attention to the two closed doors she'd passed along the way. One must have opened onto a bathroom, and now Eran was standing just outside of it, drying his hands on a towel and looking at her like there was nothing in the world more ordinary than Brynna lurching down a basement hallway while wrapped in a sheet.

"Yes," she managed. "Back h-home."

"To your apartment?" He shook his head and draped the towel over the edge of the sink, then came toward her. "Nope. Not a good idea."

"Mireva—"

"Is fine. I've been in so much contact with Ramiro and Abrienda that they're starting to think I'm stalking them. In fact, I just talked to him about twenty minutes ago. They have family visiting for a week and their place is crammed with people. It's the perfect way to keep her safe. She hasn't been by herself in days."

Days?

"How long . . ."

Eran cocked his head and let his gaze travel down to her swollen feet and blistered ankles. "Four days. I'd say you're only about halfway there, Brynna. You need another four—at least—to get you back to preroasted condition."

"Four days," she echoed. Her shoulders sagged. That seemed like so long, and she didn't know if she was talking about how long she'd been out or how long she still needed to heal.

"Come on," Eran said, and moved alongside her to guide her back the way she'd come. "Back to bed with you. You've come a remarkable distance already—and completely freaked out Father Murphy, by the way—so let's not screw it up by moving too fast. Besides, Gavino knew where you lived and he probably told Lahash. I don't know if their kind collaborate with Hunters, but I'm willing to bet it's time for you to relocate."

Not a pleasing thought, but she'd deal with that later. Besides, she wasn't going anywhere until the business of Mireva completing her divine task was finished. And right now she had to admit Eran was right. She was far too tired to do anything but go back to sleep.

"HOW IS SHE?" FATHER Murphy was sitting behind his oversized desk in the large, spacious office directly off the entrance to the rectory. Sunlight shone through the translucent curtains at the windows, washing over the old golden oak trim that surrounded the tall windows and built-in bookcases.

"Good," Eran answered. He settled himself onto the left one of two leather chairs facing the desk. This was the more comfortable of the pair and his favorite—he'd become very familiar with this office and its furnishings over the last four days. The matching couch centered on the wall opposite the windows was hard and cold, a bitch to sleep on even with a thick quilt as padding. Having done just that for the last four nights, Eran had yet to find a single yielding spot on the damned thing. "She was awake when I went down, actually trying to leave. I sent her back to bed."

The priest frowned. "Leave? Why?"

"The girl," Eran reminded him. "Mireva. I told you the story."

And he had, from start to finish . . . except, of course, for certain details of the relationship between himself and Brynna. He wasn't sure what this Catholic priest would think of him once he learned that Eran had made love with a demon. Eran wasn't sure what he thought of *himself*.

"I'll have her out of here in a couple more days, I promise."

Father Murphy pushed back from his desk and regarded Eran. He looked tired and older, as if the past few days, along with the knowledge he'd gained—*if* he believed it—had tripled the effects of gravity on him and dragged his skin downward. "She can stay here as long as she needs to. I told you that."

Eran nodded. "I know. But I get the feeling that you really don't believe anything I told you, and that means you think . . . well, I don't know what you think. That I'm crazy, maybe. Delusional." He paused as a new option occurred to him. "Or that I hurt Brynna and brought her here to hide her or something."

Father Murphy held up a hand. "I don't think either of those things, but you're right in that I'm having a difficult time accepting the other things you talked about. Angels, demons—everything I've been taught is that these are elements of God's universe that are not seen by humans.

They're taken on *faith*, not personal experience. They may be in God's realm, but they don't exist in our reality. At least not anymore."

"But what if they *do*, Father? Doesn't faith work the same way for that, too?"

"What do you mean?"

"You can't *see* God, yet you have faith that He exists. Doesn't the fact that you haven't seen an angel or a demon in the flesh put them in the same category—beings believed in as a matter of faith, not fact?"

Father Murphy's gaze was level. "Every religion has a history upon which its faith is based."

"An accounting of history is not necessarily factual," Eran pointed out.

"Even so, the older a history is, the more that history *serves* as fact," Father Murphy said. "In this case, the Bible, or the Koran, or—"

"You mean the less likely it is that there's any chance that anyone can prove it's *not* fact," Eran interrupted. "As in 'I can't prove God exists, but you can't prove He doesn't.' The ultimate stalemate."

When the priest was silent, Eran sighed. "Look, I know it must all sound crazy, and you're right—I don't have a written history or witnesses. But you see how quickly Brynna is healing. You have to admit that a normal person wouldn't be able to do that. Don't you think that's indicative that something's different here, or that it might at least be smart to consider the possibility that what I'm telling you is true?"

"If you're asking if I can accept that the woman downstairs is an extraordinarily rapid healer, then yes, I can do that. But the flipside is you telling me she's not human, that a trio of street criminals set her on fire in the alley and she changed into a demon in order to survive the attack. That she grew *wings*." When Eran started to say something, Father Murphy held up his hand. "Then you go on to tell me tales of nephilim and serial killers and some kind of divine plan regarding the children of angels, and the deeper you go into your story, the more fantastic and outlandish it gets."

"If you think I'm that damned insane, then why not tell me to get out?" Eran couldn't help the frustration in his voice. "Or call the cops—my division captain, or just 911. Why put up with it?"

"I may not be an expert, but I've dealt with a lot of people and I really don't believe you're dangerous," Father Murphy said. "Or that you had anything to do with that woman's injuries. And frankly, it's not my job to judge. Only to help as best I can."

Eran didn't know what else to say. If the priest wasn't going to believe him, there wasn't much he could do. It certainly wasn't like Brynna could snap her fingers and *presto-change-o* into the being she'd been in the alley. Or maybe she could. Even if she would, there were, provided he understood things correctly, real dangers associated with doing just that. Dangers like the Hunter in the alley that could just as *presto-change-o* kill whoever got in its way.

He didn't know why it was so important that Father Murphy believe him, or what it would accomplish if he did. A sense of validation? Camaraderie? Or sanity? In any case, there was nothing the priest could do to help other than provide a sort of "safe house" if they needed it. And even that wasn't permanent—they couldn't stay here forever.

"A couple more days," Eran finally said. "Then I think I can move her to my place."

"And the men who attacked her? You said she's crossed them before." Concern showed in Father Murphy's green eyes. "If they learn she survived, they might try again."

"Definitely a consideration. But I worked with Ramiro Cocinero, Mireva's uncle and the man who owns the taco place, and we identified two of them. My partner and I picked up both yesterday morning and charged them with attempted armed robbery. We're still looking for the leader, but there's an APB on him so it's just a matter of time."

The other man folded his hands on the desktop. "You mentioned a partner—"

"Bheru Sathi. Yeah, we've been together a long time, almost a decade."

"What does he think of Brynna and all this?"

A corner of Eran's mouth lifted. "He was much more open-minded right from the start. He saw a lot of the strange things that Brynna could do, the unexplainable results, the way she heals. He has an acceptance of it all that took me awhile to find."

Father Murphy gave a small nod. "I see."

Eran stood, and the priest did likewise. "Listen, thanks again for all your help. I hope we didn't cause too much grief. I know you had to reschedule some stuff to keep folks away."

"No problem." Neither man said anything for a moment, then Father Murphy came around the desk and touched Eran on the arm. "I'm not shutting out the possibilities, Eran. But you have to understand that in my business—religion—a lot of people make a lot of claims about a lot of miracles. And that, in essence, is exactly what you're doing. The Church has a strict policy about miracles, and it's a tough one. It *has* to be." He gave Eran a lopsided grin. "Otherwise every piece of toast and moldy sink sponge that shows up on eBay would end up in the Vatican."

Eran had to laugh, but then his expression turned serious again. "Okay. But I have a feeling that someday you'll be looking at Brynna in a whole different way."

"I DON'T THINK THIS is a good idea," Brynna said. She was standing in Eran's living room, feeling awkward and jumpy while his dog snuffled warily in Brynna's direction. The place was spotless and rather sparse, with painted black furniture and plain cushions that gave it an almost industrial feel. There were a few pictures on the walls, but they looked like they'd been chosen as afterthoughts, something to fill the too-large expanses. The windows were covered with white metal mini-blinds that did little to block the light and only accentuated the officelike atmosphere. A thin, cream-colored throw covered most of the couch, but there were no knickknacks or family photographs.

"Of course it is," Eran said. "Come on in, make yourself comfortable." He motioned toward the couch. "Sit—you're not a hundred percent well, you know. Don't overdo it."

Brynna did, then jumped in surprise as the huge white dog climbed on the couch and settled next to her, regarding her with sky-blue eyes. They stared at each other for a long moment, and Brynna finally asked, "What do I do?"

"Pet her," Eran said, sounding amused. "She's a Great Dane and her name is Grunt. I'm sure she's glad to see us. I've been gone so much of the time she was starting to think of me as a stranger."

Brynna extended her hand and scratched Grunt's head; to her surprise, the dog pushed herself into the gesture then squirmed on the couch until she could rest her big head on Brynna's thigh. Grunt made a little grumbling sound in her throat, then sighed in enjoyment. In her entire existence—a monumental amount of time—Brynna didn't think she'd ever touched a dog like this. It was kind of pleasant, comforting. Were cats like this? The dog had instantly liked her yet expected nothing in return. No wonder humans liked pets. "She's certainly friendly. Nice doggy."

"She can't hear you," Eran said. He was flipping through a stack of mail that he'd picked up on the way inside. "Born deaf."

"Interesting." Still stroking Grunt's neck, Brynna decided to turn the conversation back to where it should be. "As I was saying—"

"There's no reason to think anyone, or any*thing,* knows where you are," Eran said, stepping right back into it. "You've never even been here before."

"They could track *you,*" Brynna pointed out. "It's not like you've been hiding."

"Why would they want to? They're not interested in me, just you."

Brynna's eyes were shadowed. "Don't underestimate the Hunters, Eran. Or Lahash. You've made it very clear that there's a connection between us. They'll use that any way they can."

"All right," he said, but she could tell he was just placating her. It must have shown on her face, because he came over and sat on the edge of the coffee table, where he could face her. "Look, this is the only place we have right now. Father Murphy was starting to have problems—he had too many things on the church's schedule and he was rescheduling enough to where people were starting to take notice. If you really don't think it's safe, then we'll find you another apartment. Obviously you can't go back to yours."

She took a deep breath, then nodded. Whether he really believed there was an issue didn't matter. That he would do something about it did. "Okay."

"In the meantime, take it easy here. There's food in the fridge, a soaking tub in the bathroom, and Grunt to keep you company. I have to go in to work. Father Murphy isn't the only one who's been putting things off."

Brynna nodded and levered herself up, earning a reproachful look from the dog. Her ankles were layered with fresh, pink scar tissue, healed on the surface but still tender beneath the skin. The scars would disappear—the ones on her shoulder were almost invisible now—but she still needed an inordinate amount of sleep. To her left was a set of open French doors, and when she walked through them, she was in a sort of dressing room. Like the rest of the place, there wasn't much furniture, just a triple dresser with a nearly empty surface, a leather chair next to a modest round table and lamp, and a man's butler over which a carefully pressed pair of slacks hung. A folded-up ironing board hung from a holder on the wall.

"Bedroom's to the left," Eran told her. "The sheets and spread on the bed are clean."

"I never doubted it," Brynna said. The queen-sized bed had no headboard or decoration, and was covered in a spread that was exactly the same as the one on the couch. A small night stand holding a reading lamp and an alarm clock stood next to it, but there was nothing else in the room. "This place is like a hospital."

Eran blinked and opened his mouth, then closed it. "I guess I haven't gotten into decorating much. Anyway, I'm off. I probably won't be back until this evening, so it'll be nice and quiet. If Grunt goes to the door, would you let her into the yard? She only needs about five minutes. Leave the outer door open and she'll come back onto the porch. If you forget to let her into the house, she'll start yelping."

"I think I can handle that."

"I put your cell on the kitchen table," Eran said. "Give me a call if you need anything."

When he was gone, Brynna checked to make sure the door was locked, then satisfied an ill-defined desire to know more about Eran by wandering through his coach house apartment. In hindsight, she was sorry she'd made that comment about a hospital—she could tell by his expression that it had stung. She might never say it again, but it was still pretty accurate. His place, though large and well lit, was oddly personality deprived. Was Eran so much into his work that his apartment was nothing but a box in which he could put his dog and his belongings? Or was there a deeper, darker meaning to a lifestyle that was so austere? Even his closet was military-neat, shirts hung according to color, shoes lined up neatly on a black shoe rack.

She'd never thought to ask him about family or his childhood. It struck her again that there were no photographs, not of friends or family, no games or sports equipment, like a baseball glove or football, in any of the closets. There was only one thing that hinted at how he spent some of his time: in the living room was an extensive collection of DVDs—in alphabetical order, of course—in a double set of bookshelves to one side of a flat-screen television. The titles were all over the board and gave no insight on the man who owned them.

Back in the kitchen, she made herself a sliced-tomato-and-cucumber sandwich, settling at the table in the center of the immaculate, roomy kitchen. Even with Grunt lying at her feet, Brynna felt odd and out of place here, something messy and unpredictable in this orderly, almost sterile room. The only trace of Eran Redmond was his detective's star lying next to the neat stack of mail he'd left on the counter. Beyond that, the surface was clear of everything but a coffeemaker. Even the knives were precisely hung according to size on a magnetic strip above the stove.

What was she but a heated catastrophe on the edge of exploding into Eran's cool and collected existence? In all of eternity, she'd never seen the union of an angel and a human endure, much less a relationship between a demon and a human—it just wasn't doable. She had no idea if redemption would ever be within her reach, but whether it was or wasn't, she was immortal and Eran wasn't. Period, end of discussion, nothing left to argue about. Eran's mortal life would pass in the blink of God's eye, and hers would go on; if she loved him—and right now, at this moment, was the very first time she'd let herself even *think* that word—how would she feel when—

Grunt lifted her head and growled.

Brynna jerked, then realized the Great Dane wasn't growling at her, wasn't even looking in her direction. Instead, Grunt had turned her head and was focused on the storm door as she sniffed the air, taking it in with rapid, frantic breaths. The soft hair along the expanse of the dog's white back had risen and every muscle in her body was taut.

"Oh, *shit*," Brynna said as a maroon shadow flickered on the other side of the glass. Her chair tipped backward as she started to rise, but it was already too late to run. Less than ten feet away, the metal handle of the door glowed a sudden, sultry red before it melted and slid downward; when the door swung inward and the room filled with the stench of sulfur, she wasn't surprised to see the Hunter slouched there.

"Time to go home, Astarte."

"No," she said, then realized it couldn't hear her over Grunt's sudden, vicious snarling. The dog was pressed against Brynna's side, snapping at the air between her and the Hunter. Her spittle flew through the air and fizzled where it splashed against the beast's skin. "No!"

The Hunter ducked through the doorway but still couldn't quite stand up straight. Its gaze swept over Brynna and stopped on the dog, then it laughed. *"Not exactly hellhound caliber, is it?"*

Brynna hooked the fingers of one hand into Grunt's collar and pulled her backward. "Go back where you came from. I'm staying here."

"You know that's not possible, Astarte." The Hunter gestured at her, making Grunt snarl more fiercely. *"I tire of this game. Lucifer awaits."* It grinned hideously. *"Anxiously."*

"Tell him to take a tranquilizer for his nerves," Brynna shot back. "I'm *not* going."

Lucifer's soldier gave a twisted shrug, then snatched at her. Brynna yanked herself out of range, but Grunt, suddenly freed of Brynna's hold, went forward; in an admirably fast move, her teeth snapped shut on the creature's first two fingers. A millisecond later Grunt released them and shook her head wildly, baying at the foul taste the Hunter's bodily liquid had left in her mouth. Before Brynna could blink, a fireball the size of an orange streaked through the air and slammed into Grunt's shoulder. The dog howled in agony and scrambled away on three legs, slipping and clawing across the linoleum to disappear into another part of the house. *"Brainless animal,"* the Hunter spat. It turned to glare at Brynna and flexed its fingers. *"I don't kill you only because Lucifer desires to do so himself. But we go NOW."*

The Hunter lunged for her, swatting aside the table and chairs as if they weighed nothing. Brynna feinted to the right then leaped left, scrambling through the living room entrance and sliding left again into the bathroom. There was no use closing the wooden door, so she didn't bother to waste time. The only thing she could think of was the window—she was on the second story, but the drop wasn't too far. The bathroom was on the backside of the coach house: a tumble to the alleyway below and she'd be off like an Olympic runner. A quick glance behind her when she reached the window and—

Where the hell had the Hunter gone?

"Damn it," she said under her breath. This wasn't right, not at all—it should have followed her, nothing in the world should have made it pause. Except . . .

Eran.

She bolted back the way she'd come, careening around the doorway and nearly tumbling over one of the upended chairs.

Sometimes she *hated* being right.

Eran had slipped into the kitchen behind the Hunter, and the beast's attention was now wholly focused on Eran and the service revolver aimed at its forehead. "Get out of my house," he told the Hunter. His voice was flat, emotionless. "Or I'll shoot you right between the eyes. I never said you could come in here."

Lucifer's soldier actually looked startled for a moment, then it belted out a grisly-sounding chuckle. *"You've watched too many movies, human. We roam where we will, and you can do nothing to stop us."*

"Then I'll just shoot you and be done with it," Eran retorted.

Brynna saw the muscles in his hand flex and gasped—she knew he'd never be quick enough. And she was right; faster than her human eye could follow, the Hunter slapped the gun to the side and wrapped one huge, cruel hand around Eran's neck. The beast lifted him in midair and held him there as though Eran weighed no more than a bag of feathers.

"Foolish human. What do you think having a soul has given you? You are no better than a cockroach, something to be stepped on and eliminated forever."

The Hunter's fingers glowed, then tightened. Brynna heard Eran choke as he flailed at the grip around his windpipe. She was frozen, her mind flipping lightning-fast through options, examining and discarding one before trying the next. Every damned thing she came up with to fight this Hell soldier would kill Eran, too, but if she didn't do *something*, he was going to die anyway, she had to *move*—

A sound roared through her ears once, then again, a rapid double instant of thunder that blotted out her thoughts and sent her reeling backward. Gunshots— Eran had never let go of his revolver, and as he'd promised, he'd brought the weapon back up and squeezed off two hollow-point rounds. One had taken off part of the Hunter's jaw and the other had gouged out a two-inch wide path of flesh through its neck.

Gagging, Eran tumbled to the floor as the Hunter staggered backward. Brynna darted forward, hammering her shoulder into the creature's rib cage, driving it back against the counter. She'd never get another chance like this one, and she wasn't going to lose it. Before the Hunter could right itself, she kicked viciously at its knees, using every bit of strength she could find, again and again, until the spindly legs buckled and sent it to the floor.

It wasn't enough—the beast was injured but nowhere

near critically. In a minute or less, it would be back on its feet and coming after her, killing Eran and taking her back to Hell. There had to be something she could do that didn't involve destroying it in a demon-sized furnace blast.

Brynna could hear Eran trying to get up. Looking for anything to use, her gaze swept the wall behind the Hunter then paused. She kicked the creature again, just to keep it miserable, then lunged over it and grabbed the biggest knife she saw off the magnetized rack. It wasn't really that great, only human-sized, but it was the best she could get her hands on. If this didn't do it, she and Eran were both more than screwed. They were *doomed*.

She came down on the Hunter like a banshee, howling and hacking as fast as she could. It fought back instinctively and she could feel the heat building in its skin, a heat that would rise to inferno level and wipe out the entire building if she couldn't stop it. The butcher knife was in her right hand, yet just stabbing at it wasn't going to be enough. She had to get to its throat, but when she wrapped her left arm across its face, the beast *bit* her, tearing through the flesh and muscle of her forearm and going for bone just like Gavino had. She screamed and tried to pull away—she couldn't help it—and it was the best thing she could have done. The movement hauled the Hunter's head, with its teeth still chewing away at her, backward and against her chest, and Brynna brought the knife forward and sawed at his throat as hard as her body would let her.

Its clawed hands thrashed and found Brynna's skin in a

dozen places, leaving long, bleeding furrows that felt like molten razor cuts. It hurt, horribly, and she couldn't stop herself from wailing, but she would not stop, she would *not*.

Heat enveloped her suddenly, and she drew strength from it, pulling just enough final energy to wrench the knife through the last stretch of resistance—

The Hunter's head toppled off its body.

But it wasn't over yet. It was never that easy.

The beast was weak and its heat was cooling, but it was still moving, already tipping sideways and reaching out with blind fingers as it tried to find its missing part. Brynna couldn't let the Hunter reassemble itself, and the only way to prevent that from happening was to destroy the head completely. *Completely*—no parts left big enough to put back together. Because of Eran, she couldn't incinerate it, so what now?

She swatted aside the Hunter's fumbling fingers and snatched its head off the floor, holding it by one of the undulating spikes that protruded from its skull, trying desperately to ignore the pain zigzagging through her arm from the bite wound. The Hunter's eyes stared at her, spiteful through the pre-cloudiness of death, and its mouth twitched and clicked although it could no longer speak. Could it still bite? She didn't want to find out.

Brynna spun and saw that Eran had managed to get to his knees; he was using the door frame to pull himself up. "Eran, I have to destroy the head," she cried. "Completely—"

"Cleaver," he croaked. He waved vaguely at the cabinets behind Brynna. "In the drawer."

She turned and yanked open the nearest drawer but saw only boxes of plastic bags and aluminum foil. As her hand closed on the next one over, pain seared through her ankle. She gasped and kicked at the Hunter—it was clawing at her ankle, trying to hobble her. She pulled too hard on the next drawer and it came free of the cabinet and crashed to the floor, scattering everything inside it. The cleaver she was looking for spun away and came to a stop against the baseboard to the right of the refrigerator. Retrieving it took her out of the Hunter's reach, and she swung the creature's head up and thunked it onto the countertop. She could stomach what she had to do next—she'd done far worse in the depths of Hell—but could Eran?

Time to find out.

Brynna lifted the meat cleaver high and brought it down on the Hunter's skull. Bone cracked and the thing's mouth stretched; a sound somewhere between a gurgle and a screech found its way out. On the floor, its body spasmed violently, then twisted and began to squirm in her direction, deadly claws seeking her legs. Then Eran was there, swinging one of the kitchen chairs, beating it back to give her back some safety.

Brynna brought the cleaver down again, then again, chopping and cutting until the countertop was covered in red and black ichor and bits of bone no bigger than an inch across. But it wasn't enough and she knew it—there could be nothing recognizable, nothing that the unholy force that powered this creature could piece back together like a diabolical puzzle. Eyes glazed almost to exhaustion, Brynna squinted at the wall above the sink and saw something so simple, so sublime and innocuous, that she couldn't believe she hadn't noticed it before.

A wall switch like the one at Ramiro's restaurant.

Eran had managed to hammer the Hunter into the far left corner. The creature was still fighting, but it was losing ground quickly—every downward slam of the cleaver had taken a little more out of its power. It wasn't the only one losing energy; there wasn't a single part of Brynna's body that didn't hurt, and she'd lost enough blood to make the room swim when she leaned sideways.

There was a crash as the Hunter got lucky and blocked Eran's next whack. The chair splintered and broke apart, leaving Eran staring dazedly at a chair leg, the only thing left in his hand. Before Eran could react, the creature flung an arm out and knocked him off his feet. Then it rolled onto its belly and scrabbled sightlessly across the floor like some kind of enormous, bloody worm, trying desperately to find Brynna.

How she felt didn't matter. If she had to drag herself sideways by her fingernails, Brynna had to finish this.

She stretched until her hand found the sink, then pulled herself toward it, using her right arm to scoop the ghastly mound of the Hunter's brains, skin and chunks of bone with her as she moved. Three feet had never seemed so far, especially when it took her that much closer to the Hunter headed toward her from the other direction. As the beast's jagged talons scraped the side of her foot, Brynna pulled the entire loathsome puddle into the sink, twisted the faucet to ON and slammed her sludge-covered hand against the switch.

The light over the sink came on at the same time the Hunter sank its claws deep into the meat of her foot.

Brynna howled and beat on it, but her blows were useless against the agony spiraling up her body as the Hunter tried to use her leg to climb upward. Eran was yelling at her, but she couldn't make out the words above her own shrieks and the sound of the running water close to her face and her ear because she was sinking, going down against the cabinet door under the gut-wrenching pain and the weight of the Hunter's headless body.

Something shoved her to one side and the Hunter went with her, clinging to her like a giant parasite. She was falling, headed for the floor, where she would die when the soldier tore out her throat. Then it would go for Eran—

The whine of a motor, high-pitched and shockingly close, split her thoughts apart. For a single unrelenting moment, the Hunter clutched the bones of her knees even tighter—

Then its claws went slack and it sagged, lifeless, across her feet.

A million miles above her head, Eran scraped the vile remains of the Hunter's head down the garbage disposal.

"THAT WAS THE MOST disgusting thing I've ever seen," Eran said. "I don't think I could have even imagined anything worse."

"I'd rather be disgusting than dead." Sitting next to him on the side of the tub in Eran's oversized bathroom, Brynna winced as she leaned over the cool water and hurriedly sponged it onto her legs and arms. He'd come up with boxer shorts and T-shirts, and they'd both changed out of their fouled clothes and decided to clean up their wounds before dealing with the enormous, smelly situation in the kitchen. They'd tended to Grunt as best they could, and as soon as they got things under control, Eran was going to load her in the car and drive her over to the vet clinic on Clark and Diversey. "What were you yelling at me back there?"

Eran gave her a grin that could only be described as sickly. "I was telling you the switch to the garbage disposal was on the other side of the sink."

"Right." She stood, but her legs were wobbly and she had to hold on to the sink before she could step over the tub's edge onto the bath mat. She was torn inside. Part of her was grateful for his help; she would've died without it because she would have never let the Hunter take her back to Lucifer. Another part was more than a little dumbfounded. "What were you doing here, anyway? I thought you were going to work."

He stepped out next to her and pulled a towel from the rack. His throat was burned, but not too badly—more like a bad sunburn than anything else. He had no idea how lucky he'd been. "I came back because I forgot my star," he said. Instead of swabbing at his own neck, he pressed the towel gently against the deep gashes where the Hunter had chowed down on her arm. "As long as I've been on the force, I've never done something so idiotic. Then again, things weren't exactly on pattern around here this morning."

"Don't you need to go back?"

"Got a few things to deal with first," he said grimly.

"Like getting Grunt taken care of, and what the hell to do with that thing's body." He looked pointedly at Brynna's ravaged legs and arm. "And you, too. Coming on top of your little barbecue, don't you think this is all a bit extensive to go untreated, even for you?"

She shook her head. "No. I've been through worse."

"As a human being?"

Brynna exhaled. "No," she admitted. "But I'll be all right, I promise." They both turned their heads at the sound of a whimper from the living room. "We have to get Grunt to the vet. Poor thing—she's like a child. She has no idea why she was hurt or why the pain won't stop."

Brynna went with him into the living room and knelt next to Grunt. The dog was lying on a blanket that Eran had put down for her, panting heavily and occasionally lifting her head to try to lick at the massive star-shaped burn on her shoulder. It was deep and looked dreadfully painful, and they could see where the fireball had burned through the skin and into the muscle below. A thin, bloody fluid leaked from the edges, dribbling down and staining the blanket. It made Brynna recall her own burns of just a week or so earlier, and she couldn't help shuddering in sympathy.

Working together, they tugged on the blanket and tied the ends so that it formed a sort of hammock. The arm that was injured was next to useless, but Brynna got her good hand wrapped around one end and helped lever the heavy dog up and into Eran's arms. She followed him down the stairs and opened the car door, wincing every time the Great Dane yelped.

"What about you?" Eran asked as he slid onto the

driver's side after getting Grunt settled in the backseat. "I hate to leave you alone with that—that *thing* up there."

Brynna managed a smile. "That *thing* isn't a problem anymore beyond cleaning up after it."

"You're sure?"

"Absolutely." She was silent as he closed the door then rolled down the window. "Eran, I can get rid of the rest of it, but I'm not at the top of my game. It's probably going to leave a mark on the floor or . . . something."

He raised an eyebrow at her pause before the word *something,* and Brynna knew he was remembering what she'd told him about getting rid of the Thai witch doctor in the basement of the jewelry store. "Do what you have to. Just please don't burn the place down. I'm sure I can come up with some bullshit about a grease fire to tell the landlord, but annihilating the entire building is a little beyond my creativity."

"Got it." Brynna watched as he pulled away, then turned back and trudged up the stairs to the coach house. She hoped Grunt would be okay, and was a little surprised at how truly sorry she felt that the dog had gotten hurt. Why? Because the animal had tried to defend Brynna. How strange that the sweet-natured pet would endanger herself trying to protect a person she'd met only an hour earlier—yet another reason why humans placed such high value on their dogs.

Standing in the kitchen, she stared numbly down at the body of the Hunter. Even with the evidence of it on the floor at her feet, she still wasn't sure she could fathom the magnitude of what she'd done. Killing one of Lucifer's Hunters . . . that was an *enormous* thing.

Anything else she'd done over the past millennia as she'd traveled the path to realizing that her true desire was redemption—all the thousands of little betrayals that she'd committed by showing tiny moments of mercy on a multitude of tormented souls—was nothing compared to this. Yes, she had killed Gavino, but her former partner would barely be aggravated about that; the snot had acted big on Earth, but in Hell Gavino had been little more than a nameless lower-echelon demon hardly worth Lucifer's time. His efforts to better himself had accomplished nothing beyond getting himself killed.

But the Hunter at her feet . . . this was a different thing altogether. Hunters were like children to Lucifer, spawned of the underworld's lava pools and a touch of his own infernal breath. With this single ruthless act, she had permanently closed the door on any possible return to an existence in Hell.

Heaven might forgive, but Hell did not . . . and Lucifer would never forget.

Twenty – three

Mireva's long – awaited science fair was held on a warm and beautiful Saturday at the Museum of Science and Industry at 57th and Lake Shore Drive. The temperature floated in the upper seventies and a light breeze off Lake Michigan kept the humidity under control; for Chicagoans, it was a perfect day to get out and enjoy their city.

To Brynna, it seemed like half the city had decided to go museum-hopping.

It had been a long time since she'd seen so many people in one place. To begin with, the concept of Mireva being at the science fair at all set her teeth on edge—it was too public, too crowded. On one hand that seemed good, in an overused more-the-merrier sort of way; on the other, there was so much that was out of her control—namely, who, what, where, and when. In short, *everything*.

On the outside, the museum reminded her of fifth and sixth century Greece, back when she had watched with interest as the humans of that region warred with each other at the same time they built incredible structures like the Parthenon, the Propylaea, and temple after temple to their gods. The architecture of the museum shared many of the same features—massive stonework, statues that were strikingly similar to the lovely caryatids and other sculptured figures created by the masterful Grecian artists, columns topped by Ionic capitals, and acroteria—the elaborately carved figures adorning the corners and tops of pediments.

The inside was another matter. Only the marble floor seemed to go with the magnificent, ancient-looking exterior; everything else had moved on into the era of technology. Banners floated overhead, advertising exhibits that covered everything from airplanes and helicopters, to molecular biology and nuclear power, to the creation of the Earth (if they only knew) and a hundred other subjects. For Brynna, it was a jarring transition. Then again, maybe it was time to leave history behind and get with the present.

The science fair, a heroic undertaking in and of itself, had been set up in a large hall situated at the right center off the main floor. To get to it, Eran and Brynna had to walk through the museum's main hallway and attraction, which for quite some time had been a presentation on *Harry Potter.* What little she saw of it in passing made her grin with delight and the secret knowledge of how magic really worked. If getting to Mireva and watching over her hadn't been such a high priority, Brynna would have had a wonderful time wandering through the exhibit.

The Chicago public school system held another science fair every March, but this was a special extension of that one, sponsored by several dozen universities around the country. There were ten prizes in total, the top three being full scholarships; partials went to second-, third-, and fourth-place categories. The massive exhibit hall had been divided by cloth-covered tables into inner and outer rectangles so that the contestants had plenty of room to work and for storage behind their setups. The entrants faced each other across a wide aisle, and the judges, along with family members, other students and the general public, flowed between the two of them. Out of nearly a thousand entries, only 150 projects had been picked to enter this final phase.

Mireva had been assigned a spot in the larger outer rectangle, midway down the room on the north wall. Washed by the blue-white light of countless overhead fluorescents, her lush, healthy plants were an expanse of luxuriant green among the more austere shades of gray and metal. People couldn't help gravitating toward her project; in the midst of all this science, Brynna thought that spoke very strongly to the spiritual attraction between mankind and the most basic, natural things of this world.

"So far, so good," Eran said. He was keeping pace with Brynna as she walked the aisle between the tables, both of them looking for anything that just wasn't quite right. Brynna doubted that Lahash would show up, at least not in the very crowded exhibition hall, but who knew if he would find another sad and sorry puppet like Klesowitch? The thought made her cringe inside; if he had, neither she nor Eran would have any idea who it was.

"Don't say that," Brynna said. "It's like tempting fate."

The corners of his eyes crinkled although a smile didn't show on his mouth. "Fate—you believe in that stuff?"

"I do," she said. "Fate, destiny—they're one and the same. But neither is completely set. I told you before, there are always choices. One small decision can affect everything."

"Like chaos theory. The butterfly on one side of the world," Eran said. "I learned that from *Jurassic Park*."

"What's that?"

"A movie based on a Michael Crichton book."

"Ah." She had no idea who Michael Crichton was, but chaos theory was as good a term as any.

"So how does that apply to Mireva?"

"The same as it applies to anyone," Brynna answered, watching the crowd with sharp eyes. "Her destiny is to complete a task preset by God, but He always gives choices. There's always the chance that a choice made by one person can affect, for good or bad, someone else."

"Like Klesowitch."

"Exactly."

They'd walked the entire hall and were now back at Mireva's table. Mireva was beaming, transformed from a normally self-conscious and studious teenage girl into a young woman totally comfortable with herself and her presentation as she explained the project to a group of adults. Brynna saw Abrienda and Ramiro moving down the tables, content to let the girl shine on her own. After a minute or so, the adults moved on and Brynna and Eran took their place in front of Mireva's table. Mireva's excited words tumbled over the question Brynna would have asked.

"Isn't it great? The judges have been around twice and I think they're really impressed." Her smile was ear to ear, her words lilting with excitement. "I have a really good feeling about this, Brynna. I really do."

Brynna smiled, but inside she could still feel her nerves jumping over one another. She wanted to believe everything was going to work out, that Mireva was going to be okay and, as they say, life would go on. But there was still that pesky little problem of Mireva completing her task. The tricky thing was knowing whether or not it *had* been accomplished. Sometimes these things were so tiny, a matter of being in the right place at the right time to do the most insignificant of deeds, that a nephilim could fulfill his or her destiny and never realize it—the butterfly effect that Eran had mentioned.

"Great job, Mireva," Eran said warmly. "All that work, and it's finally going to pay off. That's excellent."

Still smiling, Mireva inhaled deeply, then let out her breath in a long, slow sigh that reminded Brynna of meditating. The girl's next words, however, were like a razor blade running down Brynna's spine. "I still feel like I've forgotten something," she said. She scanned her table, the plants, the poster presentations hanging on the easels behind her. "But I've gone over my checklist a dozen times and I can't find where anything's been left off."

"Excuse me," a female voice said from behind Brynna.

Brynna turned, then her eyes widened. The last time she'd seen the blond-haired teenager standing before her was over a month ago, and she hadn't been looking particularly energetic after a go-around with a group of prostitutes in a holding cell. This young woman was clean, pretty, and well dressed; the only evidence of that ugly late-night encounter was a line of faint pink scars along one cheek. They were carefully covered with makeup and would probably fade away in another six months. With all the dirt gone, Brynna could see the girl's Irish heritage in her lightly freckled skin and blue eyes.

"Hi," the girl said. "Do you remember me?"

"Of course," Brynna said. She glanced at Eran, who was looking from the girl to Brynna with a pleased expression on his face. She was puzzled for a moment, then she realized how seldom he probably saw someone who'd been in a jail cell reappear in any environment other than a courtroom. She wasn't sure what was next or what she was expected to say, but the girl took it from there.

"My name's Kodi. I never got a chance to say thank you for helping me that night."

"Brynna always seems to be helping people," Mireva put in before Brynna could respond. "What did she do for you?"

Brynna shot Mireva a glance but Mireva stubbornly refused to look at her. Kodi surprised both Brynna and Eran by answering truthfully. "I snuck out of the house and went to a party with a bunch of friends. Things got kind of out of control—they were doing X and drinking, and the neighbors called the police. I wasn't into the illegal part, but I freaked out and tried to run away when the cops showed up. Of course I got caught. I'd lost my purse and didn't have any ID, so I didn't have any proof I was underage. When they tried to call my dad, he and my mom had gone out and he'd forgotten his cell phone. I ended up in jail for the night."

Mireva's expression had gone from inquisitive to alarmed. "Yikes."

"Yeah, well, getting thrown in jail was the easy part. *Staying* in there turned out to be a totally big problem. I got beat up and she—Brynna, right?—stopped things before they got *really* bad." She sent Brynna a grateful glance. "I wish I could do something for you in return. My dad said you probably saved my life."

Brynna shrugged. "No problem." She wasn't sure why, but she felt a little embarrassed at being thanked in front of people like this. Stuff like this was supposed to be low key, not public. "I'm glad you're all right."

Kodi smiled. "A cracked rib and some bumps and scrapes, but they're all healing." She touched her scarred cheek. "I sure won't do something like that again."

"That's an awesome story," Mireva put in.

"So what are you doing here?" Eran asked. His timing was perfect in redirecting the conversation before Mireva could dig deeper, and Brynna couldn't help feeling relieved. She didn't think the story of how she'd landed in jail because she was talking to that first nephilim when he was shot in the head was a great subject for conversation.

"My dad is head of the museum's committee on local events. He takes a big interest in the science fairs because he also teaches environmental science at U of I. He was telling me about your project, so I thought I'd come over and take a look." She grinned and looked again at Brynna. "So you guys know each other, huh? Small world?"

"He noticed my exhibit?" Mireva's eyes were bright.

Kodi nodded, then gave Mireva a smile that could only be described as secretive. "Oh, yeah. A lot of people did."

"Really," Mireva breathed. "That's great." She looked down at her table and its careful arrangement of plants, each with a meticulously lettered placard that corresponded to the complicated ecological plan on the posterboard behind her table. "I'm gonna run to the restroom for a minute."

Brynna frowned. "You all right?"

"Yeah. My stomach's just a little funky—nerves, that's all. It's been building ever since I got the notice that I'd won an exhibition slot here." She shrugged. "My own fault for obsessing too much over it. I'll be glad when it's all over."

"Hey," Eran said. "Anyone would. It's a big deal."

"I'll be right back." The girl started to slip out from behind the table, but an adult voice made her stop.

"Now's not a good time to leave your exhibit, miss," said an older man with glasses. A tag on the lapel of his jacket read *Dave N., Science Fair Staff.* He looked down at a piece of paper on a clipboard. "Mireva Cocinero, right? You're one of the finalists, and the judges are doing their last walk-through. You really need to be here in case they have any questions."

He moved on without waiting for a response, and Brynna saw Mireva's shoulders tense. "Mireva?"

"I really need to take a quick break," she said unhappily. "I should've gone ten minutes ago, and now . . ."

"I'll stand in for you," Kodi said. She leaned around Brynna and Eran, peering down the center aisle. "I've been to dozens of these things, and they don't move that quickly. You've got at least ten minutes, and even if they get here before you return, I know every person on the panel. I know I can persuade them to hold off, maybe talk to one or two others and then come back."

Mireva looked relieved. "Really?"

"Sure." Kodi turned the other way, where Dave's retreating figure could just be glimpsed heading out of the exhibit hall. "I've never seen that guy before. He's probably just some new clerk on a little control trip—do this, move here, don't breathe. You know the type." She looked back at Mireva. "Go. Turn right when you get out of the exhibition hall. You'll see the coal mine room, and the restrooms are to the left of it."

"Thanks," Mireva said. "Just give me five minutes."

Then she was out from behind her table and slipping into the crowd. Brynna watched her go as Eran regarded Kodi. "So," he said. "That was quite the experience you had over at the precinct, huh? You know, I never got the full skinny on what happened."

"Oh, God," Kodi said. "You aren't kidding. I *never* want to go through something like that again. I must've had VICTIM invisibly tattooed across my forehead, because those women went after me the second I got put in there. If it hadn't been for Brynna—"

Brynna heard the conversation, but she wasn't really listening. Her thoughts were twisting around and around, like a bunch of mental snakes trying to become untangled. How strange was it that Kodi, whose name she'd never bothered to learn at the police station, had turned up here at Mireva's science fair? The idea that it was a "small world" was bullshit; with over eight million people, the city of Chicago was the third largest in the country, and the odds of meeting Kodi again when you had completely different lifestyles were astronomical. Add to the situation that Kodi's father was involved with the museum and the girl knew the judges . . . well, it was pretty solidly on the side of not-a-coincidence. Then there was Dave, the staff member Kodi had never met and who'd told Mireva she couldn't leave her table. Yet because of her ties at the museum, Kodi had been here to let Mireva do just that.

Everything happens for a reason.

Kodi would not have been here had Brynna not been at the police station to pull her out of the piranha-infested holding cell. Mireva would have sucked it up and stayed put, not wanting to chance that the judges would knock her out of the running on the basis of a few unanswered questions.

Brynna scowled, thinking about how Mireva had said her stomach was bugging her. That just didn't seem right—nephilim never got ill, were never plagued by the multitude of biological ailments that generally tormented a normal human's body. She squinted toward the hall's main entrance, but there was no sign of Mireva, or of the elusive Dave. Who was he? Just another new employee? Or someone else, another tool being wielded by Lahash? There was too much at stake here—namely Mireva—for Brynna not to make sure everything was copacetic.

"I'm going to check on Mireva."

Eran looked at her in surprise. "What—is something wrong?"

Brynna was already moving, and he followed without hesitating. Kodi watched them go, her expression bewildered. "I hope not," Brynna said over her shoulder. "But I'm going to make damned sure."

><+>-०-<+><

IT WAS UNSETTLING HOW quickly the lie had come out of her mouth.

Mireva hurried toward the women's restroom, weaving smoothly among the people milling in front of the tables. There wasn't a thing in the world wrong with her, and it was a good thing her mom and uncle hadn't been around to hear that complete fabrication about her nerves and the science fair making her stomach disagreeable. Had she been nervous? Well, duh. But she'd never been physically sick a day in her life.

There were even more visitors milling around the museum's huge central foyer, drawn, no doubt, by the *Harry Potter* exhibition. Maybe when the science fair was over, for better or worse—and she sure hoped it would be for better—she could go up front and take a look. Normally she wouldn't have been able to afford it, but the science fair contestants had been given a special day pass. She'd like to take a look at the baby chick hatchery too.

The restrooms were right where Kodi had said they'd be, and Mireva hurried into the women's room, still not sure why she'd felt so strongly that she had to get here. And to lie about it? Wow—she'd never been a liar. Hearing those words come out of her own mouth had been like having her brain taken over by aliens or something. Plus, now that she was inside, well . . . hey. It looked perfectly normal, like countless other women's restrooms she'd seen. Tiled walls and a water-splashed floor beneath a row of sinks with mirrors above them, paper towel holders, square trash bins, a row of stalls. Mireva's need to get in here had been all-consuming, like a firefighter responding to a midnight alarm. So where the hell was the fire?

There was a woman washing her hands at a sink while another lady a few feet away refreshed her lipstick. Feeling self-conscious, Mireva went to an empty sink and smoothed her hair, trying to look like she had a reason for being there when in reality she thought she was acting like some kind of weirdo. Mrs. Lipstick finished up and walked out, while the first, a pleasant-looking woman in her midfifties, was still studiously scrubbing her hands; she reminded Mireva of the way surgeons on reality medical shows scrubbed up. She had dark hair that was starting to go silver at the temples, and when she glanced at Mireva and smiled, her brown eyes were warm and friendly. An expensive leather bag that Mireva assumed belonged to her was resting on the narrow metal shelf beneath the mirror. "Enjoying the museum?"

Mireva made herself smile back. "Yes, thank you." Why did she suddenly feel so tense?

"I saw you in the science fair, didn't I?" When Mireva nodded, the woman continued, "That's the whole reason I came downtown on a Saturday, you know. I'm a professor at Wright College. I teach human and organismal biology. I've been through the museum a dozen times, but I'm always interested in the competitive science fairs, especially at the precollege level. Seeing what the high school students come up with is like looking through a telescope into the future." She finally rinsed and gave her hands a shake, then turned and stepped toward the paper towel dispenser. "Refresh my memory, please. What's your project—"

It happened so fast that Mireva almost didn't make it. One wrong step, the slightly off-balance turn of a

low-heel shoe, the smallest pool of water in front of one
of the sinks.

The professor's hip twisted and she fell sideways as her
foot slipped forward. Nothing in the restroom was soft,
but Mireva was there before the older woman lost it completely; faster than she'd ever thought she could move,
both hands shot out and Mireva grabbed the woman by
the shoulders and pulled her forward. Momentum carried
them both down but Mireva's hold softened the impact.
The landing was still hard enough to make Mireva's teeth
click together, but nothing, on either of them, was broken. The professor's breath went out of her in a gasp, then
her eyes widened when she turned her head and realized
that her temple had missed the sharp corner of the metal
trash bin by scarcely half an inch.

"Wow," Mireva said as she untangled herself. "That
was close. Are you okay?"

"I am, thank you very much. Banged my knee pretty
hard, though." The professor shook her head. "That was
certainly . . . embarrassing."

Mireva gave the woman a shaky grin and got to her feet,
then extended her hand. It was so ridiculous—was being
here to stop this teacher from hitting her head the whole
reason she'd felt such an urge to get to the restroom? First
of all, it didn't make any sense; secondly, if that *had* been
it, why didn't she feel any better? The woman reached for
the hand Mireva offered. "My name is Lydia D'Amato.
And you—"

"Hel-*lo*, ladies."

Mireva's head snapped around at the sound of the
oily male voice. Beneath her fingers, she felt Professor

D'Amato's hand stiffen. "What are you doing in here, young man? The men's room is down the hall." The professor grabbed the side of the sink and started to pull herself up, but Mireva instinctively stepped backward, cutting her off and forcing her to stay on the floor. She looked up at Mireva, surprised. "Would you help me up, please?"

"Yeah, Mireva. Help her up, why don't you?" The guy had let the restroom door swing shut behind him and now he blocked it with his foot. He looked young and gang dangerous; despite the air-conditioning he was sweating heavily and the dark, curly hair that was bunched under his baseball cap was stringy and wet. The eyes that regarded her from beneath the cap's brim were black as coal and callous, utterly without feeling.

Mireva's brow furrowed and she stared at him. Instead of giving the professor some room, she let go of the woman's hand and crowded her even more, pinning the woman against the tiled wall. "Who are you? How do you know my name?"

He shrugged one muscular shoulder, and the movement reminded her, strangely, of Gavino. "Let's just say we have a mutual *amigo*."

Stress was making Mireva's temples pulse, but still she tried to sort it out. A mutual friend? Who? Gavino was dead, and this hoodlum sure wouldn't be on Facebook terms with Brynna or Detective Redmond. So who—

Her stomach twisted as a not-so-long-ago conversation with Brynna flashed through her memory. It had to be Mr. Lahash, the creep who'd masqueraded as a sponsor from Purdue University, and who Brynna said had sent Gavino, and that crazy serial killer, to try to murder her. This guy must be Lahash's latest mercenary. "Look," she said. "What's the deal with all this, anyway? I'm nobody. There's nothing to be gained by killing me." Her words triggered a sharp breath from the professor, but Mireva still wouldn't budge.

"You got that right." The guy pulled a knife from his pocket and flipped it open. Mireva inhaled, but instead of coming after her, he leaned back against the door and started scraping at the filth under his fingernails with the tip.

Behind her, Professor D'Amato tried again to push her way free. "Mireva—that's your name, right? Mireva, get out of the way and let me talk to him."

"No," Mireva hissed. She reached back with one hand and easily pressed the older woman back down. People were always surprised at how strong she was, had even said she was stronger than she should be. But Mireva had always taken her strength for granted. After all, she was over six feet tall—of course she was strong. "You stay *there*."

The guy's snakelike gaze fixed not on Mireva but on the woman on the floor behind her. "As I was saying, you're right. Our friend isn't much interested in you anymore." He dug below another fingernail and Mireva grimaced inside; his nails were sharp and long—too long for a man—and so dirty they were discolored. For some reason she knew they were very, very strong. "See," he continued, "I was supposed to get over here and take care of you before you met up with the old lady. You weren't even supposed to get to the bathroom. Sadly, I'm late." He made a *tsk* sound with his lips. "Gotta love the Saturday crowds."

"So go away, then." Mireva lifted her chin. She was dizzy, her breath coming in short, shallow inhalations that were just shy of hyperventilating. But she would not show fear to this piece of street garbage. "If you blew it, then there's nothing—"

"Oh, but there *is*." He smirked. "The man don't take failure for an answer, you get my meaning? He said if I'm late, then I have to do a two-for-one once I find out who you're talking to. So now I know. That means Grandma goes first, then you." The guy straightened and flipped the knife around and up. The movement had a fluidity to it that spoke of way too much practice. "I don't usually work that cheap, but this time it seems I gotta make an exception. Because, you know, witnesses have big, noisy mouths."

Mireva watched him come toward her, but for some reason, she was no longer afraid. Her racing pulse had calmed, and the lightheadedness that had been seeping through her a moment ago was also gone. Instead, everything had become clear and crisp, like she was suddenly seeing the world through an ultrasharp camera lens. This, she realized, was somehow the single most important moment of her life. She didn't know how she knew that, or why, but everything that had happened, everything that was *her*, had led up to right now.

"Get out of the way," he said.

"No."

The restroom wasn't that big and he was across the few

feet that separated them in barely more than a second. He
drove forward with the knife but Mireva caught his wrist
and swept it aside, fingers clamping onto his flesh with
every bit of strength she had. His weight slammed her
backward and vaguely she heard Professor D'Amato cry
out. She tried to bring her knee up and into his crotch but
there wasn't enough room, so she settled for smashing the
heel of her shoe against his instep.

He cursed when he couldn't yank free of her grip,
then punched her in the side of the head with his other
fist; Mireva didn't feel it. She was as tall as he was and
her right hand was jammed between her chest and his.
As they grappled with each other, jerking back and
forth, she managed to wriggle her hand up until her
fingers were just past his jawline. When the tips of her
nails grazed the stubble-covered flesh of his face, Mireva
curled her fingers into hooks and dug in as deeply and
viciously as she could. He howled and tried to jerk
back but she followed, plastering her body against his
and propelling him backward in an attempt to put as
much distance as possible between him and the professor. Beneath her attacker's bellows of rage was another
sound—Professor D'Amato was screaming, filling the
small room with the shrill sounds of attention-drawing
panic.

The two of them ricocheted off the stalls and sinks
until they finally crashed against the door. She still had
a lock on his knife hand, was still trying her best to maul
the bastard's face, when he whipped his head to the left
and his teeth clamped down on her fingers. She shrieked
and he seemed to feed on the sound of her agony, grinding

down, scraping bone, then shaking his head like a wild dog. Mireva wasn't prepared for the pain. It was overwhelming, all-consuming, like nothing she'd ever experienced. Even the noise of someone hammering on the other side of the metal bathroom door wasn't enough to keep her mind focused on anything but the complete and utter agony ratcheting through her hand and up her forearm. Now *she* was the one trying to pull away and he was following *her* as the door was being shoved open. They were headed back toward where Professor D'Amato was—

No!

She had no choice but to let go with her left hand.

Mireva brought her hand up, driving her palm against his cheekbone and jamming her thumb deep into his right eye. He staggered, braying with pain; she kept pushing backward, harder and harder. They were moving back and forth in an insane dance and she was determined to keep the distance between him and the professor. Something flashed once in the corner of her eye, then again, and he was still biting her, he was going to bite her damned fingers right *off,* but she was too wrapped up in the anguish of that and the overwhelming need to keep this wannabe killer away from the woman behind her to know what it was. Everything about her had condensed into this single instance in time, and she would not fail, she *could* not.

And even as the left side of her neck went numb and cold and she heard Brynna and Detective Redmond shouting, Mireva was still holding on to her assailant and trying to drag him down to the cold, cold tile floor.

⊱⊰◦⊱⊰

BRYNNA WOULD HAVE KILLED Juan if Eran hadn't gotten into the room first.

When the door gave way, he almost fell into the restroom. Then he was moving forward and catching Juan's bloody, upraised hand, fast but still not fast enough. There was so much blood—Brynna saw streaks of it running down Juan's face, splatters on both of Mireva's hands, a glistening red sheet of it falling from the girl's neck downward—

Dear God, Brynna thought. Her *neck*!

Eran spun Juan away from Mireva and slammed him face-first against one of the stalls. For a single, shocked moment Mireva just stood there, perfectly balanced with her hands still up in a fighting stance. Brynna felt more than saw Eran's head turn toward the teenager; when Mireva toppled forward, Brynna caught her and let her go gently to the floor, cradling her and feeling the girl's life rush past her in a breeze of sweet, sun-filled ocean air that no one else in the room could smell but her. Mireva's eyes, always so dark, lightened to a sparkling tan for just an instant, and Brynna knew that somewhere on the other side of eternity, the girl was seeing the face of God.

Brynna pulled Mireva closer and pressed her cheek against the girl's hair. And for the first time in all of her long, long existence, Brynna cried.

Epilogue

Brynna had never experienced grief like this.

There was sorrow in Hell, of course, but it was selfish, the sorrow of the soul as it realized too late the wrongs done and the eternal damning of itself. No soul banished to Hell thought of those it had wronged or hurt or murdered; there was only the punishment to be endured, the never-ending pain of the now and the seemingly endless torment to come.

Yet here, on an afternoon bursting with summer sunshine, birdsong, and the too-strong scent of roses and carnations, the anguish of Mireva's family seemed to rival the worst of what she'd ever seen in Lucifer's Kingdom. Their loss was so huge it was nearly suffocating; it coupled with the pain that Brynna was still feeling and left her bewildered and confused, helpless to sort out her own emotions as she struggled, with abject inexperience, to find something comforting to say to Ramiro and Abrienda.

"All that," Eran said in a low voice, "and it still ends like this."

They were standing on the other side of Mireva's grave, giving the family their own space as the light blue casket was slowly lowered. Green felt had been draped over the edges of the hole to hide the dirt, but Brynna doubted that made anyone feel better—it was still a cold, dark hole in the earth. To humankind, Brynna suspected this was the worst part. It must be so very difficult for them to hold on to faith and the promise of God's eternal light while at the same time consigning the remains of a loved one to the indifference of darkness.

"She fulfilled her destiny," Brynna told Eran quietly. "She did what He required, and her soul is in God's hands now."

Eran's eyes were shadowed and fixed on the small mantle of roses at the head of the casket, watching as it disappeared from sight. "Did she? How can you be sure?"

"I felt it," she said. "She died in my arms, and I saw her whole task and why." He looked at her, his eyes troubled. "The woman in the bathroom, Professor D'Amato—did you notice that she went back to the science fair after all the police and medical personnel left?"

"No. I got her statement but then I had to deal with Juan." He practically spit out the name.

"I think she was just trying to clear her head, and she wanted to take one more look at Mireva's project—the girl had just saved her life. A couple of tables over was a young man who'd been trying for a scholarship for three years but never quite made it. Like Mireva, he's smart and hardworking, but he doesn't have the money to go to college. He always fell just a little short on his studies because he worked—his mother is disabled."

"What does this have to do with Mireva's task, or whatever you call it?"

"This was his last attempt," Brynna said quietly. "He was going to give up this time, get a job and go to a community college part-time." Brynna raised her head and gazed at the sky, feeling the sun on her face. "Professor D'Amato stopped at his exhibit while he was packing up. She convinced him to try one more time, told him that nothing good should ever been given up on."

Eran scowled. "That's it? Mireva died for *that*?"

"I could see what's going to happen in my head," Brynna said with a faint, sad smile. "You see, next year he'll win the scholarship, and someday he'll be a doctor in the same field as that professor. They'll meet again and she'll mentor him, and eventually the research that he does will be pivotal in discovering a major treatment for AIDS. Without Mireva's intervention, the professor would have died and he would have never become more than . . . what do you call them? A physician's assistant."

Eran said nothing, and Brynna knew he was turning this over in his mind. It was hard to refute the result, the sacrifice of one for the good of many, but that didn't lessen the pain when you had come to care for the sacrificial lamb. For her own part, Brynna sought redemption and had chosen this path to find it, yet she had never bargained for the affection she had learned as a human, had never considered that as a result of protecting a nephilim, the nephilim might die anyway. She'd never thought it would ache like this, down to her very core. Was the redemption she so desired worth the pain of caring for these humans?

"Do they always die?" Eran asked suddenly. "Is that how it always ends?"

Brynna blinked. "No. I have no idea how many go either way, but . . . no. They don't always die."

He went silent again and she watched him surreptitiously as he thought about her answer, and she thought about him. Her affection for him was growing, day by day, dangerously so—she wanted to be with him, looked forward to seeing him, *missed* him when he wasn't there. Yet he was so fragile, so temporary, and just being around her put him in constant danger. Lahash was still out there. He might be beaten for a time, but he would lick his wounds and return—they always did. To the cutthroat soldiers of Hell, Brynna was a walking example of what Professor D'Amato had told that young man: a prize you shouldn't stop trying to get.

"Look," Eran said suddenly. "It's Kodi."

Brynna followed his pointing finger and saw the blond-haired girl standing off to one side, away from the family and alone in her misery. A small bouquet of flowers was bunched in her fists and even from this distance, Brynna could see the young woman's face was swollen and red from crying. "Come on," Brynna said. "Let's go talk to her."

Kodi stared at the ground as they walked up, too miserable to look at them. Before either Brynna or Eran could say anything, she blurted, "It's my fault, you know. Who said I had to be the good guy and watch her damned table? If I hadn't done that, she couldn't have left. She would have never gone to the bathroom, would have never—"

Brynna put her hand on the girl's arm and squeezed. "Everything happens for a reason, Kodi. If Mireva hadn't gone to the bathroom, that guy would have killed Professor D'Amato. It seems to me that God's purpose was for Mireva to be *there,* not the other way around. And that means He meant for you to be where you were, too."

Kodi sniffed and dragged the fingers of one hand across her eyes, wiping angrily at the moisture. "I wouldn't take you for a religious person."

Brynna smiled. "You'd be surprised at just how religious I am."

Kodi looked back at the grave site, where the family had turned and were slowly making their way back to their cars. Crying had made the scars on her cheek darken, and another tear glided over them. "Then you believe she's okay, right? I mean, wherever she is."

Brynna slipped her arm around the girl's shoulders and hugged her, feeling strangely fulfilled that she could offer an honest bit of reassurance. "Yes, Kodi. I really do."

AFTER KODI LEFT, BRYNNA and Eran walked back to his car without speaking. What was he thinking right now, this human man who was trying so stubbornly to pin his heart to hers? She didn't know, but she thought that in time, he would tell her. *In time . . .* it was such a complicated concept. She could fight until the end of eternity, but she would never be able to eliminate all the demons under Lucifer's control. Yet if she could make one small difference for someone, make things somehow *better,* then perhaps it had all been worth it.

Eran came with her to the passenger side and unlocked

the door, but as he reached to open it for her, he hesitated, then peered at her shoulder. "How did that get there?"

She turned her head. "What?"

"Your feather."

Her eyes widened and she carefully lifted the snow-colored feather from her shoulder. She held it up and they both stared at it.

"No," she said softly. "I still have mine." She turned slightly and slipped her other hand inside her blouse. When she pulled it back out, her angel feather was between her fingers, a twin to the one that had drifted onto her shoulder. Held close together, their radiance intensified, shimmering with a glow that could never be replicated on Earth. "I think this is a . . . gift."

"So now you have two," he said thoughtfully. He gave her a small, crooked smile. "At this rate, you have a long way to go before you get your wings back."

But Brynna only smiled. "It's not the quantity that matters, Eran. It's the quality."

She tucked the two feathers safely away and slid into the car, content for a time and knowing that she was, indeed, on the path to redemption.